THE PEASANTS

SUMMER

THE
PEASANTS

A TALE OF
OUR OWN TIMES

IN
FOUR VOLUMES

AUTUMN

WINTER

SPRING

SUMMER

THE PEASANTS

SUMMER

FROM THE POLISH OF

LADISLAS REYMONT

ALFRED · A · KNOPF

NEW YORK   MCMXXV

PG
7158
R4
CS13
1924
v. 4

PUBLISHER'S NOTE

The Peasants has been translated from the
original Polish by Michael H. Dziewicki,
Reader of English Literature at the University
of Cracow. I wish to make special acknowl-
edgment to Dr. A. M. Nawench of Columbia
University for his invaluable assistance in seeing the work through the press.

A. A. K.

THE PEASANTS
SUMMER

CHAPTER I

THUS did Matthias Boryna die.

With dreadful yelps and howls, and leaps against the door to be let in, Lapa awoke the sleepers in the cabin, who were enjoying their Sunday rest; and then he pulled them by their clothes, and ran out a little, looking back again to see if they followed him, till Hanka took notice.

"Go, Yuzka, and see what that dog would have us do."

She ran out after him in good spirits, skipping along the road.

He led her to her father's body.

On beholding it, she uttered such awful shrieks that they all came out at once, and found him cold, rigid, lying on his face just as when he had passed away, his arms stretched out crosswise in a last fervent prayer.

Still attempting to revive him, they bore the body to the hut.

All their endeavours were fruitless: what lay before them was a corpse, and nothing more.

A bitter lamentation rose up: Hanka rent the air with cries; Yuzka cried not less wildly, and dashed her head against the wall; Vitek and the little ones wailed aloud, and Lapa howled and barked outside. Pete alone, who had been coming and going about the yard, glanced at the sun, and went back to his bed in the stable.

Matthias now lay on his couch, stiff and stark, as lifeless as a sun-dried earth-clod or a felled trunk. He still held a little sand fast in his clenched fist. In his wide-open eyes, gazing afar into some heavenly region, there was a look of wondering rapture.

Nevertheless, there emanated from that body an effluence

3

of mortality so sombre, so profoundly sad, that they had to cover it with a sheet.

His death was immediately known throughout the village; and barely had the sun appeared over its roofs, when visitors came pouring in one after another, raised the sheet, looked into his eyes, and knelt down to say a prayer for him. Others, stricken with awe at this example of God's dominion over human life, stood wringing their hands in mournful silence.

Meanwhile the mourners' lamentations continued resounding unceasingly.

And now Ambrose came, turned away the crowd outside, closed the cabin door, and, together with Yagustynka and Agata (the latter having crept in to pray beside the body), set about rendering the last services to the deceased, which he always did willingly, and in general with plenty of witticisms; but this time he felt somehow heavy at heart.

"So much for the happiness of any man!" he muttered, as he undressed the body. "Dame Crossbones, as often as she has a mind, will clutch you by the throat, slap you in the face; and ye, turning up your toes, are borne away to the 'Priests' Cow-byre'; and is there any able to resist her?"

Even Yagustynka was grieved, and said, in no merry mood: "Poor man! they neglected him so in this world that 'twas better for him to die!"

"Indeed? And who, then, did him any harm?"

"Nay, were they so very good to him?"

"And who on earth has all to his liking? Why, even a squire, even a king, must suffer trouble and pain."

"He had not to bear either hunger or cold: we can say no more."

"Ah, good Mother, what is hunger? The heart-ache gnaws far worse."

"True. I have felt it. And Yagna cut him to the heart: nor did his own children spare him."

"But," Agata put in, interrupting the prayers she was saying, "he had children that were good, and did him no wrong."

Yagustynka turned snappishly upon her. "Say your

prayers, you! ye were best. What? will she drone dirges
for the dead man, and listen all the time to the talk?"

"Well, but if his children were bad, would they mourn for
him so? Only hark to them!"

"Had he but left you so much, ye would move heaven
and earth with your lamentations!"

Here Ambrose interfered. "Be quiet," he said; "here
comes Yagna."

She rushed in, but stood transfixed in the middle of the
room, unable to speak.

They were then attiring the body in a clean shirt.

"What! . . . gone?" she said at last, with eyes fixed on
him. Fear was gripping at her throat and her heart; her
blood ran cold and she could scarcely breathe.

"Did they not tell you?" Ambrose inquired.

"I was asleep at Mother's: Vitek came to call me but
now.—Is he dead truly and indeed?" she asked suddenly,
approaching him.

"Surely 'tis for a coffin, not for a wedding, that I am attiring him."

She could not make it out, and staggered up against the
wall; she fancied herself in a deep sleep, the prey of some
nightmare.

Several times she quitted the room, but always returned:
to keep her eyes away from the body was impossible. Now
and again she would start up to go out, and yet stayed on;
at times she went out as far as the stile, and looked far
across the fields with unseeing gaze; or she would seat herself outside, but close to the room and to Yuzka, who was
weeping, tearing her hair, and for ever crying:

"Oh my father, my lost father! lost!"

There was great wailing and sobbing, not only in, but
also around, the cabin. Of the mourners, Yagna alone,
though quaking in every limb, and stirred to the inmost
depths of her being, could not shed one tear, could not utter
one cry. She only walked to and fro with eyes gloomily
bright, with an expression of stern awe.

It was a good thing that Hanka presently recovered herself and, though tearful yet, was able to see to everything, and felt quite calm on the arrival of the blacksmith and his wife.

Magda wept; the smith asked for particulars, which Hanka gave him.

" 'Tis well that the Lord Jesus has sent him so easy a death!"

"Poor man! Running out afield to flee Dame Crossbones' embrace!"

"Yestereve I went to look at him; he was as quiet as usual."

"And did he not speak? Not a word?" the smith asked, wiping tearless eyes.

"Not a word. So I pulled the down covering over him, gave him to drink, and came away."

"What? and so he got up alone! Peradventure, then, he might not have died, had any been there to watch over him," said Magda, between her sobs.

"Yagna was sleeping at her mother's. She always does so, now the old dame is so very ill."

"It was to be!—And it has been!" said the blacksmith. "These three months and over he has been a-dying. Whoso cannot be healed, better let him die quickly. Let us thank the Lord God that he suffers no longer."

"Aye, and well ye know how much the physicians and medicines cost us in the first days . . . and all to no purpose."

"Ah!" Magda lamented; "how good a farmer he was! how able a man!"

"What grieves me is that Antek should not find him alive, when he comes back."

"He is no child, nor likely to weep on that account.—Rather bethink yourself of the funeral."

"True, true.—Oh, what a pity that Roch is away just now!"

"We can do without him. Be not troubled: I will see to all," the smith replied.

He showed a sorrowful face, but was evidently masking

some hidden thought as he set to help Ambrose to fold up
the dead man's clothes. For a long time he ferreted in the
store-room amongst hanks of spun wool and odds and ends;
then he went up the ladder—for the boots which hung there,
he said. The fellow panted as loud as a pair of bellows,
pattered prayers for the dead man louder than Agata,
and was continually recalling the good actions of the deceased. But his eyes were meanwhile wandering about the
room, and his hands gliding about under the pillows, or
groping in the straw of the mattress.

At length Yagustynka said tartly: "Are ye looking for
aught in particular?"

"One cannot find, unless one seeks!" he answered. And
then he began to search quite openly; nor did the arrival
of Michael from the organist's, in hot haste for Ambrose,
hinder him in the least.

"Come at once, Ambrose: four babies wait in church to
be christened."

"Let them wait; I must first of all get him neat and tidy."

"Nay, ye had better go, Ambrose," said the smith, who
wanted to get rid of him.

"What I have offered to do, I will do. I shall not soon
lay out such another as he. Take my place in church,
Michael," he added, turning to the lad, "and let the god-
fathers and godmothers go round the altar with lighted
tapers: they will drop you kopeks in plenty.—What!" dis-
paragingly; "ye are to be an organist, yet cannot serve at
a simple christening?"

Hanka now brought in Matthew, to measure Boryna for
his coffin.

"Do not grudge him room in this last dwelling of his,"
said Ambrose, in a sad tone; "let the poor man have some
comfort, at least after death!"

"Lord, Lord!" Yagustynka whispered; "when he lived,
he had not enough with all his many acres; and now four
boards will suffice him amply!"

Agata, interrupting her prayers, here faltered tearfully:
"He was a landowner, and shall be buried as such; but

some poor creatures know not under which hedge they are to die. . . . May light perpetual shine upon you! May——" And here she broke down again.

Matthew said nothing, but nodded, and after taking the measure, said a prayer and went out. Though it was Sunday, he set to work directly. All the necessary tools were in the hut, and some seasoned oaken planks that had long been in readiness lay upstairs. He had presently set up his workshop in the orchard, and was hard at work—and making Pete, who had been told to assist him, work hard too.

The day had dawned long ago, and the sun was shining with jocund burning rays. It had been quite hot ever since breakfast-time; all the fields and orchards were being slowly plunged in a vapour-bath of whitish simmering air.

In some places, the languishing trees stirred their leaves, as birds overwhelmed by heat might flutter their wings. The lull of the day of rest had pervaded all the village; nothing moved but the swallows darting over the pond, and the carts bearing people to church from some neighbouring hamlet, with clouds of dust in their wake. . . . Every now and then one of them stopped in front of Boryna's, where the disconsolate family were sitting, to greet them and sigh heavily, looking in through the open windows and door.

Ambrose made good speed, and hastened the preparations: soon the bed was out in the orchard, and the bedding spread on the hedge to air; and now he called upon Hanka to bring him juniper-berries to fumigate the mortuary chamber.

But just then she heard nothing. She had wiped the last tears from her eyes, and was looking down the road, in the hope that she might at any moment see her Antek.

But, as the hours passed, and he did not come, she wanted to send Pete to town for news of him.

"Nay," objected Bylitsa, who had just come in from Veronka's hut; "he will bring no news and only tire the horse."

"But they must know something at the police bureau."

"No doubt; but it is closed on Sundays. Besides, they will tell you naught, if their palms be not greased."

"Alas!" she complained to her sister, "I can bear this no longer."

"Oh, he will yet be a thorn in your side," hissed the blacksmith, darting a glance at Yagna, who was sitting under the eaves. And, his fruitless search for the money having stirred his bile, he added spitefully: "His legs must be stiff with the irons he wore; how, then, can he make haste home?"

She replied nothing, and went to look out upon the road again.

As the Mass-bells were ringing, Ambrose made for the church after ordering Vitek to grease the dead man's boots well, for they had got so dry that they could not be put on him.

The smith, together with Matthew, went off to the village; and now there remained no one in the cabin but the women and Vitek, busily greasing the boots, softening them over the fire, and at times casting a look in the direction of Yuzka, whose sobs were growing fainter.

There was now no movement at all upon the road, the people being in church; nor was anything to be heard in Boryna's cabin but the voice of Agata within, saying the litany for the dead. It rose up like the chirruping of a bird, along with the volumes of juniper smoke, with which Yagustynka was perfuming the hut and the passage.

They heard the service begin. Audible in the noonday hush, the chants wafted from the church, and the sound of the organ came to them in high-pitched undulations, pleasant and remote.

Hanka could find no rest within doors, so she went to the stile, to get through her prayers there.

"Dead, dead, dead!" she thought, as the beads slipped slow through her fingers.—But she prayed with her lips only; her brain, her heart, were full of manifold puzzling thoughts, and not a few misgivings.

"Thirty-two acres. Also pastures. And a bit of forest. And the outhouses, and the live stock!" She sighed and cast a look of affection on the broad acres before her.

"If we could but pay them off, and keep all the land together!—And be just what his father has been!"

Pride and ambition filled her heart; she gazed sunwards, smiled fearlessly, and went on telling her beads, her bosom swelling with agreeable hopes.

"No, I will not give up even half the land. Half the cabin is mine, too. Nor shall the others get a single one of my milch-kine!"

She went on very long in this way, saying her prayers, flinging tearful glances over those lands, clad with sunshine, as if it were a tissue of gold, where the rye, in its growing luxuriance, waved its rusty-red drooping ears; where the darker barley-patches stood shining in the light, glossy and shimmering; where the bright green oats, thickly sprinkled with yellow-flowering weeds, stirred and quivered in the parching heat; where over the blossoming clover that lay spread out on the hill-slope, like a blood-red kerchief, a great bird was hovering, balanced on its outstretched wings, and where the broad beans stood, with their thousands of snowy flowers, keeping watch and ward over the young potato-plants, and a few plots of flax in the hollows gleamed blue with delicate flowers—childlike eyes that seemed blinking in the glare.

All was so wondrously beautiful! The sun grew hotter and hotter meanwhile; and the warm breeze, laden with the scents of the blossoms that glowed in countless numbers, breathed from the fields with delicious life-giving might, dilating the souls of men.

"O native soil, O holy soil, most holy!" she said, bending down to kiss it.

She heard the church-bells tinkling, twittering in the air.

"O my dear Jesus! all's for Thee—yea, all things in the world!" she murmured fervently, and again betook herself to prayer.

But close to her she heard a rustling noise, and looked

around her cautiously. Beneath the cherry-trees, leaning
against the trellised fence, Yagna stood, absorbed in unpleasant thought.

"What, never one moment of peace!" Hanka complained; for, at the sight of her, sharp memories arose—
sharp as stinging nettles.

"Yes, there's the donation made to her. 'Tis a fact!
Aye, six whole acres! Oh, that thief!" She turned her
back upon her, but could not take up her prayers again.
Like hounds that not only barked but bit deep, the wrongs
and outrages of former days came back and beset her.

Noon had passed; the shrunken shadows were beginning
to creep out once more from under the trees and the houses.
In the corn which bent slightly towards the sunbeams, the
grasshoppers played their faint shrill music, a beetle
hummed by at intervals, or a quail piped. And the weather
was all the time growing more and more intolerably hot.

High Mass was now ended, and the women came out of
church to take off their shoes by the pond, and there was
no more solitude for Hanka; the roads swarmed so with
men and wagons that she went home.

Boryna was at last lying in state.

In the middle of the room he lay, on a wide bench, with
a cloth over it and burning tapers around. He had been
washed, combed, and clean-shaved, but his cheek bore a
deep gash from Ambrose's razor, which a bit of paper concealed. He was arrayed in his very best clothes: the white
capote that had been made for his wedding with Yagna,
striped breeches, and all but quite new boots. In his over-
worked withered hands he held the image of Our Lady of
Chenstohova.

A large barrel of water stood by to keep the air cool; and
upon earthenware tiles there lay juniper-berries, smoulder-
ing and exhaling their aromatic smoke, that filled the whole
cabin with a bluish haze, through which the awful majesty
of death was mistily visible.

So lay, then, in silent state, the body of Matthias Boryna,
an upright and an able man, a thorough Christian, a farmer

and the son and descendant of farmers—the foremost man in Lipka.

He was in readiness, about to depart, to bid farewell to his kinsfolk and all that knew him, and set out on the Great Journey!

His soul had already passed before the Judgment-seat: it was but his worn-out body, the empty shell his soul had once inhabited, that lay there, feebly smiling, amongst lights and smoke-wreaths and unceasing prayers.

In came the people then, in an interminable procession, sighing, beating their breasts, musing profoundly, or weeping; and the sounds of their stifled sobs and faint whispers was like the pattering of autumnal rain. They came and went without end: all Lipka came, rich and poor, young and old, men and women.

In spite of the magnificent weather, his death made the whole village gloomy and wretched; everyone was in deep sadness, everyone greatly given to moralize over "the unhappy fate of mortal man."

Many of the dead man's friends lingered about the hut, and some of the goodwives remained to attempt consoling Hanka and Magda and Yuzka in words of homely comfort, condoling and weeping heartily along with them.

To Yagna nobody said one word. Though indeed she cared little for their pity, she felt nevertheless pained at being so pointedly left alone; so she went out into the garden, where she sat listening to Matthew at work hammering the coffin.

"That creature!" the Voyt's wife hissed after her. "To dare show her face at all!"

"Oh, let her be!" said another; "it is no time now to think of her misdeeds."

"Aye, leave them to the Lord Jesus, who will judge them hereafter," Hanka added mercifully.

"And for the bitter things ye say, the Voyt will reward her abundantly," the smith remarked, with a sneer, and went away, the miller having sent for him. Luckily; for

the goodwife was swelling with rage like a turkey, and
ready to fly out at him.

He broke into a croaking laugh, and hurried off. The
others lingered on to talk, but the talk flagged, partly
through their sorrow, partly on account of the intense heat.
It was indeed so hot that all the flowers and plants were
fading, and the walls shedding tears of resin.

Of a sudden a bellow, long-drawn and plaintive, was
heard, and a peasant, driving a cow, passed by on the
farther side of the pond.

He pulled her hard by the rope, while they looked on in
dull silence.

"Taking her to the priest's bull, I suppose," Yagustynka
said; but no one took any interest in her remark.

The bells rang for Vespers and they took leave of Hanka,
who then sent Vitek to ask the smith to go with her and
arrange with the priest for the funeral expenses. He presently returned, saying that the smith was in conference with
the Squire and the miller, and taking afternoon tea together;
his stallions were outside, pawing the ground in the shade.

"He with the Squire!—How strange!" But she could
not wait, and accompanied by Magda, dressed in her best,
she went to the priest's house.

He was in the farm-yard, and sent them word he would
see them there.

He sat in the shade, close to the fence. In the middle of
the yard, not far from a rather fine cow that a peasant held
fast with a rope, a powerful dappled bull was turning round
and round her, kept back with difficulty by the priest's
farm-servant, pulling at the end of his chain.

"Valek! Just wait a little: he is not ready yet," the
priest called out. Then, mopping his bald head, he called
the women to him, and asked about Boryna's death, and
consoled and comforted them with the greatest kindness.
But when they inquired about the funeral fees, he stopped
them short, saying impatiently:

"Of those things later. I am no extortioner. Matthias

was the biggest farmer in the village; he cannot have a mean
funeral. No, I tell you, he cannot," he repeated fiercely,
as was his way.

They embraced his feet, not venturing to insist.

"Ah!" he cried suddenly. "You little blackguards! I'll
give it you! Look at them, those bad boys!" He was addressing the organist's sons, peeping surreptitiously over
the hedge.—"Well, and what think ye of my bull, hey?"

"A splendid beast!" Hanka replied. "Finer than the
miller's."

"The two differ as much as a bull differs from a wagon!
Only look at him!" And he came nearer with them, and
patted the flanks of the animal, that now was approaching
closer to the cow.

"Oh, what a neck! what a back! what a splendid chest!
what a dewlap!" he cried, breathless with enthusiasm.
"Why, 'tis no bull, 'tis a bison!"

"Indeed, I never saw so fine a one."

"No, ye never did. It is a thoroughbred Hoilander.
Cost me three hundred roubles."

"So great a sum as that?" they exclaimed in amazement.

"Not one kopek less. Valek, let him go . . . but cautiously now; the cow is but a puny thing.—She will be
mated in an instant. . . . Aye, the bull is exceeding dear.
But then the Lipka folk—if they want to have a breed of
first-rate kine, will have to pay not less than one rouble,
and ten kopeks for my man besides!—The miller is wroth,
but I was disgusted with the miserable beasts his bull is
accountable for.—Now then, run away!" he said, noticing
that the women averted their faces with shame. As they
went, he called after them: "To-morrow we bring the
body to the church!" and set to helping the peasant, who
had much ado to hold his cow.

"You'll very soon thank me for a calf such as you did
never yet see in your life.—Valek, take him away to rest
awhile. Though indeed he can scarcely be in need of any
rest at all . . . Such a trifle!" he boasted.

The women had repaired to the organist's, because they

had to make a separate agreement with him. And as they
had to take coffee there, and talk for some time afterwards,
the cattle were coming home when they returned to their
huts.

Mr. Yacek puffed at his pipe, standing in the porch with
Matthew, whom he tried to engage to build Staho's hut,
but who seemed hardly pleased at the offer, and would say
nothing definitive.

"As to cutting up the timber, that's no great affair; but
as to building the hut . . . Do I know? I have enough
of the country and may be going somewhere far away.—No,
I cannot say for sure." As he spoke thus, he glanced at
Yagna, who was milking her cow outside the byre.

"Well, well, I shall finish the coffin to-morrow morning,
and then we may talk the matter over," he concluded, and
hurried away.

Mr. Yacek, entering the room where Boryna lay, prayed
for him long and fervently, wiping away many a tear. He
said to Hanka afterwards: "May his sons but resemble
him! He was a good man, a true Pole; was with us in the
insurrection; came of his own accord, and did not spare his
blows: I have seen him in action. Alas! it is through us
he has perished! . . . There's a curse upon us," he added,
as if speaking to himself. Though Hanka could not make
out well all he said, yet his words were so full of kindness
that she fell at his feet and embraced them out of gratitude.

"Never do that!" he exclaimed angrily. "What am I
more than one amongst you?"

Once more he cast a look at Boryna, lit his pipe at the
taper, and left the place, without answering the salutations
of the blacksmith, just then entering the passage.

"What, so proud to-day?" the smith cried; but as he was
in good spirits this vexed him but little. Seating himself
by his wife's side, he talked to her very low:

"You must know, Magda, that the Squire is seeking to
come to terms with our village—and looks for me to help
him. Of course I shall make a good thing of it. But mum!
not a whisper of this, wife of mine: 'tis a big affair."

And he went off to the tavern, inviting men to come there and confer with him.

Along the western horizon the sky looked like a sheet of rusted iron, but a few clouds still glowed above in golden light.

When all the evening duties had been done, the people assembled around the dead body. More and more tapers were lit about Boryna's head; Ambrose snuffed the wicks again and again, and chanted out of a book; and all present joined in the responses, weeping and lamenting one after another.

The neighbours came too, but, as it was very close within, stayed outside, droning out the long sorrowful notes of the Litany as they knelt.

This continued till late at night, when they retired, leaving only Ambrose and Agata to watch the body till morning.

This they did, at first chanting in a loud voice. But when all noise and movement around had ceased, they felt drowsy, and even Lapa, coming in and licking the grease off his master's boots, failed to wake them up.

About midnight, all became extremely dark, not a single star shone. Withal, there was a deep dead stillness, unbroken save by the faint whispering of a tree, or some eerie far-off sound—neither a shout, nor a crash, nor a call—remote and fading away in the distance.

No house in Lipka had any light at all now, save Boryna's, with the pallid illumination of the tapers, and the dead body just visible in the yellow flames, only blurred by the smoke of the perfumes, and seen as in a cloud of bluish fog. But Ambrose and Agata, with their heads pressed against the body, were both sound asleep and snoring loud.

The short summer night was soon over, as if hurrying to depart before the first cock-crow. One after another, all the tapers went out except the largest, which still sent up its long waving flame, like a blade of gold.

At last the grey mist-clad dawn looked into the room and into Boryna's face, who seemed somehow to have awaked from his heavy sleep, and to be listening to the first twitterings of the nestling birds, and through discoloured lids eyeing the still remote daybreak.

Now the mill-pond sighed, with drowsy undulations; now the forest began to loom out darkly, looking like a range of black earth-hugging clouds, as the fading night grew phosphorescent, and the trees scattered here and there stood out distinct like tufts of swarthy plumes on the brightening sky-line, while the first morning breeze sprang up, playing with the orchard trees and murmuring in the ears of the sleepers outside the huts.

Few, however, opened their eyes as yet, being somewhat languid, as is usual after Sunday or a fair.

Then came the day, misty before sunrise, but with the lark chanting his matins, the waters bubbling their joyful carol, the corn giving forth its melodious many-sounding voices; and presently with the plaintive bleating of the sheep, the screaming of the geese, human calls resounding, gates creaking, horses neighing, and all the bustle and movement of those rising to their daily work. But everything was still and quiet yet in Boryna's hut.

They were sleeping, overcome by the grief that had wrung their hearts so sorely.

In came the wind through open windows and doors, whistling and blowing the old man's hair about, and tossing the flame of the last taper in every direction.

And he lay still as a stone, no longer ready to rush to work himself, nor to urge others to toil: deaf to every call now for evermore!

The wind was rising higher, streaming through the orchard with great force, making the trees shake and rustle and sway and toss, and seem peeping in through the windows at Boryna's ashen face. So did the tall slender hollyhocks, bending and bowing at the windows, not unlike red-cheeked country lasses. Now and then a bee from the Manor hives looked in, or a butterfly, glancing in the light; a swallow would dart in and out with a hesitating twitter; and flies and cockchafers, and every kind of living creatures came likewise: so that the room was filled with a quiet buzz and drone and whirring hum—the voices of all these things, repeating:

"Dead—dead—he is dead!"

The sun rose—a huge red-hot globe, stilling all those voices; and then it suddenly veiled its glorious all-powerful and life-giving face, now hidden behind dense-volumed vapours.

The world grew grey; in a minute it began to rain abundantly in warm tiny drops, and soon their fall was heard through every field and orchard, pattering continually.

The roads cooled and exhaled the peculiar smell of rain; the birds sang loud and lustily to welcome it; the world was bathed in its greyish tremulous spray; and the thirsty cornfields, and the shrivelling leaves, and the trees, and the rills with their dry parched throats, and the baked clods of earth —all drank deep and heartily, uttering, as it were, a silent thanksgiving.

"Thanks, Brother Rain! Thanks, Sister Cloud! We all thank you!"

Hanka, who slept by the open window, was waked first by the rain driving in her face, and ran at once to the stable.

"Up, Pete! the rain has come.—Run and heap the clover in cocks—quick, or it will mowburn and rot!—And you, Vitek, lazy boy! drive our kine afield.—All the other folk's kine are out by now."—As she spoke, she let the geese out of the fowl-house, and they hastened to splash joyfully in the pools of water.

While she was thus engaged, the smith came, and they settled together what would have to be purchased in town for the funeral feast next day. He took the money; but on starting in his britzka, he called her and whispered:

"Hanka, let me have one-half, and I'll never breathe a word about your robbing the old man!"

She flushed red as a beet-root, and cried out in a passion:

"Say what ye will, and to the whole world!—Look at that man! He thinks that all are like himself!"

He glared at her, pulled at his moustache, and drove off.

Hanka was very busy indeed, and her voice was soon heard giving orders everywhere.

Two fresh tapers having been lit at Boryna's side, a sheet was spread over the body. Agata went on praying, and every now and then putting more juniper-berries on the hot coals.

After breakfast, Yagna came from her mother's, but was so frightened of the dead man that she never went in, and only wandered outside, watching Matthew as he worked at the coffin. He had done hammering now, and was just painting a white cross upon the top, when he saw her at the stable-door, silent and looking upon the black coffin-lid with a great sinking at heart.

"Yagna!" he whispered compassionately, "you're a widow now—a widow!"

"Yes, yes, I am!" she returned in a sad subdued voice.

He felt much pity for her; so worn, and pale, and unhappy-looking, and like a child that has been ill-used.

" 'Tis the common lot!" he told her, gravely.

"A widow! a widow!" she repeated. Tears welled up to her dark-blue eyes; a deep sigh burst from her bosom. She ran out into the rain and wept there so plentifully that Hanka came to bring her within doors.

"Of what use is weeping? We too have much to bear. But to you, forlorn one, it is in truth a still greater blow," she said kindly.

Yagustynka, always the same, here observed:

"Weep away! But ere the year be out, I'll sing you such a new wedding-song as will make you dance like mad."

"Such jests are ill-timed now!" Hanka said reproach-fully.

"I say true; 'tis no jest! Why, is she not wealthy and lovely and young? She will need a stout stick to keep the men away from her!"

Hanka, going out to take the pigs their wash, looked along the road.

"What," she thought with misgiving, "can the matter be?

He was to be set free on Saturday: it is Monday now, and there's no news of him!"

But she had no time for brooding. Her assistance was wanted to make the rest of the hay and all the clover just mown into cocks, for the rain never left off, and was falling in torrents.

In the evening, the priest came with the organist and the Confraternity, bearing lighted tapers, to lay Boryna in his coffin. Matthew nailed it down, the priest recited some prayers, sprinkled holy water over it, and it was taken to church in procession, Ambrose tolling the funeral bell the while.

How empty, how fearfully quiet the hut seemed on their return! Yuzka quite broke down. Hanka said:

"He was just like a corpse for so many a day, yet we felt there was a master amongst us!"

"But Antek will come," Yagustynka assured her, "and there will then be another master!"

"Would it were soon!" she sighed.

But as in this rainy weather there was a great deal of work to do, she dashed her tears away. "Come, good people!" she cried. "Should the greatest man in the world die, he is like a stone in the depths of the sea—never to be fished up again; and the land will not wait, and we must toil and till it."

Then she took them all to earth up the potato-plants, Yuzka alone staying at home to take care of the babies, and because the sorrow, which she had not yet got over, had made her ill. Lapa was constantly by her side, watching over her, and also Vitek's stork, that stood on one leg in the porch, as if on guard.

When the downpour, heavy and warm as it was, had lasted for some time, the birds ceased from singing, and all the beasts listened in silence to the purl and gurgle and drumming of the torrential rain. Only the geese made a riotous noise, swimming merrily about in the frothy pools.

"To-morrow we shall surely have fine weather," people said, on coming back from the fields, seeing the sun shine

bright at evening, and peer out with his fiery eye over the
country-side.

"Would it might still rain to-morrow! it will be worth
much gold to us!"

"Aye, our potatoes were all but destroyed."

"And how dried up the oats were!"

"Things will look better now."

"If it could but rain for three days running!"

And so on.

It had kept pouring steadily till nightfall, and the peasants had the pleasure of standing outside their huts to
breathe the cool and deliciously fragrant air. Meanwhile
the Gulbas lads were urging all the boys and girls to sally
forth and kindle the "Sobotki" [1] fires on a neighbouring
eminence. But the weather was far from pleasant, and
only a few bonfires gleamed that evening along the skirts
of the forest.

Vitek wished very much for Yuzka to go with him to the
Sobotki. But she said: "No, I will not. What care I for
amusements now . . . or for anything in the world?"

Still he pressed her to go. "We will only light a bonfire,
leap over it . . . and come home again."

"No! And you too shall stay at home: else Hanka shall
know of it," she said, threatening him.

He went notwithstanding—and came back too late for
supper, famished, and most shockingly bespattered with
mud; for the rain had been falling all the time. Indeed, it
only gave over the next day, at the time of the funeral
service.

Even then the weather was cloudy and foggy, setting off
still better the bright green of the fields, threaded with silver
brooklets everywhere. It was fresh, cool, pleasant: the
lands, all drenched and soaked, seemed fermenting with intense life.

A votive Requiem Mass was celebrated by the parish
priest, who afterwards, in company with his Reverence of

[1] The "Sobotki" correspond to the St. John's Eve fires.—*Translator's Note.*

Slupia, and the organist, seated in pews on either side of
the sanctuary, chanted the *Officium Defunctorum* in Latin.
High on a catafalque lay Boryna, amid a grove of burning
tapers. Around him the whole village knelt humbly, praying and giving ear to the long-drawn, melancholy dirge,
that now sounded like a cry of terror, making their flesh
creep and wringing their hearts; now gave out subdued
murmuring syllables, low thrilling moans, that caused the
tears to start unwilled; and now again would soar on high
in unearthly rapture, like the hymns of angels in everlasting
bliss; and the hearers would wipe away their tears, or burst
into uncontrollable fits of weeping.

This lasted a full hour. At last Ambrose took the tapers
out of their sockets to distribute them amongst the congregation; and the priest, having prayed before the body, gone
round it, swinging his silver thurible until all the air around
was blue with incense-smoke, and sprinkled it with holy
water, walked forward to the door, the cross preceding him.

Then was there within the church a confused din of cries
and wailing and sobbing, as several husbandmen of the
highest standing, shouldering the coffin, bore it to the cart
outside, the basketwork of which was crammed with straw.
Yagustynka (furtively, lest the priests should see and prevent this superstitious act) thrust under it a big loaf,
wrapped up in clean linen.

The dismal knell burst forth, the black banners were
raised and the lights flared and flickered. Staho having
lifted the cross, the two priests intoned:

"Miserere mei, Deus . . ."

The dread strains, the chant of death—the dirge of infinite sorrow—began to sob forth, and they wended their
way towards the burying-ground.

In front of the procession, the black flag bearing the skull
and crossbones, fluttered like a bird of horror: following in
its wake came the silver cross, a long line of taper-bearers,
and the priests, arrayed in black copes.

Then appeared the coffin, high in view, and the loudly

lamenting mourners, and all the village in the rear, walking in sad dreary silence. Even the sick and the crippled had come.

The grey clouds hung low in the sky, almost resting on the tops of the poplars, and motionless, as if intent on the chants that were sung. When a breeze arose, the trees shed their tears over the coffin, while the corn in the fields bent low as though to salute their master, leaving them for ever.

Floating through the air with the voices of the groaning bells, the dirge rolled a stillness as of death on the hearts of the listeners; while the mourners wailed, and the banners flapped, and the cart-wheels creaked—and the lark sang, far away in the fields.

And once again the *Miserere* resounded, with a magical effect on the feelings of those present.

Their hearts were as dying within them; their eyes strayed over the land and up to the grey sky, begging for mercy. Their faces had grown pale with the strain on their emotions; trembling had taken hold of them; and more than one whispered his prayers out of livid lips, with fervent sighs and beatings of the breast, and hearty repentance of sin. And over them all loured that heavy sense of irreparable loss, and a feeling of immense woe, bringing forth most searching desolating thoughts, so that they could not but give way and mourn aloud.

They mused on the inevitable fate of man; on the fruitlessness of all his endeavours; on the utter vanity of his life, his joys, his possessions, his hopes—all mere smoke, dust, illusion, nothingness!—on his folly in setting himself above any creature whatsoever—he that is a mere whiff of wind that comes none knows whence, blows none knows why, goes none knows whither; or the impossibility—were a man lord of the whole world, and enjoying all imaginable pleasures—of avoiding death: and wherefore, then, doth the soul of man drag with it this torpid body? To what purpose doth man live?

Such were the meditations of the people, as they walked in procession, gazing around upon the verdant fields with looks of sorrow unutterable, faces set hard and souls shuddering within them.

But nevertheless, they knew well that their refuge—their sole refuge—was in the infinite goodness and mercy of the Lord.

"Secundum magnam misericordiam tuam!" . . .

The mysterious Latin words fell upon their hearts like clods of frost-baked earth; and as they walked on, they bowed their heads instinctively to the sounds, as men must bow to the inexorable scythe of death. Now they felt absolutely resigned to all that might come—as indifferent as those rocks they saw cropping out of the fields close by them, in their hard grey strength; or the fallows and flowery meadows, and the mighty trees which may at any time be blasted by the thunderbolt, and yet which raise their heads to Heaven boldly, with a silent song of gladsome life!

Thus they traversed all the village, each one so lost in serious thoughts that he felt as if alone in a boundless desert, and seeing with his mind's eye all his forefathers borne to the churchyard, visible through the great poplar trunks.

And now, to the dreary tolling of the bells, it came in full sight, rising out of the corn with its clumps of trees, its crosses and its graves, opening before them that terrible insatiable abyss into which all the generations were slowly dropping. Peering through the air, dim with rain, they fancied they could see coffins borne from every hut, funeral trains crawling along every road, and everybody weeping, lamenting, sobbing for the loss of some dear one, till the world was full of mourning, and drowned in bitter tears.

They were already turning off to the churchyard lane, when the Squire came up with them, got down from his carriage, and accompanied the coffin on foot—a thing of some difficulty, because the road was narrow, and planted thickly with birch-trees on either side of the surrounding cornfields.

When the priests had done chanting, Dominikova, who

was led by Yagna, and walked bent down, almost blind,
struck up as well as she could the psalm: "He that dwell-
eth . . . ," which they all sang with great fervour, reliev-
ing their depressed spirits with this declaration of un-
bounded trust in God.

And thus they entered the burial-ground.

The foremost husbandman now carried the coffin, the
Squire himself lending a hand to hold it up as they went
along the yellow pathway, past grass and crosses and graves,
till beyond the chapel they came to the tomb just dug
amongst hazel-trees and elder-bushes.

At the sight, the wailing broke forth again, and still
louder. The tomb was surrounded with banners and lights,
and the people thronged with sinking hearts to gaze into
that empty pit of sand.

Now the priest mounted a heap of sand thrown up, and
he turned round and lifted up his voice, saying to the people:

"Christian folk and men of Lipka!"

Every sound was instantly hushed, save the distant tolling
of the bells, and the sobbing of Yuzka, who had put her arms
round her father's coffin and held it embraced.

The priest took snuff, wiped the tears from his eyes, and
spoke thus:

"Brethren, who is it ye are burying this day? who, I ask?

"Matthias Boryna, ye will answer.

"And I will tell you, it is also your foremost husbandman,
and an honest man, and a true son of the Church, that ye
are now burying.

"I, who have known him this many a year, can testify
how exemplary and religious his life was, how regularly he
confessed and went to Communion, and how he helped the
poor.

"How he helped the poor, I say," the priest repeated with
emphasis, and stopping to draw a long breath.

As he paused, the crying broke out again more loudly.
And now he resumed in a sad voice:

"Poor Matthias! And he is with us no longer!

"Gone!—Taken by death, that wolf that chooses for himself the goodliest ram in the flock—in broad day, unhindered by any.

"Like the lightning that strikes a lofty tree and cleaves it in twain, so the cruel hand of death has struck him down.

"But, as Holy Scripture saith, he has not died altogether.

"For behold him, a wanderer from this earth, standing at the gate of Paradise, and knocking, and crying pitifully to be let in, till at last Saint Peter asks him:

" 'Who, then, art thou, and what wouldst thou have?'

" 'I am Boryna of Lipka; and I pray God in His mercy . . .'

" 'What! have thy brethren tormented thee so that thou couldst live no longer?'

" 'I will tell thee all, Saint Peter,' quoth Matthias; 'but prithee set the gate ajar, that I may warm me a little in the heat of God's mercy, for I am icy cold after my sojourn upon earth.'

"So Saint Peter set the gate ajar, but did not let him enter yet, saying:

" 'Now speak the truth to me, for there is none whom lies can deceive here.—Speak hardily, good soul, and say wherefor thou hast left this earth.'

"Then did Matthias drop down on his knees; for he heard the Angels singing, and the little bells ringing, as during Mass at the Elevation; and answered with tears:

" 'I shall speak the truth, even as in confession. Lo, I could not stay upon earth any more. Men are there like wolves to one another, and quarrels are rife, and dissensions, and sins against our Lord.

" 'They are not men, Saint Peter, not human creatures, but mad dogs, as it were. . . . Behold, they are so evil that I cannot say all the evil they do. . . .

" 'Gone is obedience, gone is honesty, gone is all mercy as well! The brother rises up against his brother, and the child against his father, and the wife against her husband, and the serving-man against his master. They respect nothing any more—neither old age, nor dignity of station, nor even the very priesthood itself.

" 'The Evil One now reigns in every heart; under his rule lasciviousness and drunkenness and spite now flourish daily more and more.

" 'Knaves, ridden by knaves whom knaves drive: such are they all!

" 'Trickery is everywhere, and fraud, and cruel oppression, and such thieving! Set but down what ye hold in your hand, they will snap it up at once!

" 'They will graze their beasts, or trample down the grass, on your very best meadow.

" 'If you possess but a strip of land, they will take it and plough it for their own!

" 'Let but a fowl run forth from your garden: they'll instantly seize it!

" 'All they do is to swill vodka, commit uncleanness, and neglect God's service. They are heathens, Christ-murderers, and the Jews their accomplices are scores of times more honest and God-fearing than they.'

"Here Saint Peter interrupted him: 'Oh, is it thus in your parish of Lipka?'

" ' 'Tis no better elsewhere perchance, but nowhere is it worse.'

"Then Saint Peter smote his hands together, and his eyes flashed. And, stretching down his fist towards the earth, he said:

" 'Men of Lipka, are ye then such? Such loathsome wretches, heathens worse even than Germans? Ye possess goodly fields, a fertile soil, pastures and meadow-lands, and also portions of the forest: and 'tis thus that ye demean yourselves? O knaves that ye are, waxed fat with too much bread!—Most surely will I tell our Lord of your misdeeds, and He will henceforth keep a tighter hand upon you!'

"Matthias, good man as he was, tried hard to plead for his people; but Saint Peter grew wroth, and cried out, stamping his foot:

" 'Say not one word in their favour: they are villains, all of them! This one thing do I tell thee: let those sons of

Judas repent and do penance ere three weeks are past . . . or if not, I will afflict them bitterly, with hunger, and fire, and sickness; and the scoundrels shall remember me well!"

The priest went on preaching in the same unsparing fashion, and dealing out menaces of God's anger against them, with such effect that the whole congregation burst into sobs of contrition, and beat their breasts in token of repentance.

Then, after a breathing-space, he again spoke of the deceased, and pointed out how he had fallen for their sakes. And he wound up with an appeal to them all to live in concord and avoid sin, since no one knew whose turn it would be next to stand before God's awful judgment-seat.

Even the Squire was seen to brush away a tear.

The priest went off with him, when the funeral came to a close. And as the coffin descended with a thud into the grave, and the sand began to stream down upon it with a hollow rumbling, there arose such a tempest of cries, such a din of tumultuous lamentations, as might well have softened the hardest heart.

Yuzka wept clamorously, and Magda, and Hanka, and all the relations, near or distant, and even many that were not related at all. But not less loud than the loudest rang the shrieks of Yagna, who felt something clutch and tear at her heart, and made her as one beside herself.

"Yes, yes! She is bellowing now: yet what pranks she used to play upon her husband!" someone muttered aside; and Ploshkova, wiping her eyes, remarked:

"She would fain find grace in their eyes, and not be expelled from the cabin."

"Does she think them such fools that they can be cozened so?" was the outspoken comment of the organist's wife.

Yagna was completely unmindful of them all. Stretched out on a mound of sand, she lay crying wildly, with a feeling as if it were she herself upon whom those heavy reverberating torrents of earth were now pouring down, for whom the bells were tolling so mournfully, and over whom the people were so sorrowfully lamenting.

They now began to disperse: some, as they went, stopping to kneel and pray for some dear departed, others wandering about the tombs in dreary meditation, and others again lingering here and there, as they saw Hanka and the smith giving invitations to the customary funeral feast.

The earth was now beaten down over the grave; a black cross had been stuck in; and all went to the cabin with the mourners in several groups, talking low, condoling with them, and at times shedding tears.

The cabin was ready for them, with tables and settles ranged along the walls; and the company, when seated, was offered bread and vodka.

They drank at first with quiet decorum, and broke a little bread. The organist read suitable prayers, and a litany was sung for the deceased, with pauses when the blacksmith went round with drinks, and Yagustynka with more bread.

The women gathered in the other apartment with Hanka, and took tea and sweet cakes; and, the organist's wife leading off, they sang strains so plaintive and piercing that hens about the orchard began to cackle. Thus did the company eat, drink, and weep to the honoured memory of him who had died, and sing pious hymns for his soul, as befitted such an occasion and such a man.

Hanka grudged neither food nor drink, and generously pressed them all to partake. When, at noon, many of them expected to depart, a dish of *kluski* boiled in milk was served, followed by broiled meat with cabbage and pease.

"Other folk," Boleslaus' wife whispered, "have not such dainties even at their weddings."

"True; but what a goodly inheritance he leaves them!"

"And no doubt a large hoard of ready money."

"The blacksmith talked of its having been in the cabin— and vanished somewhere."

"Aye, he complains, but knows full well where he has hidden it."

The organist, who by this time was somewhat flustered, now stood up, and, glass in hand, set to extolling the late

Boryna in such high-flown terms and such a wealth of Latin quotations that, little as they understood, they wept copiously, as they did at a sermon hard to make out.

The noise increased, the faces grew flushed, the glasses clinked in fine style: some were groping for these with one hand and, with the other arm round their neighbour's neck, babbled and stammered pitiably. Some still attempted to keep up the sad tone due to such an occasion; but no one paid any heed to them. Each turned to the companions he preferred, talking with them most affectionately, and drinking to them again and again.

Ambrose alone was that day unlike his usual self. He had indeed drunk as much as any, nay, perhaps more, having taken all that he possibly could get; but he sat moping in a corner now, wiping his eyes and sighing heavily.

Some of them endeavoured to put him in a gay humour.

"Draw me not out, I am in no mood," he growled. "I am soon going to die. To die! Over me there will be only the dogs to whine; or perhaps an old woman may clink a broken pot for me," he mumbled, whimpering.

"Yea, I was at Matthias' christening, and made merry at his first wedding, and buried his father. Oh, well I remember that day! O Lord! And how many others I have laid in their graves, and sounded their funeral knell. Now 'tis time for me to go!"

And getting up suddenly, he went out into the orchard. Vitek afterwards said that the old man had sat down behind the cabin and wept for ever so long.

But he was not one to trouble much about. Besides, just as twilight was at hand, the priest, accompanied by the Squire, came in unexpectedly.

His Reverence consoled the orphans, patted the childrens' heads, and drank some tea, made for him by Yuzka; while the Squire, after some words exchanged with various people, took a glass which the smith offered him, drank to them all, and said to Hanka:

"If anyone has cause to regret Matthias, it is surely I. Were he living now, I might come to an agreement with

Lipka. And perchance," he added in a louder tone, glancing
round, "I might even agree to all your demands. But with
whom am I to make terms? With the Commissioner [1] I can
have naught to do, and there is no man amongst you now
who can represent Lipka."

They listened with deep attention, weighing every one of
his words.

He talked on for some time, and put a few questions; but
he might have spoken to a wall with as much effect. No one
thought of letting his tongue run freely, or so much as
opening his mouth.

They only nodded and scratched their heads, and looked
at one another. . . . At length, seeing that he could not
break down that barrier of suspicious caution, he went out
along with the priest, and all the visitors saw him to the
gate.

It was only afterwards that their surprise and bewilderment found tongue.

"Well, well! The Squire himself coming to a peasant's
burial!"

"He fawns on us; therefore he has need of us," Ploshka
said.

Klemba took his part. "Wherefore should he not have
come as a friend?"

"Years have brought you no wisdom. When did ever a
Squire come to the peasants as a friend? Say when!"

"Since he seeks an agreement, there must be something
kept back."

"Only this: that he needs it more than we do."

"And that we are able to hold off!" cried Sikora, who
was tipsy.

"Ye may be able: not all of us are!" angrily exclaimed
Gregory, the Voyt's brother.

They began to quarrel, each man airing his own view.

"Let him give up both timber and forest-land, and then
we'll come to terms."

[1] The representative of the Russian Government.—*Translator's
Note.*

"We need not do so at all. There will be a sentence, and all will be ours by law."

"Mother of dogs! let him go a-begging; 'twill serve him right!"

"Because the Jews have got hold of him, lo, he comes whining to us peasants for help!"

"And once his only cry was: 'You peasant! get out of my way, or 'ware my horse-whip!' "

Here some one quite drunk cried out: "Never trust him, I tell you; he and his likes only plot the ruin of us peasants."

Then the blacksmith shouted: "Farmers, hear my words —words of wisdom! If the Squire wants to make an agreement, make one by all means, taking what ye can get, and not seeking pears of willow-trees, as the saying is."

Gregory seconded him strongly.

" 'Tis God's truth!—Come with me to the tavern, all of you, and let us talk the matter over."

And presently they all left the premises together, accompanied (as it was late) by the gaggling of geese and lowing of herds coming back from the fields, and many a shepherd, playing on the flute.

They went along noisily, more than one screaming at the top of his voice, merely to give vent to his satisfaction after the feast and (so to speak) blow off the steam.

Meantime, at the Borynas', when the hut had been tidied up, all was silent and dreary and eerie.

Yagna was bustling about in her own room, like a bird beating its wings in the cage: but marking how stupefied with grief all the others were, she went out and said no word to them.

The place then became still as a tomb. Supper over, and the evening household duties performed, they all felt oppressed with sleep; but no one cared to leave the big room. Sitting by the fire, they looked into the dying embers, and gave a timorous ear to every sound they heard. It was quiet outside; only the wind whistled at times, and made the trees rustle, the fences creak, and a pane jingle now and again. Or Lapa would growl, his hair stiffening all down his back with terror; and then the dull interminable stillness would once more come over them.

There they sat, shivering with ever-increasing fear, and so scared that more than one crossed himself and said his prayers with chattering teeth. All felt sure that Something was moving about, walking in the loft above, making the rafters creak, fumbling at the door, peeping in at the windows as it passed, rattling at the latch, and going round the whole cabin with a heavy tread.

On a sudden, a neighing was heard in the stable. Lapa, barking violently, flung himself against the door, while Yuzka cried out in uncontrollable anguish: "'Tis Father! O God! 'tis Father!" in an outburst of affrighted tears.

Thereupon Yagustynka thrust her fingers forth three times, and said gravely:

"Do not weep. Weeping only keeps a soul longer upon this earth: you would prevent him from departing in peace. Open ye the door, and let the wanderer flee away to the fields of the Lord Jesus.—May he go, and peace be with him!"

They threw the door open, and presently all was as still as death. Only reddened eyes glanced about in fear, while Lapa smelt in every corner, with a whine from time to time, and a wag of his tail, as though fawning on someone . . . someone unseen. They felt now, more strongly than ever, that the dead man's soul was straying somewhere about in their midst.

At last Hanka thought of the Evening Hymn, and intoned, in a trembling husky voice.

> "All our actions, done this day,
>   At Thy feet, O Lord, we lay!" . . .

which the others took up heartily, and to their great relief.

CHAPTER II

IT was an ideal summer's day.

About ten in the morning: for the sun stood half-way between east and south, and ever with hotter fires. And all the bells in Lipka belfry had begun to peal with might and main.

The loudest was the one they named Peter. It boomed full-throated: as when a peasant, somewhat in his cups, goes swaying from side to side of the roadway, and his deep roar tells all the world how merry he is.

The second, a little smaller, that (according to Ambrose) had been christened Paul, took up the strain with livelier and more high-pitched tones, ringing long and clangorously, in ecstasies of joy, like a maiden in the glow of love on a spring day, who runs out afield and, darting through the rye, sings from a full bosom to the winds, to the lands, to the clear sky, and to her own joyful heart.

And the third, the *Sygnaturka*, which announces that Mass begins, poured out its notes, like a bird, doing all that it could (though in vain) to outvie the other two with a hurried babbling tinkle.

All three, sounding together, formed a grand orchestra —a roaring bassoon, a warbling violin, and a jingling cymbal, with shrill quivering notes: their music was very solemn and very pleasant to the ear.

It was the day of the local Feast—Saint Peter and Paul— and it was for this that they called the people so joyfully.

In the bright dazzling sunshine and the burning heat, the dealers had ever since dawn been setting up their shady booths, and the tables and counters beneath them, on the large open space in front of the church.

And no sooner had the bells sent their merry peals over

34

the country-side than all sorts of vehicles came rolling in
through clouds of dust from as far as the eye could reach,
with great crowds of people on foot. All the roads, lanes
and field-paths were red with women's dresses or white with
men's capotes.

Still from the brazen throats of those bells did the notes
pour forth, and they rolled sunward their chants and their
loud invocations:

"Kyrie!—Kyrie!—Kyrie eleison!"

"Madonna!—Madonna!—Most holy Madonna!"

"To Thee, O God!—To Thee I cry—I cry—I cry aloud!"

All the huts were decorated with greenery; and in the
whole aspect of the village, on this noted day of high solemnity, there was an atmosphere that lifted up the heart and
filled it with rapture.

Every thoroughfare was soon encumbered with foot-
passengers, horses and wagons: the travellers within these
gazing about them in wonder at the scenery, so beautifully
adorned by nature for so great a festival.

All the landscape was given over to an inundation of wild
flowers. Along every pathway there reigned a wonderful
profusion of soft white and gold and violet hues. The
larkspur and the convolvulus put their perfumed heads
forth from their hiding-places in the cornfields: bluebells
and corn-flowers were seen in every patch, and the hollows
where water had been now teemed with forget-me-nots, making the dells look like bits of blue, fallen from the sky.
There were clumps of vetches without end, buttercups and
dandelions innumerable, and the purple flowers of the thistle
and clover, and daisies with camomiles—and countless
others, of which only our Lord knows the names, since
they were blooming for Him alone. And as sweet a perfume
came up out of the fields as when his Reverence in church
offers incense to the Holy Sacrament!

The new-comers smelt all those perfumes with intense
pleasure, but nevertheless hurried on, not sparing the whip;
for the heat was too great to bear, and simply overwhelming.

And shortly all Lipka was crowded, even to the skirts of the forest.

Whenever there was the slightest shadow, wagons were drawn up, horses unharnessed; and as to the space in front of the church, it was all but impassable.

The pond was lined with women come to wash their feet clean from the dusty road, put their shoes on, and make themselves fit for church. Mature peasants were exchanging neighbourly greetings; and the younger generation—lads and lasses—went together with wistful looks past the booths, or thronged very thick around a barrel-organ player, on whose instrument sat a strange little beast from beyond the seas, clad all in red. It had a snout not unlike the face of an old German, and leaped about so, and performed such antics, that they all held their sides with the fun of it.

The music played was so merry, they could scarce hold back from dancing where they stood. But then it was accompanied by a very different tune at the same time: the begging hymns droned out by the *Dziads*, who formed a double row, from the church-porch to the lich-gate, where sat another of them, a fat man, always led by a dog. He it was who sang most fervently, and dragged out the words with the slowest drawl of them all.

At the signal for High Mass, the whole assembly rushed to the church like a torrent in spate; in an instant it was full—so terribly full that the people felt their ribs crack. There was an awful crush indeed, and even a few sharp words, and the greater part of those come had to stay outside, by the walls, or under the trees.

Several priests had come over from the nearer parishes. They at once took their places in confessionals, set up beneath the trees, and began to shrive the people.

It was most fearfully sultry weather, the wind having died away, but the multitudes thronged patiently round the confessionals or swarmed in the churchyard, seeking in vain some protection against the extreme heat.

Mass had just begun when Hanka came along with Yuzka. But to get even so far as the church-door was out of the

question; so they stood out in the full blaze, not far from
the churchyard-wall.

The organ pealing announced that High Mass was in
progress. All knelt down piously, or seated themselves on
the grass to pray. It was just noon now, and the heat in
the still air was tremendous. The sky hung overhead like
a white-hot oven tile, so dazzling that it plucked the eyes
out. The earth, too, underfoot, and the walls around, glared
with heat; and the poor people knelt motionless, hardly able
to breathe—baked, as it were, in the sun's pitiless glow.

From within came the music of the organ, mingling with
the pattering of their prayers; now and then rose a distant
voice from the altar; or the tiny bells were rung; or the
organist sang loud and hoarsely. Then came long intervals
of relative silence in this furnace, while the incense-smoke
came out by the church-door, weaving bluish odoriferous
festoons round the kneelers' heads.

But in the bright incandescence of the day, this open space
and the churchyard, strewn with garments of many a dazzling hue, had the air of a great garden of flowers. And
so they were—these worshippers, humbly prostrate at this
hallowed hour before their Lord, hidden beneath the veils
of that burning sun, and of the sacred silence which en-
veloped them!

Even the *Dẓiads* had ceased from their importunate begging. Only from time to time one of them would wake up
from somnolence, say a "Hail Mary" and ask alms in a
louder key.

The heat was now almost that of a conflagration: the
fields and orchards seemed ready to burst into white flames.

The hush, too, was yet more slumber-compelling than
before; some nodded, falling asleep as they knelt; others
withdrew, no doubt to refresh themselves, for a well-sweep
was heard to creak.

They only quite woke up when the church rang to the
tones of the whole congregation, singing within; when the
banners came out waving, followed by the priest beneath
the crimson baldachin, holding the Monstrance aloft, and

supported only by the Squires of the parish as he went
forth for the procession, with all his parishioners behind
him. Slowly, to the sound of the chants that rose up to
Heaven with grand and mighty fervour, the procession—
a river of humanity rolling in full flood—flowed round the
church-walls, resplendently white, and radiant in the sun.
And thereon floated the crimson baldachin, quite hidden in
the smoke from the thuribles: only now and then did a rift
in those clouds give a glimpse of the sun-like ostensory,
with its golden rays. The banners, like huge birds, flapped
their wings over the heads of the swarming multitudes, the
feretories, wrapped in mist-like gauze, tottered forward
with their bearers; and the organ thundered, and the glad
bells boomed, and the whole people sang together from the
bottom of their hearts, enchanted, carried away—far away—
towards Heaven, towards Him, the Sun of Righteousness!

.   .   .   .

The service was over at length. The Squires had come
out of church, seeking in vain a little shade, until Ambrose
made room for them under one of the trees, and brought
them chairs for their greater convenience.

The Squire of Vola had also come, but did not sit down
with them, and was perpetually moving about. Whenever he
saw a known face of some Lipka villager, he went up and
spoke to him as a friend. Happening to meet Hanka thus,
he pushed his way to her through the crowd.

"Is not your goodman back yet?"

"Alas! no."

"Ye went to bring him, of course?"

"I went directly after Father's funeral, but was told he
was only to be released in a week: that is, on Saturday
next."

"And the bail—what of the bail? Have ye paid the
money in?"

"Roch is seeing to that," she replied, with cautious reserve.

"If ye cannot pay, I am willing to vouch for Antek."

"Thanks, most heartily," she said, bending down to his feet. "It may be that Roch can arrange all things by himself, if not, he will be forced to take other measures."

"But remember: should need arise, I'll vouch for him."

He went farther, and perceived Yagna, sitting close to the wall near her mother, and deep in prayer; unable to invent any topic or pretext of conversation, he only smiled at her, and returned to his own people.

Her eyes followed them, she being very much interested in the young ladies, who were clad in such sort that she could not but wonder, marvelling also at the whiteness of their faces and the slimness of their waists. Lord! and they breathed forth such sweet fragrance, sweet as the perfumed whorls from a censer!

And the thing they flirted to cool their cheeks! why, it was just like a turkey's tail!—And how those young Squires came and ogled them! And they laughed so loud that the people around were shocked!

Then, from the end of the village, perhaps from the bridge near the mill, there came a sudden clattering and rumbling, while volumes of dust rose above the trees.

"Come too late for Mass!" Pete whispered to Hanka.

"Just in time to put out the candles!" someone said with a laugh.

Others peeped over the wall to look out on the road that skirted the pond.

Very soon, in a tempest of noisy barking, a long line of great white-tilted vans came in sight.

"The Germans! The Germans from Podlesie!" was the cry.

It was true. There were fifteen of these vans, more or less, drawn by stout draught-horses. Women and children, sitting within, and a complete assortment of domestic furniture, were visible under the canvas coverings. Beside these vans marched a lot of burly red-headed Germans, puffing at their pipes. Great dogs ran by their sides, often showing their teeth and barking back at the Lipka dogs, which attacked them furiously.

The people drew near to look at them, several even leaving the churchyard to see them closer.

They drove by slowly, making their way with difficulty through the jumble of wagons and horses; but, on passing in front of the church, not one of them so much as doffed his cap. Their eyes were glaring, their beards bristling—with hatred, no doubt. And they eyed the people with murderous looks.

"Ha! ha! Long-Trousers! . . . Carrion!"

"Ye horse-begotten ones!"

"Droppings of swine!"

And other epithets fell, thick as hail.

"Well?" Matthew called out to them. "Who has won the day, O Fatherlanders?"

"Who is forced to leave, you or we?"

"Our fists are too heavy; is it not so?"

"Come, stay awhile; 'tis our local feast.—We'll make merry with you in the tavern."

They replied nothing, but lashed their horses to urge them on.

"Not so fast, or your breeches will come tumbling down!"

Here a boy threw a stone at them, and several seized bricks to follow up the blow, but were stopped in time.

"Let them alone, lads, and allow this plague to go from us."

"A sudden death carry you off, ye ungodly hounds!"

And a Lipka woman stretched out her fist, screaming after them:

"May all of you perish like mad dogs!"

So they passed by, and vanished on the poplar road, as the clattering of their carts faded away with the column of dust they had raised.

The people of Lipka were overjoyed, and could pray no more, but came clustering around the Squire in increasing numbers. This pleased him vastly, and he talked gaily with them and offered them snuff.

"Ah!" he said at length; "so you have smoked them out and the swarm has flown, hey?"

Gregory replied, in tone of mock pity: "Our sheep-skins do not delight their nostrils. And then they are too delicate folk to dwell nigh us: if we come to loggerheads with any of them, why, down he goes straightway."

The Squire asked with curiosity: "What, have you fought together at any time?"

"Why, no . . . not a fight exactly . . . but Matthew here just gave one of them a tap for not returning his greeting, 'Praised be Jesus Christ!' And behold, the fellow was at once covered with blood, and well-nigh gave up the ghost!"

"They are a soft-limbed people," Matthew explained blandly. "To the eyes they look strong as oak-trees; but put forth your fist, 'twill feel as though it had struck a feather-bed!"

"And in Podlesie they had no chance. Lost their kine, it is said."

"True, they have not brought even one away with them now!"

"Kobus might tell us something . . ." one of them was beginning, when Klemba cut in sharply:

"They died—as all know—of rinderpest."

The men shook with suppressed laughter, but kept it down well, while the smith pressed forward, and said: "If the Germans have gone, we owe it to his Honour the Squire."

"Because I prefer to sell my land to my own countrymen, no matter on what terms," the latter asserted with great energy; and went on to assert that his grandfather and great-grandfather had always held with the peasants.

Sikora grinned to hear this, and said in a lower tone: "Aye, 'tis a fact, and the Squire his father scored it on my back with a horse-whip to remember! I bear the marks yet!"

But the other had apparently not heard him, and was telling what trouble he had had to get rid of the Germans. The peasants listened with civil assent; but, as to his kind feelings, they kept their own opinion.

"Surely butter would not melt in our benefactor's mouth,"

Sikora sneered; and Klemba bade him hold his tongue.

Whilst they were thus complimenting one another, a clergyman in surplice, with a plate in his hand, pushed his way into the group.

"If 'tis not Yanek, the organist's son!"

It was he, but now wearing the priest's cassock, and making the collection. He greeted everyone, and collected with great success; for they knew him, and it was impossible to let him pass without offering something. So each man undid the bundle his money was knotted in, and often a silver *zloty* jingled amongst the coppers on the plate. The Squire flung down a rouble, the young ladies of Vola small silver coins in plenty. Yanek, streaming with perspiration, red as fire, but happy and radiant, went on collecting indefatigably all through the churchyard, passing no one by, and saying a good word to everybody. He met Hanka, and saluted her so cordially that she gave twenty kopeks. But when he came face to face with Yagna, clinking the money in his plate before her, she raised her eyes—and was struck dumb with amazement. He too was so taken aback by her confusion that he at once and without a word passed on farther.

She had even forgotten to make an offering, lost as she was in the contemplation of the young man—the very image, she thought, of the saint painted above one of the side-altars: so young, so slender, so beautiful to look upon! Oh, what a spell those gleaming eyes of his had cast on her! . . . Vainly she rubbed her eyes, and crossed herself again and again to get rid of it.

Around her ran whispers:

"Only an organist's son, yet how well he is clad!"

"And his mother is as vain as a turkey about him."

"Ever since Eastertide, he has been at the school for priests."

"His Reverence sent for him to make the collection to-day."

"For his son, at least, the grasping old skinflint is liberal enough."

"Surely, for will not the glory of the priesthood do honour to him too?"

"Aye, and no small profit will be his likewise."

But Yagna, following him with fascinated eyes, heard no word of what they said.

The service being quite at an end, the congregation was now dispersing, and Hanka was moving towards the gate, when Balcerkova came up to her with important news.

"Know ye that, between Simon, son of Dominikova, and the girl Nastka, the banns have just been published?"

"Oh, but what will Dominikova say to that?"

"There will, of course, be another quarrel."

"She cannot do anything to prevent it: Simon is in the right—and of age besides."

"There will be a perfect hell in the hut," Yagustynka observed.

Hanka sighed: "Are there too few quarrels and sins against God as it is?"

"Have ye heard," Ploshkova asked her, "the news about the Voyt?" And she brought her large belly and bloated face unpleasantly close.

"I have had so much trouble with the funeral, and so many other cares of late, that I know naught of what goes on in the village."

"Well, the head man at the office told my goodman that the village accounts were short by a great sum. And now the Voyt is going about everywhere and whining to get money lent to him; for there may be an investigation any day."

"Father-in-law used to say it would surely end in that wise."

"Aye, he was puffed up, and proud, and played the great man; now he must pay for his greatness."

"Can his land be taken from him?"

"Of course it can; and if it should not suffice, he must go to jail," Yagustynka said. "The rogue has had his fling: let him have his punishment!"

"I could not understand why of late he never showed his face at our cabin, even for the funeral."

"Oh, 'twas not Boryna but Boryna's widow he cared for!"

But Yagna, holding her mother by the hand, was passing by, and they held their peace. Nevertheless, and though the old dame walked stooping and with eyes still bound, Yagustynka could not refrain from a hit at her.

"When is Simon's wedding to be? What we heard to-day from the pulpit was so unexpected! . . . Though indeed, now the lad is tired of doing a girl's work, it is hard to forbid him his manhood. And," she added mockingly, "Nastka will do that work now for him."

Dominikova drew herself up suddenly, and addressed Yagna in a hard voice:

"Take—take me away, else that viper will sting me again."

She went sobbing away, and Ploshka chuckled.

"Blind as she was, she knew well who you were!"

"She's not so blind but that she can see to tear Simon's hair out!"

"Ah, God grant she may harm no one else besides!"

There was no more talking; they were in the great crush close to the gate, and Hanka was separated from the others: not much grieved to be spared that cruel backbiting they enjoyed so. To each of the *Dʒiads* she gave a kopek, and five to the blind one with the dog, saying: "Come and dine with us, *Dʒiad!*—At the Borynas'!"

He lifted his head, and rolled his sightless eyes. "I think ye're Antek's wife.—God reward you!—Surely I shall come . . . and speedily."

Without the gates, the throng was less dense; but there too sat more *Dʒiads*, in two parallel rows, uttering various complaints. At the very end was a young man, with a green shade over his eyes, singing to the accompaniment of his fiddle ballads about the "kings of olden time," and surrounded by a large audience: coins were frequently dropped into his cap, his performance being a decided hit.

Hanka, who stood close to the churchyard, looking for

Yuzka, most unexpectedly happened to see her father.

He was amongst the *Dziads,* holding out his hands for alms, and begging with the usual whine of the class!

At first she thought her eyes were mistaken, and rubbed them, and looked again. No! it was—it was—he himself!

"My father a *Dziad!* O Lord!" She flushed burning red with the shame of it, drew her kerchief far over her brows, and crept round to him from behind the wagons by which he was sitting.

"What, oh, what do ye here?" she groaned, crouching behind him lest she should be seen.

"Hanka! . . . Yes . . . it is I."

"Come with me!—Come home!—Instantly!—O Lord Jesus, such a disgrace to us all! Come."

"I will not . . . long have I thought to do this. . . . Why should I burden you, if kindly folk will come to my aid? . . . I will go along with the others . . . see the world . . . visit the sanctuaries . . . hear about new things.— Aye, and I will bring money home to you. See, here's a *zloty:* buy a toy for little Peter therewith.—Here!"

She seized him firmly by the coat-collar, and almost by main force dragged him out of the jumble of wagons.

"Home with me this instant, I say!—What, have ye no shame?"

"Unhand me, or I shall be angry with you!"

"That wallet, throw it away! And quickly, lest any behold it!"

"Look ye, I will do just as I choose. Wherefore should I be ashamed? 'The wallet's his mother, who has Hunger for brother.'" At those words he jerked himself free from her, darted away among the horses and carts, and disappeared.

It was out of the question to think of following him in such a crowd as there was all round the church.

There the people, though drenched with perspiration, half choked with dust, half roasted by the heat, were all the same enjoying themselves to their hearts' content, in this seething cauldron!

The barrel-organ played lustily, the *Dziads* cried aloud,

the little ones whistled in the earthenware birds they had bought; horses were biting each other and squealing, being more than usually tormented with flies that day; and men talked with their friends, or went in company to look at the booths, besieged especially by girls, who were swarming there like bees about a hive.

The articles sold were more or less those on sale at the annual fairs: pictures of saints, victuals and homely dainties, clothing, ribbons, beads, etc.; and at every booth there was a great concourse of people, stopping there on their way from church.

Some went afterwards to the tavern, some straight home. Others, overcome with sleep and weariness, just laid themselves down under the wagons or about the orchards and farm-yards to refresh themselves and to rest.

In so intense a heat that they could scarcely breathe, few cared much to chat, or even to move: many felt stupefied, almost swooning. And as just then the villagers sat down to their meal, the place grew quieter at last.

At the priest's house, they had made a grand dinner for the clergymen and the Squires, whose heads were to be seen through the open windows, out of which floated the noise of talk and the clinking of glasses, together with such delightful aromas as made the mouths of them that passed by to water.

Ambrose, arrayed in his very best, and wearing all his military decorations, was continually moving about the passages, and heard frequently crying out in the porch: "You riff-raff away, or I thrash you within an inch of your lives!"

But his threats served him in no way; the urchins were like sparrows, perched all over the fences; and the boldest even crept under the windows. He could only scold, and threaten them with his Reverence's stick.

Hanka, in search of her father, came to him just then, and asked whether he had not seen him.

"Bylitsa?—Why, 'tis so tremendously hot, he must be

asleep somewhere in the shadow.—Ah! ye little wretches!"
he cried, and went stumping after the urchins.

Greatly upset, Hanka returned home, and told the oc-
currence to her sister, who had come to dine with her.

But Veronka only gave a shrug.

"His having joined the *Dziads* will not cost him a king-
dom, and it will make things easier for us. Better men than
he have ended likewise!"

"But, good God! what a disgrace to us, to let our own
father go a-begging!—And what will Antek say?—And the
others, our neighbours, will they not cry out that we have
turned him out to beg?"

"Let them yelp as they please! Anyone can wag his
tongue; but who will offer help? No one."

"And I—I will not allow my father to beg."

"So high and mighty? Then take him and feed him
yourself."

"So will I!—You, you grudge him a few spoonfuls of food.
—Oh, I see now! . . . 'tis you that have driven him to
this!"

"What? what? is there too much of aught in my home?
Am I to take the food out of my children's mouths, and give
it to him?"

"Yet remember: he has a legal claim to be fed by you for
the land he made over."

"To give what I have not, I will not rend my bowels."

"Rend them, but give: Father comes first! He has more
than once complained to me that you starve him, and care
less for him than for your swine."

"Most true. I starve my father, and live myself like a
rich lady! So stout am I that my petticoat slips off my
hips, and I have hardly strength to crawl."

"Do not talk so: folk might think ye spoke the truth."

"But I do! Were it not for Yankel, we should not even
get the potatoes and salt we eat.—Ah, 'tis a true saying:
'Goodman Bellyful thinks no one is hungry.'"

She was going on in this way, and growing more and more

querulous, when the blind man, led by his dog, appeared on the premises.

"Sit ye down here by the hut," Hanka said, and hurried away to get him his dinner.

Dinner had been already served under the trees, and the smell of the dishes came to his nostrils.

"Groats and fat bacon: very good indeed. May it profit you!" the beggar muttered, sniffing the scent of it, and smacking his lips.

His dog sat close to the house-wall, panting with wide-open jaws, and tongue lolling out; for the heat was so great as to melt them all to nothing. In the hot sleepy stillness, only the scraping of the spoons was heard, with (at times) a swallow twittering under the eaves.

"Oh, how cooling would a little dish of sour milk be!" sighed the *Dʒiad*.

Yuzka answered at once: "Be easy, I shall fetch you some."

"Well, has your whining brought you in much to-day?" Pete asked, tapping the dish lazily with his spoon.

"Lord have mercy on all sinners, and remember not their ill-treatment of the *Dʒiads!*—Brought me in much, quotha! —Whoso sees a *Dʒiad* must needs stare into the sky, or turn down another road. Or, drawing forth some miserable small coin, he will wish he had change for a five-kopek piece. We shall die of starvation!"

"But," Veronka objected, "this year the hard times before harvest press sorely on all of us."

"They do; but for all that, no man goes short of vodka."

Yuzka here put a porringer in his hands, and he began to sup it eagerly.

Presently he said: "They tell us the Lipka folk are to come to terms with the Squire to-day: is it so?"

"They may do so," Hanka said, "if they get their rights granted."

"And do ye know," Vitek put in, "that the Germans have gone from amongst us?"

"Oh, may the plague stop their breath!" the *Dziad* burst
out, clenching his fist with fury.

"Have they, then, injured you too?"

"I went to them last evening: they set their dogs at me!
. . . Scum of the earth, dog-begotten miscreants! . . . I
hear the men of Lipka have made it too hot for them to
stay. . . . Ha! I would flay them alive, leave not a rag
of skin upon any of them!" he said, as he emptied the porringer, and, after feeding his dog, prepared to depart.

" 'Tis your harvest now, and ye must go and gather it in,"
Pete said sarcastically.

"I must, indeed. Last year we were only six in all here;
now we are four times as many, and my ears tingle with
the din we make."

Yuzka said: "Pray spend the night with us."

"May our Lord give you health, O you that remember
the poor starveling!"

"A fine starveling indeed! With such a belly that he can
hardly drag it!" sneered Pete, seeing him waddle ponder-
ously in the middle of the road, groping for obstacles with
his staff.

And then they all went out again: to hear Vespers, and
enjoy the sweet tones of the organ, and weep their fill in
church, and then visit the booths once more, were it only to
feast their eyes on the splendours they displayed.

Simon had bought a string of amber beads for his Nastka,
and ribbons, and a bright scarlet kerchief: all of which she
immediately put on. And then they went from booth to
booth, arms round waists, overflowing with gladness and
intoxicated with joy.

Yuzka followed them, trying here and there to cheapen
some article for sale, and ever more ruefully counting her
money—only one wretched *zloty* in all!

Yagna, not far from them, affected not to see her brother,
and walked alone, sorrowful and forlorn. All those fluttering ribbons now failed to rejoice her; and the barrel-organ's
tunes, and the crowd and the hubbub, failed too.

She walked along, carried on by the multitudes, and stopping where they stopped, knowing neither why she had come nor whither she was drifting.

Matthew glided up to her, and whispered softly:

"Do not drive me away from you!"

"And have I ever done that?"

"Once surely. And with words of upbraiding!"

"Because you had said what you should not—and I had no choice.—Someone had——"

She broke off suddenly; Yanek was slowly pushing through the crowd towards her.

"He's here, then?" whispered Matthew, pointing to the young cleric, whose hands people wanted to kiss, and who smilingly refused the honour.

"He behaves like the son of a Squire! And how well I remember him, not so long since, running after the kine!"

"He, tending kine?—Never!" she exclaimed, hurt by the very thought.

"I have said. I recollect perfectly how the organist thrashed him one day for letting the kine graze in Prychek's oat-patch, he asleep under a pear-tree the while."

Yagna left him, and timidly made her way towards the young cleric, who smiled at her, but (finding himself the observed of all observers) turned his eyes away at once; and having purchased some tiny engravings of saints at a booth, he set about distributing these to anyone who cared to get them.

She stood rooted to the spot, gazing on him with ardent eyes. And to her vermilion lips there came a smile—bright, calm, and very sweet, like honey.

"Here is your holy patron, Yagna," he said, handing her a picture of St. Agnes.—Their hands just touched, and fell apart, as from the smart of a burn.

She, shaking all over, durst not utter one syllable. He added a word or two, but she remained speechless, her eyes drowned in his.

The crowd drove them asunder. She placed the engrav-

ing in her bodice, and looked about her for some time. He
was not visible any more, having entered the church, where
another service was going on. But still she saw him in
fancy.

"How like he is to that saint above the altar!" she said,
uttering her thoughts aloud.

"And that's why all the girls stare at him so!—They are
foolish. 'Not for dogs, I'm afraid, are sausages made.'"

She looked round quickly: Matthew was by her side!

Murmuring some inarticulate words, she tried to get away
from him, but in vain; he followed her step by step. It
was some time, however, before he ventured on putting this
question:

"Yagna, what says your mother about Simon's banns?"

"What can she say? Let him marry, if he choose: his
will is his own."

He made a wry face, and asked hesitatingly:

"But tell me, will she make over to him his portion of
land?"

"How should I know? She has said naught to me. He
can ask her himself."

Simon and Nastka then joined them, with Andrew, who
appeared suddenly, the five thus forming quite a group.
Simon spoke first:

"Yagna, do not take Mother's part; she would do me an
injustice."

"No, it is your part I am taking.—But, good heavens!
how you have changed in these last few days! . . . 'Tis
wonderful!" And, indeed, the brother she now saw before
her was quite a dashing young fellow—clean-shaven,
straight-backed, with a hat tilted on one side, and a snow-
white capote!

"Because I am my mother's drudge no longer."

"And are you better off in your freedom?" she inquired,
pleased at his spirit.

"Ask the bird you let go out of your hand: ye will see!
. . . Did you hear the banns published?"

"And when is the wedding to be?"

Here Nastka answered, nestling tenderly to his side, and passing her arm round his waist:

"In three weeks, before harvest-home."   And she blushed deeply.

"And the wedding shall take place, were it in the tavern: I will not beg to use Mother's cabin."

"But have you a place for your wife?"

"Certainly; I shall remove to the side of our cabin opposite Mother's. I shall not seek lodgings amongst the villagers. Let her but give me the land that's my due—I shall do well!" he said, swelling with self-confidence.

"And we," Matthew declared, "are not going to send Nastka away empty-handed. She will get one thousand *zloty* in cash!"

Here the smith came up, took him aside, whispered a word, and hurried away.

They went on talking, and filling up imaginary details. Simon thought with sparkling eyes what a good farmer he would be, once come into his own, and how he would settle down to work. Oh, they would soon see what a man he was!—Nastka gazed on him, open-mouthed in wonder. Andrew talked in the same sense; Yagna alone was absent-minded, hearing barely half of what they said. It did not interest her.

"Yagna!" Matthew cried. "Come over to the tavern; the band will be playing."

"I care no more for such amusements," she replied, sadly.

Her eyes were dimmed. He shot a glance into them, pulled his cap down, and rushed off, jostling those in his way. In front of the priest's house he met Teresa.

"Whither away?" she asked him timidly.

"To the tavern. A meeting has been called by the smith."

"I should go with you gladly."

"I neither thrust you aside, nor is there lack of space. But take heed lest they speak evil of you for the glances of your eyes!"

"They speak as it is, and tear me to pieces, as dogs tear a dead sheep."

"Then wherefore give them occasion?" he asked, now growing impatient.

"Wherefore? Well, you know wherefore!" she replied in a husky voice.

He walked forward, and so fast that she could hardly keep up with him.

Suddenly turning round on her, "Now then!" he cried; "there ye are, shedding tears like a calf!"

"Nay, nay! 'twas but a little dust in mine eyes," she returned.

Unexpectedly, he moderated his pace, and, walking by her side, spoke to her with much gentleness:

"Here is a little money: purchase something for yourself at one of these booths.—And come ye to the tavern: we will dance together."

She would fain have fallen at his feet to thank him.

"For the money I care not; but your kindness, how great it is!" she faltered, her face red as fire.

"Well, come then; but later. Until the evening I shall be much engaged."

And with a farewell smile on the tavern door-step, he went in.

There were plenty of people there, and it was stifling hot. The great room was full of people, drinking and chatting with one another; but the private parlour contained the best youth of Lipka, with the smith and Gregory, the Voyt's brother, at their head. There were several of the older farmers, too: Ploshka, the Soltys, Klemba, and Adam, cousin to Boryna. Even Kobus, though uninvited, had found means to enter.

When Matthew came in, Gregory was speaking very earnestly, and writing with chalk on the table.

By the proposed agreement, the Squire promised to give four acres of the Podlesie farm for each one of the forest they made over to him; also to let them have as much more land, to be paid by instalments. Moreover, he was to give them timber on credit for building the huts.

All this Gregory set forth, article by article, calculating in

figures how the land should be divided, and how much each
was to get.

" 'A promise is a toy made to give fools joy!' " grumbled
Ploshka.

"But this—this is a fact, not a promise. He is to sign
everything at the notary's—and do not forget it! So much
land for us folk! Each family in Lipka will have an ad-
ditional holding: think of that, my masters!"

The blacksmith here repeated what the Squire had directed him to say.

They listened attentively, in silence, looking hard at the
white figures on the table, and reflecting.

" 'Tis all right—a golden opportunity; but will the Commissioner give his consent to it?" asked the Soltys, first
to speak, and running his fingers through his shock of
hair.

"He must!" Gregory thundered. "When our assembly
has decided, we shall ask no official's leave: he cannot help
himself! We will have it so!"

"Leave or no leave, there's no need to shout so loud.
Will one of you see whether the policeman is not listening,
close outside the wall?"

"I saw him drinking at the bar this minute," Matthew
affirmed.

"And when," someone asked, "has the Squire said he
would sign?"

"To-morrow, if ye will," was the answer. "Let us but
accept, he will sign at once, and we can measure the ground
out afterwards."

"Then, directly after harvest-home, we might enter into
possession?"

"And give it proper tilling in autumn?"

"Ah! splendid! . . . How the work will go on then!"

All began talking excitedly together. They were full of
joy; their eyes shone with the consciousness of success, and
they stretched their arms forth as if to seize upon the long-
wished-for holdings.

Some fell to humming tunes, some to calling on the Jew

for vodka, out of sheer gladness. Some talked no little
nonsense about the division of the portions they were to
have, and everyone had visions of the new lands and riches
and happiness that were to be theirs.

They were like men drunk: they babbled, they drummed
on the table with their fists, on the floor with their feet: the
uproar was tremendous.

"Ah! then—then the local feast at Lipka will indeed be
a grand affair!"

"And how many weddings we shall have every Carnival!"

"Why, all the Lipka girls will not suffice!"

"We shall send to town for more, hey?"

"Be quiet, boys!" old Ploshka exclaimed, thumping on
the table for silence. "Ye make such a hullabaloo as do
the Jews in their synagogue on the Sabbath.—What I would
say is this: is there not some trick in the Squire's offer?"

They all became silent suddenly: it was a bucket of cold
water thrown over their enthusiasm. At last the Soltys
spoke:

"I too can in no wise understand what makes the man so
very lavish."

"Aye," one of the older men chimed in; "there must be
something wrong about it: else how could he give up so
much land almost for nothing?"

Gregory flew into a passion, and cried out:

"This I say: ye are a lot of drivelling fools!"

And once more he set to explain everything, till he was
all in perspiration. The blacksmith, too, put things as
strongly as he could: but there was no convincing old
Ploshka. He only wagged his head and smiled sceptically,
till Gregory leaped at him with fists clenched and trembling
with restrained fury.

"Say your say, then, since you think ours to be worthless!"

"So will I.—Well do I know that set of hounds; and I
tell you: believe naught till ye see it down in black and
white. They have from all time grown fat by wronging
us; and now they mean to make money by some other
wrong."

"If ye think thus, ye may withhold your vote; but do not prevent the others!" Klemba cried.

"And you—you, one of them that went up against him to the forest: do you now take his part?"

"As I went then, so will I go once more, if needful! I take not his part, but am only for a just agreement that shall advantage us all. Only a fool cannot see that such a contract is for the good of Lipka. Only a fool will refuse what is offered him."

"'Tis ye that are all fools! Ye would sell your breeches for a pair of braces.—Aye, and doubly fools! for if the Squire will give so much, he will perchance give yet more."

They went on disputing, while others took Klemba's part, and the noise grew so deafening that Yankel came in, putting a bottleful of vodka on the table.

"Come, come, good farmers all!" he cried. "Here's to Podlesie—a new Lipka!—And be ye all masters there!" And he passed the vodka from one to another.

This caused a still greater din; but everyone was now in favour of the agreement—except old Ploshka.

The smith—he must have been well paid for his good offices—spoke the loudest of all, extolling the Squire, and his honourable intentions; and he stood drinks to the whole company—now vodka, now beer, now rum with so-called "essence."

They had thus enjoyed themselves a good deal—some indeed too well—when suddenly Kobus, who had hitherto not uttered one single word, started up and attacked them all with a savage onslaught of abuse.

"And where do we *Komorniki* come in?" he shrieked. "Are we mere cat's-paws? We all who are not landowners stand up against this agreement. What, shall one have a belly so great he can hardly walk, and another die of starvation? The lands must be meted out equally to all.—Ye are all of you carrion and Squires!—Look at them, those bare-backed ones, who yet hold their heads as high as if they sneezed at us all!" He screamed so loud, and with such

foul language, that they put him out of doors; but outside
the tavern he still continued his invectives and imprecations.

They then separated, some to go home, and some to enjoy
the dance, for the music had just struck up.

Evening was falling now. The sky, all in flames, tinged
the orchard tree-tops and the ears of corn with crimson and
gold. A soft damp wind had sprung up, and the croaking
of frogs and the piping of quails resounded; the grasshoppers' shrill notes were heard in the fields, mingling with
the everlasting rustling of the cornstalks, the rumbling of
the carts driving off, and now and then the drunken song
of a man on his way home.

These noises gradually subsided. The villagers sat outside their huts, enjoying the quiet and the cool of the
evening.

Boys were bathing near the mill, splashing and bawling;
in the enclosures, the lasses were singing country songs.

There was next to no one at the Borynas'. Hanka had
gone out with the children; Pete had absented himself
somewhere, and Yagna had been away since Vespers.

Only Yuzka, busied with the evening household cares, was
there with the blind *Dziad*. He, sitting in the porch, in-
haled the cool breeze and, while mumbling a prayer, lent
an attentive ear to the approaches of Vitek's stork, that was
sidling up for a surprise attack on his legs with its beak.

"Ah, you villain, a murrain on you!—How hard it pecks!"
he grumbled, drawing his feet under him, and waving his
long rosary. But the stork only retreated a few paces, and
again, with its long stretched-out beak, advanced in another
direction.

"Oh, I hear you well! You shall not get at me this time.
—A clever fowl, though!" he muttered. But just then he
heard someone fiddling in the yard; so he drove the stork
away with several cuts of his rosary, in order to listen with
more pleasure to the sounds.

"Yuzka, who is it playing so featly?"

"Only Vitek! He has learned to play from Pete; and

now he is for ever playing, till one's ears tingle.—Vitek, have done, and give the colts their clover now!" she called to him.

The fiddle was silent. But a thought had struck the *Dʒiad* and when Vitek came in, he said to him in a most friendly tone:

"Here's for you. Such good playing is well worth a five-kopek piece."

Vitek was immensely gratified.

"Can you play pious tunes as well?"

"Whatsoever I hear, I can play."

"Ah, but 'every fox praises its own tail.'—Now, prithee, play this air." And he bleated out something in his professional line, shrill, slow, and quavering.

Vitek brought his fiddle before the *Dʒiad* had done, and after first imitating him exactly, then repeated the tune with such variations as he had heard in church. The *Dʒiad* was astounded.

"Why, lad, you could even become an organist!"

"Oh, I can play anything—from the music heard in the Manors to the songs they sing in the taverns." So Vitek boasted, and went on playing snatches of what he had heard, till the fowls at roost set to cackling, and Hanka, who had come back, sent him off to help Yuzka with her work.

Hanka then sat down in the porch, suckling her little ones, and conversing with the *Dʒiad*, who spun incredible yarns for her all the time; which she did not call in question, but listened, with sad eyes looking out into the night.

Yagna was not back yet. She had gone out to see some girl friends; but, agitated by the spirit of unrest, she could stay nowhere. Again and again she had felt forced to leave their huts, and in the end she wandered alone about the village. She gazed long upon the waters, now dark, yet visible as they trembled to the breeze; on the gently stirring shadows; on the cottage lights that shot over the surface of the pond and died away in the distance. Then, impelled onward, she cast a glance beyond the mill at the meadows, wrapped in warm white mist, while the lapwings flapped about, flying over her head.

There she gave ear to the waters that rolled through the sluices down the river's murky throat, beneath the lofty slumberous alder-trees; and she fancied the sound was a mournful call—a tearful melodious complaint.

From one end of Lipka to the other she wandered, lost like those waters that can find no outlet, and beat for ever sadly between impassable rocky walls.

Something was gnawing at her heart. It was not sorrow, not yearning, nor the sensation of love. Her eyes were burning with an arid glow, and she felt an awful sob swelling her bosom as if about to tear it asunder.

Now, after a time—she knew not how—she found herself close to the priest's house. A carriage and horses were outside the porch; she heard them pawing restlessly. There was a light in one room only, where the visitors were playing at cards.

On all this she gazed idly to her heart's content; then passed along the fence between Klemba's lands and the priest's large garden. She slipped close to the quickset hedge, in great nervous agitation: the overhanging boughs dashed the dew from their leaves into her face. On she moved mechanically, never thinking where her steps were leading her . . . till the organist's one-storied house rose up barring the way.

The four front windows were all open and lighted.

She crept along, hugging the shadow of the hedge, till close enough to look in.

A lamp hung from the ceiling; under it the father and mother were taking tea with their children; but Yanek was walking about the room, and talking to them.

She could catch every one of his words, every creak of the boarded floor, the ceaseless tick of the clock, and even the organist's heavy breathing.

Yanek was speaking of things so much beyond her that she could not make out one word.

But, fixing her eyes on him as on the picture of some

saint, she drank in every sound of his voice, sweeter to her
than the sweetest honey. As he walked, he at times was
unseen, towards the end of the room: then again he re-
appeared, coming into the lamp-lit circle. Several times
he stopped by the window, and she shrank back, fearing to
be seen; but he always looked only up into the star-
besprinkled sky, saying a few pleasant words that brought
a laugh to the others' lips and bright looks into their eyes.
At last he sat down by his mother's side, and his little sisters climbed upon his knees, clinging to his neck, while he
hugged them fondly and caressed them, and played with
them till the cabin echoed to their innocent laughter.

The clock struck. His mother rose, saying:

"You are for ever chattering, but 'tis bedtime; and you
have to start by daybreak to-morrow."

"True, Mother dear.—Alas! how short this day has
seemed to me!" he complained.

Yagna's heart was wrung so sorely that the tears welled
up to her eyes.

"But," he added, "our vacation is nigh; and the Rector
has promised to let me go home sooner, if his Reverence
will but write to ask him."

"I shall beg him to do so; fear naught, he will write,"
said his mother, who was making a bed for him just opposite the window.

Their farewells were long and loving; his mother held
him to her breast, as she kissed him.

"To bed now, my dearest, and sleep sound."

And now at last he was alone!

Yagna saw how they walked on tiptoe in the other rooms,
and spoke in whispers, not to disturb him. They closed
the windows, and soon the whole house was noiseless, that
Yanek might sleep more soundly.

Yagna too would have gone home, but for something that
kept her rooted to the spot; and she stood spellbound, staring into that last open lighted window.

Yanek read for some time out of a great book; then,
kneeling down by the window, he crossed himself, clasped

his hands in prayer, raised his eyes to Heaven, and began
in an impressive whisper.

It was dead of night. Silence reigned; the stars were
twinkling in the heights of heaven. A warm fragrant
breath came from the fields, and at intervals there sounded
the rustling of a bough, the faint warbling of a bird.

Yagna was now growing more and more beside herself.
Her heart throbbed madly, her eyes glowed with fire, her
full lips were burning hot. Instinctively, she stretched her
arms out to him; though at the same time she was shrinking
back within herself, she felt a strange resistless agitation
take hold of her, and had to lean against the fence that
creaked again to her trembling.

Yanek looked out of the window and around, then went
on with his prayer.

What then took place within her, she was never able to
understand. Such a fire ran through all her limbs, and with
such penetration, that she was ready to cry aloud with the
delicious pain of it. Shudders came over her like swift
lightning flashes; she felt a burning whirlwind rushing away
with her; wild cries, impatient to break forth, thronged all
her being, tense with an unspeakable longing. She wanted
to crawl towards him—nearer—nearer—but only to lay her
lips on his white hands—kneel to him—gaze on him close
at hand—pray to him as to some holy image! Yet she held
back, deterred by a feeling of mystic dread, and the vague
fear of some horrible evil.

"O Jesus! O merciful Jesus!" escaped her lips in a
stifled moan.

Yanek rose, bent out of the window, and said, as though
he had perceived her:

"Who is there?"

In mortal alarm, she held her breath. Her heart stopped
beating, she was paralysed with a sort of sacred terror.
Her soul, as it were, fluttered in her throat, as it fluctuated
in the throes of suspense—and rapturous disquiet!

But Yanek saw nothing save the fence. He shut the
window, undressed quickly, and put out the light.

Then the night fell upon her. She still remained there a long time, gloating upon the blackness of the silent window. The chill of the darkness struck through her, sprinkling its silver dew over her hot desires, quenching the ardour in her blood, and shedding over her a sense of unutterable happiness! A sweetly solemn calm pervaded her soul—the calm of the flowers which dream before sunrise—and she burst forth into a wordless prayer of bliss—the marvellous sweetness of that ecstasy which the mind's unsullied dreams bring forth—unspeakable joy like that of a spring day which dawns—and with it came glad tears in big beads —beads from the rosary of thanksgiving offered to the Lord!

CHAPTER III

"PRAY, Hanka, may I go home?" Yuzka entreated, laying her head down upon the pew-seat.

"Aye, do: run about everywhere like a silly calf!" said Hanka, rebuking her, and looking up from her rosary.

"But I feel so faint, so weary!"

"Do not be so restless: it will be over soon."

His Reverence was just ending a low Mass for Boryna's soul, which the family had retained for the octave of his death.

All his nearest relations sat in the side-pews. Yagna and her mother alone were kneeling in front of the altar. Somewhere in the choir, Agata, was pattering prayers aloud.

The church, cool and quiet, was dark, except for one streak of light that shot in through the open door, and lit up the place as far as the pulpit.

Michael, the organist's pupil, served Mass, jingling the tiny bells very loud, as usual, and also as usual continually turning his head about after the swallows which were darting in and out of the place.

The priest having ended Mass, they all went out to the churchyard; but as they were going past the belfry, Ambrose called them.

"His Reverence wishes to speak to you."

And he came up almost at once, with his breviary under his arm, and wiping his bald crown. Having welcomed them kindly, he said:

"My friends, I want to say how well you have acted in having a Mass said for the deceased: it will help his soul towards its eternal rest. It will, I assure you."

He then took snuff, sneezed violently, and asked them if they intended dividing the property that day. And, on receiving the answer that this was the date after the funeral on which the division was usual, he continued:

"Then I may say a few words about it to you. In dividing the property, remember to do all things by common consent, and to act justly. Let me hear of no quarrels, no dissensions. If Boryna knew that you tore—as wolves tear a sheep—that estate to the prosperity of which he gave his whole life, he would turn in his grave. Moreover, God forbid that ye wrong any one of the orphans! Yuzka is but a simple child as yet; Gregory is far away. Let each have his own, even to the uttermost kopek!—Also, when making the division, have a care to respect his known will. His soul, peradventure, sees you at this very moment! . . . As I am always telling you in my sermons, concord is the great thing—it upholds all in the world: naught was ever done with discord—naught but sin and the transgression of God's law.—Further, ye should not forget the church. He was always liberal, and neither for lights nor for Masses, nor for any other need, did he ever grudge his money. Wherefore did God bless the work of his hands."

He continued for some time in this strain. They embraced his knees with grateful thanks. Yuzka, weeping loudly, fell on her knees to kiss his hand. He took her to his bosom, kissed her on the crown of her head, and said soothingly:

"To weep is foolish, little one: the orphan is God's especial care."

Hanka, deeply touched, whispered: "Her own father could not have been more loving." He was very much moved himself, for he hastily brushed a tear away, offered snuff to the blacksmith, and changed the conversation.

"Well, are ye coming to terms with the Squire?"

"We are; five of us go to the Manor this very day."

"God be praised! I will say a Mass to that intention on my own account."

"I think the village ought to have a Votive Mass sung

with the greatest solemnity. What! Does not each of us
get a new farm—as it were for nothing?"

"You are right, Michael. And I have said a good word
for you to the Squire.—Now, go your ways, and remember:
Concord and justice!"

"And—hist, Michael!" he called after the smith, who
was leaving; "come ye round later to see about my curricle:
the right spring is bent and grazes the axle-tree."

"Oh, the bulky priest of Laznov has weighed it down;
'tis very like."

And so they all went to Boryna's, Yagna the last, going
with her mother, who could scarcely drag herself along.

It being a work-day, there were but few people on the
mill-pond road: only a few children playing about. Though
early in the morning, the sun was hot, but agreeably tem-
pered by the wind, which blew hard enough to make the
orchards toss their branches about, laden with ripe red
cherries, and the corn beat against the fences in boisterous
waves.

The huts stood open, and their gates as well; the bedding
lay spread upon the hedgerows, and everybody was out in
the fields. Some were bringing in the last of the hay, which
filled the nostrils with aromatic scent, and left long strips
that waved like streaming Jews' beards, from the trees the
heaped-up wagons passed under.

They walked along, pondering the question of how the
property should be divided.

A ditty rose, wafted on the wind—possibly from the fields
where they were at work on the potatoes; from the mill came
the beating of the water-wheels, mingling with the strokes
of a washerwoman's batlet hard by.

"The mill is continually grinding now," Magda remarked.

"Aye, the days before harvest are the miller's harvest."

Hanka sighed. "Times are much harder this year than
last. Everyone complains bitterly, and the *Komorniki* are
really starving."

"And the Koziols," the blacksmith added, "are prowling
about to snap up anything they can lay hands on!"

"Say not that. The poor creatures keep themselves alive as best they can. Yesterday Koslova sold her ducklings to the organist's wife, and got some money thereby."

"They will soon drink it all," Magda returned. "I will say no word to their hurt; but 'tis strange that my boy found the feathers of the drake I lost during father's funeral, behind their cow-byre."

"And who was it," Yuzka asked, "that made off with our bedding that very same day?"

"When is their suit against the Voyt to come off?"

"Not so soon. But Ploshka is for them, and they will make things hot for the Voyt and his wife."

"Ploshka was ever a meddler with other folk's matters."

"Our friend, hoping to become Voyt, is currying favour everywhere."

Here Yankel passed by, dragging and pulling at the mane of a hobbled horse, that lashed out and resisted with all its might and they laughed and made merry at his expense.

"Oh, 'tis well for you that ye can laugh! What trouble I have with the beast!"

"Stuff it with straw, fix a new tail on it, and take it to some fair: it will never do as a horse, but ye may sell it for a cow!" the smith bawled. Their laughter became a roar, for the horse had jerked himself free, leaped into the pond, and, in spite of threats and entreaties, lain down wallowing in the water.

"A remarkable brute. Bought of a gipsy, no doubt?"

"Set a pail of vodka before it: ye may then perhaps tempt it out!" joined in the organist's wife, who sat by the pond, watching a flock of ducklings, as downy as yellow catkins, while a hen ran cackling along the bank in dismay.

" 'Tis a fine lot.—From the Koziols, I suppose?"

"Yes. But they are always running away to the pond." And she tried to call them back, flinging them handfuls of Turkish wheat into the water.

Seeing them, however, making for the other bank, she went after them in a hurry.

As soon as they had arrived, and Hanka was busy over the breakfast, the blacksmith set to prowl about every corner of the cabin and all the premises, even exploring the potato-pits. At last Hanka could not help observing:

"Think ye any potatoes are missing?"

"I never," he answered, "buy a pig in a poke."

"Ye know the place of everything better than I do myself," she said, stiffly, pouring out the coffee. "Come, Dominikova! Come, Yagna! Come and join us!"

For those two had, on arriving, shut themselves up in the opposite room.

No one was at first willing to open the conversation. Hanka, extremely cautious and guarded, pressed them all to eat, and poured out coffee abundantly, but kept her eyes carefully all the time on the smith, who was prying about from his place, darting glances in every direction, and clearing his throat again and again. Yagna sat louring and mournful, her eyes glistening as if they had been quite recently full of tears. At her side, Dominikova talked in whispers. Yuzka was the only one to chatter freely, which she did just as usual, as she flew from one pot to another, full of boiling potatoes.

After a long tedious pause, the smith broached the subject.

"Well. How shall we divide the property?"

Hanka gave a start; but she at once recovered herself, and replied with calm and evidently after having thought it out well:

"How are we to divide it at all? I am here only to watch over my goodman's estate, and have no power to decide aught. When Antek returns, he will see to the division."

"But when will he come back? And things cannot drag on so."

"They must! As they did during Father's illness, so they shall until Antek's return."

"But he is not the only inheritor."

"But, he being the eldest son, the land comes down to him from his father."

"He has not more right to it than any of us."

"Ye also may have your share of the land, if Antek prefers it so. I shall not quarrel over this with you: the decision is not mine."

"Yagna!" her mother urged; "say a word about your claim."

"Why should I? They know of it well enough."

Hanka turned a deep red, and kicked Lapa, that had curled up beneath her feet. She hissed between her clenched teeth:

"Aye, the wrong done to us, we remember it well!"

"As you say. Wild words are of no account here, but the six acres are—those made over to Yagna by her late goodman."

"If the deed of gift is in your hands, none can snatch it away," Magda growled angrily. She had hitherto been sitting speechless and giving suck to her baby.

"True; and we have it duly signed and attested."

"Well, all must wait, and Yagna with the rest."

"Of course. But she may take away her personal belongings at once: her cow, her calf, her swine, her geese . . ."

"No!" the smith interrupted in a hard voice. "All those things are common property, and to be shared equally by all."

"By all? Is that your will? No one can take from her my wedding-present!" And, raising her voice, "Perchance," she cried, "ye would likewise divide her petticoats amongst you—and her feather-bed likewise . . . eh?"

"I did but jest; and ye fly out at me at once!"

"Because I know you to the bottom of your heart!"

"But now," he went on, "to what purpose is all this prating? You are right, Hanka; we must needs wait till Antek comes back.—And I have presently to go in haste and meet the Squire: I am stayed for." And he rose.

But, having caught sight of his father-in-law's sheepskin, hanging in the corner, he offered to pull it down.

"This would be just the thing for me."

"Touch it not: it is hanging there to dry," Hanka said.

"Well, then, let me have those boots. Only the uppers are in good condition, and they too are patched," he pleaded, trying to get them down.

"Not one thing is to be touched. Should you take aught, they will say that half of the household goods have been carried off. Let an inventory be made first, and officially. Till then, I will not allow one stake to come out of a hedge."

"Ha!" said Magda; "but Father's bedding is gone, and will not be down in the inventory."

"I have told you what came to pass. Directly after his death, I spread it on the hedge to air; and one came by night and stole it. . . . I could not see to everything, all alone."

"Strange that a thief should have been so ready at hand!"

"Do you mean by that I am lying now, and stole it then?"

"Be quiet, Magda, no quarreling. . . . He that stole it, let him have his winding-sheet cut out of it!"

"Why, the feathers alone weighed thirty pounds!"

"Hold your tongue, I say!" the blacksmith shouted at his wife, and asked Hanka to come out with him into the farm-yard: he wished, he said, to look at the swine.

She went with him, but well on her guard.

"I would fain give you good advice."

She listened attentive, wondering what it could be.

"Ye must, one of these evenings, and ere the inventory is made, drive two of the kine to my byre. We can entrust the sow to our cousin, and stow away all we can at our acquaintances'.—I will let you know with whom.—Ye will declare in the inventory that the corn has all been sold to Yankel: give him a couple of bushels, and he will bear witness to anything. The miller will take one colt, and it may

feed in his paddock. Of the vessels and implements, some
may be hidden among the potatoes, some in the rye-fields.
. . . 'Tis friendly advice I am giving you! . . . They all
do the same—all that are not fools. . . . You have been
working to death: 'tis just ye should get a larger share.
. . . To me you need only give a few crumbs. And fear
nothing: I will help you through the whole business; aye,
and make it my affair, too, that ye shall get all the land
for your own! . . . Only hearken to me: none can give better advice than I.—Why, even the Squire takes mine gladly.
—Well, what say you?"

She answered in slow tones, looking at the man stead-
fastly and with scorn:

"Thus much: even as I will give up naught that's mine, so
too am I not covetous of aught else!"

He staggered as if from a stunning blow—then glared
at her in fury and hissed:

"Besides, I would not breathe a word to anyone of how
ye despoiled the old man!"

"Breathe what ye choose to whom ye choose!—But I will
tell Antek of your advice, and he shall speak to you on
the matter!"

He scarcely could swallow down an imprecation. But
he only spat on the ground, and walked off hurriedly, calling
to his wife through the open window:

"Magda, have an eye to all things, lest there be yet
more thefts here!"

But as he passed, with what disdain Hanka eyed him!

Maddened by her scorn, he made off, but meeting the
Voyt's wife, who just entered the enclosure, stopped to confer with her for some time, angrily and with clenched fists.

She came bringing an official document with her.

"''Tis for you, Hanka: the policeman has brought it in
from the bureau."

"About Antek, perchance!" she thought in great trepidation, taking the paper in her apron-covered hand.

"I think it concerns Gregory. My goodman is out—

gone to the District office—and the policeman only said there
was something about Gregory being dead, or . . ."

"Jesu Maria!" Yuzka shrieked, and Magda started to
her feet in horror.

Helplessly, seized with overwhelming fear, they turned the
ominous paper about.

"You perhaps, Yagna, could understand it," Hanka said
beseechingly.

They stood round her, choking with suspense and dread;
but Yagna, after a long try at spelling it out, gave up the
attempt.

"I cannot read it: 'tis not written in our language."

"Nor penned in her presence either!" the Voyt's wife
sneered. "Other things there are, however, in which she
is more learned!"

"Go ye your ways," Dominikova snarled, "and let quiet
folks be."

But the Voyt's wife would not miss the opportunity to
strike a blow at her.

"Ye are good at rebuking your neighbours. But ye had
better have kept your daughter from lying in wait for
other women's husbands!"

"Peace, peace, good woman," Hanka interfered, fore-
seeing what was coming; but the Voyt's wife only grew
more enraged.

"Oh, I will say my say now, if never again!—Her, who
has poisoned my life so, I never will forgive till my dying
day!"

"Well, then, say your say! A cur will bark louder than
you can!" Dominikova growled. She took it coolly, but
Yagna flushed red as a beet-root. Yet, though overwhelmed
with shame, she nevertheless took refuge in reckless stubbornness; and as if to spite the other, she held her head up,
and fastened her eyes upon her enemy with a taunting expression and a malicious smile.

The look, the smile, infuriated the other, and she de-
nounced her lubricity in a torrent of invectives.

"Your words are frenzy, you are drunk with hate!" the
old dame said, to draw her anger away; "your husband will
answer grievously before God for my daughter's misfortune."

"Misfortune!—Aye, 'tis an innocent young maiden he
has seduced! . . . Ha, such a maiden that with everyone
and under every green bush . . ."

"Hold your wicked tongue, or—blind as I am—my hands
will surely find their way to your hair!" the old woman
cried threateningly, her hand tightening its grasp on her
stick.

"Oh, will you try?—Only touch me! Only dare!" she
repeated, with a defiant scream.

"Ha! will she, who has waxed fat upon wrongs done to
her neighbours, venture now to beset and pester them—as
hard to shake off as a bur?"

"Say, you, in what thing have I ever done you wrong?"

"That you will know, when your husband shall be con-
demned to jail!"

The Voyt's wife rushed at her with lifted fists; but Hanka
caught her back, and said sternly to them both:

"Women, for God's sake!—Would ye turn my cabin into
a tavern?"

This instantly put a stop to their brawl. Both breathed
hard and were panting. Tears came streaming from under
the bandages that covered Dominikova's eyes, but she was
first to come back to her senses, and say, sitting down with
hands clasped and a deep sigh:

"God be merciful to me a sinner!"

The Voyt's wife had rushed out in a fury; but, returning,
she put her head in at the window, crying out to Hanka:

"I tell you, drive that wanton from your house! And do
so while there yet is time, lest you rue it sorely! Let her
not stay one hour more beneath your roof, or that hell-born
pest will make you go yourself! O Hanka, defend yourself—and for that, be merciless, be without pity for her.
She is only lying in wait to entrap your Antek. . . . Don't
you see what a hell she now prepares for you?" She leant

further into the room and, stretching her fist towards
Yagna, shouted with the most intense hatred:

"Yet a little, yet a little, you devil from hell! I shall
not die in peace, I shall not go to Holy Confession, until I
have seen you driven with cudgels out of Lipka!—Oh, get
you away to the soldiers, you drab, you swinish jade!
Your place is with them!"

She was gone, and over the cabin there came a silence
like that of the grave. Dominikova shook with a dumb
passion of weeping; Magda rocked her little one; Hanka,
plunged in torturing thought, looked into the fire; and
Yagna, though she still had on her face the same hardened
reckless expression, the same wicked smile, had turned as
white as a sheet. Those last words had cut deep into her
soul; she felt stabbed as though by a hundred knives, each
stab streaming with her life-blood: an inhuman torment
that was impelling her to shriek out at the top of her voice,
or even dash her brains out against the wall. But she con-
trolled herself, pulled her mother by the sleeve, and said in
an agonized whisper:

"Mother, come away. Let's flee this place. And
quickly!"

"Right; for I am broken and shattered. But you must
return and watch over what is yours."

"I will not stay here! I so loathe the place that to stay
is beyond me.—Why did I ever darken these doors? Better have broken a limb than have ever come here!"

"Were you, then, so evilly dealt with?" Hanka asked
quietly.

"Worse than a chained-up dog! Even in hell there must
be less pain than I have suffered here!"

"Strange, then, that you could bear it so long: no one
imprisoned you here. You were free as air to go!"

"So I will. And may the plague choke you, for being—
what you are!"

"Curse not, or I may cast my own wrongs in your teeth!"

"Why are ye all—as many as dwell in Lipka—all of you
against me?"

"Live rightly: none will say one word of bitterness to you!"

"Peace, Yagna, peace; Hanka bears you no malice!"

"Let her too howl with the rest. Aye, let her! As dogs, dirt to me is all their howling. And what have I done to them? Whom have I robbed or slain?"

"What have ye done? Have you the front to ask?" Hanka exclaimed, in stupefaction, standing up opposite her.

"Do not drive me too far, or I may speak!"

"Speak, prithee! I dare you to speak! What do I care for you?" Yagna vociferated, now in a towering passion, that spread within her like a conflagration; and she was ready to do anything—even the very worst that offered.

The tears had instantly sprung to Hanka's eyes at the remembrance of Antek's infidelity, that rose up before her with a pang so acute that she could hardly stammer out:

"What have ye done with him—with my husband, say? Ye never would let him be, but followed him everywhere, like the rampant piece of lust ye are!" . . . Her breath failed her, and she broke into sobs.

Like a she-wolf set upon in her den, at bay, and ready to tear anything she meets with to pieces, Yagna sprang up. Burning with the most furious hate, and frenzied to the uttermost extreme of rage, she lashed her adversary with stinging words, that came each of them from her lips like the strokes of a whip.

"Indeed?—So 'twas I who pursued your man, was it? Yet there is none but knows how I always drove him from me! How, like a cur, he would whine outside my door, that he might have but the mere sight of a shoe of mine!—Yes, and he took hold of me by force, till I was bereft of sense, and let him do all his will, for my brains whirled.—And now will I tell you all the truth . . . but you will rue the telling! He loved me—loved me more than tongue can tell! And you he shrank from, even to loathing; his gorge, poor man! rose at the thought of your love; 'twas in his throat, as rancid reasty fat, ancient and musty and unbearable; and at the memory of you, he would spit with sheer disgust!

Nay, not to see you any more, he willingly would have done
himself a harm. . . . You sought the truth; you have it
now!—And, moreover, I will tell you—and do not forget
it—if I should but say the word, when you would kiss his
feet, he'd spurn you from him, and go following me throughout the world!—So weigh my words, and never dare to think
yourself my equal.—Have you understood?"

Towards the end, though loud and passionate in speech,
she had become mistress of herself, fearless, and more
beautiful than ever. Even her mother listened to her with
astonishment, mingled with dread; for now another woman
stood revealed before her, as terrible, as evil, and as danger-
ous as the dark cloud that bears the lightning within it.

Her words pierced Hanka, wounded her almost to death.
They struck her without mercy, crushed and trampled her
down. She felt strengthless, mindless, almost as unconscious
as a tree that falls struck by the thunderbolt. She was
scarcely able to breathe; her lips grew very white, and she
sank back on a bench. Her anguish, it seemed to her, was
rending her to pieces—nay, crushing her to grains of barren
sand: even the tears had vanished from her face, grown
ashy with the throes of that fierce ordeal, though her bosom
still was shaken with deep dry sobs. She stared out into
space as if in terror—into the abyss which had opened suddenly before her eyes; and she trembled as trembles an ear
of corn, that the wind whirls on to destruction.

Yagna had long ago gone with her mother to the other
side of the house; Yuzka was with the ducklings at the
mill-pond; but Hanka still sat motionless in the same place,
like a bird bereft of her fledgelings, unable to scream out,
to defend itself, to flee anywhither, only now and then
stirring its wings, and uttering a mournful cry.

But Heaven had pity on her and granted her a little relief. She came to herself again, knelt down before the
holy pictures, and with abundant tears made a vow to go
on pilgrimage to Chenstohova, if what she had heard should
prove untrue.

She was not even angry with Yagna any more; she only

dreaded her; and, hearing her voice now and then, crossed herself, as if to keep off a fiend.

Then she set to work. Her experienced hands worked almost as deftly as usual, little as her thoughts accompanied them; but she never remembered that she took the children out of doors and set the cabin in order that day.—At length, having prepared dinner and placed it in vessels for the field-labourers, she sent it to them by Yuzka.

And now, being quite alone, and no longer agitated, she sat down to reflect over every word said. Intelligent and kind-hearted though she was, she could not put from her mind the blows dealt at her self-respect as a wife; more than once their memory made her burn with indignation, and her heart writhed under the torment it gave her; more than once the thought of some awful revenge filled her mind. But at last she came to this conclusion:

"Truly, as to good looks, there is no comparison between me and her. But I am his wedded wife; I am the mother of his children"; and her confidence returned at the thought.

"And should he even go astray after her, he will return again to me!—And at any rate," she added to comfort herself, looking out of the window, "he can never marry her!"

Afternoon was melting into evening, when the thought of a step that must be taken flashed suddenly across Hanka's mind. She considered for a minute or two, leaning against the wall; then, wiping her eyes, she strode out into the passage, flung open the door of Yagna's room, and said, loud but calmly:

"Get out, out!—Out of this cabin instantly!"

Yagna, starting up from her settle, faced her for many seconds with a steady look. Then Hanka, taking a step or two back from the threshold, repeated in a hoarse voice:

"Take yourself away this instant, else will I have you thrown out by our farm-servant!—This instant!" she said once more, with stern emphasis.

Here the old dame would have interfered, eager to bring forward explanations and excuses; but Yagna merely shrugged her shoulders.

"Not a word to her—to that wretched wisp of straw! We know what she would have."

She took a paper out of the bottom of a chest.

"'Tis the donation you'd have back, and the six acres therewith: take them, eat them, fill your belly with them!"

Flinging the paper in her face, she added scornfully:

"And choke yourself to death in the eating!"

Then, paying no heed to her mother's remonstrances, she speedily set about packing up all her things and carrying them outside.

Hanka felt dizzy, as if she had received a blow between the eyes; but she picked up the paper, and said, threatening her:

"Quicker than that, or I will set the dogs on you!"

Meanwhile, she nevertheless felt overwhelmed with amazement. What! throw away six whole acres of land as one might cast away a broken pot?—How could she? The woman must be moonstruck, she thought, and eyed her over with astonishment.

Yagna, paying no more attention to her, was now taking down her own pictures, when Yuzka entered with a loud outcry.

"Give up the coral necklaces: they are mine from my mother—mine—mine—mine!"

Yagna was just unfastening them, but stopped.

"No," she answered, "I will not. Matthias gave them to me: mine they are!"

Yuzka shrieked and stormed, until Hanka was forced to silence her. Then all became calm again; Yagna seemed to have become deaf and dumb. After having taken all her things out, she hurried away to get her brother's help.

Dominikova made no further opposition, but replied to no word either from Hanka or from Yuzka. Only, when all her daughter's things were on the cart, she rose and shook her fist, and said:

"May the worst of all possible fates not pass you by!"

Hanka winced under the curse, but took it quietly, and called after her: "When Vitek brings the cattle home, he'll

drive your cow to your hut. And send someone for all the
rest in the evening, to drive them home to you."

She gazed for a long time upon them as they departed in
silence, wending their way round the pond. She had no
leisure for reflection, for the hired labourers came in presently: so she stowed the deed away carefully in her chest,
under lock and key. But she was subdued and depressed
the whole evening, and it was with but small pleasure that
she listened to Yagustynka's praises of what she had done.

Then, after the men had returned once more to their
work, she took Yuzka with her to weed the flax, which was
in places quite yellow with wild flowers. She worked with
great diligence to shake off old Dominikova's menaces from
her mind; but unsuccessfully; and she was especially uneasy about what Antek would say on his return.

"How he will knit his brows when I show him the deed!
—Oh, the fool!—Six whole acres! 'tis all but a farm by itself."

"Ah! Hanka," Yuzka cried, "we have forgotten the letter
about Gregory!"

"Aye, so we have.—Yuzka, leave off your work: I shall
go to the priest and ask him to read it."

The priest, however, was not within doors, and when she
saw him at a distance among the field-workers, with his
cassock taken off, she felt afraid he might rebuke her pub-
licly for her act. "For no doubt," she thought, "he must
know about it by this time." So she went to the miller,
who was just then trying how the sawmill worked, along
with Matthew.

"My wife told me just how ye have smoked out your
stepmother. Ha, ha! Ye look like a wagtail, but have the
claws of a hawk!" Laughing, he set to read the letter, but
at the first glance at it, he cried out: "Oh, what awful
news!—Your Gregory has been drowned.—'Twas as far
back as Eastertide. . . . They write that ye can get his
things by applying at the District Office."

"Gregory dead!—So strong a man!—And so young!—He

was not over twenty-six.—And was to have come back this
harvest-time.—Drowned! O merciful Jesus!" she moaned,
wringing her hands at the mournful news.

"Well," Matthew remarked, with bitter animosity, "heri-
tages seem to be coming your way. Ye have but now to turn
Yuzka out upon the world, and the whole estate will be
yours and the blacksmith's!"

"Are ye already off with the old love of Teresa, and on
with Yagna's new love?" she interrupted him; and thereupon he was suddenly absorbed in the machinery, while the
miller burst into a loud guffaw.

"Oh, what a good tit for tat!—And what a brave little
woman!"

On her way home, she dropped in to tell Magda, who wept
copiously, and uttered many an ejaculation of grief:

" 'Tis the will of the Lord. . . . Ah! a man like an oak-
tree. . . . Few his equals in all Lipka! . . . Oh, lot of man,
oh, unhappy lot!—Here to-day, gone to-morrow! . . . Then
his belongings go to his family: Michael will go to the
office to-morrow and fetch them. . . . Poor fellow! And
he so eager to be home again!"

"All is in God's hands. . . . He was always unlucky with
water. Remember how once he was near drowning in the
pond, and was saved by Klemba. . . . Surely it was written
that he should die no other death!"

They mourned together, and wept—and parted; for they
both, and Hanka especially, had plenty of work to do.

The news spread about very fast. The men who came
back from the fields were already talking about Gregory
and Yagna: all heartily sorry for the one, but not all for the
other: concerning her, opinions were divided. The women
(the older ones in particular) were very decidedly on Hanka's side, and violently hostile to Yagna; while the men,
though hesitatingly, inclined to take the other's part. This
even gave rise to some disputes.

Matthew, on his way home from the sawmill, heard them
talk. At first he merely spat in token of contempt, or let

out a curse under his breath; but, hearing what they said
outside Ploshka's hut, he could not help crying out indignantly:

"Hanka had no right to expel her: she has property there
of her own."

Here Ploshka's wife, red-faced and stout of figure, turned
upon him.

"Nay," she cried, " 'tis well known that Hanka does not
deny her right to the land. But she has other fears, for
Antek may come home any day. Who can watch a thief
living in the house? Was she to sit still and take no heed
of their doings? Was she?"

"Fiddlesticks! all that has naught to do with the case.
Your unbridled tongues are wagging, not for the sake of
justice, but from envy and spite!"

When you thrust a stick into a wasps' nest, they all fly
out at you: so did the women at him.

"Oh, indeed! what is there in her to envy, say? That
she's a light-o'-love and a wanton? That ye all run after
her like dogs? That you long for her, every one of you?
That she is a cause of sin and a shame to all the village?
Shall we envy her those things?"

"Perchance ye do: ye are beyond man's understanding.
Worn-out old besoms ye are, who would hate the very light
of the sun! Had she but been like that Magda, the tavern
wench, and done the worst of things, you would have for-
given her; but simply because she is the fairest of all, you'd
all like to drown her—aye, and in a spoonful of water too!"

This caused such a storm that he was glad to make his
escape, crying as he went:

"Ye foul jades, may your tongues rot in your heads!"

Passing by Dominikova's house, he looked in at the open
window. The room was lit, but Yagna could not be seen,
and he was unwilling to go in; so he regretfully passed on to
his own hut, on his way to which he was met by Veronka.

"Ah, I was at your home just now.—Staho has dug the
new foundations and made the trunks ready, so that you

might cut them into shape now: when are ye coming?"

"On Tib's eve perhaps. I am disgusted with this village, and may any day throw everything up—and go over the hills and far away!" he cried angrily, as he went past.

"Something," she wondered, as she went her way to Boryna's, "must have stung the man pretty sharply: what can it be?"

Supper was done, and Hanka told her all at leisure. Yagna's expulsion interested her deeply; but on hearing of Gregory, she only observed:

"His death will make one the fewer to share the property."

"It will.—I never thought of that."

"And with what the Squire has to give for the forest, you will get hard upon seventeen acres apiece! . . . To think of it! Even other folk's death is a gain to those already rich!" she sighed ruefully.

"What care I for wealth?" said Hanka. But when she went to bed, and thought the matter over, she felt a secret joy in her heart.

And afterwards, kneeling down for her evening prayer, she said resignedly:

"Since he has died, it is the will of our Lord." And she prayed fervently for his eternal rest.

The next day, about noon, Ambrose came to her cabin.

"Where have ye been?" she inquired.

"At the Koziols'. A child there has been scalded to death. She called me in, but there is naught needed for it save a coffin and a few clods."

"Which of them is it?"

"The younger of the two that she brought from Warsaw this spring. It fell into a tub of boiling water, and was all but boiled."

"Those foundlings, as it seems, do not get on with her."

"They do not.—But she is no loser: the funeral expenses are paid.—I came to you on another business, however."

She looked at him uneasily.

"Dominikova, you must know, has gone to the law court

with Yagna—to complain of your having turned her out,
I suppose."

"Let her. I do not care."

"They went to confession this morning, and had later a
long conference with the priest. I could not catch half they
said against you, but what they said made him shake his
fist with anger!"

"A priest—to poke his nose into other folk's business!"
she blurted out. All day long, however, the tidings stuck
in her memory painfully; she was full of fears and evil surmises, and quite at a loss what to do.

At nightfall, a cart stopped in front of her cabin. She
ran out, breathless and terrified; but it was only the Voyt,
sitting there behind his horses.

"You know about Gregory already," he began. " 'Tis a
calamity; but there's nothing to be said.—Now I have also
some good news for you. To-day—or to-morrow at the
latest—ye shall see Antek again."

"Are ye not beguiling me?" she asked; the news was too
good to believe.

"When the Voyt tells you so, ye may believe him. They
informed me in the Bureau."

" 'Tis well he comes back; it was high time indeed," she
returned, coolly; it seemed, with no joy at all. And then
the Voyt, after a moment's reflection, began talking to her
as a friend.

"That's a bad business ye have made with Yagna! She
has laid a complaint against you, and may make you smart
for having used violence and taken the law into your own
hands. Ye had no right to expel her from her own apartment.—A pretty thing it will be, when Antek comes back,
and ye are thrown into jail for it, both of you!—Now take
my sincere friendly advice: make matters up. I'll do all
I can to get the complaint withdrawn; but ye must yourself
make amends for the injury done."

Hanka stood erect before him, and told him her mind
thus:

"Are you speaking as the defender of my victim, or of your mistress?"

His whip struck the horses so hard that they bounded away at a gallop.

CHAPTER IV

HANKA could not sleep a wink that night, after such manifold and painful experiences. She continually thought that she heard someone creeping about the premises, along the road, or even close to the cabin. She listened. All the inmates were sleeping sound. The night was still, though the trees murmured; but not very dark, for the stars gave a dim light.

It was stiflingly close within. The ducklings, put to rest under the bed, smelt unpleasantly, but Hanka would not throw the window open. Her bed and pillows were hot beneath her, burning hot; she tossed from side to side, more and more agitated, full of multitudinous thoughts swarming in her brain, and drenching her with streaming sweat. At last, her fears growing uncontrollable, she started out of bed, and went out barefoot, in her shift, and bearing a hatchet .that she had snatched up at random—out into the yard.

Everything stood wide open there. Pete lay sprawling outside the stable, snoring hard. The horses were munching their provender and clinking their halter-chains; the cows, that had not been tethered for the night, either wandered about the yard or lay chewing the cud with moist dripping muzzles, and lifting towards Hanka their ponderous horned heads and the dark balls of their unfathomable eyes.

She went back to her bed and lay down open-eyed, listening attentively, and at times quite sure that she could hear voices and distant steps.

"Peradventure the folk of some cabin hard by are awake and talking," she said, attempting to explain matters; but no sooner had the panes turned grey from black than she rose and went out again, this time with Antek's sheepskin thrown over her.

In the porch, Vitek's stork was standing asleep, with one leg drawn up under him, and his head thrust beneath his wing; and their flock of geese, huddled together in the enclosure, formed a dim white mass.

The fields beyond were flooded with low-lying greyish fogs, out of which only the highest tree-tops surged, like pillars of thick black smoke.

The pond glistened in the darkness like a huge sightless eye, fringed with lashes of alders that rustled around it, while all the neighbourhood slept, wrapt in the fog's opaque invisibility.

Hanka sat down close to the house, leant back against the wall, and fell into a doze. When she again opened her eyes, she saw with astonishment that the night had gone; the clouds were all burning red like a distant conflagration.

"If he has but started early enough, he will be here directly," she said to herself, looking down the road. Her short spell of slumber had so much refreshed her that, to while the time away till sunrise, she took out the children's clothes to wash in the pond, while the light grew stronger and stronger.

The first cock crowed, quickly followed by others, making a loud noise throughout the village. Some larks too were heard, but at rare intervals, while the whitewashed walls and the empty dew-drenched roads gradually became distinct.

Hanka was busy washing, when a sound of stealthy steps drew her attention; and as she looked around curiously, a shadow passed out of Balcerek's enclosure and slung away among the trees.

"Yes—'tis a visitor to Mary! who can it be?" She could by no means make sure, for the shadow had vanished directly. "Ah! So proud a girl! One so vain of herself and her beauty—to let in a sweetheart by night!—Who would have thought it?"

She was scandalized. On looking about her again, she

perceived the miller's man, gliding by, at the other end of the village.

"He is coming home, no doubt, from the tavern where his Magda lives!—Those men! like wolves prowling in the night!—What doings, alas!" She sighed, but a restless feeling quickened her senses now and stirred her blood. This, however, presently passed away as she went on washing in the cool water; and in a voice which, though subdued, thrilled with intense fervour, she began the hymn:

> "Soon as dawn blushes in the sky,
> To Thee, O God, my voice shall cry!"

And the chant rolled over the fallen dew, and made one with the approaching daybreak.

It was time now to rise: opening windows, clattering clogs, and loud cries showed that the villagers were awakening.

Hanka spread out upon the fence all the things she had washed, and ran to wake her people. But they were so heavy with sleep that their heads but just rose and fell back on the pillow.

To her intense indignation, Pete shouted at her: "Mother of dogs!—'Tis too early! I'll sleep till sunrise!" And he refused to stir.

The babies were crying, and Yuzka whined: "Yet a little, Hanka dear! I went to bed but a minute ago!"

She then lulled the little ones to rest, drove the poultry into the yard, waited patiently for a few minutes more, and then—just before the sun had risen, when the heights of heaven were one mass of flame, and the mill-pond reddened in the dawn—she returned to the charge, and made such a din and uproar that the sleepers could not but get out of bed. And when Vitek came scratching himself drowsily, and rubbing his back against the corner of the hut, she chastised him well with sharp words.

"You'll wake up fast enough with a first-rate drubbing! —Aye, and why, you young hound! why did you not

fasten the kine to the mangers last night? Would you have
them gore each other's bellies in the dark, hey?"

He answered her back, but whipped out of sight in time,
for she made a fierce rush at him. Then, looking again into
the stable, she set upon Pete:

"The horses are mumbling their empty racks!—And you!
you are lying abed even till sunrise! O you idle one!"

"Ye scream as a magpie ere it is to rain," he growled
back. "Why, all the village can hear your noise!"

"Let them hear! Let them all know what a sluggard,
what a lazy drone, what a dawdler you are!—Oh, but the
master will be back now, and he'll keep you in order, I
promise you!"

"Yuzka!" she now shouted from the other end of the
yard. "Spotted One's udders are swollen hard: milk her
carefully, and let not half the milk remain, as you did
last time.—Vitek! take your breakfast and be off; and if
you let the sheep stray—as you did yesterday—I'll know the
reason why!" . . . So she went about, giving orders, bustling everywhere, and all the time hard at work herself:
feeding the fowls, and the swine that were standing close to
the cabin; giving a pail of thin batter to drink to the calf
just weaned; throwing the ducklings boiled groats, and
driving them off to the mill-pond. Vitek received a slap
on the back, and his food in a wallet. Nor was the stork
forgotten; she set a pipkin before him, full of potatoes
cooked the day before; and he *klek-kleked*, plunged his
beak in, and ate with a hearty appetite. Hanka was everywhere, and seeing to everything, and managing all in the best
way.

As soon as Vitek had gone off with the cows and sheep,
she went over to Pete, whom she could not bear to see idling
about.

"Take all the dung out of the byre!" she ordered; "it is
bad for the cows at night, and fouls them all over: they're
as filthy as swine."

Just then the sun's red burning eye peeped at them from

afar, and the *Komorniki* arrived to pay with their work for the flax and potato-fields they had rented.

She set Yuzka to peeling potatoes, gave suck to her babies, put her apron on over her head, and said:

"Keep an eye on everything here! And should Antek come, let me know: I shall be in the cabbage-field.—Come, good folk, while it is still cool and dewy. We shall first earth up the cabbages, and set to yesterday's work again after breakfast."

As they walked on down by the old disused peat-diggings, a few lapwings circled over their heads and some storks were wading about the low marshy ground, stepping carefully, and thrusting their heads forward. In the air there was a marshy smell, mixed with that of the sweet flag and the sedges, with clumps of which the old peat-diggings were overgrown.

Then they set to work, beginning their talk (of course with the inexhaustible topic of the weather) while they earthed up the cabbage-plants, that had grown well, but were greatly infested with weeds—towering dandelions, rank duckweeds, and even forests of thistles.

"'What man needs not nor sows, most abundantly grows,'" said one woman, knocking the earth from the roots of a weed.

"And all evil things likewise," said another; "sin is sown by none, yet the world is full thereof."

"Because its life is sturdy!" Yagustynka struck in, to air her peculiar views. "My dear! so long as man lives, sin shall live. Do they not say: 'If sin you destroy, you kill all our joy'? and again: 'But for sin dearly cherished, long ago man had perished.'—It must, then, be good for something, just as this weed is: our Lord made them both!"

This theology was sternly rebuked by Hanka. "What! . . . Our Lord make evil? It is only man that, like a swine, mars all things with his rooting snout." And they said no more.

The sun was up in the sky now, and the mists had all

disappeared, when troops of other women came along from
the village.

Hanka laughed at them.

"Fine workers! Waiting till the dew shall dry, lest they
wet their feet!"

"Not all are so eager for work as you are."

"And not all are forced to work so hard," she answered
with a sigh.

"Well, your goodman is coming back: then will ye rest."

"I have vowed, if he returns, to go to Chenstohova for
the day of Our Lady of Angels. And the Voyt tells me he
is coming to-day."

"The folk at the Bureau must know: so the news will be
true.—But what a number of people are off to Chenstohova
on foot this year! The organist's wife is to be a pilgrim
too, they say; and she tells me that the priest is to come
with the pilgrimage."

Yagustynka made fun of the idea. "Who will carry his
guts for him? He will never do so by himself.—Nay, 'tis
only a promise, as usual with him."

"I have been there several times, with the others, and
should long to go every year," sighed Filipka—she from
over the water.

"Everyone longs for a spell of idleness."

"Oh, heavens!" she went on, paying no attention to the
jeer; " 'tis all delight: everything along the road is so pleasant, so sweet to look on! And ye gaze out upon the world,
and hear so much, and pray so much besides! . . . And
one thinks for a few weeks that one has got rid of all woes
and all cares. One feels as though born again!"

"True, and many have told me the same," said Hanka.
"One is specially under the loving influence of God's grace."

A girl was hastening towards them, slipping along between
the bulrushes and the thick clumps of alder. Hanka shaded
her eyes, looked, saw it was Yuzka, and heard her from afar
crying, as she waved her arms:

"Hanka, Hanka! Antek is home!"

She flung down her hoe, and sprang up as if about to fly away like a bird; but she mastered her feeling, let down her skirt which she had tucked up, and, in spite of her rapture and her throbbing heart that made her almost unable to speak, said as quietly as if she had not heard any news at all:

"You will go on working without me, and come round to the cabin for breakfast."

The women looked at one another.

"Her calm," Yagustynka said, "is only outside, lest folk should laugh at her for wanting her goodman so badly.— I could not have mastered myself so!"

"Nor I!—But God grant that Antek do not go wrong any more!"

"As he will now no longer have Yagna at close quarters, it may be that he will keep straight."

"O my dear! when a man scents a petticoat, he'll follow it all over the world!"

"'Tis a truth. There's no beast so greedy to its own hurt as some men are."

So they talked, letting the work flag and all but come to a standstill. Hanka meanwhile went on, conversing both with Yuzka and everyone she met, though she knew but little of what either she said to them or they to her.

"Has Roch come with him?" she would ask again and again.

"How many a time have I told you yes?"

"And how is he looking?—How?"

"How can I tell you that?—In he came and asked at the very threshold: 'Where's Hanka?' So I told him and ran to fetch you—and that's all."

"And he asked after me!—May the Lord . . . ! May he . . ." She was incoherent, beside herself with gladness.

From a distance she perceived him, sitting with Roch in the porch, and as soon as he saw her, he went out to meet her in the enclosure.

She advanced more and more slowly, catching at the roadside fence not to fall, for her legs were giving way under her. She felt choked with sobs, and her brain whirled so, she could only utter these words:

"You here!—Here at last!"—And she could speak no more for the tears of joy that choked her.

"Here at last, Hanka dear!" He clasped her to his breast in a mighty hug, full of the deepest affection and love. She nestled to his side with an uncontrollable impulse, while her happy tears went streaming down her pale cheeks, and her lips trembled, and she surrendered herself all to him with childlike simplicity.

It was long before she could speak at all; but, indeed, how could any speech ever express what she felt? She would have knelt to him, kissed the dust at his feet; and when a word or two burst from her lips, they were but like flowers falling before him as an offering, fragrant with happiness, bedewed with her heart's blood; and these her faithful eyes, brimming over with illimitable love, would lay down at his feet, with the fidelity of a dog that lives only in his master's will and favour.

"You do look poorly, dearest Hanka!" he said, stroking her face with the tenderest affection.

"No wonder, having suffered so much and waited so long!"

"Poor woman!" Roch here observed; "she has been worked sadly beyond her strength."

"Ah! and ye too are here, Roch! How could I forget you so?" And she welcomed him, and kissed his hands, while he said, with a smile:

"Very easily!—Well, I wished to bring you your goodman home; and now here he is!"

"Aye, here he is!" she cried, standing up before Antek and eyeing him in admiration. For he was so much whiter now—so much more refined in his strength—so beautiful, so lordly—as if he were someone else! She looked at him in bewilderment.

"Have I changed in aught, that your eyes examine me so?"

"No, not changed . . . and yet somehow not the same at all!"

"Oh, when I set to field-work again, I shall soon be once more just as I was!"

And now, making a dart into the hut, she came out, bearing her youngest-born.

"You see him for the first time, Antek!" she .cried, as she lifted up the boy, roaring lustily. "Just look: he is as like you as two peas."

"A fine youngster!" He wrapped him up in the skirt of his capote, and rocked him to and fro.

"I have given him the name of Roch!—Here, Peter, go to Father"; and she pushed forward the other boy, who clambered on to Antek's knee, prattling childishly the while. Antek caressed him as tenderly as the other.

"Dear little things! darling mites!—How Peter has grown!—And he talks a little already . . ."

"Oh, and he takes such notice, and he's so clever! Can he but get hold of a whip, he wants at once to crack it at the geese!" She came kneeling down beside them. "Peter! Come! Try to say 'Dad'!"

He indeed said something dimly resembling the word, and continued cooing to himself, and pulling his father's hair.

"Yuzka," Antek said, "why do you eye me askant so? Come hither."

"But I dare not," she said.

"Come to me, silly one, come to me!" And he folded her in a kind brotherly embrace.

"And now you will obey me in all things, even as you did once obey Father. Fear not: I shall never be harsh to you, and from me you shall suffer no wrong."

The girl burst into a flood of tears, remembering her lost father and her brother who was drowned.

"When the Voyt told me of his death," Antek said, "I was quite stunned with grief. How dear he was to me! I never dreamed . . . And I had already arranged how we should divide the land; I had even thought of a wife for him!" he said, sorrowfully; when Roch, to turn away their thoughts from so sad a subject, exclaimed, rising from his seat:

"Talking is all very well, but not when the stomach cries famine!"

"Dear, dear! I had forgotten all about that.—Yuzka, just catch me those two yellow cockerels. . . . *Tsip, tsip, tsip!* come along! . . . Will you not begin with eggs? Or a bit of new bread, and butter made but yesterday?—Yes, cut off their heads and scald them in boiling water! . . . I shall have everything ready in a moment.. . . What a ninny I was to forget!"

"Let be, Hanka; the cocks will come in later. I would have something more homely just now; something of the country, I am so fed up with town food: give me potatoes and *barszcz* of all things!" And he laughed merrily. "Only get something else for Roch!"

"Thanks heartily; but both you and I have the same tastes as to that."

Hanka went off to get things ready. But the potatoes were on the boil by now, and she had only to fetch from the larder a huge sausage for the *barszcz*.

"This I was keeping on purpose for you, Antek. 'Tis from the pig ye sent me word to kill for Easter."

"And a splendid festoon it makes, too; though with the Lord's help, we shall get through it!—But where are the presents, Roch, say?"

The old man hauled forward a large bundle, out of which Antek took a variety of articles.

"Here's for you, Hanka, whenever you would fare any-whither." And he handed her a woollen shawl—just like the one the organist's wife had!—a black ground, with red and green chequers.

"For me! O Antek, how good of you not to forget!" she cried, overwhelmed with gratitude.

"Roch reminded me," he confessed, "or I should have for-gotten. We went together to make our choices and pur-chases."

They had bought a great many things: he had shoes for her besides, and a silk kerchief for a head-dress: azure-blue, with tiny yellow flowers. Yuzka got another just like it, but green; also a frill and several rows of beads, with a long ribbon to tie them. There were gingerbread cakes for the children, and mouth-organs as well; and there was even something that he set apart unopened, for the blacksmith's wife. Nor had he forgotten either Vitek or the farm-servant.

And how they all exclaimed with admiration at each new marvel as it came forth, and looked it over, and measured its size! How the tears of joy ran down Hanka's cheeks! and how Yuzka caught her head in her hands with bewildered amazement!

"Well have you deserved all these presents. Roch told me how perfectly everything has been managed on the farm. —Be quiet now, I did not come to be thanked!" he cried, for they were all crowding to embrace him in their gratitude.

"I should never have dreamed of buying any such beautiful things," Hanka said, still in the melting mood, as she tried on her new shoes. "They are a little tight for me, now I go barefoot; but in winter they will be just the thing."

Roch asked her about the doings in the village. She answered, but in a desultory way, being very busy with the food. In a short time she had set before them a large dish of boiled potatoes, plentifully seasoned with fat bacon, and another one, not a whit smaller, of *barszcz*, in which there swam a huge sausage, looking for all the world like a floating wheel.

And they fell to with an excellent appetite.

"That's the food I like," he cried, merrily; "lots of garlic to give the sausage a taste! After that, a man feels he has something inside him. But there, in jail . . . they fed me so—devil take them all!"

"Ah! poor dear! how famished you must have been!"

"Aye, aye! towards the end I had no taste for anything!"

"The boys told us only a starving dog could eat what they gave them: it is so?"

"There's some truth in that; but the worst was staying locked up. In the cold weather it was still bearable; but when the sun shone warm, and I smelt the smell of the land

—oh, then, how I raged! I even tried to tear out the window-bars; but they prevented me."

"Is it true," Hanka asked in a trembling voice, "that they beat folk there?"

"No doubt. But then the place is full of such villains, 'twere but justice to flog them daily.—Oh, no one ever dared to lay a finger on me! If anyone had . . . well, I'd have made short work of him."

"Yea, in truth! Who on earth could overcome you, you mighty one?" she said, with eyes gloating over him, and attentive to the least signal he should give.

They had soon finished their meal, and went out to sleep in the barn, where Hanka had already carried them beds and pillows.

"I declare," Antek said, laughing, "we shall both melt away like dripping in that place!"

She closed the great barn-door upon them, and then gave way to her feelings: to hide them, she went and weeded the parsley-bed, every now and then looking around her, while the tears welled up. They were tears of joy, shed—why? Because the sun beat hot upon her shoulders; because the green leaves were fluttering over her; because the birds sang, and fragrance filled her senses; and she felt so happy, so serene, so blissful within her soul!—As if she had just returned from confession—perhaps happier still!

"Thou, O Lord Jesus, hast done all this," she murmured, raising her moist eyes to Heaven, her soul filled with the deepest and most ineffable gratitude for the great boon she had received.

"And all things have changed so wonderfully!" she sighed in ecstasy.—All the time they slept, she remained as in a sweet trance. She watched over them, as a hen does over her chickens; took the children far out into the orchard, lest they should awaken the sleepers; and drove all the animals out of the farm-yard, heedless if the pigs should root up the new potatoes, or the fowls go scratching over the sprouting cucumber-plants.

The day was painfully long, but there was no help for

that. Breakfast-time, dinner-time passed: still they slept.
She sent all the people to work, caring little whether they
should or should not be lazy, with her not by, and stood
continually on the watch, or continually tripping between
cabin and barn.

And many, many a time did she take out the things he
had brought her, and try them on, and cry out:

"Is there in all the world another man so kind and so
thoughtful as he is?"

At last, however, she sped away to the village; and every
woman she saw she accosted with:

"Do ye know, my goodman has come back! He is sleeping in the barn now!"

Her eyes and face were radiant with smiles; everything in
her breathed such joy and exhilaration that they were all
astounded.

"What spell can that jail-bird have thrown over her?
Why, she is beside herself about the man."

"She will grow proud and stuck-up in a very short time:
you will see!"

"Oh, but let Antek go back to his old ways again, and she
will be taken down finely!" So they gossiped.

Of all they said, she heard not one word.—She was back
home presently, and preparing a first-class dinner. But
hearing some geese scream in the pond, she ran out to silence
them with a volley of stones; which nearly brought about a
quarrel with the miller's wife, their owner.

She had scarcely sent the field-labourers their afternoon
meal, when the two men came out of the barn. Dinner was
spread for them in the cool shadow in front of the house.
Beer and vodka were not lacking there, nor even a desert—
half a sieve full of ripe red cherries, brought from the
priest's house.

"A noble dinner!" Roch said, smiling; "quite a wedding-
feast!"

"And should the Master's return be a second-rate festival?" she answered, busily serving them, and eating very
little herself.

Dinner was hardly over, when Roch went out into the village, promising to look in again in the evening; and Hanka said to her husband:

"Will you look at the farm?"

"Certainly! My 'holidays' are over; I must buckle to work now.—God! how little did I think I should inherit my father's land so soon!"

He sighed, and followed her. She took him first to the stable, where three horses and a colt were snorting and stamping; then to the empty cow-byre, and the granary, full of new-mown hay. He looked into the sties too, and into the shed where all the various implements and tools were stored.

"That *britzka* must be taken in to the threshing-floor: its paint is peeling off with the heat here."

"So I told Pete more than once; but the fellow does not mind me."

She called the pigs and poultry round her, priding herself on their numbers; and then she told him about the field-work; what had been sown, and where, and how much of each crop. When she had finished, he said:

"I can hardly think that you have done all this by yourself."

"For your sake, I could have done still more!" she whispered, overjoyed at his praise; and the whisper came hot from her heart.

"You have backbone, Hanka . . . and plenty of it too!—I did not expect it of you."

"I had to, and needs must when the devil drives."

After looking about the orchard, with its half-ripe cherries, and the plots of parsley and onions, and the young cabbage-plants, they came back; and as they passed the side where his father had lived he peeped in at the window.

"And where's Yagna?" he asked, seeing with surprise that the room was empty.

"At her mother's. I turned her out," she replied in a firm voice, looking him full in the face.

He knit his brows, pondered awhile, then lit a cigarette, and said quietly and with seeming indifference:

"Dominikova is a bad animal; she will not be ousted without a lawsuit."

"I hear they both went to lodge a complaint yesterday."

"Well, well, 'between complaint and sentence, there is a good long distance'; but we must consider things well, and not let her play us any tricks."

She told him how it had all come about—of course, omitting many a detail. He heard her out, put no question, and only frowned heavily. But when she handed him the paper, he gave a sarcastic laugh.

"With that paper ye may as well . . . why, 'tis worth absolutely naught!"

"How so!—It is the very same paper your father gave her!"

"What's the use of a broken stick?—Had she annulled the deed at the notary's, that would have been something. It was in mockery she flung it to you!"

He gave a shrug, took little Peter on his arm, and made for the stile.

"I am going to look at the fields and come back," he said over his shoulder, and at the hint she stopped short, much as she had longed to go with him. As he passed the stack, now repaired and filled with new hay, he glanced at it from under heavy eyelids.

"It was repaired by Matthew!" she called out to him from the stile where she stood. "The roof alone required some scores of straw trusses."

"Good, good!" he grunted in reply, and strode away through the potatoes along the pathway, uninterested in such trifles.

The fields on that side of the village nearly all bore autumn-sown crops this year: so he met but few people, and those he met he saluted curtly, and passed on. But soon he walked more slowly, for Peter was beginning to feel heavy, and the hot still weather acted strangely upon him.

He stopped to examine almost every field in particular.

"Ha! that weed is simply choking the flax!" he cried, observing the patches of flax, azure-blue with flowers, but thickly strewn with the yellow blooms of some weed.

"She bought her linseed unsifted, and sowed it unsifted too!"

Then he stopped close to the barley, stunted, parched and scarce visible for the thistles, and camomile plants, and sorrels which grew there.

"They have sown in too wet soil.—That swine! he has ruined the field! The rascal ought to have his neck twisted for tilling the land so. And how it has been harrowed! Dog-grass and couch-grass everywhere!" He was much displeased.

But presently he came to a vast expanse of rye, waving in the sunshine, with heavy billowy ears of corn, sounding and rustling. This was a set-off: it had grown magnificently, the straw was thick in the stem, and the ears were full.

"It grows like a forest of pines! Ah, that was Father's sowing. . . . Even the Manor could show naught better!"— He plucked an ear, and rubbed it in his hands. The grain was full and fine, but soft as yet, liable to be ruined by a hailstorm.

But where he stopped longest to admire and feast his eyes was over the wheat. The growth was not quite regular—in clumps here, in hollows there—but the ears were all glossy, darkish in hue, dense-growing, and large in size.

"A first-rate crop! And, though on rising ground, it has suffered not at all from the drought. . . . 'Tis a harvest of pure gold!"

On arriving at the boundary, he gazed back. Away by the churchyard they were mowing the clover, and the scythes moved flashing over the meadows, like gleams of lightning. On the fallows flocks of geese were feeding; men swarmed about like ants; and higher and farther still he could descry lonely houses, trees hunched up, gnarled and drooping over the roads; and again more and more vast lands fading into the distance, as into a flood of bluish trembling water.

All was hushed in profound silence; the sultry air vibrated; it was, as it were, an atmosphere of white flame, through which a stork might be seen walking up and down, or poising itself on dropping wings; or a crow flying past, with beak wide open, gaping with the heat.

On high there was but the intense dark azure, with a few white clouds straying across it. But below, the dry burning wind made sport: now whirling and staggering about like a drunken man; now starting up with a sudden loud whistle; or, again, lurking somewhere away out of sight, and then bursting out unexpectedly in the corn, which it teased and dashed to and fro, and drove hither and thither in lofty billows—to disappear again as suddenly, no one knew where, while the cornfields murmured in low voices, as if complaining of its rough behaviour.

Antek, having reached his fallow at the skirt of the forest, had another burst of indignation.

"Not yet ploughed up or manured! Our horses stand idle, the dung is wasted in heaps . . . and what does it matter to him, the dirty scamp?—May all . . ." he swore fiercely, drawing nigh to the cross by the poplar road.

But here, tired, slightly dizzy, and with his throat full of dust, he sat down in the shadow of the birch-trees by Boryna's Cross. Little Peter had gone to sleep: he laid him down on his capote; and then, wiping away streams of sweat from his brow, he looked out upon the landscape, and fell into a reverie.

The first afternoon shadows of the forest were hesitatingly creeping down to the corn. The tree-tops, glowing in the sun, were conversing one with another, while the thickets of hazel and aspen below shook like men sick with an ague. Woodpeckers pecked on incessantly; magpies were shrieking somewhere unseen. And at times a bee-eater would flash athwart the old moss-grown oak-trees—a flying fragment of rainbow!

A cool breath was wafted from within the quiet woodland recesses, into which the sun but rarely shot his keen darts; it came, redolent of mushrooms, of resin, of pools simmering in the hot blaze.

Suddenly a hawk was seen above the forest, circled over the fields, and, poising itself for an instant, swooped down into the corn.

Antek sprang forward to balk it, but too late: a stream of feathers was floating down, and the robber fleeing through the air, while below partridges piped plaintively, and a terrified hare fled at random, its white scut bobbing up and down.

" 'Twas most featly done! A bold thief!" Antek thought, returning to his seat. "Well, hawks too must get their food somehow. Such is the law of the world!" he reflected, as he covered little Peter with his capote; for there were numberless black wild bees and bumble-bees buzzing around them.

He recalled those days of the near past, when he was longing so fiercely, with such insatiable thirst, to be back in his fields once more.

"How they tormented me, the villains!" he said with a curse. Then he became quite motionless.—Just in front of him, a few quails, calling to each other, put their heads timorously out of the rye, but popped back at once, on hearing a band of sparrows alight upon a birch-tree, fluttering, bickering, fighting, and flying down into the sand beneath, with a great racket and hubbub . . . when suddenly they all were silent, as if rooted to the spot.—The hawk flew past again, so near them that its shadow glided over the field beneath!

"Little brawlers! he has struck you dumb pretty quickly!" Antek mused. " 'Tis just the same with men. How many need only a threat, and are hushed at once!"

Some wagtails came out upon the road, hopping so near that with a sweep of his hand he almost caught one of them.

"I but just missed getting one of the silly creatures for the boy."

And now crows came, one after another, flocking out of the forest, pecking at anything they could find. Scenting a man, they began, cautiously and holding their heads awry, to peer about and go round him, hopping ever nearer and nearer, and opening their gruesome beaks.

"Oh, no! I am not to be a feast for you," he laughed, throwing a clod at them; and they, like thieves found out, fled away in silence.

But after a time, while thus gazing out on the country-side, his whole soul attentive to every one of its sounds and sights, all the creatures about him began to draw near him boldly. Ants ran over his back, butterflies again and again settled in his hair, lady-birds walked about his face, and great green caterpillars of the wood explored his boots with lively interest; squirrels too, peeping forth from the forest, their brownish-red tails high in air, seemed deliberating whether they should not approach him. He, however, noticed none of them, plunged as he was in a sort of dreamy state, which the sight of the country had caused in his mind, and that filled him with indescribable sweetness.

He felt as though he were himself the very waft of the wind through the corn, the very gleam of the soft green fleece of the grass, the rolling of the streamlets over the heated sands, athwart the meadows redolent of new-mown hay; he felt himself one with the birds flying high above the earth, and crying to the sun with the great incomprehensible clamour of Life: as if he had become the murmur of the fields, the tossing of the pine-forest, the rush and mighty impetus of all growing things; also the mysterious potency of that hallowed Mother, the Earth, who brings forth all in joy and gladness. And he knew himself, knowing that he was all these things in one—both what he saw and what he felt, what he touched and understood, and what he could not even seize but by the merest glimmering—that which many a soul will only see clearly at the instant of death—besides that which only looms vaguely within the human soul, and gathers and lifts it up to the unknown region where it weeps tears of ineffable sweetness, and yet is weighed down as with a stone by an insatiable craving.

But all these thoughts passed through his mind like clouds: before he could grasp one clearly, another had taken its place, as absorbing as the former and yet harder to understand.

He was awake, and yet he had a drowsy sense as of sleep coming to his eyes; he was led somehow into a land of ecstasy, where he felt as one feels at the most holy moment of the Holy Mass: when the soul floats away in adoration, towards some garden where angels dwell, some happy land —Paradise, or Heaven!

Though his was a hard tough nature, by no means given to sentiment, he was nevertheless, during those unearthly moments, ready to fall prostrate on the earth, kiss her with burning kisses, and take her to himself in the most loving embrace.

"What is it that has wrought upon me so? It must be the change of air—nothing else," he grunted to excuse his feelings, rubbing his eyes and knitting his brows. But indeed an overwhelming Power had seized upon him: it was by no means possible to crush down that jocund serenity which now flooded all his being.

He knew himself back in the land—*his* land—yea, the land of his father, of his forefathers: was it strange that he should feel his soul glad, and that every throb of his heart should cry out aloud and joyfully to the whole world: "Here I am once more, and here do I remain!"?

He pulled himself together, bracing himself to take up this new life, to walk in his father's ways and those of his ancestors before him: like them, he bowed his shoulders to the yoke of heavy toil, to be borne bravely, unweariedly, until little Peter should step into his place.

"It is the order of things that the young should succeed the old and the sons the fathers, one by one, continually, so long as it shall be Thy will, O merciful Jesus," he thought, in deep meditation.

He bent his head over his hands, bowing it low; for many and various thoughts had now come into his mind, mournful recollections which the accusing voice of conscience now brought before him—bitter painful truths that humbled him in the dust, as he acknowledged his multitudinous transgressions and sins.

It was a hard thing, this confession of his, and he found it no easy matter to appease his conscience; but he fought down his stubbornness, conquered his pride, and looked back on his past life with true repentance, examining every act with the utmost severity and fairness of judgment.

"I have been naught but an infamous fool!" he thought with deep sadness, while a bitter smile writhed his lips. "All in the world must take place in due order. Aye, my father spoke wisely: 'When all carts go the same way, woe to him that falls from one; he will be crushed under the wheels.'—But every man has to realize this by himself, with his own reason; and this may cost very dear indeed."

Sounds of lowing now floated from the wood; the cattle were coming home amid great volumes of dust; oxen, sheep with their attendant dogs, careful to keep them away from the corn; squealing herds of pigs, driven home with many a blow; calves plaintively seeking their lost mothers; a few herdsmen on horseback, and the others on foot with the flocks, striking, shouting, and keeping up a stream of noisy talk.

Antek had remained with Peter on one side to let them pass, when Vitek saw him and came up to kiss his hand.

"I see you have grown pretty well in these last times."

"I have in truth. The trousers I got in autumn now come but just beyond my knees."

"All will be well; be sure that Mistress will give you a new pair.—Is there grass enough for the kine?"

"Alas! no, it is all sere and drying up. If mistress had not fodder for them at home, they could give no milk at all.—Pray let me have Peter, for a little ride," he added pleadingly.

"But surely he will fall off the horse!"

"Why, no: how often and often have I taken him about
on our filly! Besides, I shall be there to hold him.—How
he loves riding and crying out at the horse!"—He took the
boy and set him on an old jade that was plodding along
with drooping head. Peter clutched at her mane with his
tiny hands, smote her flanks with his bare heels, and
screamed aloud with pleasure.

"A fine little fellow! O you dear boy of mine!" Antek
exclaimed admiringly.

And he at once turned off from the road, taking a short
cut that led straight to his barn, as the descending sun
painted the sky with gold and pale emerald-green, and the
wind went down, and the falling dew made the ears of corn
to droop.

He walked slow, with many memories at his heels:
Yagna among them, as vivid as in life. He rubbed his eyes
to get rid of the vision; but in vain. In spite of him, she
walked on by his side, as she once had done; and as then,
she seemed to shed around her such a delightful glow that
it made the blood rush to his head.

"Peradventure 'twas well Hanka drove her away! She
is to me as an ulcer in the flesh—a rankling ulcer!—But the
past will never be again," he said, a strange pain gnawing
at his heart; and he added, with stern reproof: "My wild
oats are all sown!" as he entered the enclosure.

In the yard they were busy over their evening labours,
Yuzka milking the cows outside the byre and singing a
shrill ditty, while Hanka made *kluski* in the porch.

As Antek went in to look over his father's apartments, his
wife followed him.

"After we have set things in order here, we shall remove
to this side.—Is there any lime to be had?"

"Yes, I bought some at the fair, and shall call Staho in
to-morrow: he will whitewash the place.—Certainly, we
shall be more comfortable here."

He peered awhile into every corner, thinking.

"Were you in the fields?" she asked him timidly.

"I was. All is in good order. Hanka, I could not have done better myself."

She coloured deeply with the pleasure of hearing him praise her.

"Only," he went on to say, "let that Pete go and feed swine, not till my ground! The good-for-nothing oaf!"

"I know him well, and have even been looking out for another farm-servant."

"Well, I shall tackle him, and—should he not be obedient —send him flying!"

Hearing the children cry, she ran to them. Antek went into the yard to continue his inspection of everything. He was so severely masterful of aspect, that—though he only threw out a word here and there—Pete felt alarmed, and Vitek, afraid to come near him, slunk about at a respectful distance.

Yuzka, was milking her third cow, and bawling ever louder and louder:

> "Still, Pretty One, be still,
>   And let me fill
>   The pail!"

"Why," he called out to her, "you screech as if flayed alive!"

She was dumb for an instant; but, bold and daring by nature, she soon struck up again, though in a less high-pitched key this time:

> "My mother begs of thee
>   This evening not to fail:
>   Still, Pretty One, be still!"

"Can you not be quiet? Master is present!" Hanka said, reprovingly, carrying some water for the cow to drink.

Antek took the vessel from her hands, and set it before the cow, saying with a laugh:

"Screech away, Yuzka, screech away; you'll drive all the rats off the premises in no time!"

"I shall do just as I please!" she answered back sulkily, in a mood to quarrel. But as soon as they had gone by, she ceased her song, though she still eyed her brother askance, with a resentful sniff.

Hanka, busy with the pigs, carried them so many heavy tubs of mash that he was sorry for her.

"That is too hard work for you; let the lads carry them," he said. "And I shall get you a wench besides; Yagustynka is of no more use to you than the whining of a dog!— Where is she now?"

"Gone to her children, to make it up with them!—A wench? Well, one would be handy; but the expense!—I could manage things by myself. But let it be as you will have it." It was surprising (so grateful she felt) that she did not kiss her husband's hand. In great glee, she added: "And then I should be able to breed yet more geese, and fatten yet another swine for sale."

After revolving the matter in his mind, he came to this conclusion:

"Now we have a farm of our own, we must behave as becomes our condition, and as our fathers have always done!"

After supper, he went outside the hut, to receive his friends and acquaintances, who had come to welcome him back with great joy.

"We were looking out for you," Gregory said, "even as the kite looks out for rain."

"Ah, well, they kept me there, they kept me, that pack of wolves! and there was no getting away from them!"

All sat down in the shadow of the hut. There were lights on every side, and bright stars overhead; the mill-pond murmured, moaning now and then; and all around it the people were enjoying the cool of the evening.

Roch interrupted some commonplace talk with: "Know ye that the head official has decided there is to be an assembly here in a fortnight, to vote for a school?"

"Is that our business?" young Ploshka cried. "Let our fathers see to it."

Gregory took him up sharply. " 'Tis easy enough to lay

all on our fathers' backs, and lie lazily on our own! The
reason things go so ill in the village is that none of us
younger men will trouble about them."

"Let them make over their lands to us, and we will!"

This was an opening for a dispute, when Antek suddenly
interposed.

"We certainly do need a school here; but we ought not
to vote half a kopek for such a one as the head official would
give us."

Roch seconded him strongly, urging them all to resist.

"Ye will each vote a *zloty*, and have to pay a rouble. . . .
What about the vote for the Law-Court Building, eh?
They have fattened finely on your money; their bellies pro-
trude with a vengeance!"

"I am decidedly against the vote," said Gregory, and,
taking up some books, he went to study quietly by Roch's
side.

There was little further talk after that; even Matthew
spoke but few words, only keeping his eye upon Antek; and
they were about to go home, when the blacksmith appeared.
He had but just come back from the Manor, he said, and
fell a-cursing both village and villagers.

"And what ails you now?" asked Hanka, peeping out of
the window.

"What, indeed?—I shame to tell it: our peasants here are
all louts and boobies! They don't know their own mind.—
The Squire behaved to them as to men and landholders;
and they, they acted like mere gooseherds. The agreement
had been made: naught was required but to sign it. Then
one of them scratches me his head and grunts: 'Shall I . . .
or shall I not?' Another would fain still consult his goodwife anew; a third sets to whining for a bit of meadow ad-
jacent to his land, that he wants given him.—What can be
done with such fellows?—The Squire is raging—will not
hear of the agreement any more, nor let any of the cattle
from Lipka graze on his lands, and will make anyone smart
that sends them there."

This unforeseen calamity dismayed them all, and they

had no words too strong for the guilty. Matthew said with sorrow:

"All this comes from the people's having no leader. We are like stray sheep!"

"Has not Michael pointed this out to them clearly enough?"

"Oh, Michael! He goes where gain is to be had, and holds with the Manor: none therefore will trust him. They listen; but as to following what he says . . . !"

Here the smith swore he cared only for the public good, even to giving time and trouble gratis, that the agreement might be made!

"And if ye should swear that in church," Matthew growled, "they still would not believe you."

"Let someone else, then, try," he retorted; "we shall see how he succeeds."

"Yes, someone else ought certainly to try."

"And who? The priest? Or the miller perhaps?" several men asked ironically.

"Who?—Why, Antek Boryna! If he cannot bring folk to their senses, we must give them up as a bad job."

"I?—I?" Antek faltered, in confusion. "Will anyone hearken to me?"

"All will! You are an able man, and the foremost amongst us."

"True it is!—Aye, aye!—You and none other!—We'll follow you!" were the cries that arose—not much to the smith's taste, seemingly. He twisted about, scratched his moustache, and grinned maliciously when Antek said:

"Well, well, they say: 'Pot-making is for others than saints.'—I can but try; and we'll talk the matter over another time."

Several, as they went away, took him aside, urging him to accept, and promising their support. Klemba said:

"We must have someone to lead us, who has wits and a strong hand, and honesty into the bargain."

"And," Matthew added, laughing, "who can command, and use a cudgel if needful."

Antek now remained alone with the smith; Roch had gone aside to pray earnestly in the porch.

They talked matters over very quietly and very long. Hanka meantime went about the hut, shaking up the bedding, providing the pillows with clean slips, and making her ablutions as for some great solemnity; combing her hair by the window, and peeping out at the two men with growing impatience. She listened attentively, too, to the smith, who dissuaded Antek from taking up such a burden, since he never could manage the peasants, and the Squire was against him.

"That's false!" she called out to him through the window. "He offered to stand bail for you in court."

"If ye know so much more about it, then let's drop the matter," he cried, surly as a dog.

Antek rose, yawning drowsily.

"But," his visitor concluded, "I'll just wind up with this: you are only at liberty till your trial; and who knows how things will go with you then? In such a position, how can you meddle with other folk's affairs?"

Antek sat down again, and was lost in a brown study. The smith did not wait for his answer, but went home.

Hanka more than once looked out at Antek, but he did not notice her. She at last called him in a tone of timid pleading:

"Come, Antek, 'tis bedtime; you must be very weary."

"Coming, Hanka, coming!" he said, rising heavily.

She began to say her evening prayers with tremulous lips, while she undressed in haste.

But he went in, sorely troubled, and thinking: "What shall I do if I am sent to Siberia?"

CHAPTER V

"PETE, bring firewood in!" Hanka called out from the cabin-door. She was covered with flour and very untidy with bread-making.

A big fire roared in the baking-oven. She raked the coals to spread them out, and hastened to roll the dough and shape it into loaves, which she carried out into the passage upon a board that she set in the sunshine, for them to rise more quickly. She bustled about in a great hurry, for the dough was almost overbrimming the big kneading-trough, covered with bedding for warmth.

"Yuzka! more wood on the fire; one end of the oven is almost black!"

But no Yuzka was at hand, and Pete did not hasten to obey. He was loading dung on a cart, heaping and pressing it down, keeping up meanwhile a conversation with the blind *Dziad*, who was occupied in making ropes of straw outside the barn.

The afternoon sun was so hot that the walls exuded liquid resin, and the wind blew like the blast from an oven, making every movement wearisome. The flies, too, hummed in myriads over the cart, and the horses, assailed, and maddened by them, came near breaking their halters, and perhaps their legs, in pulling and straining to avoid their bites.

The yard was so flooded with the heat, together with the pungent effluvium of the dung, that even the birds in the orchard close by could sing no longer; the hens had lain down half dead under the hedge, and the pigs wallowed squealing in the mud by the well. All at once the *Dziad* fell a-sneezing furiously: a whiff yet more noisomely offensive had reached him from the cow-byre.

"God bless you, *Dziad!*"

111

"That's no incense-smoke, I wot; and used though I am
to the smell, it is stronger than snuff in my nostrils."

"But use makes all things pleasant."

"Fool! don't you think I ever smell aught but dung?"

"I was but repeating what my old grandsire told me when
my drill-sergeant gave me slaps in the face."

"Ha, ha, ha!—Did you get used to that, pray?"

"I soon had enough of such drilling, and meeting the ruf-
fian one day in a quiet corner alone, I made his face swell
like a pumpkin . . . and he never slapped mine any more!"

"Did you serve long?"

"The whole of my five years! I could not purchase my
discharge; so I had to—shoulder arms.—At first, ere I knew
a thing or two, anyone who would could ill-treat me, and I
had to suffer want . . . till my comrades taught me to snap
up anything I needed . . . or get some maidservant to give
it me, whom I promised to marry. And what nicknames
those Russian soldiers gave me! and how they laughed at
my speech and at my manner of prayer!"

"Did they dare laugh at that, the plague-spotted
heathen?"

"Aye, till I punched their ribs for them, one after another, and made them leave off!"

"You must be a strong fighter!"

"Not especially," he answered with a boastful smile; "but
I could drub any three of them at a time!"

"Have you seen warfare?"

"Of course. Against the Turks. We thrashed them
soundly, we did!"

"Pete!" Hanka called out to him; "where's the wood?"

"Where it was," he muttered inaudibly.

"Your mistress is calling you," the *Dziad* said.

"Let her call! What, am I to wash up the pots for her?"

"Are you deaf?" she shouted, running out of the house
towards him.

"I shall not feed the fire; 'tis no duty of mine!" he
shouted back.

She began thereupon to rail at him to the best of her ability.

He, on his side, railed back at her, nothing loath, and when she presently gave him a harder home-thrust, he planted his pitchfork in the dunk and cried angrily:

"Ye have not to do with Yagna now: your screaming will not.scare me away."

"But what I will do, you shall see . . . and remember!"

She went on scolding the insolent fellow, while she carried the loaves of dough into the porch, or flung the logs into the oven, or looked after the children. But the labour and the intense heat were wearing her out terribly; for it was stiflingly hot within and in the passage on account of the fire in the oven. The flies, too, that swarmed on every wall, were so insupportable that she almost wept with rage as she beat them off with a branch, all streaming with perspiration, exasperated, and ever more impatient and slower at her work.

She was just patting the last loaf into shape for the oven, when Pete prepared to drive out of the yard.

"Wait a moment and take your afternoon meal!"

"Whoa!—Yes, I may as well: my stomach is empty enough after dinner."

"Had you too little to eat?"

"The food is so wretched, it goes through the bowels as through a sieve."

"There's insolence for you! What, you must have meat? And am I munching sausages in corners, say? No other farmers can at this season give their men what you get. Look at the *Komorniki*, how they feed!"

· She set down in the porch a pot of sour milk and a loaf, and he began to cram himself gluttonously, now and again flinging a morsel of bread to the stork, that had hurried in from the orchard, and stood now, like a dog, watching him eat.

"Poor stuff.—As thin as buttermilk," he grumbled, when pretty well filled.

"Naught less than cream would do for you, belike?
Wait till you get some!"

When he could eat no more and had taken the reins to
start, she said to him sarcastically: "Take service with
Yagna; she will fatten you!"

"Surely. When she ruled here, no one starved in the
hut!" And he gave the horse a stroke with the whip, and
the cart a push with his shoulder, to set it in motion.

He had wounded her to the quick, but was off before she
could find words to answer him.

The swallows were twittering under the thatch, and a
flock of pigeons alighted cooing in the porch. She drove
them away; and then, hearing a grunt, rushed out, fearing
her pigs were at the onion-bed. Fortunately, it was but the
neighbour's sow, rooting beneath the fence.

"Just put your snout inside our enclosure, and I shall dis-
pose of you in a fine way!"

But no sooner was she returning to work than the stork
hopped on to the porch, lurked about there for a moment,
cocked first his right eye at the loaves, then his left . . . and
set to dig into the dough, swallowing it by large morsels!

Uttering a loud cry, she rushed at him.

He fled away with wide-open beak, making frantic efforts
to get the dough down; but when she caught up with him to
give him a beating, he flew up and alighted on the top of the
barn, where he remained for a long time, rapping out his
klek-klek and wiping the dough from his beak on the thatch.

"O you thief! let me but catch you, and I'll shatter you
to bits!" she threatened, filling up the hollows the stork's
beak had made.

Yuzka came in then, and all Hanka's anger was poured
forth on her.

"Where have you been, you gadabout?—Always running
hither and thither, like a cat with a bladder tied to its
tail!—I'll tell Antek what a worker you are!—But get the
embers out now, and quickly!"

"I was only at the Ploshkas' with their Kate. All are

afield, and the poor girl has no one to fetch her water even!"

"What ails her, then?"

"The small-pox, I think; she is flushed and burning hot."

"And if you have caught it from her, I will take you off to the hospital."

"Is it likely? I have sat by a sick-bed already, nor ever got any hurt. Have ye no mind how I tended you, when you were lying in?" And so she went on after her fashion, prattling away in her absurdly thoughtless fashion, driving the flies off meantime and preparing to take the embers out of the oven.

Hanka interrupted her as she worked: "Ah! you must take the food to the people in the field."

"Instantly, instantly!—Shall I fry some eggs for Antek?"

"Do; but take heed not to put in too much fat!"

"Oh, do ye grudge it him?"

"How could I? But it might not agree with him."

Yuzka loved a run; so she did her work quick, and was off, before Hanka had closed the oven, with three vessels of sour milk, and bread done up in her apron.

Hanka cried to her from the window: "See whether the linen spread to bleach is dry, and wet it on your return: it is sure to be dry before sunset."

But the little chit was over the stile by then; the song she was singing floated back, and her hemp-coloured hair was seen bobbing along through the rye.

On the arable land, by the forest, the *Komorniki* were scattering the dung brought previously by Pete, while Antek was ploughing it in. The stiff clay soil, though it had been harrowed not long ago, was hard as stone and baked in the sun; the horses had to pull with such mighty efforts as to strain their harness to breaking-point.

Antek, seemingly glued to his plough-handles, drove his way on with dogged pertinacity, his mind concentrated on his work: now and then clacking the whip on the horses' hind quarters, but mostly encouraging them with a smack of his lips; for the work was really very wearisome. With

a firm steady hand he directed the plough, cutting furrow
after furrow, in long straight strips, such as it is the custom
to make for wheat-land.

Crows hopped along by the furrows, picking up earth-
worms; and the bay colt, that had been out to graze on the
field pathway, again and again pressed to its mother's side,
eager to suck her milk.

"Milk at its age! What can have come over the greedy
thing!" Antek growled, striking at its legs with his whip.
It ran off, tail in the air, while he went on ploughing patiently, only at times breaking the silence with a word or
two to the women. He was cross and tired out, and, when
Pete arrived, gave vent to his feelings.

"These women," he cried, "have been fain to stop working because of you; and you come on now slow as a rag-
picker!—Wherefore have ye stopped so long at the edge of
the forest? I saw you!"

"The 'wherefore' is there still; ye can see it; it will wait."

"A curse on your saucy tongue!—Vee-o, old fellow,
Vee-o!"

But now the horses went slower, foam-flecked and worn
out. He himself, stripped to his shirt and drawers, was
perspiring profusely, and his hands too were feeling the
stress of the work. So that, on perceiving Yuzka, he cried
out very heartily:

"Good now, 'twas high time ye came; we are all famish-
ing!"

He finished the furrow up to the pine-wood, took the
horses from the plough and turned them loose to graze on the
verdant road by the forest: then, flinging himself down
at the border of the wood, ate like a ravenous wolf, Yuzka
all the time chattering away until he had enough of it.

"Let me be.—I care naught for your tittle-tattle," he
said peevishly, and she, answering as peevishly back, ran off
to pluck berries in the wood.

The pine-forest was quiet, dried up, aromatically scented,
and, as it were, dying in the sun's fierce outpour. Only a
very little verdure was to be seen, and out of its depths

there blew a breeze laden with resinous fragrance, and carrying on its wings the warbling of birds.

Antek, stretched out on the grass, lit a cigarette and, looking into the distance, saw, as through a thickening fog, the Squire on horseback, leaping across the Podlesie fields; and some men with him, bearing poles for land-measuring.

Huge pines, with trunks as of red copper, rose above him, flinging down wavy and slumberous shadows. He would presently have fallen fast asleep, had it not been for the quick clatter of a wagon—the organist's servant, carting trunks to the sawmill—and then the sound of the familiar greeting: "Praised be Jesus Christ!"

One by one, the *Komorniki* were coming home from the forest, each with a load of firewood on her shoulders. At the very end of the file, Yagustynka dragged herself along, bowed almost to the ground beneath her burden.

"Rest ye here.—Why, your eyes are almost starting from their sockets."

She seated herself opposite him, leaning her load against a tree, and scarce able to breathe.

"Such labour is not for you," he told her with compassion.

"Yes: I feel quite crushed now," she replied.

"Lay those heaps closer, closer!" he cried to his farm-servant Pete, and went on: "Why does not someone take your place?"

She answered only with a surly look, and turned away her red eyes full of anguish.

"Ye are now so changed!—Ye give way so. . . . Quite another woman."

"'Even a flint will break under the hammer,'" she moaned, hanging her head. "And: 'Suffering consumes man faster than rust eats iron.'"

"The present season is hard even for well-to-do farmers."

"Hard! Let none talk of times being hard, so long as he has wild marjoram to eat, cooked with bran."

"Good heavens! come round this evening: we shall find two or three bushels of potatoes for you still. When harvest comes, ye can work the price out."

She broke down in a fit of crying, and could hardly speak to thank him.

"Perchance, too," he added kindly, "Hanka may have something else for you besides."

"Had it not been for her, we should have died of starvation!" she declared, sobbing. "Yes, I'll work for you whenever you may want me. May God reward you! I am not speaking for myself; I am accustomed to hunger. But my dear little mites are crying out: 'Grandam, give us to eat!' —and there is naught for them! I tell you: to feed them, I would cut off my own arms, or steal things from the altar, and sell them to the Jew."

"Then do ye live once more with your children?"

"Am I not their mother? Can I leave them in such misery? Every misfortune seems to have fallen on them this year. Their cow has died; all their potatoes have rotted (they even had to buy seed-potatoes); the gale blew their barn down; and, to crown all, my daughter-in-law has been ailing ever since her last child was born. They are all left to God's mercy."

"Aye, but why? Because your Voytek always reeks of brandy and only cares for the tavern."

"If at times he has taken too much, 'twas misery drove him that way," she said, eager in defence of her son. "Never, while he had work to do, did he even look in at the Jew's. But to a poor man, every glass is reckoned as a crime.—Alas! the Lord has dealt with them bitterly, very bitterly.—Is it right He should thus dog the steps of a poor foolish lout? And for what? What harm has he done?" she muttered, raising to Heaven her eyes, full of indignant challenge.

"But what! have ye not laid your curse on them?" Antek said, with strong signifiance. "Often and often ye have!"

"Ah, was it possible that our Lord should ever have listened to my senseless outcries?" But she added, in a tone of secret uneasiness: "Even when a mother curses her children, her heart never really wishes them evil.—'Wrath and woe make tongues go!' Aye, indeed. . . ."

"Has your Voytek farmed out his meadow yet?"

"The miller offered a thousand *zloty* for it, but I would
not allow it. What that wolf has once got in his grip, not
the devil himself could wrest out of it!—And perhaps someone else might be found with the cash?"

"It is surely a lovely meadow—can be mown twice a
year. Had I only ready money just now!" He sighed, licking his lips with strong desire.

"Matthias would have been glad to get it: it lies so
close to Yagna's land."

The name uttered gave him a start. He paused, however,
and then inquired, with an indifferent look, his eyes wandering over the country-side:

"How are they getting on at Dominikova's?"

But she guessed what was in his mind, and smiled with
thin lips, drawing closer:

"The place is a hell for them all! All there have funeral
faces: they are chilled to the marrow with the gloom which
fills it. They cry their eyes out, and live on, waiting upon
God's Providence. Yagna especially——"

And she set to weave him a story about Yagna's sufferings
and miseries and lonely life—adding all kinds of flattering
things besides, to draw him out. But he remained mute,
though such a raging desire for Yagna had sprung up within
him that he was quivering all over.

Luckily Yuzka, coming back from the forest, made a
diversion. She poured out into his hat the berries she had
plucked, took up the empty vessels, and scampered away
home. And Yagustynka, without waiting for any confi-
dences, rose to go away, moaning with pain.

"Pete!" he ordered curtly. "Take her back with you in
the cart!"

Once more he grasped the plough-handles and set patiently
to cleave the baked and stubborn clay, bending forward like
an ox under the yoke, and putting his whole soul into the
work, but unable to stifle the desire that surged up.

The day seemed very long to him. Many a time he
looked to see the sun's height, and measure the length of

the fields, of which much still remained to be ploughed. His trouble of mind increased, and he beat the horses, and cried furiously to the women to work faster. His agitation, too, was getting beyond bearing; and his brain swarmed so now with countless thoughts that his hands could no longer drive the plough steadily, and it would deflect against the stones. Hard by the forest, it went so deep under a root that the coulter was wrenched off.

To do any more work was out of the question. He took the plough away on a light sledge, to which he put one of the horses, and made for home.

The cabin was empty, and everything there untidy and soiled with flour: Hanka, in the orchard, quarrelled with a neighbour.

"The woman! She has always time enough for brawling!" he growled, on entering the farm-yard. There he grew still more angry: the other plough, which he took out of the shed, was quite out of gear. He worked at it a long time, losing his patience as he heard the quarrel going on, and Hanka raising her voice to a scream.

"If ye pay for the damage done, I'll give you back your sow: if not, I'll bring an action! Pay for the linen she tore in spring on the bleaching-ground; pay for my potatoes she has eaten now! I have witnesses to prove what has been done.—Oh, a clever woman this is!—Thinks to fatten her sow at my expense, does she? But I will not give up my rights!"

So she went on, and the neighbour giving her as violent language in return, the quarrel was waxing venomous, both of them stretching out their fists over the hedge.

"Hanka!" shouted Antek, heaving the plough on to his shoulders.

She at once ran to him, out of breath, and ruffled like an angry hen.

"Why, what a din you do make! All the village can hear you."

"I'm standing up for my rights!" she cried out. "What,

shall I suffer another man's swine to root in my garden? So much harm done—and am I to say no word?" But he stopped her short, with a sharp sentence.

"Dress yourself, and try to look like a creature of God."

"What now? Must I dress up for work as for church?"

He eyed her with disdain, for she looked as though some-one had swept the cabin floor with her. Then he walked away.

The smith was busy at work; his hammers were heard from a distance, loudly and tunefully clinking; and the forge, hot as hell, was uproarious with the tempestuous streams from the bellows that puffed in cadence.

Michael himself was working with his assistant, forging long bars of iron; and his face looked like a blackamoor's, and he beat on the anvil, as it were, out of sheer spite against it, smiting unweariedly.

"And for whom are those thick axle-trees?"

"For Ploshka's wagon. He is to cart timber for the saw-mill."

Antek rolled a cigarette and sat down by the door-step. The hammers went on with pertinacious fury, smiting rhyth-mically again and again on the red-hot iron, slowly chang-ing its shape beneath their strokes, as they bent it to the will of those who wielded them; and the smithy vibrated.

"Would ye not like to cart timber as well?" asked Michael, thrusting the bar deep into the flame, and working the bellows.

"I suppose the miller would not be willing. I hear he is the organist's partner, and hand in hand with the Jews."

"But you have horses," he said with bland friendliness; "horses and all that is needful. And your Pete does naught but lounge about your farm-yard.—And they pay pretty well."

"No doubt a little money before the harvest would be a good thing; but then, am I to go and beg the miller to do me a service?"

"No: arrange matters direct with the dealers."

"Whom I do not know!—If you would speak for me . . ."

"Since you ask me, I am willing—and shall go to them this very day."

Antek went out hurriedly; for now the hammers were playing, and a deluge of sparks of fire flew on every side.

"I shall be back this instant, and am only going to look what kind of timber they are bringing in."

At the sawmill, likewise, the workers were lively; the logs were being hewn into shape one after another; the saws rasped harshly through the great trunks, while the water, pouring out of the wheels into the river, boiled and bubbled and foamed, swirling along the narrow mill-tail banks. Rough pine-logs, with their boughs scarcely lopped off, thundered down out of the carts, till the earth shook; while half a dozen workmen were busy with their axes, squaring them for the mill; and others were carrying the sawn boards out into the sunshine. Matthew was foreman there, and Antek could see him busily engaged, both working himself and directing the work of the others.

They met with hearty good-fellowship.

"Why, what's become of Bartek?" Antek asked, looking round him.

"He had enough of Lipka, and is gone from us."

"Some folk must needs be always on the move!—Ye seem to have work for a long time in advance, with so much timber here!"

"For a year, perchance, or yet longer. If the Squire come to terms with all of us, he is going to cut down and sell the half of his woods."

"Ah! I saw them measuring the land out again on the Podlesie farm."

"Yes: someone comes to terms every day.—The silly sheep! They would not make an agreement one and all together, because they hoped the Squire would offer more. And now they make it apart and in secret from the others, each one striving to be first!"

"Some men are like donkeys, which, if you would have them go forward, you have to pull their tails. Yes, indeed, they are silly sheep.—And of course the Squire makes a good profit out of this state of things."

"Have ye taken possession of your property as yet?"

"No, it is too soon after Father's death, and we may not divide the land; but I have already overhauled the whole property carefully."

A face just then appeared amongst the alders on the farther bank of the river. Antek fancied it might be Yagna. The thought made him restless, and though the talk continued, his eyes wandered a good deal towards the bank of the stream.

"Now," he said presently, "I must go and bathe: the heat is unbearable"; and with that he went away down-stream, making as if in search of a convenient place. But as soon as he was out of sight, he mended his pace to a run.

Yes, it was she herself, with a hoe on her shoulder, going out to work on her cabbage-plot.

He soon reached and greeted her.

She looked round cautiously and, recognizing him as he bent forward amongst the parted sedges, stopped short, alarmed, bewildered, and uncertain what to do.

"What! don't you know me?" he whispered eagerly, trying at the same time, though unsuccessfully, to pass the river.

"Was it possible not to know you?" she answered low, looking apprehensively behind her towards the cabbage-plot, on which several women made red splashes afar.

"Where are you in hiding? I cannot find you anywhere."

"Where? Your woman drove me from the cabin: I am staying with Mother."

"Concerning that matter, I desire speech with you. Come, Yagna, and meet me by the churchyard this evening. I have something to say to you. Do come!" And he begged her very earnestly.

"Yes?—And what if someone should see me with you once more?—Of what has been I have enough already!" she answered. But he begged and entreated so hard that she felt her heart melting, and was sorry for the man.

"What new thing can you say? and wherefore do you call me?"

"Am I, Yagna, so altogether a stranger to you now?"

"No stranger; but yet not mine! I think no more of such things."

"But come only, and you'll not rue it!—Do you fear the burying-ground? Then come to the priest's orchard. . . . Have you forgotten where, Yagna? Have you forgotten?"

Yagna averted her head, for her face was suffused with crimson.

"Talk not foolishly; you shame me!" She was exceedingly confused.

"Come—come—come! I shall be waiting till midnight!"

"Wait, then!" And she turned away and fled to the cabbage-field.

He gazed after her greedily, full of such craving, and burning with such fire in every vein, that he longed to pursue and seize her in the presence of all—and could barely hold back from doing so.

" 'Tis naught—only the great heat has inflamed me mightily," he thought, and undressed quickly to take a bath.

The cool water calmed him down; its chill brought him to his senses, and he began to reflect.

"How miserably weak I am, for a trifle to upset me so!"

He felt humiliated and looked round, fearing lest someone might have seen him with her; and then he carefully passed in review all he had heard said against Yagna.

"A pretty creature you are, indeed!" he thought, in contempt not unmingled with sorrow. But suddenly, as he stopped beneath a tree, a vision of her came before his eyes, in all her dazzling and marvellous beauty. And he cried:

"There's not another like her in the whole wide world!"

This he said to himself with a groan, yearning terribly to see her but once again, to gather her in his arms, to press her to his breast, and take his full of those red lips of hers, and suck her sweet honey to the very last drop!

"Only, O Yagna! for this one last time! this once, this once only!" he cried aloud to her as if she had been present. For some time afterwards he rubbed his eyes, and gazed upon the trees around him, before he could muster sufficient strength to go back to the forge. Michael was alone, working at Antek's plough.

"Will your cart," he asked him, "be able to bear such a great weight of timber?"

"Let there be but the timber for it to bear!"

"I have promised: 'tis just as if you had it on your cart already."

Antek set to ciphering on .the door with a bit of chalk.

"I find," he said with much pleasure, "that I may earn about three hundred *zloty* ere harvest-time."

"It will," the smith remarked casually, "come in handy for that affair of yours."

Antek's face clouded over at once, and his eyes looked gloomy.

"Say that nightmare of mine! When I but think of it, I feel all broken, and care no more even for my life."

"That I can well understand; but not your having failed as yet to seek some means to preserve yourself."

"But what can I do?"

"Something must be done. What, man! the calf gives its throat to the butcher: will you do so too?"

"None can butt through a stone wall with his head," Antek returned, sighing bitterly.

Michael went on working with great energy; Antek sat plunged in disquieting and fearful thoughts, which made his face dark with changing expressions, till he started up and looked out in dismay. His brother-in-law let him suffer so for a considerable time, watching him with eyes full of cunning; but he finally said in a low voice:

"Casimir of Modlitsa found a way."

"He that fled to 'Hamerica'?"

"The same. A clever dog!—Aye, and a resolute one: who knew what he had to do, and did it!"

"Did they ever prove that he slew the gendarme?"

"He did not wait so long. No fool he, to submit to rot in prison!"

"He could flee: he was single."

"A man saves himself as he can. See, I do not advise you in any wise: I only say what others have done. But Voytek Gayda of Volitsa came back from penal servitude only last Eastertide.—Ten years. Well, 'tis not a whole lifetime, and one can survive it."

"Ten years! O Lord God!" Antek murmured, clutching at his hair.

"Yes; it was hard labour for that space of time."

"I could bear anything but that! God! I was there but for a few months, and came near losing my wits."

"Whereas ye could be beyond the seas in three weeks: ask Yankel."

"But it is so horribly far! How can I go—throw up everything—leave home, children, land, my village, and flee so awfully far—and for ever?"

He was absolutely panic-stricken.

"But yet so many have gone there of their own accord; and none of these ever dreamed of returning to this Paradise of ours."

"And I cannot bear even to think of it!"

"True. But take a look at Voytek, and hear what he tells about his penal servitude: ye will find it still more unbearable to think of. Why, the man is not forty yet, but quite hoary, and bent, and tottering: he spits blood, and can hardly move, and all can see he is bound for the 'priest's byre' soon.—But I need say no more: ye have your reason, and must decide."

And for the time he was silent; having sown trouble in the man's mind, he could safely leave it to grow up in time, and bring forth the harvest he expected. So, having repaired the plough, he said lightly:

"And now I am off to the dealers. Have your cart ready to carry the timber.—As for that other business, do not trouble. What is to be—is to be; and God is merciful.—I shall see you to-morrow evening."

Antek, however, could not forget his words. He had swallowed the bait of friendship, and it stuck in his throat, just as a hook sticks in the poor fish that has taken it and chokes. What pangs he felt—what sufferings he had to bear!

"Ten years! Ten years! Oh, how can I ever bear ten years!" The very thought palsied and benumbed him.

Arriving at his home, he trundled the cart into the barn, to have it in readiness for the next morning; but feeling a deep sense of weariness come over him—of the utter inutility of all his efforts—he only called to Pete, who was watering the horses at the well.

"Grease the cart's axle-trees, and have it in readiness for to-morrow. To-morrow you'll have to bring timber from the forest to the sawmill here."

Pete, who cared but little for such hard work, swore violently when he heard the order.

"Keep a civil tongue in your head, and do as I tell you. —Hanka, give the horses three measures of oats for provender to-morrow, and you, Pete, get them fresh clover from the meadow: they must have plenty to eat."

To Hanka's questionings he gave only a mumbled answer, and presently went round to Matthew, with whom he was now on a very friendly footing.

The latter, who had but just come home from his work, was supping a dish of sour milk outside his cabin, to cool him after the heat of the day.

Antek could hear, somewhere near, a sort of trickling sound—a querulous heart-broken wailing.

"Who is making that noise?"

"Who but my sister Nastka? I have enough of her love affair!—Her banns are all published now, her wedding is to take place next Sunday—and lo! Dominikova has sent word to us through the Soltys that the holding had been left to her alone; that she will not let Simon have a single strip of land, nor even enter her cabin! And the old woman will keep to what she says: I know her well, that creature!"

"And Simon? What has he to say to that?"

"What should he say? Ever since the morning, he has been sitting in the orchard as dumb as a post, and says not one word even to Nastka. I am afraid his mind must have given way!"

"Simon!" he cried out into the orchard. "Come this way. Boryna is here to see us; perchance he can give some good advice."

After a minute, he came and sat down, without any word of greeting to either of them. He looked very much broken down, and as thin as a plank of aspen wood. Only his eyes burned; and on his thin face there was a look of desperate resolve, from which nothing on earth could turn him away.

"Well," Matthew asked him in a kindly tone, "what have you made up your mind to do?"

"To take an ax and kill her like a dog!"

"Fool! keep such wild talk for the tavern!"

"As there's a God in heaven, I will kill her. What—what else remains for me to do? She drives me off my father's land, turns me out of my hut, gives me no money whatever —what am I to do? I am an orphan, cast destitute on the world; and whither shall I go—whither? My own mother has wronged me so awfully!" he groaned, brushing away a tear with his sleeve. Then, suddenly starting up: "No!" he cried out; "in the name of all mothers of dogs, I will not forgive this, I will not—not if I should rot in jail for it!"

They quieted him. He sat still, but sombre, and in such a state of dumb fury that he would not so much as answer Nastka's sobbing whispers. The others conferred together, thinking how they could be of use to him; but they found no means, because Dominikova, with her hopeless obstinacy, blocked the way. But at last Nastka took her brother aside, and pointed out a plan to him.

"She has hit on an excellent thing!" he exclaimed in great joy, on returning. "She says: Let him purchase six acres of the Podlesie farm from the Squire, to be paid by instalments.—Is't not a good thought?"

"As good as any, indeed.—But . . . whence shall the money come?"

"In any case, for the outset, and as an earnest, Nastka has her thousand *zloty* of ready money."

"True; but whence will the live stock come, and the cabin, the implements and the seed to sow?"

"Whence?—From these!" Simon cried suddenly, springing up and waving both his arms.

"'Tis good talk, that; but can you accomplish it?" Antek asked, in doubt.

"Let me but have it—the land to work on . . . and ye shall see!" he exclaimed with great energy.

"Then we have but to talk with the Squire and buy the land."

"Wait a little, Antek, wait a little; let us consider this in all its bearings."

"Ye will see how well I shall do everything!" said Simon, speaking hurriedly. "Who was it ploughed Mother's ground? Who reaped for her?—I alone! And was it work badly done? Am I a sluggard, tell me? Let the whole village answer—nay, let even Mother bear witness! . . . Oh, if I only have the land! . . . Help me to get that, O ye my dearest of brethren, and I shall thank you to the day of my death!" he cried, weeping and laughing by turns—intoxicated, as it were, with the joy of the hope which had come to him.

As soon as he was a little calmed, they set to deliberate and to talk over the idea and see what was to be done.

"Provided," Nastka said, with a sigh of fear, "provided the Squire be willing to accept instalments."

"I think he will, if Matthew and I guarantee their being paid."

Nastka, for his kindness, was ready to kiss his hands.

"I myself have had sufferings, and know how they taste to other folk," he said, rising to take leave; for it was dark upon the earth: only the sky was yet alight, and the evening glowed in the West.

Antek hesitated awhile in which direction to turn his steps, but at last bent them towards home.

He walked on very leisurely, and at length was close to

his cabin. The windows were open and alight, the children wailing within, Hanka raising her voice and Yuzka retorting shrilly. He could not quite make up his mind, till Lapa came joyfully whining and leaping up. Then—following a sudden impulse of ill humour—he gave the dog a kick and walked back to the village, going down the lane that led to the priest's orchard. He passed along the organist's premises so silently that not even a dog gave tongue; and gliding on outside the priest's garden, he was presently on the wide field-pathway which divided Klemba's land from that of his Reverence.

He was completely hidden in the dark shadow of the trees.

The moon, a sharp thin sickle, already glittered in the shadowy sky. Stars peeped out in ever greater and greater numbers; and the evening, though hot, was shedding dew upon the earth. Quails flew out of the rye; droning beetles whizzed over the fields, and the scent and silence of the meadows made the brain whirl in a sort of stupor.

Yagna was not in sight.

Instead, about half a furlong away, the parish priest, clad in a white dust-coat, walked about saying his prayers, and apparently so intent upon them that he took scant notice how his horses, from grazing on his own miserable fallow land, had crossed to Klemba's rich clover meadow, that rose high and dark, with lush growth and countless flowers, on the other side of the path.

The priest walked on, now whispering his prayers, now looking up to the stars, now stopping to listen intently. And whenever he heard any the faintest murmur in the direction of the village, he would turn round quickly, in seeming anger against his horses.

"You Grey One, whither have you wandered? Into Klemba's good clover, hey? Fond of other folk's property, are you not? What, shall I baste your flanks soundly, will you have me do it, hey!" And his voice sounded very stern.

But the priest's horses were eating with so good an appetite that he could not find it in his heart to stop them, in spite of the harm they were doing: so, looking round him, he reasoned thus with himself:

"Let them take a little, each one of them, poor creatures! I shall put up some prayers for old Dame Klembova's everlasting rest—or make the loss up in some other way!—Oh, the greedy beasts! how fond they are of that clover!"

And once more he paced back and forth, and said his prayers and kept watch, never dreaming that Antek was watching him, and listening, and ever awaiting Yagna more eagerly.

Some time passed thus. At last it occurred to Antek to go and confide his troubles to the priest.

"So learned a man must surely know some way out of them!" he thought, slipping away in the shadow of the barn, to appear thence boldly round the corner, and step out into the field-way, clearing his throat noisily.

The priest, hearing someone come near, called out to his horses:

"You mischievous creatures! You foul beasts! Cannot I take my eye off you for one instant, but ye must be at once on my neighbour's land? O ye swine!—Off with you, Chestnut!" And plucking up his long skirts, he drove them away very speedily.

"Oh! Boryna!" he cried, when the man was near enough. "Well, how goes the world with you?"

"I came to speak with your Reverence, and had been at your house already."

"Yes, I had strolled out to say my prayers and look after the horses: Valek has gone to the Manor house. But those misbegotten beasts of mine—Heaven save the mark!—I can do nothing with them. Look how magnificently Klemba's field of clover has grown. . . . Like a forest! And from the very same seed as my own. . . . And mine has been so frost-bitten that there's naught in my fields but camomile weeds and thistles." He sighed heavily, seating himself on a stone.

"Sit down; we'll talk together. What splendid weather

we have!—In three weeks we shall hear the sickles clinking.
I tell you we shall."

Antek sat down and tried to unburden his mind, while
the priest listened attentively, now shouting at the horses,
now taking pinch after pinch of snuff, and sneezing with
great violence.

"Whither! Whither!—'Tis not our land!—Behold what
perverse swine they are!"

But Antek did not make any headway; he stammered and
wandered a good deal in his explanations.

"I see you're in evil case.—Now tell me—tell me all
frankly: it will ease your heart! To whom can one speak
openly, if not to a priest?"

He stroked his head, and offered him snuff; and Antek,
encouraged, at last made a clean breast of it.

The priest heard him out, and then said with a deep
sigh:

"For the slaying of the forester, I should have given
you only a canonical penance. You were fighting to save
your father; and, moreover, the man—a libertine and an
unbeliever—is no very great loss. But the courts will not
let you off so. Ye will get at least four years of hard
labour! As to escaping . . . True, men can live in
America. And they get out of jail likewise.—But, between
the two evils, the choice is a hard one!"

And now he was for Antek's escaping instantly; now he
advised him to stay and work his time out; and said in
conclusion: "One thing is undoubtedly to be done: have
trust in God's Providence and wait upon His mercy."

"But they will put me in irons and drive me to Siberia!"

"Well, men come back thence: I myself have seen some."

"Aye, but in what state shall I find my farm—after so
many a year? How will my wife be able to keep things
going?—All will go to rack and ruin!"

"With all my heart I wish I could do something for you;
but what can be done?—Wait a little: I shall say Mass
for you at the altar of the Transfiguration here!—Pray drive

me these horses into the stable; it is high time—yes, yes, it
is high time to go to bed."

Antek was so greatly upset that he had forgotten all
about Yagna, whom he did not remember till he left the
priest's yard, and hastened to find her.

She was awaiting him, crouched in the shadow of the
granary.

"Oh, the time has been long—how long!"

Her voice was changed and hoarse . . . perhaps with the
falling dew.

"How could I slip away from his Reverence?" he asked,
with an attempt to embrace her; but she thrust him away.

"I am in no mood now for that sort of thing!"

"You are so changed, I know you no longer!" Her behaviour hurt him.

"As ye left me, so I am!"

"Were you another, you could not be more different!"
He pressed closer to her.

"Can you marvel, after such long neglect?"

"Never did I neglect you; but could I fly to you out of
prison?"

"I was alone—alone with my remorse and with a living
corpse!" And she shuddered with cold.

"And did you never think to come and visit me? Oh,
no, your head was full of other thoughts!"

"O Antek, Antek!" she exclaimed incredulously; "did
you ever expect my coming?"

"Can I say how much?—Like an idiot, I was hanging at
the bars every day, looking out for you." He stopped,
shaken with sudden anguish.

"My God!—And your curses on me—there, beyond the
haystack? And your rancour of old days? And when
they took you away, did you speak to me—look at me even?
Ye had a kind word for all, even for the dog—I marked
it well—but none for me!"

"Yagna, I bore you no grudge whatsoever. But a man
whose soul is tortured forgets both himself and the whole

world." They were speechless awhile, standing shoulder to shoulder, hip to hip, the moon shining straight into their faces. Both breathed heavily; both were torn with memories that seared them, and their eyes brimmed with unshed tears of agony.

"Not so did ye receive me, once upon a time," he said gloomily.

All at once she fell a-weeping with abundant tears, like a little child.

"And how shall I receive you, pray? Have you blasted my life and wronged me too little as yet, now that all men look upon me as on a dog?"

"I blasted your life?—Was't through me?" He was hot with anger.

"Yea, through you! On your account did that harridan—that offal—drive me from your door! And on your account have I become the laughing-stock of all Lipka!"

"Oh, and do ye no longer meet the Voyt? and the others besides? Ha?" he broke out grimly.

"All that—all!—came about because of you!" she hissed, pierced by his words to her inmost heart. "Wherefore did you force your will on me as on a dog? Had you no wife of your own? I was senseless; you had so befooled me that I saw no one in the world but you. And why did you leave me then, a prey to all men?"

But he, in a frenzy of bitterness, muttered between his set teeth:

"Did I constrain you, forsooth, to become my stepmother? And did I force you to be afterwards the prize of any that cared?"

"Ah! why did you not lift a finger to prevent me? Had you loved me, you would never have left me to myself, but saved me . . . as others would have done!" Her regret was so clear, so sincere and unfathomably deep, that he found no word to defend himself. All his former acrimony vanished from his soul, and he again felt love stirring there.

"Hush, my Yagna, hush, my little one!" he whispered tenderly.

"And this wrong besides have I suffered, that you—you, of all men!—should rise up against me with the others!" she sobbed, her head against the barn.

He led her away to the field-path, gathered her to his bosom, fondled her, caressed her silky locks, and wiped her wet cheeks, and kissed her trembling lips, and her eyes, welling with briny tears—those dear sorrowful eyes of hers! He showered every endearment on her, and presently her weeping grew fainter; she leaned her drooping head upon his breast, and put her arm round his neck with child-like trust.

But Antek's blood was by now all on fire; his kisses grew fierce and stormy, his embraces tightened to a crushing hug.

She at first did not realize what was coming on, nor what was passing in herself. It was only when she felt completely helpless, and knew again the power of his hot kisses, that she attempted to break loose, begging him in terror, almost with tears:

"Let me go! Antek, for God's sake, let me go!—I shall cry out!"

But escape was impossible: his wild impetuosity crushed all resistance down, and prevailed utterly.

"For the last—the very last, last time!" he ejaculated, in a hoarse breathless voice.

And the world turned round them both, and they both went down headlong into the boiling whirlpool. Both loved passionately, as they once had loved before—fainting, swooning, near to death.

As once—as of old—as in the past!

They forgot all—all save the tempest of fire that was carrying them away—all save their own insatiable desire. As the thunderbolt unites with the tree which quenches its fire and is itself consumed, so they each destroyed the other's passion in the tempest of their own. And for that one short minute of a rapture soon to expire for ever, after this last exuberant outburst, their former love had revived.

A moment afterwards, they were again seated side by side, feeling their souls very dark within them. Each glanced at the other by stealth, and as if in terror: each shunned meeting the other's eyes that spoke of shame and regret.

Once more, with lips eager for kisses, he sought her lips, but without success: she turned away from him with aversion.

In vain he whispered in her ear the sweet names of endearment he had once given her. She looked up at the moon, and replied not a word. In him, this bearing of hers aroused resentment, cooled passion down, and brought petulance and ill humour in its stead.

They sat together, unable to speak, each impatient of the other's presence, each waiting for the other to rise and go.

Yagna's flame was out to the last spark; nothing was there but ashes now; and she spoke first, with barely concealed animosity.

"In truth, ye did take me like a robber—by sheer might and main."

"Well, Yagna, and are you not mine—mine?" He would have embraced her again, but she pushed him violently from her.

"Neither yours nor anyone's!—Understand that!—No, nor anyone's!"

She fell a-crying once more, but this time he neither fondled nor soothed her. After some time, however, he asked her very seriously:

"Yagna, will you flee with me?"

"And whither?" she returned, her wet eyes looking him full in the face.

"Why not to 'Hamerica'? Would you go, Yagna?"

"But what would ye do with your wife?"

He started as though stung.

"Tell me true: will you give her poison?"

He caught her round the waist, showered kisses over all her face, and begged and entreated her to run away with him—somewhere—and be with him for evermore. He spoke a long while of his plans and hopes; he had suddenly caught hold of that idea—flight with her—as a drunken man catches at a fence to steady himself. He talked, too, like a drunken man, for he was carried away by his feverish excitement. She heard him out, and then said, with frigid scorn:

"Because ye have forced sin upon me, do ye think me such a fool as to believe this nonsense?"

And though he swore he was but telling her the truth, and swore it by all holy things, she would not even listen, but shook herself free of him, and said:

"Not even do I dream of going. Why should I? Am I so ill off, though alone?" Throwing her apron over her head, she looked cautiously round. "'Tis late; I must hurry away."

"Wherefore in such haste? Will anyone come from your home for you?"

"But for you 'tis time: Hanka has made the bed, and yearns sorely!"

The words made him snarl like a dog.

"Of him that is waiting for you down there at the tavern," he said venomously, "I do not remind you."

"Know, then," she said, with biting emphasis, "that more than one is waiting: aye, and are ready to wait even till morning! You would have it you are the only one, forsooth! You are too saucy!"

"Then off with you—go! Go, even to that old Jew!" he almost spat the words at her.

But she stood there still. They were both together, panting heavily, staring one at the other out of eyes full of hate, each seeking what words might wound the other most deeply.

"Ye had something to say to me: say it now, for never will I meet you again."

"Fear not: never will I ask you!"

"I would not, were you to come whining at my feet!"

"Without doubt; you are too busy, having to meet so many every night."

At that, crying: "May you die the death of a dog!" she leaped over the stile and into the field.

He did not follow, nor call after her, but looked on as she

ran through the fields and disappeared like a shadow among the orchards; rubbed his eyes, as if only just waking, and grumbled in sullen ill humour:

"My wits are clean gone from me! Lord! how far astray a man can be led by a woman!"

On his return to the hut, he somehow felt extremely ashamed. He could not pardon himself for what he had done: it obsessed and haunted him cruelly.

His bed—made in the orchard, the heat and flies within doors being intolerable—was awaiting him.

But he could not sleep. He lay looking up at the stars that twinkled overhead, and listening to the quiet footsteps of the night . . . and . . . making up his mind about Yagna.

"Neither with nor without her can I live!" He cursed her under his breath, and sighed in pain, turning from side to side, throwing off his covering, and wetting his feet to cool them in the long dewy grass. But no sleep came, and his thoughts persecuted him as before.

In the hut, one of the children set up a wail, and Hanka murmured some words. He lifted his head; but soon all was still again. And then his mind began to swarm with thoughts; the memories of past joys came floating about him, like fragrant spring breezes. But he was not now to be their slave any more; now he could resist their charms, and contemplate them with calm deliberation, and in their very presence take a firm resolve, as solemn as if he were at Holy Confession.

"This must cease—and for ever!—'Tis a foul offence against God!—Would I have folk speak about me anew?— Am I not a landed man, a father?—Aye, I must—I must— end all this now."

He felt the resolve to be unutterably painful to keep; but he took it nevertheless.

And a bitter but deep reflection occurred to him: "Let a man but once go wrong, he may come to cling so to iniquity that even death itself will not part them!"

It was dawn now, and the sky seemed covered with a

mantle of grey cloth, but Antek was yet waking: and as
soon as the daylight had come, Hanka appeared at his side.
He looked at her with eyes full of sadness, but wonderfully
gentle; and when she told him what the smith had called
to let her know late the evening before, he passed his hand
kindly over her unkempt hair.

"If the carting pays, I'll buy you something at the fair."
Such gracious behaviour on his part made her radiant
with joy, and she pressed him hard to get her a glazed side-
board, "such as the organist possessed."

"And soon ye'll be thinking of a sofa like those at the
Manor!" he said, laughing; but, promising her all she
wanted, he rose early, to put his neck under the yoke again,
and take up the work which waited for him at all times.

He had a further talk with the blacksmith, and directly
after breakfast sent Pete to cart dung afield, while he
himself went to the wood with a couple of horses.

In the clearing, the work was going on with great alacrity.
Many men were busy shaping the wood cut down in winter-
time; the ceaseless strokes of the axes and rasping of the
saws put one in mind of woodpeckers, tapping everlastingly.
In the long grass of the glades, the horses of Lipka were
grazing, and the smoke of their fires curled upward.

He recalled the scene which had taken place there, and,
seeing the men of Lipka now working together in amity
with the "nobles" of Rzepki and the others, he nodded his
head.

"Misery has taught them its lesson: a needful one, was it
not?" he said to Philip, Yagustynka's son, who was squaring a pine-log.

"But who was at fault save the Squire and the farmers?"
the man growled sullenly, continuing to lop off the boughs.

"Rather, much rather, foolish spite and bad blood!" said
Antek.

He stopped at the place where he had killed the forester,
and swore softly to himself; for he felt the passion of yore
stirring within him anew.

"The wretch! it is he that has brought me to this!—If I

could, I would serve him worse still!"—He spat angrily, and set to work.

All day long he went on carting timber to the sawmill, working as if for dear life: yet he could neither drive from his mind the remembrance of Yagna nor of his impending trial.

A few days after, he heard from Matthew that the Squire was willing not only to accept instalments, but to let them have other wood in addition to the big timber; and so Nastka's wedding had been put off until such time as Simon should be settled on his own land.

But other folk's affairs interested him little now; and the blacksmith, who visited him almost every day, was constantly terrifying him, speaking about his unhappy position, and promising him pecuniary help to escape, should he be in sore straits.

Antek was at such moments quite ready to throw everything up and flee; but again, looking round him at the countryside, and reflecting that flight would mean leaving all that for ever, he was panic-stricken, and would have preferred even the worst of prisons.

Yet the thought of a prison, too, filled him with despair.

All these inward struggles weighed him down, made him grow haggard and bitter, and harsh and fierce with those at home. What had come over him? Hanka did her very utmost, but to no purpose, to find this out. She had instantly suspected him of renewing relations with Yagna. But her own close scrutiny, and that of Yagustynka (whose fidelity was well paid) and others besides, assured her that the two were quite apart now, and never met: so she was at ease on that score. And yet, no matter how faithful a servant she proved herself, giving him the best food with the most exact punctuality, making the cottage a pattern of neatness and cleanliness, and the farm stock the very perfection of success—all would not do. He was always sullen, morose, ready to upbraid her for the slightest cause, and more than miserly of kind words. And it was worse still when he went about speechless, dreary, sad as an

autumn night—not angry, not ill-tempered—only sighing
deeply; often spending his whole evening with his acquaintances in the tavern.

She durst not question him openly; and Roch vowed that
he was aware of nothing wrong. It might well be the truth.
The old man was now seen at their cottage only at night.
The whole day he was going about with his books, teaching
the peasants to pray to the Sacred Heart of Jesus—a devo-
tion which the Russian Government had severely forbidden
in church.

One evening, all being together at supper, the dogs set
to barking furiously along the mill-pond. Roch laid his
spoon down and listened attentively.

"Some stranger.—I'll go and see who it is."

He returned in a minute, very pale, and saying:

"Sabres are flashing along the road.—If I should be asked
after, I am in the village."

And he slipped away amongst the orchard-trees.

Antek, white as a corpse, started to his feet. Dogs barked
outside the fence; and men, heavily tramping, were heard
in the porch.

"Have they come to fetch me?" he faltered, terror-
struck.

They were all petrified: the gendarmes appeared on the
threshold.

Motionless, Antek glanced at the open doors and windows. Luckily, Hanka had presence of mind enough to
offer them settles and beg them to be seated.

They answered with civility enough, and at once threw
out hints about supper, so that she had to prepare some
scrambled eggs for them.

"Where are ye going so late?" Antek at length made
bold to ask them.

"On duty! We have much to do," their leader returned,
with a glance round him.

"After thieves, no doubt!" he continued, with more as-
surance, bringing a bottle out of the store-room.

"After thieves—and others. . . . Drink to us, goodman."

He did so. And then they set to upon the scrambled eggs, till their spoons scraped together the empty dish.

The inmates sat silent, like terror-stricken rabbits.

After cleaning the platter, they took another glass of vodka; and their leader, wiping his moustaches, said impressively:

"Is it long since ye were let out of prison, say?"

"Surely your Honour can answer that best."

He stirred impatiently; then, on a sudden:

"Where is Roch?" he asked.

"Which Roch?" was Antek's reply, who had understood on the spot, and felt much more at his ease.

"A certain Roch, I am told, is living with you."

"Can your Honour be speaking of that beggar who haunts our village?—'Tis true, his name is Roch."

The gendarme fidgeted again, and said with a threatening look:

"Play me no tricks, he is known to dwell with you!"

"Surely, he had his abode here at times, but elsewhere likewise. Where he happens to find himself, there he spends the night: 'tis his way. Now in the cabin, now in the byre, and oft beneath the hedges.—Is your Honour in any wise interested in the man?"

"I? In no wise: I ask to be informed."

"A good honest man he is," Hanka put in here; "nowhere does he trouble the waters."

"We know, we know well what manner of man he is!" he grumbled emphatically, and continued to seek for information about him by various arts—even going the length of offering them snuff. But they all answered so that he was just as wise as before; and in the end, finding himself no farther on the trail, he got up in a rage, crying:

"And I declare that the man dwells in your cabin!"

Here Antek blurted out: "Think ye I have him in my pocket?"

"Boryna!" the gendarme returned fiercely; "I am here on duty: understand that!"—But he took leave in more friendly fashion, carrying with him as a present a dozen eggs and a very large pat of fresh butter.

Vitek followed them on their way step by step, and said afterwards how they had been at the Soltys's and the priest's, and had also tried to look in at several windows yet alight; only they could make no discoveries for the barking of the dogs, and had gone away as they came.

Now this incident had upset Antek to such a degree that, no sooner was he alone with his wife, than he told her his trouble.

She did not interrupt him by one single word, until at last he told her there remained nothing for him to do but to sell everything and go abroad—even to "Hamerica."

Then she stood up before him, pallid, ashen-white.

"I will not go!" she cried, with a dark frown. "No, nor let my children go either, to destruction! Not I! And if you think to force me, I'll cleave their skulls with an ax and leap down the well myself. And I am speaking the truth, so help me, O Lord God!" she screamed, kneeling down before the holy images, as one does to take a solemn vow.

"Hush, hush, dear!" Antek said. "I never meant it!"

She caught her breath, and continued, with difficulty restraining her tears:

"You will work out your time and come back. Fear nothing: I will manage all, and not lose one strip of land. Ye know me not as yet!—No, I will keep a firm grip on everything. And our Lord will help me to pull through with this affliction too." Then she wept silently.

He too was mute for a long while. At last he said:

"God's will be done! I must await my trial here."

And thus did all the blacksmith's scheming and treachery prove a dead failure.

CHAPTER VI

"LIE still once for all, and trouble me not!" Matthew growled, rolling over on the other side in a bad temper.

Simon was quiet for a minute; but as soon as ever Matthew was snoring again, he slipped away behind the corn-bin; for they were sleeping in the barn, and he fancied he could see the first faint streaks of morning light.

He got at the tools that had been laid ready the evening before, groping for them in the dark; and he made such haste that some fell to the floor with a loud thud, and Matthew swore in his sleep.

Darkness still reigned over the land, though the stars were paling, and a little light glimmered in the east, and the first cocks were crowing, flapping their wings.

Simon carried off all his belongings in a wheelbarrow and, creeping stealthily by the hut, made his way round the pond, where all was still, save for the bubbling of the water through the lifted sluices.

The roads lay in the shadows of the orchards, so dark that scarcely a white wall was visible in places, and the mill-pond could only just be made out by the reflected stars.

As he passed his mother's cabin, he went slower, listening intently. Someone was going to and fro in the enclosure, muttering incessantly.

"Who's there?" He recognized his mother's voice.

He stood mute, with bated breath, not daring to stir until the old woman began to move once more, without waiting for his answer.

"She prowls by night, like a tormented soul!" he thought with a mournful sigh, and glided past in dread.

He could just see her—a shadow gliding on from tree to

tree, feeling her way with her stick, and mumbling some litany as she went along.

"The wrongs she has done me is gnawing, gnawing at her heart!" he said, with a strange sense of relief at the bottom of his soul, and went out into the broad road, all ruts and hollows. Once there, he walked on speedily, as if driven onwards, caring nothing either for ruts or for holes.

He never stopped till he got to the cross where the two roads leading to Podlesie met. It was too dark to do anything yet; so he sat down by the crucifix to wait and breathe a little.

"Plague on the hour, that lets one not distinguish field from wood!" he grumbled, casting his eyes around him. All about him was palpitating darkness: only above were there a few pale gold streaks.

Waiting was irksome, so he tried to say his morning prayer, but ever and anon, laying his hand upon the dew-drenched soil, forgot what words to say because of the pleasant thought which then would rush in upon him—that he was now on his own land, his own farm!

"I hold you now, nor ever will let you go!" he thought; and full of the courage and joy and infinite determination given by love, he let his ardent glances wander over the dark blurred expanse by the forest, where the six acres the Squire had sold him awaited his tillage.

"Dear orphan land, I will take you unto my heart, and never, whilst I have life, will I forsake you!" And as he spoke, he wrapped his sheepskin closer over his ragged garments. The cool of the night had been somewhat penetrating: he leaned back against the cross, and soon fell into a sound but noisy slumber.

When he leapt again to his feet, the fields were just growing visible, though yet indiscernible from a grey sheet of water, and the corn dripping with dew had touched him with its drooping wavy ears.

"'Tis broad day!—To work!" he said, stretching his limbs and kneeling down for a prayer before the cross; but this time not mechanically, as he usually did, to get it over

speedily. To-day it was otherwise, and he most fervently
besought the Lord's help. With all his soul, embracing the
feet of the Crucified Jesus, he entreated Him, his eyes
earnestly fixed upon that sacred suffering face.

"Help, O merciful Jesus! My own mother has wrought
me grievous wrong. I am Thine, I, a poor destitute orphan:
come Thou to mine aid! Yes, I am sinful; but succour
me, O Lord of mercy!—I shall order a Mass to be said—
nay, two! Also I shall bring tapers; and—if I do well
enough—will have a baldachin constructed for Thy service!"
So he vowed, pressing his lips lovingly to the crucifix; and
then walked round it on his knees and kissed the earth
humbly—to rise up unspeakably refreshed and fortified.

And then, to the holding he was now entering upon, he
cried out joyfully: "You shall see! Ha! You shall see!"
It was situated at the edge of the wood, one side of it joining the fields of Lipka. But, Lord! what land! what land!
A mere stretch of desolate wilderness, pitted all over with
hollows from disused clay and sandpits, and overgrown
with wild pear-trees, surrounded everywhere with thorns and
brambles. On each eminence, torchweed, wild camomile,
and dockweed grew in rank abundance, with (in places) a
scraggy stunted pine-tree, or a clump of alders or juniper-
bushes. On the lower grounds and in the swampy parts,
there were reeds and bulrushes in luxuriant growth. In
short, it was a piece of land that, as the saying is, "a dog
might weep over." Even the Squire himself had advised
Simon not to buy. He, however, had stood firm.

"'Tis just the thing for me! I shall make something
of it!"

Matthew too, appalled at the sight of the bleak dreary
waste, dissuaded him from purchasing it. "It was a bit of
sterile moorland, fit only for the farm-yard dogs to celebrate
their nuptials upon."—But Simon held out stubbornly, and
ended the matter by saying:

"I have decided. Any soil is good, when there's a good
pair of hands to work at it!"

He had taken it because of the low price—only sixty roubles per acre—and the Squire had promised besides to help him both with timber and otherwise.

"And what I said then, I stand by now!" he cried, and gazed round with beaming eyes. Setting the barrow down on the pathway, he walked round the borders of his territory, marked off by branches stuck into the ground.

Pacing on slowly, full of deep joy, he settled in his mind the order of his work: what to do, and with what to begin. It was for himself, for Nastka, for the whole future race of Paches, that he was about to work, and he felt as fiercely ravenous to begin as the wild wolf that has just seized a lamb and tasted its quivering flesh.

He then proceeded to choose carefully the situation of his cabin.

"Best build it over against the village, with the forest close on one side of it: so, 'twill be storm-protected, and the timber not so far to bring."

Having decided this, and marked the place of the four corners with stones, he threw off his sheepskin, crossed himself devoutly, spat on his hands and set himself to level the ground and fill the hollows left by the uprooted trees.

And now the day had risen, golden: cattle bellowed, well-sweeps creaked, and the fresh breeze, running over the corn, brought with it as usual the clatter of carts and the hum of voices. To none of these things did Simon pay any heed, but plunged furiously into his work, only at intervals stopping to straighten his back for a moment and wipe the sweat from his forehead. . . . Then he repeated his onset, with the clinging and insatiable pertinacity of a leech: all the while, according to his custom, talking to each object as if it were animated.

If he had to get a rock out of the earth:

"You," he would explain to it, "have lain and rested long: come, help to sustain my hut, 'tis high time."

Cutting down a blackthorn bush, he would remark, with a jeer:

"No use resisting, foolish one: you cannot withstand me. What, should I leave you standing here to tear my galligaskins?"

And to the wild old pear-trees he would say:

"Ye grow too close together, and must be moved; but ye shall make a floor for my byre, as good as Boryna's!"

Sometimes, stopping to breathe, he would gloat over the land with eyes of love, and whisper to it: "My own—oh, my own!"

For that soil, so weedy and barren, uncultivated and forsaken by all, he was full of pity, and would say caressingly, as though speaking to a child:

"Patience, have patience yet awhile: I'll till you, I'll make you fat, and you'll bear fruit like the other lands around you. Fear not: you shall be satisfied and rejoice."

The sun, now rising, shone straight into his eyes.

"Thanks, O Lord God!" he exclaimed, blinking; and added: "We shall still have dry hot weather for some time!" For the sun rose as red as red could be.

Far away, the Mass-bell rang, and the chimneys of Lipka were crowned with plumes of blue smoke.

"Have you a good appetite, eh?" he said to himself, and drew his girdle tighter, sighing mournfully. "But Mother will never bring you your breakfast any more!"

Other parts, too, of the Podlesie farm were now swarming with people, like him at work on their newly bought lands; and he saw Staho Ploshka, ploughing with a couple of strong horses.

"Oh," he thought; "dear Lord! if I could but have one of them!"

Joseph Vahnik was carting stones to lay the foundation of his hut; Klemba and his sons were digging a ditch round their holding; and Gregory, the Voyt's brother, was busy measuring something with a pole near the highway cross.

"That," Simon observed, "would be the very best place to build a tavern."

Gregory, having driven in stakes to mark off the places he had in mind, came up to greet Simon.

"Ho, ho!" he cried, his eyes round with amazement; "you're working as hard as ten, I see!"

"Can I do otherwise? what have I in the world? One pair of breeches and these two bare hands!"

He was surly, and would not interrupt his labours to talk. Gregory gave him some advice and went back to his own ground. After him came others, some to encourage him, some to gossip, some merely to smoke a cigarette and have a laugh; but they made Simon impatient, and he ended by flying out at Prychek:

"Ye might as well do your own work and not hinder others! Holiday-making on work-days—too much of a good thing!"

So they came no longer, and he remained alone.

It was blindingly bright, broilingly hot; and the sun had wrapped the world in a shimmering haze of light.

"Oh, but ye'll not drive me away so easily!" he said, addressing the sun; and then, perceiving Nastka, who was coming with his breakfast, he went to meet her, and pounced on the porringer with greedy hands.

Nastka, very far from cheerful, surveyed the fields.

"Why, what can ever grow on such wastes and moorlands?"

"Everything!—As you'll see. There will even be wheat for you to bake cakes of!"

"Oh, yes!—'While the grass grows, the steed starves!'"

"It will not, Nastka. We have our own land now; 'tis easier far for us.—Six whole acres!" he reminded her, eating away at full speed.

"Can we eat the earth?—How shall we get through the winter?"

"That's my affair: do not trouble. I have thought it all out, and shall find means."

He thrust away the empty pot, stretched himself, and led her off to see all and hear his explanations.

"This," he cried out gaily, "shall be the site of our cottage."

"Our cottage? Built of mud, perchance, like a swallow's nest?"

"Of wood and branches, and clay and sand, and whatsoever we can get: to last for a couple of years, till we are better off."

"Quite a Manor house, I see, you have in mind!" she replied in an unpleasant tone.

"Better dwell in one's own hovel than live in another man's house."

"Ploshka's wife desires us to spend the winter with her: she has offered us a room with a willing heart."

"A willing heart!—Willing, I know, to do anything to spite my mother, with whom she is always at odds.—Fear nothing, Nastka; I'll build you a hut, with window and fireplace all that is needful. You shall see: in three weeks from now, had I to work my arms to the stumps, it shall stand there, like Amen at the end of 'Our Father': yes, stand it shall."

"And, of course, you'll have to work by yourself?"

"Matthew will help: he has promised."

"Would not your mother," she faltered, "come in any way to your aid?"

"I would die rather than ask her!" he burst out; but at once, seeing how dejected she looked, he felt sorry and, sitting down at her side by a rye-field, stammered an explanation.

"How can I, Nastka? Me she has thrust out, and you she loads with curses!"

"But, good God! if she would but let us have one cow! We are like the very lowest of *Dziads:* with naught in the world! 'Tis fearful to think of."

"But, Nastka, there will be a cow: I have one already in mind."

"No hut . . . no cattle . . . nothing whatsoever!" she wailed, with her head upon his bosom, while he wiped her eyes and stroked her hair. All the time, he felt so sad that it was a wonder he himself could keep back his tears.—All at once he seized his spade, sprang to his feet, and cried in feigned anger:

"Woman, fear God! There's so much work to do—and you do nothing—only complain!"

She, sorely troubled, rose with him, but care was gnawing at her heart, and made her say:

"Even should we not quite starve, the wolves will eat us in this wilderness."

This time, he felt seriously angry. Turning away to work, he threw her these sharp words:

"Better stay at home than come here to talk nonsense and whimper!"

She wanted to appease him, but he pushed her away.

"Dear Lord!" he thought. "Indeed, a woman is of the some blood with a man; but she hath not reason such as a man hath. Wealth falls from heaven, not by lamenting and wailing, but by working with our hands.—They are all like children, now weeping, now laughing, or drooping, or full of malice.—Dear Lord!"

He went on grumbling thus, till his work had absorbed him so that he forgot all else on earth.

And so things went with him day by day. He would rise at grey dawn, and go home late in the evening, and many was the day when he exchanged no word with any living soul. Teresa or someone else now brought him his meals; for Nastka was working at the priest's potato-field.

People came to see how he worked; but at a distance, for he disliked talking. His unwearied activity made them wonder.

"There's plenty of grit in the fellow: who'd have thought it?" Klemba grunted.

"And is he not of the seed of Dominikova?" someone replied with a laugh. But Gregory, who had watched him all along closely, observed:

"True it is, he works like an ox; but we, we ought to make things easier for the man."

"We ought," they assented; "and we must, for he de-

serves help." But no one put himself forward, everyone
waiting for him to ask them first.

That Simon would not do, nor had even thought of doing.
And so he was one morning in much amazement, seeing a
cart come his way.

It was driven by Andrew, who called out merrily:

"Aye, it is I. Tell me where I am to plough!"

It was some time before Simon could believe his eyes.

"You, to have dared so greatly!—But you'll get beaten,
poor fellow!—You'll see!"

"I care not. And if she beats me, I will come over to you
for good."

"Did you get this thought all by yourself?"

"All by myself! For a long time I had been fain, but
they watched me at first.—Yagna too advised me not to
come."

He told him the whole affair in detail, while preparing to
work; then they ploughed all day together; and, on going,
he promised to return the next day.

So he did, with the rising sun. Simon noticed some slight
discoloration on his brother's cheeks, but only questioned
him after the day's work was done.

"Did she hurt you very much?"

"Oh, she's purblind, and cannot catch me easily; and then
I do not put myself in the way of her claws," he answered,
somewhat ruefully.

"And Yagna . . . she did not give you away?"

"Indeed no; she is not that sort."

"Ah, can anyone make out what a woman may take it
into her head to do?" He sighed deeply, and told him not
to come again.

"I can manage alone now. Later, at sowing-time, you
will help me."

So he was alone again, working out his days one after
another, like a horse turning a threshing-machine, and heedless both of the dreary solitude and the heat. For now it
was growing hotter than it had ever been—a glow like hell,
a conflagration. Scarcely anyone could work in the fields:

the skies poured down living fire. They were one sheet of
scorching incandescence: no breeze blew, no birds sang, no
human voice resounded, while the sun went steadily on from
east to west, raining down heat and drought.

Yet Simon worked every day just as at the beginning;
even sleeping afield of nights to lose no time in coming
over. Matthew endeavoured to restrain him, but to no purpose. He replied, curtly:

"I shall rest on Sunday."

On Saturday evening he went home, but was so tired out
that he fell asleep over his meal; and he slept almost the
whole of the next day. He did not rise from his straw bed
till the afternoon, when, dressing very finely, he sat down
to a dinner of plentifully heaped-up dishes, with all the
women in attendance about him, as about some grand per-
sonage, attentive to his least sign, and ever supplying him
with more and more to eat; then he, having filled himself
to the utmost, loosened his girdle, stretched his limbs in
lordly fashion, and cried merrily: "Many thanks, good
Mother!—And now, let us go and enjoy ourselves in some
measure!"

So he started for the tavern with Nastka; and Matthew
went too, along with Teresa.

Before him, the Jew bowed down to his waist, set vodka
on the table without being asked, and called him "Master!"
which puffed Simon up not a little. He drank as much as
behoved him to drink, thrust himself amongst the foremost
men there, and gave his opinion about everything.

The tavern was full, and the band playing to increase the
enjoyment; but dancing had not as yet begun. They only
drank one to another, and complained of the drought, of
the hard times, and so on, as usual.

Even the Borynas and the smith and his wife came; but
these engaged the private bar, where they must have enjoyed
themselves pretty well; for the Jew was again and again
taking vodka and beer in to regale them.

"Antek is staring at his wife to-day like a dog at a
marrow-bone: he's not the same man any more!" Ambrose

grunted sullenly, glancing towards the parlour bar, from whence there arose a pleasant sound of joyful voices.

Yagustynka's reply came pat: "Because he prefers his own clog to a boot that goes on all men's feet!"

"Aye," someone returned; "but such boots do not pinch!" And the whole tavern was in a roar; they all knew well who was meant.

Simon had not heard and did not laugh. Somewhat the worse for liquor, he was putting his arms round Andrew's neck, and saying to him:

"And you must now remember what I am, and be obedient to me!"

"I . . . I know well," the other stammered, with maudlin tears. "But then, Mother commands . . . commands . . ."

"Mother counts no longer! I am a landholder: hearken unto me!"

But now the band had struck up a dancing-tune; and as heels began to stamp and boards to resound and couples to spin, Simon seized Nastka by the waist, threw his capote open, set his cap at an angle, and, bawling "Da dana!" with the best of them, and stamping the loudest of all, he launched into the dance, whirling giddily and rolling along, blithe, noisy, clamorous—like a torrent in spate!

But, after a dance of two, he let the women take him home, where—presently completely sobered—he sat down outside the cabin. Yagustynka joined him and had a good long talk with him; and it so fell out afterwards that, although the hour was late, and Simon had thought of returning, he was no longer in any hurry, but waited, hovering and dangling about Nastka, and sighing like a furnace.

At last her mother said to him!

"Stay with us, spending the night in the barn: whereunto should you trudge about by night?"

"I'll make him a shake-down in the shed," said Nastka.

"Do not be so hard on him, Nastka!" Yagustynka said with a leer.

"What . . . what are ye thinking of? What next, I wonder!" she rapped out, greatly troubled.

"Hey-day! Is he not your swain? To forestall the wedding a day or two is no harm. . . . And then, the poor man, who works for you like an ox, ought surely to have some reward!"

"Oh, how true! Nastka! Nastka!" he cried, as she fled, and leapt after her and caught her, with many a kiss and entreaty, and held her fast.

"Would you drive me from you, Nastka darling? drive me away on such a night?"

Her mother had suddenly something to do in the passage; and Yagustynka withdrew, saying:

"Forbid him not, Nastka! There's so little happiness on earth: what comes—rare as the grain of corn a blind hen finds—pass it not by!"

In the enclosure she crossed Matthew, who, making a shrewd guess, called out to Simon within:

"I should never have had your patience!"

But next daybreak saw Simon hard at work again, and indefatigable. Only, when Nastka brought him his breakfast, he was even more greedy for a kiss from her cherry lips than for the porringer.

"If you do betray me, you'll be scalded soundly!" But while she threatened so, she was nestling to his bosom.

"Nastka, mine you are, and never will I let you go!" he bleated earnestly; and, looking into her eyes, added in a low voice: "The first must be a boy!"

"A simpleton you are! But who put all these naughty thoughts into your head?"—And, pushing him away, she ran off, her face all scarlet. Not far off, Mr. Yacek had appeared, pipe in mouth and violin tucked under his arm. He came up, "praised God," and asked him a few questions. Simon, much elated, bragged about what he had achieved, but stopped all at once, rolling the eyes of bewilderment. Mr. Yacek had laid down his violin, taken off his coat, and set to work, stirring and softening a mass of clay! Simon's shovel fell and his jaw dropped.

"What is't ye wonder at?"

"What, shall Mr. Yacek work with me?"

"I shall, and will help you to build your hut. Think you I cannot?—You will see."

Henceforth they worked together. The old man had indeed not much strength, and was little wont to labour; but he had such ingenious ways that the work went on far better and more swiftly. And Simon obediently followed all his directions, now and then muttering:

"Heavens! this is unlike anything ever seen! A Squire!"

Mr. Yacek only smiled, and then, entering into talk with him, told him such wonderful things about this world of ours that Simon, had he only dared, would have fallen at his feet in wonder and gratitude. And in the evening, he ran to tell Nastka all about it, concluding:

"Folk call him silly: yet he is as full of wisdom as any priest!"

"There be some that talk wisely, yet act foolishly. What, would he come peradventure to aid ye if he had all his wits? And would he tend Veronka's kine?"

"That, indeed, I cannot make out."

"Save by saying he has lost his senses."

"At any rate, he is the best man in the world."

Simon was immeasurably grateful to him for his kindness. Yet, for all their working together, and eating from the same vessel, and sleeping beneath the same covering, there was nothing of familiarity in their fellowship.

"He always belongs to the race of the Squires," Simon said to himself, with profound respect and thankfulness. With his help the hut rose up, even as a loaf rises which has been leavened; and when Matthew had likewise come to assist them, and Adam, son of Klemba, brought all they required from the forest, the building was soon to be seen distinctly from Lipka, so splendidly did it get on. Matthew worked hard for nearly the whole week, directing the others' toil; and when (on Saturday afternoon) it was quite finished, he put up a cluster of green boughs on the chimney-top, and went off to some other work of his own.

Then Simon whitewashed the cottage, and swept the shav-

ings and rubbish away. And Mr. Yacek came with his
violin under his arm, saying with a smile:

"The nest is ready: bring the mother-bird!"

Simon answered: "Our wedding is to-morrow after
evensong," and fell at his feet to thank him.

"Oh, but I have not worked for nothing! When they
send me away from the village, I come to lodge with you!"
And, lighting his pipe, he strolled away to the forest.

Simon, though all was finished, still pottered about the
hut, stretching his weary limbs, and gazing upon it with an
unexpected intensity of joy.

"Mine! Aye, mine!" he repeated; and, apparently not
believing his own eyes, he would touch the walls, walk
round, peep in at the window, and sniff the raw pungency of
the whitewash and the clay. It was late in the evening when
he returned to Lipka to get ready for the next day.

Everybody knew about his wedding, and Dominikova had
been informed by a neighbour, though she made out not to
have caught what was said.

Early on Sunday morning, Yagna several times slipped
away from her mother's hut, carrying various articles in
bundles quietly out through the garden, and taking them
over to Nastka. The old dame, though quite conscious of
what was going on, did nothing at all to prevent it, but
went to and fro in silence, with so sombre an air that Andrew only ventured to approach her after High Mass.
Which he did with great caution, and not very close.

"Mother, I am going out."

"Better drive the horses to clover!"

"Know ye not? . . . 'tis to Simon's wedding."

"Praised be God, 'tis not yours!" she answered bitterly.

"——Well, but only get tipsy, and you'll see what I'll do
to you!" With that threat, she groped her way out to a
neighbour's, while the young man put on all his finery.

"Yes, I will! . . . I will get tipsy, if only to spite her!"
he growled, scurrying fast to Matthew's cottage, just as they
were all setting out for church. But it was a very quiet

wedding: neither songs nor shouts nor music. In the church, too, there were only a couple of tapers: Nastka shed many a tear of shame, and Simon shot angry challenging glances round him at the few that were present. Luckily, when it was all over, the organist played them out with such a strain of music as almost set their feet a-dancing, and made their souls within them merry and jocund.

The wedding over, Yagna went back at once to her mother, and only looked in from time to time; Matthew performed on his fiddle, Pete accompanied him on the flute, and another beat the kettle-drum for them with fierce energy. They began to dance, even within the little cabin, and so many of the guests as felt inclined tripped it also to and fro outside, amongst the tables that had been set up. There was some eating, some healths drunk and conversation enough. All was quiet, though; for in broad daytime and with unflustered heads, they felt in no mood for noise.

Simon clung close to his wife, taking her into corners and kissing her so violently that they made fun of him; and Ambrose, in a bad temper, grunted:

"Poor fellow! enjoy yourself to-day; to-morrow you shall have to pay your score." And as he spoke, his greedy eyes followed the glass as it went round.

There was really no great life in the party; besides, no considerable merry-making could be expected, since many, having taken a little and sat for some time, as the rules of good breeding demanded, retired to their homes as soon as sundown set the sky on fire. Matthew, however, was very blithe and jolly, playing, singing, pressing girls to dance with him, and passing the vodka round; and when Yagna showed her face, he was her constant companion, ogling her, and talking, and utterly careless of the tears that glistened in Teresa's eyes.

Yagna, indifferent to the man, had no reason to hold off. She merely listened patiently to him, while on the watch for the coming of the Borynas, whom she wished not to meet. Fortunately they did not come; nor, indeed, did any of the first-class landholders. These, nevertheless,

not having refused the invitation, had (as was proper) sent
various presents in aid of the wedding-feast. Their ab-
sence being remarked upon, Yagustynka made a character-
istic reply:

"Had there but been dainties in plenty, and a cabin all
reeking with vodka, there would have been no keeping
them out, even with a stick! But dry tongues and empty
paunches please them not."

She was by this time somewhat elevated and mischievous:
so, having noticed Yasyek Topsy-turvy sitting in a corner
by himself, sighing miserably, wiping his nose, and eyeing
Nastka from a distance, she drew him out to address her
and so make sport.

"Dance with her, and take what may be had! Your
mother would not let you marry her; but frisk around her
now she has a goodman, and she may requite your love!"

Then she poured forth such talk as made the ears tingle;
and when Ambrose, having got enough to drink by now,
began to wag his tongue likewise, they set the ball rolling
together, and made everybody shake with mirth, till the
short summer night, spent in fun and frolic, came unexpectedly to an end.

And now no one remained but the family (and Ambrose,
bent on draining the very last drop left in the bottles). The
young couple decided to start at once for their new home.
Matthew wished them to stay a little longer; but Simon,
who had borrowed a horse and cart of Klemba, would not
hear of it. So he bundled lockers and vessels and bedding
into the cart, seated Nastka in state on the top, knelt down
for her mother's blessing, and, with a kiss for his brother-
in-law and a profound salute to the others, crossed himself,
whipped up the horse, and started off: the whole family
accompanying him.

They walked on in silence, till, close to the mill, a couple
of storks were seen circling high in air above their heads.
The old dame clapped her hands at the sight, and said:

"Knock on wood! Here's the best foreboding for you,
and ye shall have children in plenty!"

Nastka, reddened slightly; but Simon, who was pushing behind the cart, whistled jauntily, and threw exultant glances around him.

When at last they were alone, Nastka, looking at her new home, burst into tears at the sorry sight. But Simon cried:

"No crying, silly! Other folk have still less: they are envying you!"

He was very much worn out, and somewhat in his cups. So he flung himself down on some straw in a corner, and was soon snoring loud . . . while she, sitting near the window and looking down at the white cottages of Lipka, went on shedding tears.

This melancholy state of mind did not, however, last very long. All the village folk seemed to have plotted together to come to her aid. Klemba's wife came first, with a hen under her arm, and a brood of little chickens in a basket. It was a good beginning; and almost daily one of the goodwives looked in, and never a one of them empty-handed.

Their kindness touched her heart.

"Dear people," she said, "how can I ever repay you?"

"A word of hearty thanks will do," replied Sikora's wife, who had brought her a piece of linen cloth.

"When ye are at your ease, ye can pass it on to someone that is also in want," added Ploshkova, producing a goodly piece of bacon from under her apron.

So many presents did she receive that she had enough for a long, long time. And one evening, at dusk, Yasyek Topsy-turvy brought her his dog Kruchek, which he tied up close to her hut, and then took to his heels, as if in fear of some harm that might come.

They laughed heartily, as they told Nastka about this; but she curled a disdainful lip.

"At the noonday rest, Nastka, he had been gathering berries for you; and his mother took them away from him!"

CHAPTER VII

YAGUSTYNKA went to the Borynas'. She had gathered some wild strawberries, and brought them for Yuzka. Hanka was then milking the cows outside the hut; so she sat down under the eaves and told her of all the presents Nastka had got.

"But," she concluded, "they all do this to spite Dominikova."

"And," Hanka corrected, "to help Nastka also.—By the by, I too ought to take her something or other."

"If ye have aught that I can take now, I'll do it willingly," Yagustynka told her. And then from inside the cabin was heard a faint voice of entreaty—Yuzka's.

"O Hanka, give her my young sow! I know I am going to die, and then Nastka will say a prayer for my soul!"

The idea struck Hanka as good; she directly told Vitek to drive the little sow over to Nastka's, for she did not feel inclined to go herself.

"Vitek," Yuzka cried, "tell her the sow is from me. And she must come quick to see me: I cannot move now."

The poor girl was very plaintive and querulous. She had been in bed for a week, sick of a fever, all her body covered with crusts and scales. At first they had let her lie under the orchard trees, for she had begged them very hard. But she had grown so much worse that Yagustynka had forbidden this.

"You must lie in the dark," she said; "the sunlight drives all the ill humours inside."

So, moaning and groaning and complaining feebly that no children nor any friends of hers were allowed to come in, she lay alone in the darkened room. And Yagustynka, now constituted her guardian, drove away any that tried to come in, even taking a stick to them!

161

on the down coverlet over her, holding it up by the ears.

"Dear little leveret, sweet little leveret, taken away from your mother!" she whispered, holding it close to her bosom, like an infant in arms, and stroking and fondling it tenderly. But the animal screamed as if tortured, and, escaping from her hands, jumped out into the passage amongst a lot of fowls that took tumultuously to flight, rushed out of the porch just in front of Lapa, that was dozing inside, and away into the orchard. The dog was hot in pursuit instantly; Vitek followed, shouting; and the noise and uproar were so great that Hanka came out of the farm-yard: while Yuzka laughed almost to split her sides.

"And did the dog get it?" she asked, with anxiety.

"A likely thing!" he exclaimed. "No; he just saw its scut and no more, when it vanished into the depths of the corn, as a stone disappears in the water.—A splendid runner it is.—Do not be sad, Yuzka; I will get you another."

Whatever he could find, he brought to her: now a lot of gold-besprinkled quails, now a hedgehog, now a tame squirrel that leapt about the room the most funnily in the world; or a brood of young swallows, twittering so very sorrowfully that the parent birds flew after them into the room, and Yuzka ordered him to restore them to the nest; and many another curious thing; besides apples and pears, as many as they both could manage to eat without their elders' knowing.—But everything at last wearied her, and she turned away tired and caring no more for anything.

"All this is naught to me! bring me something new!" she would murmur, turning even from the stork, as it strutted about the room, poking its beak into every pot and pan, or placed itself in ambush for a sudden thrust at Lapa in the doorway.—Once only, when he brought her a rainbow-hued bee-eater, caught alive, did she enjoy the sight a little.

"What a magnificent bird! It looks as if painted!"

"Only take care lest it peck your nose: 'tis an ill bird to tackle."

"But it does not even try to get away.—Is it tame?"

"No, but I have bound its wings and legs."

The bird amused them for some time; but it pined away, sat motionless, and, refusing to eat, died shortly, to the great sorrow of all in the household.

So the days went by.

Outside, it was slowly getting hotter and hotter still: men could hardly do anything in the fields by day; nor was the night anything but a stifling time spent in a vast oven: even out of doors and in the orchards, it was so. The drought was swiftly becoming a disaster. The cattle came back to their sheds, lowing and hungry from the pasture-lands. Potatoes were withering to the size of hazelnuts; there were fields wherein the stunted oats rose but a few inches above the ground; the blades of barley were sere; and the rye, untimely dried up, was white with grainless ears. In deep trouble, therefore, they would look, each sunset, in desolate hope, for some indication of a coming change in the weather. But not a cloud hung in the sky. Above them there was only a glassy whitish glare; and the sun would go down unveiled by the faintest shadow of vapour.

Many a one now wept fervently at the altar of our Lord's Transfiguration, before the holy images; but unavailingly. The fields grew ever more parched, more scorched; the fruits fell unripe from the trees; and so little water now went down the stream that both flour-mill and sawmill stood closed, silent and dreary: while the people, reduced to desperation, united, each man paying his quota for a grand votive Mass, with exposition of the Holy Sacrament!

So heartily and so fervently did they put up their prayers that not even a heart of stone could have remained untouched.

And indeed our Lord did have mercy on them. True, the next day was so sultry, so perspiring, so fiercely glowing that birds fell fainting to the earth, oxen lowed plaintively over the pasturelands, horses would not come out from their stables, and men, wearied and worn, crawled about the dried-up orchards, unwilling to quit the shade. But it met Yagna, carrying a hoe and a basket. He greeted her cordially; she glared at him like a wolf, and passed on in silence.

"So haughty as that?" he grumbled angrily; and then, seeing Yuzka in the enclosure, rated her soundly for being out in the damp.

She was indeed so much better by now that they had permitted her to lie in the orchard all day long. Her sores were healing beautifully, and leaving no scars, and it was only in secret that Yagustynka continued to anoint her as before, Hanka grudging so great a consumption of butter and eggs.

So she lay, getting well slowly, almost all day long by herself, Vitek now tending the cows again. Only now and then did a girl look in for a while, or Roch sit with her for a little; or old Agata would come to say, as usual, that she was going beyond doubt to die in harvest-time, in Klemba's cabin, and as a peasant dame should die. But her most frequent companion was Lapa, that always watched by her side, the stork, that would come at her call, and the birds which flew down to her for crumbs.

One day, when no one was in the hut, Yagna came to her with a handful of caramels; but before Yuzka had time to thank her, she had taken to flight on hearing Hanka's voice somewhere, crying over the hedge:

"May they do ye good!"—She had vanished.

She then ran over to her brother's, carrying something for him.

She found Nastka beside a cow that was drinking water out of a tub. Simon was building an outhouse close by, and whistling with all his might.

"What!" she exclaimed, very much surprised; "have you got a cow so soon?"

"We have: is she not a beauty?" returned Nastka, very proud of her.

"Really, a very fine one: she must be of Manor stock. Where did ye buy her?"

"Though we have not bought her, yet she is ours! I'll

tell you all—but you'll never believe me.—Yesterday at
dawn, I was aware of something that rubbed against the
cabin wall, and thought it might be some hog driven out to
the pasture-lands, that was cleaning its sides from caked
mire. So I lay down anew, but was not yet asleep, when I
heard a faint sound of lowing. I went out; and behold,
there stood by the door a cow, tethered, with a bundle of
clover in front of her, her udders full, and her face turned up
to me. I rubbed mine eyes, thinking this to be some dream
of the night. But no: 'twas a live cow, lowing and licking my fingers. Then I felt sure she had strayed from some
herd; and Simon too said they would be coming for her in
a trice. Only there was one thing:—she was tied up.
Could a cow tie herself up in any wise?—But noon came,
and no one to take her away, and the milk was oozing from
her udders by then: so I eased the poor beast. I asked
through the village; no one knew anything of a cow lost.
Old Klemba said it might well be some thieves' trick, and
I had better take her to the *gendarmie*. I was sorry, but
what else was I to do?—Then, when noon came next day,
Roch came too, and said:

"'You are honest and you are needy; therefore hath the
Lord Jesus blessed you with a cow!'

"'A cow falling from the sky! Not even an idiot can
believe that.'

"Roch laughed, and, preparing to depart, said:

"'The cow's your own: have no fear! None shall take
her from you.'

"Then I thought she was his gift, and fell at his knees
to thank him; but he shrank back.

"'And if you should meet Mr. Yacek,' he continued
with a smile, 'beware of thanking him: he's a man to lay
about him with a stick, for he loves not to be thanked.'"

"Then 'twas Mr. Yacek who gave you the cow!"

"Is there another man in the world so kind to poor
folk?"

"True, it was he gave Staho the timber for his hut, and
helped him in so many other ways."

"A holy man he is, no doubt, and daily I will pray for him."

"But take heed lest any should steal her from you!"

"What, steal my cow? I would go over all the world to seek her, and tear the thief's eyes out! Our Lord would never permit such a wrong!—While Simon is building the shed, I'll have her in to sleep with us every night. And Yasyek's dog, Kruchek, will take care of her.—O my dear one, O my darling!" she cried, taking her round the neck and kissing her pink muzzle; while the animal uttered a faint gurgling sound, the dog barked with joy, the fowls cackled for fear, and Simon whistled louder than all.

"Beyond all doubt, then, ye are blessed of the Lord," Yagna said, looking intently at them both, with a sigh of something like compunction. They both seemed changed beyond recognition; Simon especially. He had always passed for an incapable fellow, who bore the blame of all that went wrong; and anyone that cared to wipe his feet on him could do so.—And now! Able in speech, wise in his acts, and dignified in his bearing, he was really not the same man! . . .

After a long silence: "Which are your fields?" she inquired.

Nastka pointed them out to her, telling her what they were going to sow, and where.

"But whence is the seed to come?"

"Simon says we shall get it; and so we shall. Because he speaks no idle words."

"He's my own brother; but what ye say seems told of someone else!"

"So good, so clever, so hard-working! . . . There's none like him, none!" Nastka declared most emphatically.

"Surely," Yagna mournfully assented.—"And whose are those fields with the mounds marking their boundaries?"

"Antek Boryna's. Not worked at present, though, for they await the division of the farm."

"There will be a goodly bit of land for them, and a most comfortable holding."

"Oh, may our Lord, for their kindness to us, render them back tenfold! Antek stood surety with the Squire for our payment of the instalments, and has helped us in many another way."

"Antek! . . . Surety for payment!" She was astounded.

"And Hanka is not less kind: she has given me a young sow. 'Tis only a sucking-pig now, but of good stock, and will grow up to be of great use to us."

"Indeed, you tell me of a marvellous thing. Hanka give you a sucking-pig? 'Tis simply incredible."

They returned to the hut, where Yagna, having taken a ten-rouble note out of her kerchief, handed it to Nastka.

"Here's a trifle . . . I could not bring it before . . . the Jew had not yet paid me for my geese."

They thanked her very warmly, and Yagna said, on leaving:

"Wait a little; Mother will relent, and let you have some of the property."

"I do not want it! Let her take the injury she has done me down to her grave with her!" Simon burst out, so suddenly and with such vehemence that she left without one word more, and went home, moody, depressed, and not a little out of sorts.

"What am I? A dry stick that no one cares for," she sighed forlornly, as she went.

About half-way home, she met Matthew. He was going to his sister, but went back with her and listened attentively to what she said of Simon.

"Not all men are so well off," he remarked gloomily.

They talked on, but he did not feel at his ease. He was longing to say something to her, but embarrassed how to say it; Yagna was meanwhile looking down at Lipka, bathed in the sundown glow.

Then he said: "In this narrow little world, I feel stifled to death!" He was almost speaking to himself.

She turned to him with a questioning look.

"What ails you? Your face is as wry as if you had been drinking vinegar!"

On that, he told her how he loathed his life and the country and all things, and was determined to go away and wander forth into the world.

"Why, if you will have a change, then marry!" she said, laughing.

"Aye, if she of whom I think would but have me!" he cried, staring eagerly into her eyes; but she, confused and unpleasantly impressed, looked aside.

"Ask her! Anyone would be glad to marry you: more than one already expects your messengers."

"And what if she should refuse me?—The shame—the pain of it!"

"In that case, you'd send your men with vodka to some-one else."

"I am not that sort. I would only have one, and cannot turn to another."

"Oh, a young man has much the same liking for every girl, and would fain come to close quarters with them all."

This he did not deny; but presently, changing his mode of attack:

"Yagna, you know that the boys only wait for your mourning-time to end; men will at once be sent to you with vodka."

"Let them drink it themselves! I'll marry no one of them!" she declared, with so much energy as to made him think deeply. She spoke her mind: she cared for none of them; only for Yanek—her Yanek!

The thought of him made her sigh, and she gave herself up to it with delight, while Matthew, baffled, went back to his sister.

And Yagna looked into vacancy with wandering eyes of unrest, saying to herself:

"What—what is he doing at this moment?"

On a sudden, someone had seized and was hugging her close in his arms. She struggled violently.

"Will you not console me for my loss?" the Voyt whis-pered passionately.

Raging, she tore herself from his clutch.

"Touch me but once more, I'll tear your eyes out and call the whole village here to you!"

"Hush, Yagna, hush! See, I bring you a present!" and he pressed into her hand a necklace of coral.

"Put it . . . !" Her exasperation may be some excuse for what she said. "All your gifts are mere rubbish to me!"

"But, Yagna, what—what means this?" he stammered, stupefied.

"It means this much: ye are a hog! And are never to speak to me any more!"

She broke away from him in a towering passion, and rushed home.

Her mother was peeling potatoes; Andrew was milking the cows, out of doors. She set herself busily to perform her evening duties, though still trembling all over with anger and unable to calm herself; and as soon as the twilight had gathered, she went out to roam again, saying to her mother:

"I am going to look in at the organist's."

Soon she beheld the windows of Yanek's room, shining bright in the darkness; there Michael was writing under the suspended lamp, while the organist and his dame sat outside the house, taking the cool of the evening.

They greeted her with the news: "Yanek is to be here to-morrow afternoon!"

The bliss of it nearly made her fall senseless at their feet. Her knees bent under her; her heart beat so fast that she could scarcely breathe. Having sat with them a few minutes for courtesy's sake, she fled away along the poplar road and towards the wood, swift as a hunted beast. . . . "Lord! Lord!" she burst out in strange thanksgiving: she stretched forth her arms, tears gushed from her eyes, and a marvellous feeling of gladness came over her, so intense that it gave her a longing to laugh, to scream out, to run like mad, and kiss the trees around her and the fields beneath, that lay silvery in the moonlight!

"Yanek is coming—is coming—is coming!" she crooned to herself, darting forward suddenly with the rapidity of a bird, and running on, impelled by her desires and her anticipations, as if towards the achievement of her destiny, and towards ineffable delight.

When she got home, it was late. All the village was dark except Boryna's hut, where many people had assembled to debate; and as she went, she thought only of the morrow and of Yanek's return.

Back in the hut, she could not fall asleep. As soon as she heard her mother's rasping stertorous breath, she ceased from tossing on her pillow, and went to sit out of doors and await there either slumber or daybreak.

She could now and again catch the sound of voices at Boryna's, across the water, and, one side of his hut being lighted, she perceived the tremulous reflection of the light in the pond opposite her.

Her eyes fixed on this, she forgot about all things . . . lost in a multitude of dreary thoughts that wrapped her about like gossamer tissues, and carried her away with them into the universe of unsatiable yearnings!

The moon was down, the country-side of a murky brown tint. Many stars shone on high; and from time to time one of them would fall with such swiftness and from so enormous a height as to thrill every limb of her with dread. Sometimes a faint breeze swept gently by, like the touch of tender hands; and then the pleasant waft, warm and odorous, coming up from the fields, made her stretch and stiffen her body in the voluptuous enjoyment of that fragrance.

Absorbed, entranced in this reverie, of which no words can tell the sweetness, she remained immobile, like a swelling shoot of some young plant, gathering within itself hoards of sap and vegetable life. . . . And the night passed on, silent and careful, as it were, not to disturb human nature in its rapturous bliss.

Within Antek's cabin, the men that held with him and Gregory were talking of the assembly that was to take place next day at the District Office, and to which the Voyt had convened all the farmers of Lipka.

There were about a score of peasants there—the whole

party of Antek and Gregory—lighted only by one small candle that glimmered on the penthouse of the chimney.

Roch, who sat in the shadow, was explaining at length the results of opening the school in Lipka as proposed; and Gregory was telling each man in particular how to vote and what to say to the head of the District.

They laid their heads together for a long time, with many objections and some opposition; but in the end they agreed entirely, and then separated before dawn, for they would have to rise pretty early in the morning.

So Yagna remained alone awake outside the cottage, still plunged in the night of her reverie, still breathing these words, like an invocation of love:

"He will come—he will be here!"

And she turned instinctively, bowing towards the eastern sky—as if desirous to know what the coming day would bring, that now peeped grey over the horizon—and she abandoned herself, with a sense of dread and yet of exultation, to that which was to be.

CHAPTER VIII

IT was near noontide, and the heat greater and greater. The people were all assembled outside the District Office; but the head of the District had not yet appeared. The scrivener had several times come out upon the threshold and, shading his eyes, looked down the broad highway, with its borders of gnarled willow-trees. Nothing was visible but the glittering pools which yesterday's shower had left—one cart crawling along, and a peasant's white capote fluttering among the trees.

So they waited patiently. The Voyt alone rushed bustling to and fro, restless and fidgety, now looking out upon the road, now urging forward the work of the men who were filling up the hollows in the square before the Office.

"Faster, lads! faster, for God's sake! He will be here ere ye have done the work!"

A voice from the crowd called out: "Beware lest ye be so scared that some accident happen to you!"

"Now, men, stir yourselves! I am here on duty: such jests are untimely."

"Our Voyt, 'tis known, fears God alone!" said one peasant, a man from Rzepki.

The Voyt, now furious, shrieked: "If any man speak one word more, I'll have him thrown in jail!"—And then he ran round to the cemetery that stood upon the height on which the District Office was perched.

It was overshadowed by many an ancient tree, through whose branches the grey church tower was seen; the black arms of the crosses bent over the stone wall, and above the road that led through the village.

Nothing was to be seen as yet. The Voyt left the Soltys along with the people, and went into the Office. Here

176

someone was continually entering, called in by the scrivener, who took occasion to remind him gently of taxes in arrears, unpaid subscriptions for the court buildings . . . and other things still more important. These reminders were truly very distasteful to each of them: how could they pay in such hard times, and just before the harvest? So they only made him a very deep bow, some even kissing his hand, and some pressing their last *zloty* into the man's outstretched palm. But they all implored him to wait till the harvest, or till next fair.

That scrivener! he was a cunning blade, a wily crafty old fox! How many a way he had of fleecing the people! To some he would make no end of promises, others he wrought upon through fear of the gendarmes; these he got the upper hand of through sheer flattery, and those, by treating them with free and easy friendliness. But he always and somehow got something out of every one of them. He was in need of oats, or he required a few young goslings for the head of the District; or he obtained a promise of some straw ropes for binding sheaves. And, willingly or unwillingly, they promised whatever he wanted. And then —just as they were leaving—he would take those apart whom he knew best, and say to them in friendly guise:

"Look ye, vote for the school; for if ye should oppose it, our head may wax angry, and peradventure cancel your agreement with the Squire as to the forest."

"How's that?" cried Ploshka, in astonishment. "Why, we made the agreement freely on either side."

"Aye, but know ye not?—'But noble with noble is hand in glove; for peasants, never noble has love.'"

Much dismayed, Ploshka left him; and he continued to call the men in, frightening each of them in a different way, but pressing them all to do the same thing.

A good many people were gathered together—more than two hundred—who at first grouped themselves by villages, each with his own acquaintances: men of Lipka with men of Lipka, and so on. But now it was known to be the head of the District's will they should vote about the school, they

began to mingle together, passing from group to group as
it suited them. (Only the "nobility" of Rzepki held proudly
aloof, looking down upon the other peasantry.) All the rest
had presently mixed together, like lentils in a dish, all
over the square, but congregating mostly in the shadow of
the churchyard trees, or about the wagons.)

But it was round the large tavern that they thronged
closest. This stood opposite the District Office, surrounded
by a clump of trees, as in a shady grove; and many a one
went that way to refresh himself with a glass of beer, after
standing so long in the hot glare. The tavern being chock-
full, quite a number of groups were lounging about under
the trees, discussing the news and attentively watching both
the Office and the other side of the house, where the scrivener
lived, and where the noise and bustle was greatest.

From time to time, the scrivener's wife thrust her fat
face out of a back window, screaming:

"Make haste, Magda! O you sluggard! may you break
both your legs!"

The girl was heard every now and then rushing about the
rooms, the panes quivering to her tread; a child would squall
with shrill vehemence; somewhere behind, the fowls were
cackling in great trepidation, and a panting constable was
hunting chickens in the corn and down the road.

"Belike they are going to feast the head official," someone remarked.

"They say the scrivener brought in half a cartload of
liquor yesterday."

"Then they'll get as drunk as they did last year."

"Oh, they can afford it. Do not the people pay, and is
there anyone to watch what their hands grab?" said Matthew: to whom another cried at once:

"Be silent! the gendarmes have come."

"They prowl about like wolves: where they go, and by
which ways, who can tell?"

So they stood mute with fear, when the gendarmes drew
up in a line before the Office, with a number of people
round them: amongst whom were conspicuous the miller,

the Voyt, and—at a little distance—the blacksmith, alert and attentive.

"That miller!—He fawns upon them, like a famished dog!"

"Wherever the gendarmes are seen, look out for the District Official!" Gregory exclaimed, passing over to where Antek, Matthew, Klemba, and Staho were talking together. Then they parted to mix with the people, holding forth and expressing their opinions with much force. They were listened to in silence; sometimes one or another of their hearers would groan and scratch his head with an embarrassed air, or cast a glance at the gendarmes, now drawing closer to one another.

Antek, with his back against the corner of the tavern, spoke curtly, but with conviction, and an air of authority. In another group, Matthew was talking humorously and making many a man laugh at his jests, while in a third crowd, nearer the cemetery, Gregory lectured with much ability, and as if he were reading out of an open book!

But their speeches all tended in one direction: to oppose the head official, to vote against the school, and not to heed those who were always on the side of the officials.

No one else uttered a word, but all nodded assent: even the greatest fools among them knew well that such a school meant nothing but the payment of new taxes for nothing: which no one cared for.

The multitude, however, were restless, shifting uneasily from one foot to the other, coughing and clearing their throats.—They were terribly afraid of opposing the head official and his satellites.

One man looked at another, secretly troubled what to do; and everyone noted carefully what the richest among them seemed to think. As to the miller and the foremost men in the other villages, they appeared to put themselves forward on purpose to be favorably noticed by the gendarmes and the scrivener.

Antek went to speak with them; but the miller said rudely: "Any man but a fool can tell how he should vote!"

and turned to the blacksmith, who was of everybody's opinion, and always gliding about from group to group, guessing shrewdly how matters would turn out. He talked to the scrivener, chatted with the miller, offered Gregory a pinch of snuff—and kept his own counsel meanwhile so well that to the very end no one knew on which side he was.

The majority were meanwhile gradually inclining not to vote for the school. They now dispersed about the square, indifferent to the noonday heat, and were setting to canvass their views still louder and more boldly than before, when the scrivener called from the open window:

"Here, some one of you!"

No one stirred.

"Let someone run over to the Manor for the fish. 'Twas to be brought here in the morning, and we are waiting still.—Come!" he shouted masterfully; "make haste!"

Here a voice uttered the bold words:

"We are not here as your servants!"

"Let him run thither himself! It irks him to drag his paunch about!" At this they laughed, for his belly was indeed as big as a drum.

The scrivener swore. But in a minute, out came the Voyt at the back of the house, who, passing behind the tavern, slipped away to the Manor by the outside of the village.

"He must have been changing the clothes of the babies at Madam Scrivener's, and cleaning them likewise: so he has gone out for a little fresh air."

"Ah, yes; Madam likes not her rooms to be noisome."

"She will soon find other services for him to render her."

"Strange that the Squire is not yet to be seen," they said in some surprise; but the smith returned, with a cunning smile:

"He has too much sense to come."

They looked at him inquiringly.

"For why," the smith explained, "should he have to vote for the school . . . or go to loggerheads with the District

Official? And he will never vote: fancy what he would
have to pay! No, he is wise."

"But you—are you with us, Michael, say?" Matthew
pressed him, eager to know.

The smith wriggled like a worm trodden upon, but, being
in a quandary, grumbled a word or two, and went over to
speak to the miller, who had come round to the peasants,
and was now talking to old Ploshka very loud, for the rest
to hear.

"My advice is: Vote as the officials wish. A school there
must be: the worst is better than none. The one you wish
for, ye'll not get: 'tis no use knocking your heads against
a wall. Won't you vote?—Then they will not ask your
leave."

"But," cried a bystander, "what can they do, if we give
no money?"

"You are foolish. They'll take it. Will you refuse?—
They will sell even your last cow, and send you to prison
for mutiny into the bargain. Is that clear?—For," he
added, turning to the Lipka folk, "ye have to do now, not
with the Squire, but with the head official: a man who is not
to be trifled with!—I tell you, do as they bid, and thank
God things are no worse!"

Such as held his views here chimed in; and old Ploshka,
after musing for some time, said on a sudden:

"Ye say true; and Roch misleads and seduces our folk."

To this, one of the Przylek husbandmen added with
emphasis:

"He is with the Manor folk, and therefore stirs us up
against the Government."

An outcry arose against him on every side; but he, un-
daunted, went on as soon as they let him.

"Those," he said, looking sagely around him, "those are
fools that help him. If anyone likes this not, let him come
forward: I'll call him a fool to his face. Such men know
not that it hath been so from all time: the gentry rebel
and drive our folk to ruin; but who has to pay, when pay-
day comes? Why, we peasants! When the Cossacks are

quartered in your villages, who will get the beatings? who
will suffer and be sent to prison? Only we peasants! The
gentlefolk will not move a finger for you; they will slink
away and leave you in the lurch, the Judases!—and, moreover, they will feast the officials in their manors!"

"Ha! What is the people in their eyes that they should
stir for them?" cried one; and another:

"If they could, serfdom would be restored to-morrow!"

"Gregory says," the former speaker continued, " 'let them
teach in Polish; or, if they will not, let us vote no schools
and no money for them.'—Very fine. But 'tis only a la-
bourer who can say to his master: 'I will not work,' throw
an insult in his face, and yet escape a thrashing by running
away. We farmer folk cannot flee, and must needs stay and
take the beating. Therefore I say it will come cheaper for
you to build the school than to resist the officials. True,
they will not teach our language; but they will never make
Russians of us for all that: we shall none of us pray to God
or speak among ourselves save as we do now, even as our
mothers taught us!

"Finally, I repeat: Stand up for your own interests only!
Let the nobles tear each other to pieces: 'tis no affair of
ours. Let them bite and fight: these are no more our
brethren than those. And a plague upon them all!"

Here he was shouted down by the crowd that pressed
about him. In vain did the miller and a few others take
his part. Those on Gregory's side came near using their
fists, and things were looking very bad, when old Prychek
cried: "The gendarmes are listening!"

This silenced them and gave the old man an occasion to
hold forth in an angry tone:

"One very true thing he has said: we must look to our
own interests!—Be quiet there! You have said your say,
let others say theirs!—These fellows bawl and bawl, and
think themselves great men!—If shrieking meant thinking,
then every loud-mouthed brawler would have a better head
than even our priest himself! You laugh at me; but I
say to you: how was it that year . . . when our noblemen

rebelled? Remember how they threw dust in our eyes,
and swore that as soon as Poland existed, we should have
our will . . . our own lands . . . and forests—and everything. And they made promises and speeches, and every
other man of us helped them; and what have we of it now?
—Ye may hearken to the nobles, if ye be fools; but I am
too old a bird to be caught with chaff!"

"Smite him on the mouth, that he may be still!" cried a
voice.

He went on nevertheless: "And now I am a noble, as
much as any of them all: I have my rights, and none dares
lay a finger on me!"

But his voice was drowned in a torrent of jeers that poured
down on him from all sides.

"You swine that grunt about your delights, and are happy
to have a sty and a full trough!"

"Once fatted, you shall feel the club on your skull, and
the knife at your throat!"

"Did not a gendarme flog him at last fair? And yet he
prates about no one daring to touch him!"

"A great noble he is, and most free to be eaten by lice!"

"Truly the straw stuffed in his boots could teach as much
wisdom as he!"

"He knows not to judge a fowl's worth, yet he comes here
to enlighten us!"

The old man was foaming with rage, but only said:

"Ye scum of the land! . . . that cannot even respect
grey hairs!"

"What then? Must a grey mare be respected, for that
she is grey?"

They roared with laughter at this; but presently their
attention was diverted to the roof of the office, on to which
the constable Joseph had climbed, and, holding to a chimney, was gazing into the distance.

"Joseph!" they cried to him in a merry mood. "Shut
your mouth, lest something fall into it!" For a flock of
pigeons was wheeling above his head. But he only shouted
with all his might:

"He is coming . . . coming! Has passed the turning from Krylak!"

The assembly now gathered close round the building, and gazed quietly along the road that as yet lay empty.

The scrivener hastily donned his very best clothes; again the air rang with his wife's outcries, and the clinking of plates, and the rumbling of displaced furniture, and the noise of many feet. In a short time, the Voyt too appeared on the scene: standing on the door-step, red as a beet-root, perspiring, breathless, but adorned with his chain of office. Casting his eyes on the crowd around him, he shouted in fierce tones:

"Silence, men! This Office is not a tavern."

"Come round here, Peter! I'll tell you what!" Klemba cried to him.

"There is no Peter here! I am an official," he answered loftily.

The words were taken up at once and made great fun of, till they shook with laughter; but, all at once, the Voyt cried solemnly:

"Make way there! Way for the head of the District!"

A coach appeared on the road, jolting over the ruts and hollows, and pulling up in front of the office.

The head official raised his hand to his cap, the peasants took their hats off, and silence followed, while the Voyt and the scrivener darted forward to assist him from the coach, and the gendarmes stood erect at attention beside the doorway.

He alighted, divested himself of his white dust-coat, turned round to gaze at the assembled crowd, stroked his blond beard, assumed a severe look, and nodded his head. Then he entered the scrivener's dwelling, into which the latter, bent like a hoop, ushered him.

The coach drove away, and the peasants thronged round the table that had been set up. They thought the meeting was now about to begin. But it was a very long while indeed before the head official showed himself: while from the scrivener's apartments there came the noise of jingling glasses, and laughter, and certain fragrant scents that made the mouth water.

They were weary both of waiting and of the broiling heat, and many a one tried to slip away to the tavern. But this the Voyt would not have.

"Do not go away!—Whosoever is absent shall be put down for a fine."

This kept them back, but they uttered many an invective, as they looked impatiently towards the scrivener's curtained windows.

"They are ashamed to be seen drinking!"

"Quite right of them: it would only make us more thirsty that we have but our spittle to swallow!"

From the lock-up, in the same building as the Office, now came the constable, dragging by a halter a large calf that resisted with might and main and, making a sudden rush at him, upset the man and set off at a run, tail in air in a cloud of dust.

"Stop thief! Stop thief!" they cried, laughing.

"Oh, the bold rascal, to break prison so, even lifting up his tail against my Lord the Voyt!"

They also aimed a good many jibes at the constable, who was not able to get the calf into the yard without the assistance of all the Soltyses present. They were not yet fully breathed after their hunt, when the Voyt ordered them all to cleanse the lock-up thoroughly; he himself saw that the work was well done, and helped them a good deal, fearing lest the District Official should make a tour of inspection.

"But, Voyt dear! ye'll have to burn incense there, or his nose will tell him who the prisoner was!"

"Have no fear: after a few drams he will scent naught in the world."

And other gibes were thrown at the Voyt, which he only received with clenched teeth and glaring eyes.—At last, however, they had enough of sun, and hunger, and waiting—and could not even jest any longer. So, in spite of the Voyt's objurgations, they all made tracks for the tavern and the trees, Gregory flinging these words at him:

"Ye may cry till nightfall: we are no dogs to follow you to heel!"

Saying this, and glad to be no longer under the gendarmes' inspection, he again went about amongst the people, reminding each man apart in what sense he should give his vote.

"And," he would wind up, "fear ye not: right is on our side. As we vote, so things shall be; and what we will not have, no man can force upon us."

They had, however, not yet begun to stretch themselves in the shade, or to eat a morsel, when each village was called by its Soltys, and the Voyt came roaring:

"Here's the head!—Come quick!—We are to begin now!"

"The smell of good things has wrought upon him," they muttered in a bad temper, walking slowly towards the Office. "We are in no hurry; let him wait!"

Each Soltys stood at the head of his own village; but the Voyt was seated at the table, beside the scrivener's assistant, who whistled to frighten the pigeons, that circled round above the roof in a white fluttering cloud.

One of the gendarmes suddenly stood at attention, and cried: "Silence!" in Russian.

To their disappointment, however, no one came out but the scrivener, holding some papers in his hand, and edging himself to a seat behind the table. The Voyt then rang the bell, and said, majestically:

"Good people! we open the meeting.—Be still there, ye men of Modlitsa!—Our secretary will read you things concerning this school: only hearken ye diligently, that ye may know all about it."

Putting on his spectacles, the scrivener began to read, very slowly and distinctly.

After a short interval of breathless silence, someone exclaimed:

"Why, we understand naught!"

"Read it in our tongue! We cannot make it out!" repeated many voices.

The gendarmes here began to fix a steady glare upon the people.

The scrivener looked very black, but went on with the document, translating it into Polish.

All now were still, listening to each word with the most concentrated attention. The scrivener continued deliberately:

"Whereas it hath been decided to found a school in Lipka, the same being also for the use of Modlitsa, Przylek, Rzepki, and the neighbouring hamlets . . ."

The rescript then pointed out how great a benefit education was; how the Government was night and day only thinking of means to aid the progress and enlightenment of the people, and to defend it from all evil influences . . . and then passed on to reckon how much would be required for the ground, for the building itself, and (yearly) for the teacher: concluding with the estimate that they ought to vote a supplementary rate of twenty kopeks per acre.—He paused, wiped his spectacles, and added as an observation of his own:

"The head of the District has assured me that, if ye vote the rate now, he will allow the building to commence this year, so that next year in autumn your children will go to school."

When he ended thus, no one made any remark. Everyone reflected with heads bent as under the weight of this fresh burden. At last the Voyt said:

"Have ye heard all that our secretary has read to you?"

"We have indeed! We are not deaf!" several voices replied.

"Then whoso is against this plan, let him step forward and say so."

No one, however, was so bold as to put himself forward first, or go beyond glances and nudges.

"Then," the Voyt proposed, "let us vote the rate directly, and go home."

"Very well," the scrivener asked, with solemn formality. "Ye do all unanimously agree to this plan?"

"No! No!" vociferated Gregory, and about a score of others with him.

"We need no such schools! We will not have them! The taxes are heavy enough as it is!—No!" and cries of opposition now resounded on every side, and ever more boldly.

At the sound, the head official came forth and stood in the doorway. At the sight, the tumult died away. Stroking his beard, he said, with much affability:

"Well, good husbandmen, how goes it with you?"

"The better that your Honour asks us!" answered the foremost men, swaying to and fro under the pressure of those behind, pushing forward to hear the District Official. Now he, leaning against the door-post, uttered some sentences in Russian; but their effect was impaired by constant hiccups.

The gendarmes started forward, crying to the people:

"Hats off! Hats off!"

A voice was thereupon heard abusing them roundly: "Get out, ye vermin, and meddle not with our business."

But the head official, though he had spoken very affably, concluded in Polish, and in a tone of command:

"Vote the rate, and at once, for I have no time to spare."

And he looked on them with an ominous scowl. Fear seized upon them; they wavered, and low timorous whispers ran through their ranks.

"Ah, shall we vote?—Say, Ploshka, what are we to do?— Where's Gregory?—The head commands us to vote!—Come, then, brethren, let us do so!"

But the tumult swelled to a storm, when Grzela came forward, and declared fearlessly: "For such a school we'll not vote half a kopek!"

"We will not! No, we will not!" a hundred voices repeated.

At this, the head official knitted his brows.

The Voyt was terror-struck, and the scrivener's spectacles fell from his nose. But Gregory met the great man's glance

without fear, and was about to speak further, when Ploshka,
pushing forward, and louting very low, said humbly:

"May it please your Honour the District Official if I speak
in our tongue, and think with our own thoughts.—As to
voting the school, we are willing; but twenty kopeks an
acre seems to us very much.   Times are hard just now, and
money is short.   And that is all."

The head made no reply, and seemed plunged in thought,
only nodding his head at times, and rubbing his eyes.   Encouraged by these gestures, the Voyt spoke strongly in favour of the school, and those of his party likewise, the miller
distinguishing himself amongst them, and scorning the in-
terruptions of Gregory's partisans, until the latter grew
angry and shouted: "We are pouring empty vessels into the
void!" and availed himself of an opportunity to step forward and ask boldly:

"We would know what kind of school this new one is
to be."

"Like all the others!" he said, opening his eyes very wide.

"That is the very sort we do not want.   We'd vote even
half a rouble an acre for a Polish school, but not a stiver
for any other."

"Those schools are good for nothing!" cried one.   "My
children learned there for three years, and do not know
their A B C."

"Be still, good folk, be still!" growled the head.

The sheep were getting lively, and the wolf was biding
his time.

"Those infernal talkers! they will talk the people to its
ruin!"

And now every man was striving to speak louder than his
neighbours, and the din became deafening, each one main-
taining his own view.   They had broken up into small
groups, disputing with one another, and getting ever more
and more excited, Gregory's party especially standing up
most stubbornly against the school.   It was to no purpose
that the Voyt, the miller, and the others of that side went

about explaining, beseeching, even threatening awful things that might come to pass: the greater part of the assembly had got quite out of hand, excited to exasperation, and talking themselves hoarse.

The District Official, who sat seemingly indifferent to the hubbub, conferred in whispers with the scrivener, and let them talk their fill; and when he judged they had enough of that senseless noise, he told the Voyt to ring the bell.

"Silence there!" thundered the Soltyses of each village. "Silence! and lend your ears."

Then, before all was quite still, rose the voice of command:

"The school, look ye! has to be built. Obey, then, and do as ye are bidden."

His tone was as hard and stern as could be; but they were no longer afraid, and Klemba answered him back on the spot.

"We force no one to walk on his head: let others likewise allow us to speak in our tongue, as God has given it us!"

"Hold your tongue!" shrieked the Voyt, ringing the bell to no purpose. "Peace, you son of a dog!"

"What I have said, I repeat: in our schools our language must be taught!"

"Karpenko! Ivanoff!" the Voyt cried to the gendarmes who stood in the centre of the throng; but the peasants pressed round them directly, and they heard a whisper: "Let but one of you touch one of us—we are three hundred —ye shall see!"

Then their ranks opened slowly to let them pass, and closed after them, surging round the head official, with the dull angry hum of a furious mob; catching their breaths, cursing low, and one or other of them every now and then uttering such words as these:

"Every creature has its own voice; we alone are forbidden our own!"

"Always commands, and naught except commands! Obey, and pay, and sweep the ground with your hat, you peasant!"

"They'll make us soon ask leave . . . to go behind the barn!"

"So mighty a man, let him command swine to sing as nightingales!" Antek cried. They laughed, and he went on, greatly excited:

"Or bid geese to low like cows! When they do, we'll vote the school!"

"They tax us, we pay; they recruit us, we go; but beware of . . ."

"Hold your peace, Klemba!—His Majesty the Czar himself has decreed in the clearest words that our schools and law courts are to use Polish! Yes, the Czar himself has decreed it: him shall we obey!" Antek vociferated.

"Who are you?" the head official said to him, with eyes intently fixed upon his face.

"Who am I?—It stands there in black and white," Antek replied boldly, pointing to the papers on the table, though he felt his heart throb as he did so. "I am no magpie's dropping!" he added with bravado.

The head spoke to the scrivener, who after a while proclaimed the fact that Antek Boryna, not being yet cleared of a criminal charge, had no right to take any part in the Assembly of the Commune.

Antek flushed angrily, but, before he could utter a word, the District Official cried out to him: "Get him out!" indicating him to the gendarmes with a significant look.

"Boys, never vote this school! Right is on our side: have no fear!" Antek shouted indomitably.

And with slow steps he went out of the village, looking back at the gendarmes following him yet more slowly still, as a wolf might glare at a couple of curs.

But the incident had brought disorder into the meeting again. Each man seemed possessed of a devil—screaming, cursing, quarrelling, threatening—no one knew why or wherefore!

Their invectives bore, not only on the school and Antek, but on indifferent and wholly irrelevant matters—just as if a sudden madness had seized upon them. Gregory and others of his party strove to calm them, but unavailingly: they were blind and deaf to everything, gobbling one at another furiously, like irritated turkeys in a poultry-yard.

At last, one of the Soltyses, seeing an empty barrel that stood under the eaves of the house, had the idea of beating upon it with his stick so frantically, so madly, and with such loud and hollow bombilation, that it partly brought them to their senses again.

Thereupon the head official, who was beside himself with rage, exclaimed: "Enough of this prating! Silence! Silence, when I speak!—Obey me.—Vote the school."

All were in a moment struck dumb with fear: a cold thrill went through them. They looked at one another, without dreaming of defying the man who stood there, grim and threatening before them, rolling savage eyes over the terrified multitude.

Again he sat down, while the Voyt and his party once more attempted to frighten the peasants into obedience.

"Vote for the school!—We must!"

"Have ye not heard? An ill thing is impending!"

Meanwhile, the scrivener read the list of names, and the cry, "Here! Here!" was heard with incessant reiteration.

This done, the Voyt ordered those who were for the school to pass to the right and raise their hands.

A good many did so, but the bulk of the assembly would not budge.

The head official then, knitting his brows, ordered the votes to be taken by name, "that all might be done with strict justice."

Gregory was dismayed on hearing this order. He was but too sure that the majority would weaken, and not venture to oppose the vote.

The polling took a long time, for the people were very numerous; but the result was given at last:

"Ayes, two hundred; noes, eighty."

Gregory's party raised a great protest.

"We have been cheated!—Vote again!"

"I said, No! and they put my vote down for the school!" one man, soon followed by many others, declared persistently; and the more zealous proposed to tear up the papers and thus annul the voting.

A coach from the Manor then passed by good fortune outside the Office, and the people had to draw back willynilly. The District Official, having read the list, handed to him by a manservant, declared solemnly: "It is well; ye shall have a school in Lipka."

No one spoke a word any more; they all stood gazing at him in silence.

He then, after signing a few papers, got into his coach and drove away.

They all bowed to the ground. He took no notice of them, even by a glance; but, having spoken a few words with the gendarmes, turned off to the Manor of Modlitsa by a side road.

Their eyes followed him in silence. At last, one of Gregory's men said:

"That lamb, so meek and mild, can show fangs that bite deeper than a wolf's—aye, and when we least expect it, trample us under his feet!"

"How could they govern at all, unless we were fools and they scared us?"

Gregory breathed hard, looked round, and whispered:

"For to-day, we have lost: it is hard; but the people have not yet learned how to resist."

"And that they will hardly learn, so long as everything can frighten them."

"My God! what a man! He tramples even the laws underfoot."

"Aye, they are for us, not him!"

Here a peasant from Przylek came complaining to Gregory.

"I meant to vote for you; but behold! when he fixed his eyes on me, I could not speak a word, and the scrivener wrote down what he pleased."

"There have been so many abuses that we might well make an appeal."

"Come all to the tavern!" cried Matthew. "May a brimstone thunderbolt smash them all!" Then, turning to the crowd, he shouted:

"Do ye know, my men, that the head has forgotten to tell you one thing?—That ye are a rabble of sheep and curs. Ye will be well paid for your obedience; but such idiots as ye are deserve to be flayed alive—not only fleeced."

They answered him back, some even abusing him roundly; but their attention was then drawn off by a cart with a Jewish driver, and Yanek sitting in it.

Yanek was soon surrounded by a crowd, and Gregory told him what had occurred. Yanek listened, talked to them for a while, and then drove on.

The others repaired to the tavern, where, after a couple of glasses, Matthew roared out:

"I tell you, the Voyt and the miller are to blame for everything!"

"Quite true," Ploshka chimed in; "they were all the time canvassing and pressing and bullying us!"

"And the head official threatened us, just as if he knew all about Roch!" someone faltered.

"If he does not, he is sure to be told. We have informers amongst us!"

"What," Gregory inquired with an uneasy glance, "what has become of those gendarmes?"

"Gone somewhere in the direction of Lipka."

Gregory for a short time lounged about the tavern with the others, but presently he slipped out unnoticed by anyone, making for Lipka by a short cut across the fields.

CHAPTER IX

ANTEK left the assembly about as willingly as a cat driven away from a bowl of milk. He was even deliberating whether he had not better return, when, perceiving the gendarmes following him, he was struck with an idea. On his way, he broke off a large bough, and set about whittling it into a stick, leaning against a fence, and eyeing the "Brown-Coats," who walked as slowly as they could, but could not help coming up with him very soon.

"Wither away, my ancient?" he asked the elder of them in a tone of mockery.

"On duty, Master Farmer.—Are we bound for the same place?"

"It would please me, but I fancy not."

Looking around, he saw that they were quite alone with him, but still too near the District Office: so he went with them, walking close to the hedge, and well on the look-out for a sudden attack.

The "ancient," cautiously disposed, continued the talk in a friendly tone, complaining bitterly that he had not eaten since early morning.

"The scrivener," Antek replied, "has treated the head official most grandly, so no doubt he had left good things for you, my ancient!—Alas! in the country there are no such dainties to be had—only *kluski* or cabbage!—and what are those things for grand folk like you?" He was jeering on purpose to irritate them. The younger of the two, a stalwart young fellow with flashing eyes, growled under his breath, but the "ancient" made no answer.

Antek, still playing with the men, now stirred his legs so vigorously that they had much ado to keep up with him,

195

and awkwardly splashed along after him through pools and stumbled into hollows.

The country-side was quite empty and deserted; a blazing sun burned. Here and there a peasant stared after them, or a few children peeped out from shady places: the village dogs alone followed them persistently and with great clamour of barking.

The "ancient" lit a cigarette, and held it between his teeth as he went on talking, lamenting over his lot: no rest either day or night with that everlasting service!

"Indeed? That means it is no easy thing nowadays to squeeze money out of the peasants!"

The "ancient" flung out a curse at him, with a foul reflection on his mother. Antek, who had no mind to bandy insults with them, grasped his stick with a firm clutch, and rejoined, now openly attacking him:

"What I say is the simple truth: your service in the villages only gets you barked at; at most, some poor fellow's last złoty may now and then find its way to your pockets!"

The "ancient," though he turned green with spite, and clenched his hand on his sword-hilt, still bore this in silence. It was only when they were just passing the last cabin in the village that he unexpectedly sprang at Antek, crying out to his comrade:

"Seize him!"

The surprise failed, however. Before they could touch him, Antek had sent them both reeling back with a couple of blows. Leaping to one side, he stood, with his back against the cabin, brandishing his stick, showing teeth that gleamed like a wolf's, and uttering bits of sentences, hoarse and incoherent:

"Go your ways. . . . Ye'll never get hold of me! . . . Even four of you would be too few! . . . Dogs! I'll break all your teeth! . . . What would ye? . . . I have done no one any harm. . . . Will ye have a fight?—Very well; but first order a cart to carry your bodies away. . . . Come on, then.—Touch me.—Let me see you try!" he growled; and his stick sang loud in the air. He was in a slaying mood.

Seeing him thus, they both stood transfixed: the man
was of such great stature, expanded to the utmost by the
towering passion he was in; and his stick hissed and hummed
and whirled in his hand with so ominous a sound!—The
"ancient" felt that an attack upon him was out of the
question, and attempted to turn the whole affair off as a
joke.

"Ha! ha! excellent! . . . Trapped! Trapped! A splendid joke we have played off on you!" He burst out laughing, holding both his sides, while they withdrew several
steps (overcome, as it were, with the fun of the thing);
but, continuing to retire, and now out of danger, he suddenly changed his tone and, shaking his fist, snarled
furiously:

"Ye have not seen the last of us, my master: we shall talk
with each other once more!"

He snarled back in reply: "May the plague carry you
both off first! Why, you are afraid lest *I* should attack
you; therefore did ye try to turn it into a jest!—And I too
shall talk with you . . . but man to man, and alone!" he
growled, as he watched them out of sight.

"Those fellows—to set upon me!" he thought. "The
fools! They were the hounds, I was the hare!"—He mused.
—"Because of what I said at the assembly! Though indeed
it could not have been much to his taste."

He was now near the Manor garden, that lay at some
distance beyond the village, and sat down there to rest
awhile and compose himself. The Manor was seen through
the wooden fence, white upon the background of a larch
grove, its open windows staring darkly, like so many grot-
toes. On the pillared veranda, there were several people
sitting: probably taking refreshment, for servants hovered
about them, and there was a clinking of crockery. At
times the sound of merry laughter was heard.

"They are well off, those folk! Eating, drinking, and
caring for nothing at all!" he thought, making a meal of
the bread and cheese that Hanka had put in his pocket.

As he ate, his eyes roved over the huge lime-trees which

bordered the road, and were now full of blossoms and
humming bees, and the soft steamy fragrance from them
filled him with delight. A duck quacked in a neighbouring
pond; there, too, frogs croaked drowsily; the thickets
around him thrilled to the many voices of living things,
and from the fields came the grasshoppers' concert, alter-
nately loud and faint: till, after a time, all these sounds
were hushed and silenced, as it were, in the sunshine's hot
downpour. Silence reigned; all animated life hid away
from the desolating heat—all except the swallows, that were
darting and dashing and flashing about evermore.

His eyes ached with the intensity of the heat, and even
in the shadow he felt parboiled. The last pools were drying up, and the blast, which blew from the all but ripe
cornfields and the parched fallow lands, was like that from
an open oven.

Antek, after resting well, walked swiftly towards the
neighbouring woods; but, passing out of the shadow and
into the light, he felt a quiver pass through him, as if he
were entering a furnace of white fire. His capote was off,
but his shirt, that clung close to his moist reeking sides,
seemed like hot sheet-iron. He took off his boots as well,
and went on with naked feet crunching the burning sand.

The stunted little birch-trees that grew here and there
gave hardly any shadow yet; the drooping ears of rye bent
down over the roadway, and the flowers also hung their
heads in the burning glare.

Sultry silence prevailed: no man was visible; no bird, no
living creature anywhere in sight. Not a leaf, not a blade
of grass trembled. It was as if the Demon of Noontide
had swooped down upon the country and, with husky lips,
were sucking all the strength out of the swooning earth.

Antek walked on, still more slowly, thinking of the
assembly: now furious with anger, now laughing with scorn,
now heavy with discouragement.

"What's to be done with such men?—The first gendarme
who comes by appals them! . . . If they were commanded
to obey a gendarme's boot, they would!—Sheep, silly sheep,

all of them!" he thought, with mixed feelings of bitterness
and compassion.

"True, we are all badly off—each one of us wriggling
like a tortured eel! And everyone is so wretched, he can
hardly breathe: why should he trouble about things that
concern him less! Ah, poor people, so benighted, so miserable! They do not so much as know what they need!"
And his heart went out to them, afflicted at the thought of
their misery.

"Swine find it hard to raise their snouts to the sky—and
so do men!" So he thought, sorely troubled, but yet got no
profit of his pain, further than the feeling that he himself
was in as bad a case as anyone else—perhaps worse.

"Only those can live their lives contentedly who never
think!"

He waved his hand with a gesture of despair, and then
walked on, plunged in so deep a reverie that he nearly
stumbled over a Jew—a rag-picker—sitting at the edge of
a cornfield.

"Resting, are ye? Indeed, the heat is terrible." he said,
stopping for an instant.

"Heat? We are in a furnace: 'tis a judgment of God!"
the Jew ejaculated. Getting up, he passed a strap over his
round old shoulders, and, thus harnessed to his wheelbarrow,
set about pushing it along with infinite toil. It was chock-
full of rags and wooden boxes; above these towered baskets
of eggs and a coop full of chickens; and, the road being
deep with sand, and the weather unbearably hot, he had
to struggle along desperately, and sit down to rest every now
and then.

"Nuchim, you'll be late, Sabbath is at hand," he solilo-
quized, chiding himself with tears. "Push, Nuchim, push
on! you're strong as a horse! Now, Nuchim!—One—two
—three! . . ." And with a cry of desperation, he would
wheel the barrow on for a score of paces, and then stop
again.

Antek was for passing him by with a nod, but the Jew
called to him earnestly:

"Master Farmer, I pray you! Help me, and I will pay you well. I can no more, in truth I can no more!" And he fell forward against the handbarrow, breathless and as white as a sheet.

Without a word, Antek turned round, threw his capote and boots on to the barrow, seized it by the handle and pushed it forward so lustily that the wheel hummed and the dust flew. The Jew trotted beside him, catching his breath as he went, and chattering by the way to interest his helper.

"Only as far as the wood: the road is good there. 'Tis not far. And I'll give you five whole kopeks!"

"Confound your kopeks! Fool, do I care for your money? But ye Jews think money is everything in the world."

"Be not angry, Master, I'll give you pretty toys for your children.—No?—Then needles, thread, ribbons peradventure?—No?—Then may I offer rolls or scones or caramels . . . or aught else? For I have everything—Or would ye, Master Farmer, buy of me a packet of tobacco? Or may I give you a glass of quite superior vodka? such as I have only for my very good friends—on my conscience, only for my very good friends."

And here a fit of coughing made his eyes almost start from their sockets. . . . Antek went a little more slowly, and the Jew, catching at the barrow, managed to drag himself along.

"We shall have a good harvest," he continued, starting another subject; "the price of rye is falling."

"Aye, and when the crop is scanty, it must bring us in less: either way, it is ill for farmers!"

"But the Lord God has granted us fine weather, and the corn in the ear is dry." He rubbed some in his hands and tasted it.

"Well and good; but the Lord Jesus is hard upon us for the barley crop: it is quite lost."

From topic to topic, they came to talk about the morning's assembly. It appeared that the Jew had special in-

formation on this point. Looking cautiously about him, he
said:

"Do ye know? The District Official made a contract as
far ago as last winter with a builder about that Lipka
school! My son-in-law acted as his agent."

"What, in winter, and before it was voted? What is this
ye tell me?"

"Was he to ask anyone for leave? Is he not throughout
his District like a Squire on his estate?"

Antek put him a few more questions, which Nuchim
answered, giving many curious particulars, and finally saying, with tolerant amenity:

"Things have to be so. The husbandman lives on the
land he tills, the tradesman on what he sells, the Squire on
his estate, the priest on his parish . . . and the official, on
everybody. It must be so, and 'tis well so. All men
should get their livelihood, should they not?"

"To my mind, that one man should fleece the others is
not well; but that all men should live justly, and as the
Lord hath commanded."

"What's to be done? Folk must live as they can."

"Oh, I know the saying: 'Every man peels his own
turnip'; but therefore do things go so badly."

The Jew nodded, but kept his own counsel.

They at last got to the wood, where the road was less
deep in sand. Antek gave up the barrow, bought a *zloty's*
worth of sweets for his children, and, when the Jew wanted
to thank him, cried out:

"You are foolish! To help you was but a whim of
mine."

And then he started off at a good pace for Lipka. He
was now in the cool grateful shadow of the trees, with only
a tiny strip of sky overhead, and a thin bright stream of
sunshine beneath. The wood—of oak, pine and birch—
was old and tall, and the trees were pressed close, with a
thick undergrowth at their feet of hazels, aspens, juniper-
bushes, and hornbeams, with here and there a few groves

of firs, pushing greedily skywards to get at the sun.

There still were plenty of pools glittering on the road after yesterday's rain; plenty of broken boughs, too, and tree-tops scattered on the ground. In some places, a slender tree had been uprooted, and lay across the way, which was quiet and cool and darksome, and smelling of mould and of mushrooms.

The trees stood motionless, lost, as it were, in the contemplation of heaven; only at rare intervals did they let a few beams slip through, like golden gossamer threads, on to the banks of moss, and the wild strawberries, sprinkled about, and red as clotted blood, amongst the pallid grasses.

Antek was so charmed with the cool and profound tranquillity of the wood that he sat down under a tree, and fell unawares into a doze, from which he only awoke at the sound of a galloping snorting horse. It was the Squire, out for a ride, and he went forward to accost him.

They greeted one another as usual, and in neighbourly fashion.

"Fearfully hot, eh?" said the horseman, soothing his restless mare.

"So it is.—In a week's time, we shall have to go reaping."

"In Modlitsa they are already cutting down the rye."

"The soil is sandy there; but this year they will everywhere be reaping earlier."

The Squire asked him about the meeting at the District Office, and stared to hear what had taken place.

"Did ye actually demand a Polish school?—and so openly, and so firmly?"

"I have said: my tongue tells no false tales."

"But what daring! To demand such a thing in the head official's very presence!—Well, well!"

"It is so written down in the laws, as clear can be; I had the right to demand it."

"But how did the idea come into your head to ask for a Polish school?"

"How? Because I am a Pole—not a German, nor of any other nation."

"But who gave you the idea?" he asked, lowering his voice, and approaching.

"Untaught, children may learn to think aright," he answered evasively.

"Ah," he went on in the same tone, "I see that Roch's work amongst you has borne fruit. . . ."

"Who, together with your Honour's *kinsman*, teaches our folk as he can."

Antek had interrupted the Squire, and, laying stress on the word "kinsman," looked keenly on him. The Squire, ill at ease, tried to turn the conversation; but Antek returned to the subject of set purpose, speaking of the peasants' many grievances, and their benighted and friendless condition.

"That's because they will hearken to no one. I know well how the clergy work for their good, and how they urge industry upon them . . . and how it is all lost labour."

"Sermons are no more good for that purpose than a thurible of incense for a dead man!"

"Then what *is* good, pray?—You have, I see, learned not a few things in prison," he retorted. The taunt made Antek's eyes blaze and his face flush; but he answered with calm:

"So I have. And, especially, that the nobility is to blame for the evils we suffer!"

"Foolish prating! What harm did they ever do to you?"

"Harm?—When Poland was free, they cared no whit for the people, only to drive them to work with a whip, and oppress them, while they themselves made merry, and danced the country to ruin: so that we now must build it all over, from the very foundations."

The Squire was a hot-headed man, so he lost his temper: "You insolent peasant! Let alone the nobles and their doings —care rather to pitchfork your dung—you had better! And keep your tongue between your teeth, and well inside, or there be those that will cut it out for you!"

And, slashing his mare, he went off down the road at a swift gallop.

Antek was not less offended and indignant.

"That race of hounds!" he muttered angrily. "Great gentlemen, forsooth! Blood of a dog! So long as he stood in need of the peasants, he was hail-fellow-well-met with them all! The vermin—himself not worth a roast louse!" Infuriated, he strode along, crushing the toad-stools on his path in his rage.

On leaving the wood for the poplar road, he heard a couple of voices that seemed familiar to him, and, peering forward, perceived a britzka covered with dust in the shade of some birches at the edge of the wood, and Yanek, the organist's son, standing with Yagna a few paces off.

He rubbed his eyes, quite sure they must be in fault. They were not. The couple, not twenty paces from him, stood gazing one at the other, with faces wonderfully radiant.

Much surprised, he strained his ears to catch what they were saying; but he could only just hear that they spoke aloud.

She had come out of the forest, and met him driving to the village: a chance meeting, he thought at first. But at that moment he was swept by a wave of suspicion, and a rankling sense of bitterness got hold of him.

"No! It cannot be but they have met by agreement."

Yet once more, scanning the innocent features of the young man, and seeing the saintly serenity that lighted up his face, Antek grew calmer, though he was still unable to explain why Yagna had dressed so carefully to go to the forest, why her azure eyes flashed so brightly, why her crimson lips trembled so, or why she was so visibly flooded with joy. He took note of her, his eyes gleaming like a hungry wolf's, as she, with swelling bosom, bent forward to offer Yanek a small basket of bark, out of which he took strawberries, eating some, and putting some in her mouth.

". . . He is almost a priest, and he wants to play like a baby!"

He whispered the words in a tone of pity, and slipped

away quickly home, for the sun told him the afternoon meal
was due.

"That ulcer of mine" (he was alluding to Yagna) "hurts
me, but only when I happen to touch it! . . . Oh, how
greedily her eyes were fixed on the lad! As if she would
have devoured him!—Well, let her! Let her!"

But, do what he would, his "ulcer" gave him excruciating
pain.

"She flees me as the plague! . . . This fellow's new sieve
for her peg.—Fortunately, she will lose her trouble with
Yanek.—Ah!" he said, now more and more wrought up;
"some women are of such nature that they will run after
any man who only whistles to them."

But, fast as he went, his burning memories went with
him. He saw no one, though several men passed by; and
he only calmed down at the village, on perceiving Yanek's
mother, sitting by a ditch, her youngest son rolling in the
sand beside her, and a flock of geese grazing between the
poplar-trees.

"You have come pretty far with your geese, Madam,"
he said, stopping to wipe his face.

"I went out to meet Yanek; he must be here at any
minute."

"I just saw him at the skirt of the forest."

"Ah, is he, then, so near?" she ejaculated, starting up and
chiding her geese for getting into the rye near the roadside,
where they were doing considerable damage.

"His britzka was standing near the crucifix; he was in
talk with some woman or other."

"Yes, he must have met an acquaintance and had a chat.
Good kind-hearted boy! he cannot even pass by a strange
dog without patting it.—And who was she?"

"I could not be quite sure, but fancy she was Yagna."
He saw the old dame purse her lips at the name, and added,
smiling significantly: "I could not tell, for they were slipping away into the thickets. On account of the heat, no
doubt."

"Saints of the Lord! what has come to your mind? Yanek!—to mix with such a one!"

"She's as good as others!" he retorted, suddenly angry. "Better, it may be."

The organist's wife bent over her knitting, and her fingers wagged more quickly.

"What! Yanek, on the very verge of the priesthood, to have anything to do with such a woman!" And then she recalled certain tales she had heard about priests, and dug a knitting-needle into her hair in perplexity, and resolved to see into this and inquire. . . . But Antek had gone; and now there came a great cloud of dust upon the road; and two minutes later Yanek was embracing her with the tenderest affection, and crying out from his heart:

"O my dear, my darling mother!"

"Saints of the Lord!—Let go, you young giant, let go: you're choking me!" But when he had let go, she fell herself to hugging and kissing, and gloating over him with eager eyes.

"Poor little mite! How thin they have made you! How pale, poor son of mine! and how wretched-looking!"

"One does not grow fat on broth of holy water!" he answered, laughing, and tossing his little brother up in the air, till he crowed with delight.

"Fear nothing; we'll stuff you and puff you out in no time," she said, stroking his cheeks with affection.

"Well, let us drive on, Mother dear, and we shall be sooner home."

"Ah, those geese! Lord, Lord! In the rye again!"

He ran to drive them off, for they were plucking at the rye-stalks and devouring the grain at will. Then he placed his brother in the cart, and walked on himself along the middle of the road.

"Look there!" his mother cried; "how that brat has smeared his face!" She pointed to the boy on the britzka.

"Yes, he has made free with my strawberries. Eat away, eat away!—I met Yagna coming out of the wood with them, and she gave me some." He coloured bashfully.

"Boryna was just telling me he had met you both. . . ."

"I did not see him; he must have passed at some distance."

"Child, folk in a village can see things through walls—
even things that have not taken place!" She laid stress on
the words, looking down on her twinkling knitting-needles.

Yanek had apparently not caught her meaning. Seeing
a flight of doves sweeping low above the rye, he aimed a
stone at one of them, saying merrily:

"They are the priest's: anyone can tell that, so fat they
are!"

"Be still, Yanek! Someone else might hear you!" she
gently rebuked him, though her thoughts already saw him
a parish priest, and herself spending her old age by his side,
and living the rest of her years in peace and happiness.

"And when is Felix coming for the vacation?"

"Why, Mother, know ye not? He is in jail."

"Saints of the Lord! In jail! What was the misdeed?
—And I always said and foretold he would come to a bad
end!—Such a scapegrace!—Had he become a scrivener of
low degree—that would have sufficed him—quite; but the
miller wanted him to be a doctor, forsooth! . . . And they
were so stuck up, so proud of their darling! Now he is in
jail—and a pretty comfort to them!" she said, trembling
all over with malevolent satisfaction.

"But, Mother, it is not that at all: he is in the Warsaw
Citadel."

"In the Citadel? Then" (she lowered her voice) "it is
some political misdeed!"

Yanek either could not or would not tell her any more,
and she went on, in a faltering voice:

"My dear child, remember never to have aught to do with
any such affairs."

"No! In our seminary, anyone who so much as speaks
of them is expelled."

"You see? They would expel you, and you would never
be a priest, and I—I should die of shame and sorrow! O
God! have mercy upon us!"

"My dear mother, have no fear for me."

"And you are aware how hard we work and strive for the bettering of your lot; what trouble we have—so many of us, and our gains always growing less; and how, were it not for the bit of land we have, our priest would drive us to die of starvation. Aye, he now settles matters directly with the peasants, both for weddings and for funerals: who ever heard of such a thing! He says Father takes too much from the peasants—and he becomes their benefactor at other folk's expense!"

"But," Yanek faltered here, "Father really did take too much!"

"What! will ye rise up in judgment on your own father? —Even were this true, for whom is he greedy? For himself? No: for you all; for you and your schooling!" She felt deeply hurt.

Yanek was going to ask her forgiveness, but he just then heard a bell tinkle on the other side of the pond, and cried:

"Hark, Mother! it must be the priest taking the Holy Viaticum to some sick man!"

"He is more likely to be ringing to prevent the bees from flying away; they are probably swarming in his garden now. He is more interested in his bees and his bull than in the church."

They were just passing the churchyard, when suddenly they heard a roaring hum, and Yanek had but just time to call out to the driver:

"Bees are coming!—Hold the horses still, or they'll bolt."

A huge swarm was flying with a loud drone about the church square, rising up like a sonorously purring cloud, and wheeling about in search of a good place to settle upon; at times sweeping low and floating amongst the trees. Behind it ran the priest, clad only in shirt and breeches, bareheaded, out of breath, and continually sprinkling the bees with water from an aspergill. Near him came Ambrose, creeping along in the shadow of the bushes, ringing and shouting with all his might. They went twice round the square without slackening their speed; for the bees, flying ever lower, seemed to want to alight on one of the cottages, from which the frightened children were already making their escape; but then, rising a little higher, they made straight for Yanek's britzka. His mother, with a shriek, and pulling her petticoat over her head, ran to crouch down in the nearest ditch; the geese waddled away; the horses would have bolted, had not the driver covered their eyes with cloths. But Yanek stood quietly, with uplifted head, while the swarm swirled on above him, and passed him towards the belfry.

"Water, quick, before they are off again!" bellowed the priest, rushing after, and, coming up with them, sprinkled them with so copious a shower that their damp wings allowed them to go no farther, and they began to settle on the belfry window.

"Ambrose! the ladder and the sieve now!—Hurry, else they are away again!—Stir your leg and hurry up!—How do you do, Yanek? Get me some live coals in a thurible: we shall have to quiet them with incense!" he cried in great excitement, incessantly sprinkling the swarm as it was settling. Before he could have said a "Hail Mary," the ladder was there, and Ambrose tinkling, and Yanek sending up clouds of aromatic smoke as from a chimney; and meanwhile the priest climbed up and, bending over the swarm, groped amongst the bees to find their queen.

"Ha! here she is! God be praised; they will not flee any farther now!—But they are dispersing: Yanek! smoke them from beneath!" he cried, taking the bees up in his bare hands and pouring them into the big sieve, the swarm being an exceedingly large one, talking to them all the while, and not in the least afraid, although they came settling on his head and crawling over his face.

"Take heed! they are getting excited, and may sting," he said, warning the others, as he came down, surrounded by a vast cloud that was eddying on all sides of him, and buzzing and humming. On reaching the ground, he raised up the sieve as carefully and as solemnly as though it had been a Monstrance. Yanek, swinging the thurible, accompanied him; Ambrose followed, now ringing, now sprinkling the bees. And thus they went in procession to the priest's apiary, behind his house, where stood in a separate enclosure some scores of hives, all humming as loud as if each of them were about to swarm.

While the priest was getting his bees into their new hive, Yanek, now very tired and hungry, slipped away quietly home.

They all rejoiced exceedingly to see him, and the noise and fuss made over him cannot be described. When the first outburst was over, they made him sit down to table, bringing him all sorts of good things, enticing and pressing and teasing him to eat, till the whole house echoed to the din and bustle, all wanting to be by the lad's side or doing something for him. In the midst of this hubbub, in dropped Gregory, the Voyt's brother, to ask them anxiously if they had seen Roch anywhere. But they had not.

"Nowhere can I find him," he said in distress, and, without staying to talk, went on to another cabin to seek for him. Scarcely had he left them, when the priest sent for Yanek. He lingered and delayed going as long as he could, but of course had to go at last.

His Reverence, who was sitting on the porch, embraced him like a father, and, making him sit down by his side, said with great affability:

"I am glad you have come: we shall say our breviary together.—But do ye know how many swarms of bees I have this year? Fifteen! And as vigorous as any of the old ones; some have already filled a quarter of the hive with honey. And I had more swarms; but I had told Ambrose to watch for the swarming, and he fell asleep, the blockhead! and where are the bees now?—In the woods and the forests!—And then the miller stole one from me; he did, I say! They flew on to a pear-tree of his, and he claimed them for his own, and would not hear of returning them. Sore about the bull, he is, and that's his revenge. . . . The robber!—What, have you heard about Felix? . . . Ah! these wretches, they sting like wasps!" he broke off all at once, brushing away with his handkerchief the flies that came settling on his bald crown.

"All I know is, he's in the citadel."

"If that were all! . . . And I warned him so! . . . The donkey would not hearken to me; and now he's in a pretty fix. . . . The old father is a loud-mouthed boor; but I'm sorry for Felix; a clever young rogue, and with his Latin at his fingers' ends, as well as any bishop! . . . What is that saying? ah, 'Touch not what's not allowed, and keep yourself from things forbidden' . . . and: 'A docile calf thrives as though it sucked two mothers.' Aye . . . aye . . ." he continued his voice growing feebler, as he went on brushing the flies away. "Recollect that, Jasio, recollect it." His head fell back, and he sank deep into his vast arm-chair. But as Yanek got up to leave, he opened his eyes and murmured: "Those bees have tired me out!—Come and say the breviary with me of an evening. . . . And take heed not to be too familiar with the peasants. Note this: 'He that mixes with chaff will be eaten by swine!' Eaten, I tell you—and there's an end."—With these words he threw a handkerchief over his face, and was asleep in the twinkling of an eye.

What the priest had said, Yanek's father thought, no doubt; for, when the farm-servant came home with the horses from the pastures, and Yanek vaulted upon one of them, the old man cried:

"Get down this instant! It is unseemly for a clergyman to ride bare-backed, or to keep company with herdsmen!"

Dearly as he would have loved a ride, he nevertheless alighted meekly and, twilight having fallen now, went into the garden to say his evening prayers. But he could not keep his mind on them. There was a girl, somewhere about, trilling a song; some women were gossiping in a neighbouring orchard, and every word came wafted over the dewy grass to him; children shouted as they bathed in the pond; in another direction, the sound of laughter struck his ears; and then came the lowing of the cows, and the metallic cackle of the priest's guinea-fowls pierced the air, and the whole place was full of sounds of every kind, and like a hive of humming bees. All this put him out; and when he had at last collected himself, and, kneeling down at the edge of a rye-field, raised his eyes to the starry heaven, and his soul to the Infinite beyond it, he heard such a sudden din of piercing shrieks and howls and curses that he ran back to the house, not a little alarmed and shaken, to ask his mother (who had just come to call him in for supper) what the matter was, and whether the people there were fighting in earnest.

"Oh, 'tis only Joseph Vahnik, back from the police office a little in his cups, and he's fighting his wife. The woman had long stood in great need of a good drubbing. Do not trouble, she will take no harm."

"But she screeches as if she were being skinned alive!"

"That's her way: if he had taken a stick to her, she'd have been quiet enough. And she'll get even with him to-morrow, she will!—Come, dearest, or supper will be cold."

He went to bed, utterly worn out, and having scarcely touched any food. But as soon as the sun rose next morning, he was on his legs: going about the fields, bringing clover to the horses, teasing the priest's turkeys till they gobbled at him indignantly, making friends with the dogs, that tried to fawn on him till they well-nigh broke their chains; scattering grain to the pigeons, helping his youngest brother to drive the cattle, and Michael to chop wood; looking whether the pears in the orchard were ripe yet; frolicking with the colt, going everywhere and greeting everything he saw with eyes of love, as friends and brothers —even the flower-dight hollyhocks, the little pigs basking in the sun, the very weeds and nettles themselves! And his mother, following his gambols with loving looks, murmured, smiling fondly at the lad:

"He's out of his wits—clean out of his wits!"

And so he wandered about, radiant as that July day: smiling, sunny, full of warmth, and embracing the whole world with intense affection . . . until, the Mass-bell beginning to tinkle, he quitted all to hasten away to church.

It was a Votive Mass, and Yanek walked out of the
sacristy in front of the priest, in a new surplice, freshly
adorned with red ribbons. The organ pealed forth, and
from the choir there came a big bass voice which made the
flames of the altar-lights tremble. Quite a number of worshippers were kneeling round the altar, when the service
began.

Yanek, though serving Mass and praying fervently between his responses and the acts of his ministry, could not
help noticing Yagna and her gleaming dark-blue eyes, fixed
upon him, and the lurking smile on her parted crimson lips.

After church, the priest took him to his house directly
and set him amanuensis work to do for him till noon, when
he was free to visit his acquaintances in the village.

He went first to see the Klembas, his nearest neighbours,
but found none of them at home. Only, looking through
the passage open at either end, he saw that something moved
in a corner, and heard a husky voice:

"Here I am . . . I, Agata!" She raised herself up, and
lifted her hands in astonishment. "Lord! 'tis Master
Yanek!"

"Pray you, do not rise! . . . What, are ye unwell?" he
asked her kindly, and, seating himself on a stump that he
brought in, looked into her face, which he could scarcely
recognize, so worn and wasted it was.

"I am waiting upon the Lord and expecting His mercy."
Her voice had a strangely solemn sound.

"What is it that ails you?"

"Naught. But Death is growing ripe within me for the
harvest. The Klembas have only taken me in here that I
might die amongst them: so here I am—praying and awaiting the end . . . waiting for Dame Crossbones to knock
and say: 'Come away with me, you weary soul!'"

"But wherefore are you not lying within—in the cabin?"

"Ah, I would not be in the way till my time comes. As
it is, they had to take their calf hence to make room for me.
. . . But they have promised to lay me in their dwelling-

room for my last hours—on a bed, beneath the Holy Images, and with the Taper of the Dying lit in my hand! . . . And to bring the priest, and dress me in my best clothes, and give me a real goodwife's funeral! Yea, and I have paid for everything, and they are honest folk: perhaps they will not play false with a poor lone old woman.—I shall not trouble them long; and they promised me this in the presence of witnesses—of witnesses!"

"But are you not weary of lying here alone?"—His voice sounded tearful and unsteady.

"Master Yanek, I am very well off indeed here. Through these doorways, I can see many a thing: folk that go along the road, folk talking one to another; some look in, some even have a few kind words for me: I might just as well be going about the village. And when they have all gone to their work, I can see the fowls scratching in the rubbish-heaps; and then the sparrows hop into the passage, or the sun looks in for a little ere he sets, or some naughty boy flings a clod my way; and so the day is gone by before I know it. . . . And . . . in the night . . . they come to me—oh, many a one! . . ."

"They? Who, ah! who is't that comes?" He bent close, and peered into her seemingly sightless eyes.

"My own folk, who died long ago: kinsfolk and acquaintances.—I tell you true, young master: they do come! —Once, too," she whispered with a smile of ineffable rapture, "once the Virgin Mother herself came and said to me tenderly: 'Lie there, Agata, the Lord Jesus will reward you.' It was she of Chenstohova: I knew her at once by her crown and her mantle, all covered with gold and coral beads. And she stroked my hair and said: 'Be not afraid, O lone one; you shall be a foremost dame in the court of Heaven, a lady of high degree.'"

Thus spoke the old woman, chirping feebly, like a bird that is dropping off to sleep; while Yanek, bending over her, looked and listened; as one who, gazing into abysmal depths, hears something hidden that bubbles and gurgles, and sees the glimmer of a mystery that is going on, beyond

the ken of the human mind! He felt terror-stricken, yet
could not tear himself away from that rag of humanity,
that withered ear of corn, that life which, trembling like a
ray that goes out in the darkness, was yet dreaming of its
forthcoming renewal and splendour! Never yet had he beheld so near as this the inexorable destiny of man, and he
was naturally appalled on realizing it. His heart was filled
with mourning, and tears welled up from his eyes; he was
bowed down to the earth with deep commiseration, and a
fervent supplication burst convulsively from his lips.

Old Agata roused herself, lifted up her head, and cried
ecstatically:

"O Yanek! O, most holy youth! Dear priest, beloved
of my heart!"

He remained for a long time afterwards, standing propped
against a wall, taking in the warmth of the sun, and feast-
ing his eyes on the bright day, and the life he saw seething
round him.

Did it matter, after all, if hard by him a human soul were
struggling in the grip of death?

The sun shone all the same, the cornfields rustled; far, far
above, the white clouds sailed past; children played on the
roads; on the boughs, ripe apples glowed crimson; hammers
beat upon the smithy anvil; they were getting ready a
wagon, and tempering a sickle for the coming harvest;
the air was redolent of fresh-baked bread; women were
chatting together, kerchiefs moved along the hedges and
fields and enclosures: humanity went on its way, as usual,
as everlastingly, swarming, bustling, full of cares and little
schemes, no one so much as wondering who would be first to
fall into the abyss!

And so Yanek soon shook off his sadness, and went on
to the village.

He stayed a little with Matthew, who was now raising the
walls of Staho's hut to a good height; had a talk with
Ploshkova, busy bleaching her linen; paid a visit to Yuzka,
who was still in bed; lent an ear to the complaints of the
Voyt's wife; looked how the smith at his forge was harden-

ing scythes and putting a jagged edge to reaping-hooks; and
he looked also into the gardens where women and lasses were
at work: everyone was glad to see him, hailed him as a
friend, and looked on him with no little pride—a child of
Lipka—one of them!

Dominikova's was the last hut he visited. She was sitting
outside, spinning, and he wondered how she could spin with
a bandage over her eyes.

"My fingers tell me if the thread is fine or thick," she
said; and, greatly pleased that he had come, called Yagna,
who was doing something about the yard.

She came at once, scantily attired in only smock and
petticoat; but on seeing Yanek, she hastily put up her hands
and ran into the cabin, as red as a cherry.

"Yagna, bring us milk: Master Yanek will surely take
some refreshment."

She brought in a full milking-pail, and a mug to drink
from. She had covered herself with a shawl, but was still
extremely confused. As she poured the milk out with
downcast eyes, her hands shook, and she turned pale and
red by turns.

All the time he was there, she said not one single word;
but, accompanying him to the gate when he went away, she
gazed after him till he was out of sight.

There was in him something that attracted her irresistibly,
and stirred her up with such power that, in order not to
follow him, she flew to the orchard, caught hold of a tree,
and embraced it with all her might, hugging it in both arms.
There she stood, breathless, almost beside herself, cloaked
and hidden, as it were, by the apple-covered branches that
bowed down over her, with eyelids half closed, and a faint
smile of happiness on her lips, though she also felt a vague
dread, and a fearful yet pleasant sense of agitation: something like what she had experienced when looking at him
through the window, that night in spring.

She too attracted him, though he was not aware of any
attraction. He would now and then look in at her cabin
for a short time, feeling an unaccountable gladness at the

visit; and, seeing her daily in church, always on her knees
during the whole of Mass, and seeming to be in a state of
fervent, even ecstatic prayer, he could not witness this without a pleasing emotion. One day he spoke to his mother
of that ardent piety of hers.

"Oh, if anyone stands in need of prayer and pardon, she
does!" was the reply.

Now Yanek's soul was as pure a white as the whitest
flower in the world, and so he failed to catch the real meaning of those words. As, moreover, she used to frequent
their house, where everybody liked her, and he saw her piety
besides to be so great, he really had no suspicion of what
she was. Only he thought it a curious thing that she had
not come once since his return.

His mother answered: "I have just sent for her; there
is much ironing to be done."

And presently she came, but so finely dressed that he
wondered.

"What? are ye off to a wedding?"

One of the girls here cried out: "Rather she has received
an offer of marriage."

"Let them but dare! I should soon send them flying!"
she replied with a laugh, blushing like a rose, for every eye
was upon her.

Yanek's mother set her to iron at once; his sisters joined
her, and Yanek went with them. In a short time they were
all very merry, roaring with laughter over the merest trifles,
and finally the old dame had to rebuke them.

"Be quiet, ye magpies!—Yanek, better go into the garden.
'Tis not fitting you should sit grinning here."

So he had to go out, according to his wont, into the fields
away beyond the village, or even as far as the boundaries of
Lipka, where he would sit reading or meditating.

Yagna knew well those haunts of his, and where to find
him, if only with the mind's eye; she was for ever flying
round him, like a moth round a candle, and could not help
herself; for she was driven towards him, and now followed
her impulse without resistance, giving way with all her

heart and soul to that gentle force, which like the rush of a foaming current impelled her onward; she never even wondered on what shores it would land her, nor how it all would end.

Whether she laid herself down to rest late in the night, or rose up at early dawn, she was continually repeating with every heart-beat:

"I shall see him—see him—see him once again!"

She was often kneeling before the altar, when the priest came out to say Mass; the organ burst forth with soul-stirring strains, the incense-smoke poured out of the thuribles, and whispered prayers went up to the throne of God; but she, with eyes full of worship, gazed only on Yanek, clad in white, slender, fair to behold, moving with joined hands amidst the fragrant vapours and the rainbow hues that streamed down from the stained-glass windows. He seemed to her like a real angel, stepping out of a picture-frame, and gliding towards her with a sweet smile. And then all Heaven would enter her soul; she would fall prone in the dust, kissing the place where his feet had passed, and, carried away by the force of her passionate emotions, would join with the others to sing the hymn: "Holy, Holy, Holy!" in a delirium of purely human bliss.

Sometimes Mass was over, and the people had gone home, and Ambrose came jingling his keys to close the church, while she was yet there, on her knees, gazing at the spot, now empty, where Yanek had been—plunged in a hallowed calm, an intoxicating joy, intensified even to pain—shedding big tears that flowed down clear as crystal.

Now was every day for her like a day of solemn festival, a great day of indulgence, with the never-ceasing joy of adoration ever thrilling her soul; and when she looked out upon the country-side, the ripe ears of corn, the sun-baked soil, the orchards bending under their burden of fruit, the far-away forests, the passing clouds, and that grand sun, like the Sacred Host, rising up over the world—all these, with one accord, sang together in her soul one and the same hymn, which reached to Heaven: "Holy, Holy, Holy!"

"At a time like this," she thought, "how strong one feels! One could wrestle with God—master death—even struggle against one's fate! To one in such a pass, life is for ever a joy; even the merest worm is beloved by him! . . . Every morning he kneels to thank the Lord, every night he blesses the day gone by: he willingly would give away all he has, for he would yet remain rich; and with each of those marvellous days, his power of loving increases!

"And how his soul rises up—up—far above all the worlds! And how he looks on the stars as on things close by! how boldly he stretches out his hand to Heaven and the day of bliss everlasting, seeing clearly that there is naught to bound his power of loving, and that naught can turn it aside!"

Meanwhile the days glided by as usual, those days of tedious preparation for the harvest. And she was bustling about and working hard, but as full of song as any lark; unweariedly joyful, blossoming all over with gladness, like a rose-bush or an exuberant hollyhock; or rather like some flower from the garden of Paradise—so winsome to see, so radiantly alluring with those wonderful eyes of hers, so perpetually wreathed with beaming smiles! Even the glances of aged men followed her with delight, and young swains again came flocking about her cabin, sighing with love. But she rejected every one of them.

"Take root here, if you will; you'll profit nothing," she said mockingly to each.

"We are all scorned by her! She is as haughty as any Manor lady," they complained to Matthew. And he only sighed bitterly: he himself, had he any greater privilege than to talk at dusk with her mother, and eye Yagna as she hurried about the cabin, and listen to the songs she sang? He looked and listened, and each time went home in a surlier mood, now more and more often repairing to the tavern, and on his return thence discharging his bitterness on everyone around him. Especially on Teresa, whom he pained so much that life was a burden to her; so much that, meeting Yagna one day, she could not forbear from a manifestation of spite—turning her back on her and spitting!

But Yagna, walking by with far-away looks, passed on without even seeing her.

Teresa, in a fury, said to the girls that were by, washing at the mill-pond:

"See ye how she stalks past—never looking at anyone, either by day or by night?"

"And," cried another, "arrayed as if it were the local feast to-day!"

"Daily she sits combing her hair till noon!"

"She's always buying ribbons and head-gear!" they chimed in, full of hate. Since some time, whenever she appeared in the village, she was followed everywhere by the women's piercing looks—sharp as cats' claws, stinging as a viper's fangs. And on every occasion they would find something to say against her. The goodwives whispered in Ploshka's enclosure, as she passed:

"It is unbearable, the way she sets herself above us all."

"And dresses like a Manor Lady: whence can the money come?"

"Has she not great favour with the Voyt?"

"Antek also, they say, is very open-handed with her."

But here Yagustynka interfered. "Oh, no, Antek cares no more for her than a dog for a fifth leg! 'Tis someone else she has taken up with now!" And she smiled with such a knowing air that they all pestered her to know who this was. She would not, and told them:

"I am no scandalmonger! Ye have eyes: find out for yourselves!"

And from that time, a hundred pair of eyes spied all Yagna's doings still more closely than ever. So many hounds in pursuit of one hare!

Yagna, thus constantly watched by prying eyes, went her way quite unconscious; nor would she have cared in any case, having the bliss of seeing her Yanek daily, and losing her whole being in his eyes.

Almost every day, she would look in at the organist's,

always when Yanek was at home. Sometimes he happened
to sit by her side, and she knew that his eyes were upon
her; and then her face glowed, all on fire, her feet trembled
and her heart would beat like a hammer. At other times,
when he was giving his sisters lessons in the next room,
she would listen, holding her breath, and so extremely attentive to the sweet sounds of his voice that the old dame
once asked her why she gave ear so eagerly.

"Because Master Yanek teaches in such learned wise that
I cannot understand anything at all!"

"And are ye so fain to do so?" she replied with a smile
of pity. "My son has learned in no mean school!" she
added with pride, and continued expatiating on her Yanek
for some time. She was fond of Yagna, and liked her to
come; the girl was handy at every sort of work, and besides
very often brought something—pears, wild strawberries,
whortleberries, sometimes even a pat of fresh butter.

Yagna listened with eager attention to all she said; but
when Yanek left the house, she would presently hurry away
—to her mother's, she said. She loved to gaze on him from
a distance; and at times, too, hidden in the rye or behind
a tree, she would gloat over him for a long time, and with
such tender emotion that the tears would fall in spite of her.

But her joy was greatest in the short warm clear summer nights. As soon as her mother was asleep, she carried
her bedding out into the orchard, where, lying on her back,
she looked up at the stars scintillating through the tree-tops,
and dreamed sweetly of the "world without end." The sultry night-winds swept over her face and the stars looked
down into her wide-open eyes; the voices out of the fragrant
darkness, the breathless whispers of the leaves, the broken
rustling of the creatures slumbering around—feeble sighs
and dull stifled calls and timid chuckling sounds—melted
within her into a weird music, penetrating her with a hot
thrill that made her catch her breath, and quiver, and fall
down, rolling on the cool dewy sward on which she lay
like a fruit fallen from the tree. There she would remain,
prone and powerless, in the clutch of the almighty force of

Nature, as did the ripening fields, the fruit-burdened branches, the broad yellow wheat-lands, ready for the sickle, the birds, the blasts, or for any fate that awaited them, indifferently expecting all!

Thus did Yagna spend the short warm clear nights and the burning days of July: they passed by her like a delightful dream, repeated again and again, and always more desirable.

And she moved about, too, as in a dream, scarce knowing whether it was day or night.

Dominikova noted that something unusual was taking place in Yagna, but she knew not what: only she was rejoiced at her unexpected and most fervent piety, and would often say:

"Yagna, I tell you: whoso seeks God, to him doth God come!"

And Yagna would then smile a quiet humble smile of expectant happiness, but said nothing.

And one day, quite unawares, she came upon Yanek, sitting by the mound that was the village landmark, book in hand. She could not take to flight, so stood there stockstill, confused and blushing deeply.

"Why, what are you doing here?" he said.

She stammered something, fearing lest he had guessed how matters stood with her.

"Sit down; I can see you are hot and tired."

As she hesitated whether to comply, he took her by the hand and seated her by his side; she, with a quick motion, hiding her bare feet under her skirt.

Nor was Yanek at his ease; he seemed embarrassed and troubled, and looked about him in perplexity.

No one was near. The roofs and orchards of Lipka rose like far-away islands out of a sea of corn, which rolled its waves in the breeze; there was a warm scent of wild thyme mingled with that of the rye. A bird was sailing high above their heads.

To break the awkward silence, he said: "It is terribly hot."

"And it was pretty hot too yesterday," she replied, in a voice so husky with joy and fear that she could hardly get the words out.

"Reaping will begin soon."

"Aye, it will," she assented, her eyes glued to his face. He smiled and, attempting a free and easy tone, said to her:

"Why, Yagna, you are growing prettier every day!"

"I pretty? No, indeed!" she faltered, turning very red, while her dark-blue eyes shot flames, and a smile of secret delight trembled on her lips.

"But tell me true, Yagna, do ye not mean to marry again?"

"Never! Am I not happy, single as I am?"

"And is there no one for whom ye care at all?" he asked, growing bolder.

"No one, no one!" She shook her head, fixing full upon him her dreamy eyes that told of blissful thoughts. He bent forward, and looked into their azure depths. In her glance there could be read a prayer, full of sweet and most profound trust—like the fervent outcry of an adoring heart at the most sacred instant of the Mass. And her soul stirred within her, as a sunbeam passing over the fields, as a bird winging its way, singing far above the earth.

On a sudden he shrank back, strangely perturbed, rubbed his eyes, and rose to his feet.

"I must be going home." He nodded farewell to her, and set off towards the village through the fields, opening his book to read as he went. His eyes happening to wander off it, he looked round, and stopped short.

Yagna was following, only a few paces behind him!

"This," she said, timidly excusing herself, "is the shortest way home for me too."

"Then let us walk abreast," he answered, gruffly, not much pleased at having her company; and on he went, reading the book to himself half aloud.

"What does it tell of?" she inquired, with a glance at the open pages.

"I'll read you some, if you wish."

There was a spreading tree not far off; so he sat down in its shade to read, while Yagna, squatting down and facing him, her hand propping her chin, listened very eagerly, drinking in all his being with greedy eyes.

"How do you like this?" he asked after a while, raising his head. She blushed, looked away, and blurted out bashfully:

"Can I tell?—It is not a story about kings, is it?"

He looked annoyed and read on, but slowly and distinctly this time, laying stress upon every word. He read about fields and cornlands . . . about a manor that stood in a grove of birches . . . about the son of a Squire who came home . . . and a damsel who sat in a garden with the children! And all that was set down in verse, exactly as in the books of pious canticles, and they sounded like a hymn given out by a priest from the pulpit. And she felt a wish to sigh and cross herself and shed tears, the words impressed her so.

But the place where they were sitting was fearfully hot. All around them stood the rye, spoiled by tangles of cornflowers and vetches and morning-glory flowers, forming a dense wall, through which no breath of air could pass to cool them. The silence was broken only by the rustling sound of the dangling ears of rye, by the chirping of sparrows in the boughs, and the drone of some passing bee. Yanek's voice sounded very sweet and melodious; but Yagna, though her eyes were fastened upon him, as upon a most beautiful picture, and her ears did not miss one word he said, yet could not help nodding from time to time, for she felt so drowsy she had much ado to keep awake.

Fortunately he left off reading then, looking her straight in the eyes.

"Say, is it not truly beautiful?"

"Aye, very beautiful; very like a sermon!"

His eyes flashed and his cheeks flamed, as he held forth

to her about the poem, and quoted many a passage, describing the fields and forests. But she broke in:

"Why, every infant knows that trees grow in the woods, that water flows in the rivers, and that men sow the fields; wherefore, then, put such things in print?"

Yanek started, astonished and displeased.

"I," she went on to say, "care only for tales of kings, of dragons, of spectres—tales which make one's flesh creep to hear them, and the heart within one burn like a live coal. . . . Such tales Roch tells us sometimes: I could listen to him all day, all night!—Have ye any books on such matters?"

"Who would read them? Mere trash, mere fables!" he ejaculated, scornfully, and very much put out.

"Fables? Why, Roch has read them to us: they are in print!"

"Then he read you falsehoods and senseless things!"

"What, are all those marvellous tales only falsehoods and made-up stories?"

"Nothing more!"

"And those about the noonday phantoms too? And those about the dragons?" she asked, more and more disappointed.

He was losing patience. "I tell you, all that is mere falsehood!" he said.

"But is all false too? About the Lord Jesus, journeying with Saint Peter?"

He had no time to answer her; for suddenly, as if risen out of the ground, Kozlova appeared, standing in front of them and looking on the pair with a wicked smile.

"Master Yanek," she said in soft tones, "they are seeking you throughout Lipka."

"What can the matter be?"

"Three carts, full of gendarmes, have come to the village."

He started up, greatly upset, and made off as fast as was seemly.

Yagna too returned to the village in deep trouble, Kozlova walking by her side.

"I fear I have interrupted you two . . . in your prayers!" she hissed.

"By no means.   He was reading to me from a book with certain tales done into verse."

"Oh.   I fancied something very different indeed.   His mother had begged me to seek him. . . . Coming this way, I look around: there is no one. . . . Then I think of giving a look under this pear-tree . . . and behold, there are my turtle-doves, cooing one to another.—'Tis a very convenient spot . . . quite out of sight!—Aye, aye!"

Yagna broke away from her in a rage, screaming: "May your filthy tongue be struck dumb for ever!"

And Kozlova cried after her: "And ye'll always have someone to shrive you!"

CHAPTER X

ON entering the village, Yagna at once could see that something out of the ordinary was going on. The dogs in the farm-yard were barking in great excitement; the little ones, hiding in the orchards, peeped out from behind the trees and hedges; the people, though it was yet far from sunset, were fast coming in from the fields; women were whispering together in groups; every face bore an expression of disquietude, and in every eye there was a look of alarm and suspense.

"What has come about?" she asked the Balcerek girl, peering round the corner of her hut.

"I cannot say; belike soldiers coming from the forest."

"Jesu Maria! Soldiers!" And her knees trembled with terror.

"Young Klemba," added the Prychck girl, as she ran by, "says they are Cossacks from Vola."

In great dismay, Yagna hurried on to her cabin, where her mother, sitting on the threshold, and spinning, was in earnest talk with several women.

"We have both seen the same thing—the men sitting in the porch, and their leader with the priest inside the house."

"And they have sent the organist's lad Michael to fetch the Voyt."

"The Voyt! then it can be no trifle. Ho, ho! something is in the wind!"

"It may be they have only come to collect the taxes."

"With such a number of men? No, they come surely for something more than that."

"Perhaps; but, mark my words, they are here for no good!"

Yagustynka came up. "I," she said, "can tell you why they have come."

All crowded round her, stretching their necks out like so many geese.

"They have come to take us women into the army!" she cried with a croaking laugh that no one took up; and Dominikova remarked sourly:

"Ye must always be making some wretched joke!"

"It is you that are always making mountains of mole-hills! You quake so, your teeth are well-nigh falling out of your heads; yet all are greedy to hear that something is to hap! Much do I trouble about the gendarmes!"

Thereupon Ploshkova, pushing forward her portly figure, began telling them how "something had come over her as soon as she saw those carts . . ."

"Be quiet! Here comes Gregory and the Voyt, running at full speed towards the priest's house."

Their eyes followed the two moving figures on the farther side of the pond.

"Aha! Gregory too is wanted!"

They were wrong. Gregory only pushed his brother in, but stayed himself to look at the carts drawn up there, and to question the drivers who were sitting in the porch. Then, in great distress, he ran to Matthew, who was working at Staho's cabin, and sitting astride on one of the roof-beams, while cutting hollows in it to fix the rafters.

"Not gone yet?" he asked, cutting away as before.

"No; and the worst is, we cannot tell for whom they have come."

"Some evil thing is certainly at hand," old Bylitsa stammered.

"Perchance they come about our meeting. The District Official threatened us then, and the gendarmes have been to and fro, seeking to find out who it is that eggs on the Lipka folk," Matthew said, slipping down to the ground.

"Then they are likely to have come for me!" Gregory rejoined, suddenly breathless with apprehension.

"No, I think they mean to seize Roch!" Staho asserted.

"True, they have inquired about him once already: how could I let that slip my memory?" He felt relieved for himself; but at once said, in distress for the other's fate:

"No doubt, if they have come for anyone, 'tis for him!"

"Well, but shall we let him be taken?" shouted Matthew. "Him, that is so truly a father to us all!"

"Alas! we cannot resist them, it is not to be thought of."

"Let him hide somewhere—and first let us warn him instantly."

"But peradventure," Staho remarked diffidently, "they may have come on some other errand—the Voyt's business, for instance."

"He must at all events be warned," cried Gregory; and, rushing out into the rye, and working around several gardens, he soon reached Boryna's hut.

Antek was sitting in the porch, putting jagged edges to some sickles on a small anvil. On hearing what the matter was, he started up in alarm.

"He has only just come in.—Roch!" he cried. "Here, we want you."

"What is it?" the old man asked, putting his head out of the window; but before they had time to speak, in dashed Michael, the organist's lad, panting very hard.

"Know, Antek, that the gendarmes are coming to you now, and are already at the mill-pond!"

"For me!" Roch bowed his head with a sigh.

"Jesu Maria!" Hanka shrieked from the threshold, and burst into tears.

"Oh, be quiet!" Antek whispered; he was thinking very hard. "We must hit upon something."

"Roch!" vociferated Michael, breaking off a large branch and looking daggers. "I'll shout the news through Lipka, and we will not give you up!"

"No fooling!—Roch! Get behind the haystack and into the rye this instant. Wiggle into some furrow, hide yourself well, and stay till I call you.—Quick! ere they are here!"

Roch snatched up some papers he had in the room and handed them to Yuzka, who was in bed:

"Hide them under yourself, do not give them up," he whispered.

And just as he was, without hat or capote, he darted into the orchard and vanished like a stone in the waters: they could just see the rye undulating slightly beyond the haystack.

"Now, Gregory, off with you! Hanka, to your work! Go, Michael—and not a word of this!" Antek commanded, sitting down again to his interrupted labour. Again he set to notching the edges of his reaping-hooks, evenly and calmly as before. Now and again he would hold the edge up to the light, glancing the while in every direction about him; for the barking of the dogs was growing louder, and in a little he could hear the heavy tread of the approaching gendarmes, the jingling of their sabres, and the sound of their voices.

His heart was palpitating, his hands were shaking; yet he managed to go on, notching evenly, regularly, with rhythmical strokes, never raising his eyes till the men were standing before him.

"Is Roch in your hut?" asked the Voyt, mortally afraid.

Antek looked around at the group, and replied with great deliberation:

"He must be in the village, I suppose: I have not set eyes on him since this morning."

"Open your doors!" thundered the commanding officer.

"Why, they are open!" Antek growled, getting up from his bench.

The officer and some of his men went in, while the others watched the orchard and outhouses.

About half the village was now outside in the road, looking on in silence, while the cottage was searched and ransacked thoroughly. Antek had to point out and open everything, while Hanka sat by the window with the baby at her breast.

The search was of course fruitless; but they sought everywhere, and were so careful to overlook nothing that one of them even peered under the bed!

Some little books, strapped together, were lying on the table. The officer pounced upon them, and set to examine them with the utmost care.

"How have ye come by these?"

"Belike Roch has left them there . . . and there they lie."

"The mistress here cannot read," the Voyt explained.

"Can anyone amongst you read?"

"No," Antek returned; "they teach us at school so well that now no one is able even to spell out the words in our prayer-books!"

The officer handed the little books to a subordinate, and passed round to the other side of the hut.

"What's here?—A sick child?" he said, taking a step towards Yuzka.

"Yes. She has been lying there for a couple of weeks: small-pox."

He retired hurriedly into the passage.

"Was Roch a lodger in this cabin?" he asked of the Voyt.

"In this or any other, according as it struck him: 'tis the *Dʒiads'* wont."

They peered into every hole and corner, even looking behind the holy images; while Yuzka followed their movements with eyes full of dread, trembling all over. One of them having approached her, she cried out wildly:

"Oh, have I hidden him under me? Seek him then here, do!"

When they had done, Antek went over to their officer, and said very humbly, with a deep bow:

"Has Roch stolen aught, I should like to know?"

The other, putting his face close to Antek's, replied with a stare, and laying stress on each word:

"Be it but found that you have concealed him, and ye shall go on a journey together, both of you!—Do you hear?"

"I hear indeed, but cannot think what all this means." And he scratched his head, as if much perplexed.

The officer shot an angry look at him, and left the cabin.

They went round to many another, looking here and there, asking questions of many a one, until sundown; when, the roads filling with home-driven cattle, they went back empty-handed.

Now the village breathed freely, and people began telling of the searches—at the Klembas'—at Gregory's—at Matthew's—and how each had seen things better than anybody else, and had not been frightened in the least, but had annoyed and bantered the gendarmes to the utmost!

But Antek, once alone with Hanka, said to her, dropping his voice:

"This is a wretched business, I see: there will be no keeping him in our cabin any longer."

"What, turn him out? So holy a man? One that does so much good?"

"A curse on it all! I am sick of it!" he cried, unable to find any way out of the quandary. But Gregory came presently, along with Matthew, and they held a consultation, locked up together in the barn: the cabin, continually full of callers for news, was no fit place.

When they came out, it was quite dark. Hanka had milked the cows, and Pete was back from the forest. Antek got the britzka and directly, while Gregory and Matthew went out, ostensibly to look everywhere for Roch, in reality to mislead the people of the village.

They were indeed all surprised at the quest, having made sure that Roch lay somewhere concealed on Boryna's premises. But the two friends gave out that he had left Boryna's directly after dinner and had not been heard of since.

"Lucky for him, or he would be journeying in chains ere now!"

So it became generally known (as they had planned) that Roch had not been seen in Lipka since noon.

People were glad, and said amongst themselves: "He guessed what was awaiting him, and is off 'to the land where pepper grows.'"

"Let him not come back, I say; we do not want him," old Ploshka growled.

Matthew snarled back at him: "Is he in your way? Has he wronged you in aught?"

"He disturbed the peace and troubled Lipka not a little. We all may yet suffer on his account."

"Then why not seize on him, you, and give him up?"

"Long ago we should have done so, had we any understanding!"

Matthew uttered a curse, and would have flown at him; they held him back, but with difficulty. And then, it being late, they went each man to his own cabin.

Antek was awaiting this moment, when the roads were deserted, and everybody was supping at home, and the scent of fried bacon was wafted abroad with the sound of merry talk and the tinkling of spoons in the dishes; then he brought Roch to the room where Yuzka lay; but he would not have a candle lit.

The old man snatched a hasty meal, put on what clothes he had left in the hut, and said farewell to the women. Hanka fell at his feet, and Yuzka wept and wailed piteously.

"God be with you! we may meet once more!" he said in a tearful voice, pressing them paternally to his breast, and kissing them on the forehead; but, Antek urging him to make haste, he once more blessed the women and children, crossed himself, and went out to the stile by the haystack.

"The britzka is waiting at Simon's hut in Podlesie, and Matthew will drive for you."

"But I must still pay a visit here in Lipka.—Where are we to meet?"

"At the crucifix by the forest, whither we are going at once."

"That's well, for I have yet many things to speak of with Gregory."

And presently he was unseen and inaudible.

Antek put the horses to, placed a bushel of rye and a whole sack of potatoes in the britzka, conferred for some time apart with Vitek, and then said, for all to hear:

"Vitek! drive over to Szymek's hut with the cart, and then come back: do ye hear?"

The lad's eyes blazed, and he started off at such a pace that Antek called after him:

"Slower, you rogue, or you'll lame the horses!"

Roch had meantime crept stealthily to Dominikova's, where he had left a few things, and shut himself up in the inner room.

Andrew was on the watch by the roadside, and Yagna every now and then looked out into the enclosure, while the old woman, sitting in the front room, listened, trembling all over.

It took him some time before he came out to talk a little with Dominikova by herself; then he wanted to take up his bag and start off. But Yagna insisted on carrying it for him, at least to the forest. He agreed, and, taking leave of the others, went out into the fields, and slowly along the narrow pathways, with noiseless caution.

The night was clear and starlit; the lands lay hushed in slumber, with only now and then a sound of fitful barking.

They were nearing the forest, when Roch, coming to a standstill, took Yagna's hand.

"Hear me, Yagna," he said in a kindly tone, "and take to heart what I am going to say."

She lent an ear, though agitated by an unpleasant sense of foreboding.

Then, just as a priest might speak in confession, he talked to her of her doings . . . with Antek . . . with the Voyt . . . and most of all with Yanek.

She listened in deep humiliation, with averted face covered with blushes; but when he named Yanek, she raised her head defiantly.

"With him I have done no evil whatsoever!"

He pointed out gently to her the temptations to which they were exposing themselves . . . the sins and scandals to which the Evil One might give occasion thereby.

But she hearkened to him no longer; her mind was full of Yanek only: unconsciously her bright red lips were murmuring with ardent and frenzied love:

"Yanek, O Yanek!"

Her glowing eyes gazed afar, and circled in fancy over his adored head.

"Oh, I would go with him to the ends of the earth!" she declared, not knowing what she said. At the words, Roch shuddered, cast one look at those wide-open eyes, and held his peace thenceforward.

At the edge of the wood, just by the crucifix, several capotes were seen to glimmer white. Roch stopped, full of misgiving:

"Who is there?"

"Only we—your friends!"

"I am tired, and must rest awhile," he said, sitting down amongst them. Yagna gave up the bag to him, and seated herself not far off, at the foot of the crucifix, in the deep shadow of the branches.

"Well, may your troubles at least come to an end here!"

"The worst of all will come," said Antek, "now that you go from us."

"But it may be, it well may be, that I shall return one day!"

Here Matthew exploded. "Blood of a dog!" he cried; "to hunt men down so . . . as if they were mangy curs!"

Gregory moaned. "And why, Lord God, why?"

"Because," Roch declared with solemn emphasis, "I want truth and righteousness for the people!"

"Hard is every man's lot; but that of the righteous is harder!"

"Do not mourn, Gregory; evil will be changed into good."

"So I think; 'tis hard to fancy that all we do is in vain."

"While we're awaiting the summer, the wolves will eat up our horses," Antek sighed, peering into the darkness at the white blot which was Yagna's face.

"But I say unto you: 'Whoso plucks up the weeds and sows good seeds, great riches shall win, when harvest comes in!'"

"And if he fail?—Such things have been."

"Yea, but he that sows, sows in the hope of gathering in a hundredfold."

"Surely, for who would care to lose his toil?"

And they pondered these things deep in their hearts.

The wind was up now, the birch-trees murmured above them; a rustling sound came out of the forest, while the voice of the waving corn rose up to them from the fields. The moon floated along a pathway in the sky, made up of a double row of white clouds; the trees flung shadows mingled with patches of brightness; goatsuckers passed over their heads with a noiseless circling flight. Their hearts were very full of sadness.

Yagna shed tears in silence: she could not have said why.

"Wherefore do you sorrow?" he asked, laying his hand paternally on her head.

But the others too, all gloomy and cheerless, sat with their eyes fixed upon Roch, whom they now held for a man of God. He was sitting beneath the cross, from which the Crucified seemed to bend forward to bless his white weary head.

Then he spoke these words to them, full of hope and confidence:

"Fear naught for me. I am only a unit—one blade of corn in a fruitful field. If they take me, and I perish, what of that?—So many more remain!—each of us ready to die for the Cause! . . . And the time cometh when there will be thousands of them, from town and country, from cottage and from manor, all incessantly giving up their lives, one after another, piled and heaped together, the stones that are to form into the Holy Church of our desire! And that Church, I say unto you, shall stand and last for ever; and no power of evil shall prevail against it, because it will be built up completely with blood and loving sacrifice!"

Then he told them how no drop of blood, nay, not one single tear, would fall in vain, nor any endeavour be without its fruit; and how on every side, as from a soil abundantly manured, new forces, new defenders, and new victims would spring forth, until that blessed day should dawn— that sacred day, the day of resurrection and of justice and of truth for all the nation!

He spoke with glowing enthusiasm; often, too, of such

high matters that they could not understand all that he said; but his fire inflamed them also, and their hearts leaped up and were exalted by his words in mighty faith and longing. Antek said at last:

"O God!—Be ye our leader: I will follow you even to death!"

"We all will follow you and trample down whatever may resist us!"

"Who can withstand us and prevail? Let him but try!"

So they all spoke, till he was forced to hush their violent words and, drawing them still closer, and whispering, say what that longed-for day would be, and how its coming would be hastened by their labours.

He told them many a thing they had not dreamed of, and they listened breathless, full of dread and joy at once; and every word of his gave them the thrill of faith which one feels at the Communion Table. He opened heaven before them, and made Paradise appear visibly to their eyes; their souls fell prostrate in deep ecstasy, their eyes beheld ineffable wonders, and in their hearts the sweet, sweet hymn of Hope was heard.

"And it is in your power to realize all this," he ended, when quite tired out. The moon was just eclipsed behind a cloud; the sky was grey, the landscape murky; the woods gave forth their inarticulate utterances, and the cornfields rustled and shook as if with fear. Afar there was a noise of dogs that barked. And still they sat there, silent and subdued, listening in rapt attention, inebriated with the words he had said, and feeling as one who has just taken some great vow may feel.

"It is time: I must go!" he said, and, rising, embraced each of them, pressing them to his heart. They could hardly keep back their tears when he knelt down, said a short prayer, and prostrated himself with both arms on the breast of that holy mother—the land which he might perhaps never see again. Yagna sobbed aloud, and the others were struggling with deep emotions.

Such was their parting.

Antek alone went straight back to Lipka, along with Yagna; the others disappeared in the shadows at the edge of the forest.

They long walked on in silence. Then he said: "Beware and say naught to anyone of that which you have heard."

"Am I, then, a pedlar of news from hut to hut?" She was offended.

"And," he added, with stern significance, "God forbid that the Voyt should hear anything of this!"

She answered only by hurrying on; but he would not let her go, and strode on by her side, again and again glancing at her indignant face, bedewed with tears.

The moon shone out again, silvering the narrow pathway where they walked abreast, and throwing across it the black distorted shadows of the trees. Suddenly his heart throbbed fast; his arms quivered with a sense of greedy desire, and he took a step nearer to her side.—He might have gathered her to his breast with a sweeping grasp. But he did not—he durst not. Her stubborn and disdainful silence held him back, and he only said to her bitterly:

"You seem as if you wanted to get away from me."

"Because I do! Someone might see us together, and tongues would wag."

"Are you in a hurry to fly to anyone else?"

"I am. What is to prevent me? Am I not a widow?"

"They say (no idle talk, I see) that you prepare to keep house for a certain priest."

Swift as the wind, she rushed away, her tears falling in torrents down her cheeks.

CHAPTER XI

ON the lighter soils, they were beginning to reap already; on the heavier, they were preparing all things for the harvest that was about to take place. It was but a few days after Roch's flight. Lipka was getting the wagons ready for use, cleaning out the barns and airing them with wide-open doors; in the shadow of the orchards, people were busily twisting bands of straw; and within doors the women were busy baking loaves and cooking food for the reapers. All this caused so much racket and turmoil that the village looked as though on the eve of some great festival.

Moreover, a great many people had come over from the neighbouring hamlets, and the roadways to and from the mill, in particular, were as crowded as on a fair-day. Most were taking their corn to be ground; and as if to thwart them, the water ran so low that only one of the falls would work, and even that very feebly. But everyone awaited his turn patiently, because all wanted the corn in their barns ground before harvest-home.

Many besides had come to the miller's to get meal, or groats; some even loaves.

The man himself was ill in bed; but he still directed everything. He would cry out to his wife, sitting outside by the open window:

"Not a kopek's worth on credit for the Rzepki folk! They have patronized the priest's bull: let the priest help them now!"

He was inexorable to all prayers and entreaties: no one that had "patronized" the animal in question was lent even half a quart of flour.

"They prefer his bull to mine," he shouted; "let them get flour out of him now!"

His wife, who was a poorly-looking querulous thing with a bandaged face, would shrug her shoulders; and, when possible, she made loans by stealth to many a one.

Klemba's wife came to ask for half a quart of millet groats.

"Cash down! I'll not sell her one grit on credit!"

This was very embarrassing to her; she had brought no money.

"Your Thomas is hand in glove with the priest: let him lend the groats ye want!"

At this, Klembova took offence, and answered defiantly:

"Aye, he holds with the priest, and still will hold; but never shall he set foot in here again!"

" 'Slight the plight, brief the grief!' Go elsewhere for your meal!"

She withdrew, but in sore perplexity, for there was not a kopek in the house. However, meeting the smith's wife, who sat by the closed forge, as she set to complain to her about the miller's behaviour, the latter returned, with a smile on her face:

"His power, let me tell you, will not last long."

"Alas! who can resist so rich a man?"

"When there's a windmill close by, we shall be able."

Wide-eyed with bewilderment, Klembova stared at her.

"My goodman," she explained, "is building a windmill. He has just set out with Matthew to the forest for timber; it will be put up in Podlesie, close to the crucifix there."

"Well!—Michael build a windmill! I never dreamed of such a thing. . . . Well, well!—But 'twill serve that extortioner right: he has waxed too fat."

Her feelings much relieved, she was hastening home in good spirits, when, seeing Hanka outside her cabin at the washing-tub, she went to tell her that same unexpected bit of news.

Antek, working at a cart just by, overheard her, and said:

"Magda has told you the truth. The smith has pur-

chased a score of acres in Podlesie, close to the crucifix. . . .
The miller will go mad with rage! But he has treated us
all so that none will pity him."

"Any tidings of Roch?"

"None whatever," he replied, turning away quickly.

"That, methinks, is strange. 'Tis the third day we have
no news of him."

"Ah, how often has he disappeared so, and yet come back
again to us!"

"Is any one of you," Hanka queried, "going to Chenstohova?"

"Yes: Eva and Matty.—A good few make the pilgrimage
this year."

"I too am going; the linen I am washing now is for the
journey."

"There will be many from the other villages too, I expect."

"And a good season they have chosen—just when the
work is hardest!" Antek grumbled; but he would not forbid Hanka, knowing well to what intention she was making
this pilgrimage.

Yagustynka joined them.

"Know ye?" she cried; "John came home from the army
about an hour ago!"

"Tereska's goodman! And she was saying he would not
be back till autumn!"

"I have just seen him; very well clad . . . and dying to
be once more in his home!"

"A good fellow, but a very headstrong one. . . . Is
Teresa at home?"

"No, at the priest's, pulling up flax-plants. She has no
idea of what's coming."

"There will be trouble again in Lipka. Of course they
will tell him all, and at once."

Antek was attentive and much interested, but said nothing.
Both Hanka and Klembova were sincerely sorry for the
woman, and feared the worst might come to pass. Yagustynka broke in on their talk, saying:

"A fig for the justice of it all! That man of hers leaves her for years and years all alone; and if aught happens to her, poor creature! he is ready to kill her! Where's the justice of that? He may do as he pleases, play the goat as he likes: no one will breathe a word against him.—Things are outrageously ill-managed in the world!—Why, is a woman not a human being just as much as a man is? Is she a block of stone or wood? . . . If she must be punished, then let him who has sinned not a whit the less, be punished likewise. Wherefore is he to have it all enjoyment, while she bears all the punishment?"

"My dear," Klembova observed, "from the beginning it has been so, and so it will be even to the end."

"Yea, so it will be—to the people's hurt, and to the delight of the Evil One; but I would fain have things ordered otherwise. Whoso took his neighbour's wife should be forced to keep her always . . . and if not—a stick for his back, and to jail with the wretch!"

Antek was tickled by her zealous ardour; but she swooped down upon him like a fury.

"Ye find it a laughing matter, do you? *For you it is!* O poisonous villains, to whom every girl is your best-beloved—till she's yours! . . . And after that, ye make a mock of her!"

"A magpie when rain's at hand makes less din than you!" Antek retorted, somewhat out of temper.

She left them, only to return in the evening, weeping bitterly.

"What ill thing has befallen?" Hanka inquired in alarm.

"What ill thing? I have tasted of human sorrow, and the draught has made me faint." She again burst into tears, and said, sobbing all the while: "Kozlova took John in hand and informed him of everything."

"Ah, well, had it not been she, it would have been some-one else: no doubt of that."

"But I tell you, that cottage will see some fearful deed done! I went there once: no one was in. Just now, I looked in again. There they sat, both of them—weeping.

On the table lay the presents he had brought for her—all
open and unpacked. Lord! a shudder went through me; I
felt as when one looks down into a grave. They are saying
naught, only weep. Matthew's mother told me all: it made
my hair rise."

"Do you know," Antek asked, "whether he said anything
about Matthew?"

"He cursed the man most horribly. No, no! he never
will forgive him!"

"Do ye think Matthew will whine to him for pardon?"
Antek answered in a surly tone, and hurried off to warn his
friend at Nastka's hut.

He found her brother deep in talk with her, took him
a little down the road, and told him all.

Matthew took in his breath with a hissing gasp, and uttered an oath.

They returned to the village together, Matthew looking
gloomy and downcast, and more than once heaving a high.

"I see," Antek said, weighing each word, "that you are
grievously troubled in mind."

"For her?—Not I! She was sticking like a bone in my
throat. No, 'tis something else that perplexes me."

Antek felt surprised, but did not like to ask questions.

"To sorrow over each particular girl of mine the time
would not suffice me. She came within my grasp; I took
her: who would not have done so? But truly, mine was but
the joy of a dog fallen down a well; she has wailed and lamented for ten women. I fled her; she came after me, just
like my shadow. Let John now rejoice with her!—I no
longer crave for love affairs, but something very different."

"True, it were time for you to take a wife."

"Nastka just now was saying so to me."

"Our village girls are plentiful as poppies, and you have
an ample choice."

Matthew blurted out the thoughtless answer: "It was
made long ago."

"Then ask me to be your proposer, and have the wedding
after harvest-home."

Somehow the idea displeased him; he asked for more particulars about John, talked of Simon's farm, and let out —inadvertently, it seemed—the information that, according to Andrew, Dominikova meant to bring an action against Antek for Yagna's rights as old Boryna's relict.

"But no one denies that Father made a settlement," Antek said. "I'll not give the land up, but will pay her its value to the full. The quarrelsome hag does this for sheer love of a lawsuit!"

"Did Yagna really give the title-deed back to Hanka?"

"Yes, but what of that? she took care not to annul it at the notary's."

This greatly relieved Matthew, who—now unable to conceal all he felt—dropped several words in Yagna's praise.

The whole manœuvre was soon plain to Antek, who only said with a mocking smile:

"Have you heard what they are saying about her now?"

"Oh, those old women are always her enemies!"

"It seems she is running after Yanek, the organist's son. And most shamelessly," he added for greater effect.

Matthew flared up, hot with anger.

"Did ye see that?"

"Nay, I am no spy on her: what is she to me? But those there are who daily see her go out to meet her Yanek . . . in the forest . . . or amongst the corn . . ."

"A good beating for one or two of them would soon put an end to such tales!"

"Try, try; ye may perchance frighten them," Antek responded deliberately, though horribly tortured with jealousy at the thought of Matthew possibly becoming her husband: it bit him with all the venom of a mad dog's fangs.

To what the latter said, though his talk was not infrequently hostile and even offensive, he made no reply, lest he should reveal what he was suffering; but, when they parted, he could not help saying with a malicious smile:

"Whoso marries that woman will have plenty of . . . connexions . . ."

And they parted, not on very friendly terms.

When Matthew had gone a little way, his face grew brighter.

"She is keeping him off; that's what makes him talk so!—Let her run after Yanek!—'Tis but a child; and she cares far more for the priest than for the man."

His thoughts were so extremely lenient, because, having heard from Antek all about the title-deed and the settlement, he had made up his mind to marry Yagna. He slackened his pace to calculate how much he would want to pay off Andrew and Simon, and have the twenty acres all to himself.

"The old woman will be no treat, but she'll not last for ever."

The recollection of Yagna's pranks, indeed, disturbed him, but he said:

"What is over is over; and if she tries new tricks, I'll soon make her give them up!"

Outside the hut, his mother was awaiting him.

"John is back!—He knows all."

"Glad of it! I shall not have to lie."

"Teresa has been in here more than once: talks of drowning herself."

"Indeed, indeed . . . she might do so!"—The thought gave him so fearful a pang that he could not touch his supper, but sat listening for any sounds from John's orchard, which was only separated from theirs by a pathway. His disquietude increasing, he pushed the dish away, and smoked cigarette after cigarette, striving in vain to overcome the fit of trembling that agitated him. He cursed himself and the whole race of women; he tried to jest at the silly business: all would not do. His terror grew more and more, tormenting him past all bearing. He had got up several times to go out and seek company—and yet there he was, remaining in the hut, and he knew not why!

Night had fallen, when he heard steps approaching, and then, coming in with a rush, Teresa had thrown her arms round his neck.

"O Matthew, save me, save me!—O God! how I have been waiting and looking out for you!"

He set her down by his side, but she clung to him like a little child; and with streaming tears she called upon him in the extremity of her despair.

"He has been told all! It never entered my mind that he would really return! . . . I was at work in the priest's flax, when someone came and told me. . . . I had like to fall dead on the spot, and went home with death in my heart. . . . You were out . . . I went to seek you, but could not find you in all Lipka . . . I wandered about very long, but at last had to go in.—He was standing there, white as a sheet; he leaped at me with closed fists . . . and asked for the truth. The truth!"

Matthew, shaking in every limb, wiped the cold sweat from his face.

"So I told it him: of what use would a lie have been? . . . He seized hold of an ax, and I thought it was my last hour . . . I cried out to him: 'Kill me! You'll make all right for both of us!' And he did not even touch me— only flung me a look, sat down by the window, and wept. . . . And now, what am I to do, wretched one? whither shall I go? . . . Save me, you, else I leap into the well, or kill myself in some wise! . . . Save me!" she shrieked, falling on the ground at his feet.

"Poor woman . . . how can I? . . . how can I?" he stammered, humbled in the dust; and she started up with a fierce cry of mad fury.

"Wherefore, then, did you take me? wherefore entice me? wherefore lead me on to sin?"

"Hush, hush! All the village will be here!"

Once more she fell on his breast, embraced and kissed him frenziedly, and exclaimed with all the might of her love and terror and despair:

"O my only one, my chosen one amid a thousand! Slay me, but repel me not!—Do you love me, say? do you love me?—Then comfort me this once, for the last time; gather me in your arms and leave me not to agony and ruin!—You are all I have in the whole wide world; yea, all! Let me

but stay with you . . . I'll serve you as faithfully as any
dog . . . aye, I'll be your slave!"

Such were the words of passion she sobbed out, wrung
from the bottom of her broken heart.

Matthew was as one held in a vice, and squirming and
writhing to get free. Avoiding a straightforward answer,
he strove to soothe her with kisses and caresses and words
of affection, agreeing to all she said, and all the while looking around with impatience and dread; for he suspected that
John was sitting on the stile just outside.

A moment later, the true state of things flashed suddenly
on Teresa's mind: she thrust him from her, with words that
struck him like blows:

"Liar and cur! You have always lied to me, but never
shall you deceive me any more! . . . You are afraid—
afraid lest John beat you; and therefore you turn and twist
now, like a trodden worm! And I trusted to him as to the
best of men? O Lord, O Lord! And John, who has been
so good to me! The presents he has brought—presents for
me!—Never yet did I hear him speak an unkind word; and
how have I repaid him? By giving my trust to a traitor,
to a villain! . . . Go your ways to Yagna!" she shrieked,
rushing towards him with clenched fists. "Go—and may
the hangman wed you both!—A well-matched pair—a
wanton and a thief!"

And with an awful shriek, she fell fainting to the ground.

Matthew stood beside her, at a loss what to do; his
mother sat whimpering by the wall.—Then John strode in
from the orchard to his wife, and spoke to her . . . words
of tender sorrowing consolation.

"Come to my home, forlorn one, come! Fear me not; I
shall do you no hurt! Oh, no! you have suffered enough as
it is.—Come, my wife!"

He took her by the hand, and helped her over the stile;
then, turning to Matthew, he thundered:

"But the wrong you have done her, never will I forgive—
never while there's life in me!—So help me God!"

Choked with shame, Matthew answered never a word. His soul was full of such bitterness, such grinding torments, that he flew to the tavern and drank all night long.

The event was at once known throughout the village, and all were full of admiration and respect for John's conduct.

"There's not another man in the world like him!" the women said, moved even to tears; but at the same time they blamed Teresa with the utmost severity; all except Yagustynka, who took her part with great zeal.

"Teresa is not in fault!" she cried, when hearing her spoken against in orchards and enclosures. "She was all but a child when John's military service began. Alone and childless as yet, she wanted some loving friend about her. And Matthew, like a hound, caught up the trail; and he flattered and fondled her, and took her out to hear the band play . . . till the poor silly girl's head was turned!"

One of them said with a sigh:

"Why is there no law to punish such deceivers?"

"He has some grey hairs already, yet runs after women as ever!"

"But how's a wretched bachelor to live, unless he takes another's property?" objected the young men, jeering.

"If she's not to blame, no more is he," said Staho Ploshka; "where there's no giving, there's no taking." For which ribaldry he was well-nigh assaulted by the women.

But the matter was not discussed very long: the harvest was at hand, the weather magnificent. On the uplands, the rye was, as it were, asking to be reaped; the barley was not much behind, and they went daily to inspect it. Already reapers were being engaged by the richer peasants.

The organist opened the harvest with a dozen or so of hired women reapers; his wife and daughters too took a hand in the work, while he superintended them all most watchfully. Yanek came only after Mass to help, and did not enjoy the fun long; his mother sent him home as soon as the noonday heat set in, fearing lest the sun might give him a headache. Kozlova grumbled:

"He's going to find shade at Yagna's—that's his game!"

At home, however, it was not only very hot, but very troublesome because of the pitiless attacks of the flies there: so he went out into the village, passing outside the Klembas'. There he caught the sound of moans, issuing from within the wide-open cabin door.

It was Agata, lying in the passage, close to the threshold; everybody else had gone a-reaping.

He carried her into the room, laid her on a bed, gave her to drink, and revived her, so that, after a time, she opened her eyes.

"'Tis the end coming, young master," she said with a childlike smile.

He would have run for the priest, but she caught at his soutane to prevent him.

"To-day the Blessed Virgin said to me: 'Be ready for to-morrow, weary soul!' So there is time still, young master! —To-morrow!—Thanks, thanks, O most merciful Lord!" she faltered, and her voice trailed away into silence. A smile flickered on her lips; she clasped her hands and, looking far away, sank into a state of profound mental prayer. Yanek, now sure that her last hour was drawing near, went to fetch the Klembas.

It was only in the afternoon that he came back there again. She lay on her bed, completely conscious. Her open locker stood beside her on a bench, and her hands, now very cold, had taken out of it all the effects she had provided for the present occasion: a clean sheet to be placed under her body; fresh bed-linen; holy water and a sprinkler still in good condition; a long piece cut off from a death-taper; an image of Our Lady of Chenstohova, to be put in her hands after death; a new chemise, a beautifully striped skirt, a cap deeply frilled about the forehead, a kerchief to bind over it, and a pair of shoes that had never yet been worn. This complete funeral outfit, got together by begging during the course of her life, she had now spread around her, delighted with every article and praising its quality to those about her; she even peeped into a looking-glass, and whispered with great pleasure:

"How grand it will be!   I look quite like a notable good-wife."

She directed them to dress her in all that splendid clothing at early dawn on the morrow.

No one opposed or thwarted her: everyone went about to make her last hours as happy as could be.

Yanek sat beside her bed till dusk, reading prayers aloud, which she said after him, smiling faintly now and then.

When they sat down to supper, she asked for scrambled eggs; but she only took one or two mouthfuls, pushed the dish away, and then lay still all the evening, only calling old Klemba to her before she went to sleep.

"All is well," she said anxiously; "I shall not trouble you long . . . not long!"

Next morning, clad as she had desired, she was laid on Dame Klemba's bed, but with her own bedding. She saw that everything was properly arranged, and with her own trembling hands smoothed down her thin feather-bed, poured out the holy water and placed the sprinkler in the basin; and then, all being ready, she asked for the priest.

He came, bringing our Lord, and, having prepared her for her last journey, desired Yanek to stay by her side till the end.

This he did, and sat saying his hours there. The Klembas too remained within doors, and Yagna soon came round and ensconced herself quietly in a corner. All were very still, and moved about like shadows, with eyes anxiously fixed upon Agata, who lay, rosary in hand, and still quite conscious, bidding farewell to all who came in. To some children that peeped in at the door and window, she distributed a few kopeks.

"That's for you," she whispered cheerfully; "but say a prayer for Agata."

Thus she lay in state, "as behoved a goodwife," on a bed, with holy pictures above her—and just as it had been the dream of her life to die! She was in a state of serene elation, of unspeakable happiness, and tears of joy were rolling down her cheeks. Her lips moved in faint but rapturous

smiles as she gazed into the depths of heaven, on the vast
expanse of fields, dotted with ringing and glittering scythes,
and heaped with sheaves of rye, heavy and ripe—and into
those farther abysses, visible only to her departing soul.

Now, as the day was just drawing to its close, and the
red glow of sundown flooded all the room, a violent shudder
came over her; she sat up, stretched out her arms, and cried
in a loud changed voice:

"Now my time has come—it has come!"

And she sank back.

A loud and mournful sound of wailing burst forth; all
knelt down beside the bed, and Yanek read the Prayers for
the Dying.   Klembova lit the death-taper; Agata, grasping
it, said the prayers after Yanek; but her voice, feebler and
feebler, died away; her eyes, wearied by life, grew dim like
that closing summer day.   The greyness of everlasting twilight spread over her face; she dropped the taper and died.

So passed away that poor beggar-woman—as if she had
been the foremost dame in Lipka!   Ambrose, who had come
in that very instant, closed her eyes; Yanck said a fervent
prayer for her soul, and the whole village flocked round her
body, to pray—to lament—and to wonder, not without
envy, at so blissful a death, so peaceful an end.

But Yanek, gazing on those lifeless eyes, and that face,
furrowed by the claws of death, and in hue like frost-
stiffened clay, felt so terribly panic stricken that he took to
flight and, running home, flung himself on his bed, pressed
his head upon the pillow, and wept aloud.

Yagna had followed close on his heels.   She was herself
unnerved and broken down, but set herself to comfort him
and wipe the tears from his eyes.   He turned to her as to a
mother, laid his aching head upon her bosom, threw his
arms round her neck, and burst into a tempest of sobs:

"O my God!" he cried; "how awful, how horrible
death is!"

And at that moment his mother came in, saw and was
filled with rage at the sight.

"What's this?" she hissed, rushing at them, and scarcely

stopping half-way. "Look at her, this tender nurse of ours! Pity—is it not?—that Yanek needs no nurse now, and is old enough to blow his own nose!"

Yagna raised her eyes, brimming over with tears, and in great perturbation set to telling her about Agata's death. Yanek also came forward, eager to explain the whole affair, and say how upset and overwhelmed he had been. But his mother had already been much nettled by the gossip she had heard, and cut him short.

"You're a silly calf! Best say naught, lest an evil thing happen to you!"

Then, striding to the door, she threw it wide open, and vociferated:

"As to you, woman—out! . . . And never set foot here any more, else I set the dogs at you!"

"But what evil have I done?" Yagna stammered, beside herself with shame and mortification.

"Off with you this instant, or I'll have the dogs loosed!— I do not mean to weep because of you, as Hanka and the Voytova have wept! You minx, you baggage! I'll teach you—I'll teach you to come love-making here—and ye shall remember the lesson!" she screamed at the top of her voice.

Yagna, bursting into tears, fled out of the room . . . and Yanek stood thunderstruck.

CHAPTER XII

ON a sudden he made a start to rush after her.

"Whither?" his mother asked grimly, blocking the way.

"Why—why have ye turned her out? Because she was so kind to me? It is unjust—unjust—and I will not have it.—What wrong thing has she done, say?" he cried, struggling violently in his mother's powerful grasp.

"Sit down quietly, or I'll call Father. . . . What has she done, hey?—I'll tell you at once. You are to be a priest: I will not see you taking a mistress under my very roof, nor load yourself with such shame and disgrace that folk will point their fingers at you as you go by! That's why I expelled her. And now you know!"

"Lord Almighty!—What is this you say?" he cried indignantly.

"What I know well. —I was aware that you had meetings with her; but, as God is my witness, I never suspected you of any wickedness! For I thought that if my son wore a priest's habit, he would not drag it in the mud—not make me curse him for ever—not force me to tear him out of my heart, and break my heart in the tearing!" As she spoke, her eyes flamed with such holy indignation that Yanek was petrified with amazement. "Kozlova," she went on to say, "was the first to open mine eyes; and now I myself have seen how this drab was trying to inveigle you!"

He burst into a flood of tears, and brokenly—between fits of sobbing and complaints of her monstrous suspicions— told her so frankly all about their meetings that her trust in him was completely restored. She pressed him to her heart, and wiped his tears, and soothed him.

"Now do not marvel if I feared for you. Why, she is the worst trull in the whole village!"

"Yagna . . . the worst . . . !" He could not believe his ears.

"It shames me to speak of such things; but for your good I must." She thereupon poured forth all the scandalous tales in circulation against Yagna, sparing him none of them.

Yanek shook with horror, and started up at last, crying:

"This cannot be; I will never believe her so vile."

"Take heed; 'tis your mother who speaks; these are no lying inventions of hers."

"But they must be lies! Were they true, it would be too horrible." And he wrung his hands in despair.

"What makes you defend her so stoutly? Answer me that!"

"I must defend anyone—anyone that's innocent."

"You're an arrant fool!" She was losing her temper; his disbelief pained her deeply.

"If ye think me so—well.—But supposing Yagna so wicked, how could ye let her come to our house?" he asked, flushing as red as an angry young turkey-cock.

"I have not to justify my doings to you, a simpleton who could not understand me. But this I say to you: keep away from her! For if I meet you with her, I will—aye, even before the whole village, I will—give her a drubbing she will not get over for a month!—And you too may get a taste of the same!"

With these words she went.out, slamming the door.

Yanek, not suspecting at all why Yagna's good name was so very dear to him, remained thinking over his mother's words, and chewing the cud of his bitter reflections till his soul was sickened with the nauseous taste.

"She that kind of woman? She, Yagna?" he groaned, with such stern abhorrence that, had she then appeared before him, he would have turned from her with angry loathing. Why, the very thought of such things had never come to his mind! And now he was forced to ponder them, with ever-increasing anguish! Many a time he was on the

point of running out to throw all those many sins and
wicked deeds in her teeth. "Let her know what folk say,
and clear herself, if she can. Let her declare that they are
all falsehoods!" He went on musing feverishly, now more
and more inclined to think that she was perhaps not in fault.
. . . Sorrow for her took hold of him; and then there was
a secret longing for her in his mind . . . and the memories
of their past meetings came back, not without a certain
sense of sweetness. . . . Then his eyes grew dim with a
bright haze of vague delight; and, with a mysterious pang
at his heart, he sprang up, crying out, as to the whole world:

"'Tis untrue—untrue—untrue!"

At supper, he did not raise his eyes from his plate,
shunned his mother's glances, and sat speechless, though
they were talking of Agata's death. Gloomy, fastidious in
his eating, tiresome to his sisters, querulous about the heat
in the house, he got up as soon as the meal was done, and
went over to the priest's. His Reverence, sitting pipe in
mouth in the porch, was busy talking of various affairs with
Ambrose. He kept away from them and walked about under the trees, in company with his painful thoughts.

"And yet, it may be true! Mother could never have in-
vented that!"

From the windows of the house, long streaks of light
played upon the lawn and flower-beds, where the dogs
frolicked and snarled in fun. Gruff voices came to him
from the porch:

"Have you seen the barley at 'Swine's Hollow?'"

"The stalks are still somewhat green; the grains are dry
as pepper."

"You must air the vestments, they are getting quite
ruined with mould.—And take my surplus and the albs to
Dominikova's for Yagna to wash.—Who was it brought his
cow here this afternoon?"

"Someone from Modlitsa. The miller met him on the
bridge and vaunted his bull, and even offered the use of the
beast gratis; but the man preferred ours."

"He was right. One rouble will give him a lifelong profit

. . . and a first-rate breed of cows.—Know ye if the Klembas are to pay Agata's funeral fees?"

"No, she herself has left ten *zloty* for her burial."

"She shall be buried, as grandly as any village dame!—Ah! by the way, tell the Confraternity Brethren that I will sell them my unbleached wax; the bleached wax they may want they must buy elsewhere. To-morrow Michael will see to the church; you must go round and tell the reapers to hurry. The weather-glass stands at 'Variable," and we may have a storm.—When are they starting for Chenstohova?"

"They have asked for a votive Mass on Thursday."

This talk getting on Yanek's nerves, he walked farther away to a low lattice-work fence that separated the orchard from the apiary, where he paced to and fro along a narrow path overhung by trees, the apple-laden boughs coming in frequent contact with his head.

It was a stifling evening, redolent of honey close by, and of the rye cut down a little farther; the sultry air was saturated with heat. The whitewashed trunks glimmered in the shadows, like shirts hung out to dry. From the Klembas', the dismal moaning of the dirges was heard.

Weary of thinking over his trouble, Yanek was going home, when his ear caught the muffled sound of persons whispering eagerly together in the apiary.

He could see no one, but stopped and listened, holding his breath.

. . . "Get along. . . . Let me alone, or I shall scream."

". . . foolish . . . why struggle? . . . I am doing nothing wrong . . . nothing wrong."

. . . "Someone may hear. . . . Loose me, for God's sake. . . . You're breaking my ribs!"

Yanek knew the voices: Pete from Boryna's and Maryna the priest's maidservant were there! He walked away, somewhat amused at their courtship, but, after a few paces, returned and listened with absorbing interest. It was impossible to see anything for the thick bushes and the dark night, but he was soon able to make out their broken words, that were now more distinct, more ardent, like spurts

of flame; at times, too, there was the sound of a tussle and
of deep-drawn breaths.

". . . as nice as any of Yagna's . . . you shall see,
Maryna . . . only . . ."

"Trust you indeed? . . . Am I such a one? . . . For
God's sake, let me breathe!"

There was a heavy fall upon the ground; the bushes
cracked and snapped; then they seemed to pick themselves
up, and whispers and chuckles and kisses went on as before.

"Sleep has quite fled from me now . . . all for thinking
of you, Maryna . . . of you, O dearest!"

"To every girl you say that! . . . I waited till midnight
. . . courting someone else . . ."

Yanek trembled like an aspen leaf.—The wind sprung up,
making the trees to rustle faintly, as if talking in their sleep;
the heavy scent of honey from the apiary oppressed him so,
he could scarcely breathe; his eyes watered, a hot thrill went
through him, an obscurely pleasurable sensation pervaded
his whole being.

". . . as far from me as any star!—'Tis to Yanek she has
an eye at present! . . ."

Mastering his emotion, Yanek bent over the fence and
gave ear, in spite of his growing excitement.

"True, she goes out to him every night . . . Kozlova surprised them in the wood together . . ."

Here everything began to turn round, his eyes saw nothing and he almost fell swooning. Meanwhile, the sound of
kisses and low laughter and whispering continued.

"If you . . . I'll scald your head with boiling water!
. . . Pete! . . . Pete!"

He had heard enough. He rushed away, swift as the
wind, tearing his soutane on the way, and reached home as
red as a beet-root, perspiring profusely, and in a fever of
excitement. Luckily, no one paid attention to him. His
mother, sitting by the fire-place, was singing under her
breath the evening hymn,

> "All our actions of this day,
> At Thy feet, O Lord, we lay,"

and spinning the while; his sisters and Michael, who was polishing the church candlesticks, joined in. His father was in bed.

He went to his room and began to say his hours. But, strive as he would to attend to the Latin words, his mind was always harking back to the whispers and kisses he had overheard. At last, dropping his head on the book, he unconsciously gave way to the thoughts which came over him like a burning blast.

"So? . . . Are things so?" he mused, with growing horror, and a thrill that was nevertheless not unpleasant. "Are things so!" he suddenly repeated aloud; and to get rid of the abominable fancies that beset him, he put his breviary under his arm, and went to his mother, telling her, in a low subdued voice, that he was going to pray by Agata's body.

"Yes, go, dearest; I will come for you later!" she returned, with a glance very full of love.

Klemba's cabin was almost empty. Only Ambrose was there, mumbling out of a book, beside the deceased who lay covered with a sheet. At the head of the bed, the death-taper burned, stuck in a small jug. Fruit-laden apple-boughs peered in at the open window; and now and then a belated passer-by peered in too. In the passage, the dogs growled low.

Yanek knelt down close to the light, and fell to his prayers with such intense fervour that he never knew when Ambrose got up and hobbled home. The Klembas had lain down to rest in the orchard.—The first cock had crowed before his mother, remembering, came to fetch him home.

But no slumber came to his eyelids there. Each time he fell into a doze, Yagna's form appeared to him with such lifelike reality that he started up in bed, rubbed his eyes, and looked around in horror—only to see that all the place was quiet, and to hear his father snoring sonorously.

"Ah! . . . Perhaps . . . perhaps *that* was what she desired?" he thought, as the memory of her scorching kisses and flaming eyes and husky voice came back to him. "And I—I thought it but . . ." He shook himself, overwhelmed with anger and shame. He leaped out of bed, opened the window wide, and, seated on the sill, pondered till day-break with profound sorrow over his involuntary offences and temptations.

At Mass the next morning, he did not venture to raise his eyes; but he prayed all the more earnestly for Yagna, in whose great guilt he now believed entirely, although hatred and disgust for her were beyond his power.

"What's the matter?" the priest said to him in the sacristy after Mass. "You were sighing so hard, you almost put out the candles!"

"My soutane makes me so hot!" he answered evasively, averting his face.

"When you are accustomed to it, 'twill be as easy to wear as your own skin!"

Yanek kissed his hand and went off to breakfast, picking out the shadows along the mill-pond, for the heat was broiling. On the way, he met Maryna pulling the priest's blind old mare along by the mane, and singing a noisy song.

His recollections of her stung him to the quick, and he went up to her in an angry mood.

"What makes you rejoice so, Maryna?" And he gazed at her with shamefaced curiosity.

"The hey-day in my blood!" she replied, showing her white teeth in a broad grin; and she went on pulling at the mare's mane and singing still more noisily.

"Merry! . . . and after what she has done!" He turned away hastily from the girl—whose skirt was tucked up almost to her snowy knees—and went on to the Klembas'. There Agata lay in high state and in the centre of the dwelling-room, arrayed in her best holiday attire, wearing her cap, deeply frilled over the brows, many strings of beads round her neck, and a new striped skirt, and shoes laced with bright red laces. Her face seemed moulded in bleached wax, and full of a marvellous joy. Her cold

stiffened fingers held the holy image, somewhat awry; two
tapers burned at the bed's head. Yagustynka was brushing
the flies away with a bough. The smoke of juniper-berries
was wafted through the room from the fire-place. Every
now and then somebody came in to pray for her soul, and
several children were playing about outside.

Yanek, not without some qualms, looked into the dark
room.

"The Klembas have gone to town," Yagustynka whispered. "As she has left them no small amount, they have to
deck themselves out for her funeral. For is she not their
kinswoman? Surely! But the body will be taken out only
this evening; Matthew has not finished the coffin yet."

The room was close; and, besides, that waxen face with its
changeless smile looked so ghastly that he must needs cross
himself and go out speedily. On the door-step, he met
Yagna and her mother entering. She stopped on seeing
him, but he passed her by without a word, not even the
usual "Praised be Jesus Christ!" It was only on nearing
the fence that he inadvertently turned round. She was still
standing where he had passed her, gazing mournfully after
him.

Going home, he would take no breakfast, pretexting a
headache.

"Go out for a walk; it may pass away," his mother advised.

"Mother! where am I to go? Ye will directly fancy . . .
who knows what?"

"Yanek, how can you speak so?"

"Why, Mother, have you not locked me up in our house?
Can I go out, if I must not speak to people?"

His nerves were overstrung, and he made his mother suffer in consequence. . . . It all ended, however, in her ban-
daging his head with a compress dipped in vinegar, and
making him lie down in a darkened room. She drove the
children out of the yard, and watched over her boy like a
hen over her chicken till he had slept well and eaten a good
meal.

"And now go for a walk; and go by the poplar road, where 'tis cooler because of the shade."

He did not reply, but, seeing that she carefully noted the way he took, chose the opposite direction on purpose. He strayed about the village, looked in at the forge and the hammers as they smote with deafening din on the anvil; he peeped into the mill, entered garden after garden, and went past the flax-fields and wherever the crimson gleam of a woman's dress was to be seen. Then he sat and talked with Mr. Yacek, tending Veronka's cows by a field-path, went on to Simon's cottage in Podlesie, where they refreshed him with some milk, and came back late in the afternoon, without having seen Yagna anywhere.

It was only the next day, at Agata's funeral, that he met her; her eyes were fixed upon him during all the service. The letters of his book danced before his eyes, and he mistook his Responses. As the body was on its way to the churchyard, she walked almost at his side, utterly indifferent to the fierce glances and loud murmurs of his mother; she felt herself melting in his presence like snow in the spring sunshine!

When the coffin was lowered into the grave and the customary lamentations broke forth, his ear caught the sound of her wailing; but he knew well that those sobs were not for Agata, and that they flowed from the fullness of a sorely pained and wounded heart.

"I must—I must have speech with her!"

His mind was made up on this point on returning from the funeral, but he could not get free at once. Many people from the other hamlets, and even some from neighbouring parishes, had come to Lipka about noon, in order to join in the pilgrimage.

This was to start the next morning at once after the votive Mass had been sung; and all were now slowly assembling, so that the road by the mill-pond was crowded with carts. A great many, too, had gone to the priest's bureau, and Yanek had to stay and help his Reverence in settling many various matters. It was only quite at evening that he found a convenient time to take his book and slip out behind the barn and to that pear-tree under which he had once sat together with Yagna.

He never opened the book at all, but threw it somewhere away into the grass. Then, looking round the fields, he entered the rye; and stealthily, almost creeping on all fours, he made his way to Dominikova's garden.

And Yagna was there just then, digging up new potatoes. She had no notion that anyone was gazing at her. Now and then she would draw herself up wearily, look about her with very mournful eyes, and utter a long and heavy sigh.

"Yagna!" he exclaimed timidly.

She turned suddenly pale as a sheet of canvas, scarcely believing her own eyes, and well-nigh regarding him as a miraculous vision.

Yanek's eyes were filled with light, and his heart with the sweetness of honey. But, mastering himself, he only sat down in silence, gazing upon her with an irresistible sense of delight.

"I feared I should never see you again, Master Yanek!"

As a scented breeze, blowing up from the meadows upon him, so was the sound of her voice to his soul, thrilled with inexpressible rapture!

"Yesterday evening, outside the Klembas' house, ye would not even look at me!"

She stood before him, flushed like a rose-bush in flower; like a spray of apple-blossoms, all drooping with desire; full of comeliness and altogether lovely.

"And I thought my heart would break!" she added, tears standing like diamonds on her long eyelashes, and veiling the dark azure of the heavens behind.

"Yagna!" he cried; it was a cry from the core of his inmost heart.

She knelt down in a furrow close by and, pressing close to his knees, fixed upon him the fiery depths of her eyes—those eyes as clear, yet as unfathomable, as the sky—those eyes whose looks went to the head like kisses, or the caresses

of a beloved hand—those eyes instinct at once with sub-
tle temptation and with absolute simplicity.

With a violent effort to shake himself free from the spell
she was casting over him, he spoke to her sternly and re-
counted all the sins and evil deeds of which his mother had
told him. She drank in all his words eagerly, her eyes
fastened upon him, but scarcely at all understanding what
he said, absorbed as she was in the one feeling and knowl-
edge and consciousness of his being by her side—he, the
chosen of her soul amongst all!—of his saying something, of
his eyes gleaming bright; and of her kneeling before him as
before the image of a saint, and praying to him with the
deep, deep faith of love!

"Say now," he concluded with energetic entreaty, "say,
Yagna, say of all this: 'Tis untrue!"

"'Tis untrue!—untrue!" she repeated, and with such
transparent sincerity that he could not but believe her.
Then she, leaning forward, rested her breast against his
knees . . . and in low trembling utterances confessed her
love. . . . She opened wide her soul to him, as if to a father
confessor, threw herself down before him as a stray worn-
out bird might fall; and with an ardent entreaty, that
sounded like a prayer, she gave herself up without reserve
to his love . . . to do with her whatsoever he would.

Yanek trembled like a leaf tossed in a furious tempest,
tried to push her from him and escape; but his mind was
dazed, and he could only whisper faintly:

"Hush, Yagna, hush! say not such things, they are sinful!"

Then she ceased from speaking, being quite exhausted.
And they both were silent; neither did they dare to look
into each other's eyes, but yet they pressed together so
closely that they could feel each other's hearts beat, and
the hot stifled panting of their bosoms. Both felt infinite
rapture and gladness; tears streamed down their pale cheeks,
but a smile played on the lips of both, and both their souls
were plunged in deep serene beatitude.

The sun had now gone down, the earth was bathed in the after-glow, as with a golden dew. All was still; all things held their peace, listening, as it were, to the sounds of the *Angelus;* everything seemed in orison—a prayer of quietude and thanksgiving for the blessing of the day that was over. —And they then went forth through the dusky fields, along the pathways overgrown with wild flowers, across the ripe cornlands, brushing aside the drooping ears as they walked; on they went, with eyes fixed upon the western fires, on the vast golden abysses of heaven, with heaven in their eyes, and heaven in their hearts, and a heaven-like aureole around them!

Not a word was spoken—not a single one; but at times their looks crossed like lightning flashes: each, wearied out in self-conflagration, was unconscious of what the other felt.

Nor were they conscious, either, of the wonderful hymn they were singing, which, having sprung up within their souls, was flying afar on every side, over the darkening fields.

Neither did they so much as know where they were, or whither going, or to what end.

A harsh hoarse voice broke upon their dreams on a sudden:

"Yanek!—Home!"

He was instantly recalled to his senses, and found himself in the poplar road, his mother standing in front of them both, grim-visaged and inexorable!—At the sight, he faltered, stammered, and uttered some unmeaning words.

"Home!"

She caught hold of his unresisting hand, and he followed meekly as she pulled him along.

Yagna, as if spellbound, was coming after them. The old dame picked up a stone from the road, and hurled it at her with all her strength.

"Hence!—Bitch, to your kennel!" she shrieked with foul-mouthed abuse.

Yagna looked round, really unaware that the words were

meant for her. When they had disappeared, she wandered
about the lanes for a long time, and when all the lights were
out, she went and sat outside her cabin till it was again
broad day.

The hours passed by; the villagers one by one rose and
went to their daily duties; and she still sat plunged in day-
dreams of her Yanek; of his speech with her, of their mutual
glances—and so near together! of their having gone somewhere and sung something . . . something she could not
remember. . . . And always, always the same dream, end-
lessly repeated!

Her mother woke her to reality; but Hanka did the waking yet more effectually. She came, dressed for her journey,
and timidly stretched out her hand to make peace with them.

"I am going to Chenstohova. Pray forgive me if I have
sinned in aught against you."

"Your words are kind, and I thank you," the old dame
growled; "but what ye have done, ye have done."

"Let us not go into that!—I entreat you most sincerely
to pardon me."

"I bear you no malice in my heart," Dominikova returned, sighing heavily.

"Nor do I, though I have suffered not a little," Yagna
said gravely; and then, as the Mass-bell was ringing, went
to dress for church.

"Do you know," Hanka said, after a pause, "that Yanek,
our organist's son, is coming with us to Chenstohova? His
mother told me herself that he has insisted on making the
pilgrimage."

Hearing these words, Yagna rushed out half dressed.

"In the company of our little priest, we shall journey
better and more respectably. . . . And so, farewell!"

They parted on friendly terms, and she went on to church,
telling her news as she went. Everybody was surprised,
and old Yagustynka shook her head, saying:

"There's more in this than meets the eye! If he goes, it
is not willingly. Not he!"

But there was no discussing the matter now: half the village was in church, and the Pilgrimage Mass had already begun.

Yanek was serving, as usual; but his face looked paler, and bore an unusual expression of pain. Then his eyes were discoloured, and still brimmed with tears, through which he saw, as through a mist, the church, and Teresa lying on the pavement all the time with outstretched arms, and Yagna's terrified glances, and his mother, sitting in the Manor pew, and the pilgrims coming up to receive Holy Communion: all these were dimly seen through his tears, while pang after pang rent his heart, overwhelmed with mortal anguish.

From the altar, the priest took leave of the pilgrims, and, as they pushed their way out of the church, sprinkled them with holy water, and gave them his blessing. The banner was raised, the glittering cross cpened the way before them, a hymn was struck up—and they set off upon their journey.

Yagna accompanied them, along with her mother and the rest of the village. She looked very ill, and her soul was quivering in the grip of agony. Swallowing down her bitter burning tears, she kept her eyes fixed on the boy who was all in all to her; but now she viewed him from afar, because his mother and brothers and sisters crowded jealously round him, and she could not even see him properly, much less have speech with him.

Matthew, her mother, and several others addressed her, but she paid them scant attention. She thought of this only: that her Yanek was going away for ever; that never, never should she see him more!

They accompanied the pilgrims as far as the crucifix at the edge of the forest; these continued their march, singing until they were out of sight, and only a cloud of dust told vaguely of their whereabouts.

"Why is this?" she moaned, dragging herself wearily back to the village.

"I shall fall down, I shall die!" What she felt within her she really took for the coming of death, so completely had the agonies she had endured shorn her of her strength.

"What, oh, what shall I do now?" she said, looking out upon the day, so desolate for her, so hateful with its dazzling light.

She longed, how intensely! for the silent hours of night; but they brought her no consolation. Until dawn, she went wandering about the premises, along the road, even as far as Podlesie and that cross where she had for the last time seen Yanek; and with eyes that smarted with the strain, she looked up the long wide sandy track, as though seeking some trace of his footsteps, the place where his shadow had passed—a clod of earth his foot had touched.

Alas! there was nothing—nothing for her anywhere—no more love no more hope!

Even her tears failed her in the end, although her eyes, full of awful desolation and despair, glittered like fathomless fountains of sorrow.

Now and then, when she prayed, there would burst from her lips the bitter complaint: "O my God! wherefore, whereto, is all this suffering?" . . .

CHAPTER XIII

LIFE was fast becoming impossible at Dominikova's. Yagna was always straying about like someone distraught, heedless of everything in the world. Andrew did his work in a slovenly way, and his absences at Simon's grew more frequent. The farm had fallen into complete neglect. Sometimes the cows were driven unmilked to the pastures, and the pigs were squealing for food all day long, and the horses gnawed at their empty racks. The old dame could not do all by herself, having to grope about with her stick, half blind and her eyes bandaged. No wonder if she almost went mad with trouble and mortification.

She hired a *komornitsa* for the work, and did all she could, both by herself and by her influence over her children. But Yagna seemed deaf to all entreaties and remonstrances; and Andrew, when threatened, would answer back insolently:

"Ye have driven Simon away: work ye by yourself. He wants you not, is in no trouble, has a hut, has money, has a wife, has a cow—and is an out-and-out good farmer!"—But, saying these words, he took good care to keep out of her reach.

"Aye, aye," she answered, with a dreary sigh; "truly, that unnatural wretch has contrived to succeed in all things."

"Yes, and he manages so well that even Nastka is astonished!"

"I must" (she spoke her thoughts aloud) "hire someone to work regularly, or take a farm-servant."

Andrew scratched his head, and said with some hesitation:

"But why take a stranger, when Simon is there, if ye'll but say the word?"

"Do not meddle when you're not asked!" she snarled; but

all the same, she felt—and it was a bitter pill to swallow—
that she would sooner or later have to give way and come
to terms with Simon.

But what made her most anxious was Yagna's state.
From her she could get no clue; and she went on piling
surmises on surmises, unpleasant fancies on fancies not less
unpleasant, till at last, one Saturday afternoon, she could
bear it no longer, and—bearing a large duck with her as an
offering groped her way to the priest's house.

She came back only at evening, in great agitation, crying
and wailing like an autumn wind at night; but, until she
was alone with Yagna after supper, she spoke no word.

Then, "Do you know," she said, "what tales are afloat
concerning you and Yanek?"

"I am no lover of gossip!" her daughter answered unwillingly, raising her eyes, that shone with a feverish glow.

"But you have to know this . . . and to learn, too, that
there's no hiding things from neighbours' eyes.—'What's
done in silence is spoken of aloud.'—They say most fearful
things of you."

Then she told her every particular that she had gleaned
from the organist's wife and from his Reverence.

". . . That very night they held judgment upon him; his
father gave him a beating; the priest added some blows
from his long pipe-stem; and he has been sent to Chenstohova, to protect him from you!—Do you hear that? Oh,
think what you have done!" she cried indignantly.

"Jesu Maria!—Yanek beaten!—Beaten!—O God, O
God!" And she started up with a mad idea of doing
something . . . but sat down again and hissed between her
teeth:

"May their arms wither, may their hands rot off! And
when the plague comes, may they not be spared!" She
then wept bitterly, with the tears streaming from her swollen eyes, like blood from a freshly opened wound.

Careless of her agony, Dominikova still continued to
lash her with her tongue; and each word was a blow. She
reminded her of all her many sins and transgressions, omit-

ting not a single one, and pouring out before her all the
bitterness that she had endured in silence for ever so long.

"Can you not see that all this must come to an end? that
you cannot live on any more in this wise?" she cried, more
and more pitilessly, though she herself was weeping, and the
tears fell under her bandage down her cheeks. "Shall you
be held the lowest of the low? Shall all men point their
fingers at you now?—Oh, what a shame for my old age,
good Lord! Oh, what a shame!" she murmured despair-
ingly.

"Ye too, I hear, were no whit better in your youth!"

This silenced Dominikova effectually.—Yagna set to
ironing some frills for the next day. It was a windy evening, with whistling sounds in the trees. The moon was
sailing athwart a sky flecked all over with cloudlets. Away
in the village the lasses were singing, while someone scraped
a jerky accompaniment on a fiddle.

They heard the Voyt's wife talking as she passed by.

"He went to the Police Bureau yesterday; since then, no
news of him."

"Yesterday evening," Matthew's voice returned, "he went
to the District Office; and the Soltys says the head official
had sent both for him and for the scrivener."

After they had passed on, the old woman spoke again,
but less harshly this time.

"Wherefore did you drive Matthew away from us?"

"He was displeasing to me; why, therefore, should he sit
here? I seek no man, nor do I need any!"

"But 'tis time—aye, high time—to provide yourself with
a goodman! Folk would then no longer attack you so.
Even Matthew—he's not to be disdained; a clever fellow,
and an honest."

For some time, and very earnestly, she held forth on this
theme, but Yagna, busy with her own work and full of her
own sorrows, made no reply. So at last her mother gave
over, and took up her rosary. It was late in the night.
All was quiet, save for the tossing trees and clattering mill;
the moon was now quite hid behind dense clouds, though

their edges were silvery, and a few sheaves of light shot out
between them.

"Yagna, you must go and confess to-morrow. You'll
feel more at ease, when rid of your sins."

"To what purpose?—No, I'll not go!"

"Not go to confession!" Her mother's voice was stridu-
lous with horror.

"No. Quick to punish, slow to help: that's what the
priest is."

"Hush, lest the Lord God punish you for those wicked
words!—And I say to you: Go to confession, do penance,
beg God's forgiveness; do so, and all may yet be well!"

"Penance indeed! Is mine slight? And for what wrong
that I have done, pray? No doubt, because I love, and because I suffer, I am rewarded thus. For me, the worst that
can be has already come to pass!" And she went on be-
wailing herself in her sullen mood of exasperation.

Alas, poor thing! she had no foreboding—no, not the
slightest—of the chastisement which was about to overtake
her: a chastisement far less foreseen, and far harsher still!

For on the next day, which was Sunday, a rumour spread
round the village before High Mass—the incredible rumour
that the Voyt had been arrested for a deficit in the village
accounts!

At first no one would believe it, and though fresh and
more dreadful particulars came in hourly, they were hardly
taken in earnest by anyone.

The graver members of the community only said: "The
idle love inventing stories and spreading them for a pas-
time."

They believed, however, when the blacksmith, home from
town, bore out every word, and Yankel told the whole
village:

"'Tis all true! Five thousand roubles of the community's money are wanting. His farm will be seized for the
sum, and should it not suffice, Lipka will have to make up
the rest!"

Thereupon a furious storm of protest arose. What! when

they all were in such straits, and misery cried aloud everywhere; when there was nothing more to eat, and many had
to borrow, that they might pull through till the harvest was
over: was it now that they must pay money for a thief?
That was beyond human patience; the whole place went
mad with rage, and curses and threats and foul names flew
about like hail.

"I was no partner of his: therefore will I not pay in his
stead!"

"Neither will I! He had revelled and caroused and had
his pleasure: must I suffer now, paying for the pranks he
has played?" So said many a one, in sore trouble, and
hardly able to keep back his tears.

"Long have I had mine eyes upon the man, and foretold
all that has now come to pass. Ye would not hearken then;
and now, here you are!" old Ploshka said, not without
ulterior intentions; and his wife, like a worthy helpmeet,
echoed his words about the place, repeating them to any
that would listen.

The tidings were so overwhelming that but few went that
day to church, but talked the matter over at home. As
the grievance was common to all, so they all complained together in huts and orchards, but especially along the mill-
pond banks. What puzzled them most was, where the man
could have wasted so much money.

"He must have hidden it somewhere; he never can have
spent such a sum!"

"Nay, he has trusted in the scrivener's uprightness, and
we know well how far that goes."

"Poor man! he has wronged us all, but himself more than
anyone," some of the graver villagers remarked: when
Ploshka's wife thrust her portly figure amongst them, and
came forward wiping dry eyes, and with assumed sympathy:

"And I say, poor wife!—she that was such a grand and
haughty dame—what will she do now? Both land and house
will be taken from her, and the poor wretch will have to go
into lodgings and work for others! 'Tis not as if she had
got some pleasure out of all that money spent!"

"Oh, but she has enjoyed herself very well as it is!" Kozlova bawled, attacking her like Ploshkova, but in a different fashion. "They have both lived like lords, the merry villains!—meat every day, and half a potful of sugar in her coffee! And they both of them drank their rum neat and in tumblers! I myself have seen them bring all sorts of good things from town—half a cartful! What else made them so big-bellied? Not fasting, at any rate!"

She was listened to in grave silence, in spite of the arrant nonsense of her closing words. But it was the organist's wife who decided the attitude of the people. She happened (it seemed a hazard at least) to be passing among them; and, listening to their talk, she observed, with apparent indifference:

"Why, do ye not know on what the Voyt has spent so much?"

They closed round her, and insisted on her telling them.

" 'Tis clear enough: on Yagna!"

This was a surprise, and they looked at one another in bewilderment.

"Since last springtime, all the parish has been talking of naught else.—I shall not say a word; but go ye, ask anyone, even down in Modlitsa . . . and ye shall hear the truth!"

Seemingly unwilling to say more, she made as to leave them; but they followed her and literally drove her into a corner. Then she told them, as a secret that was to go no farther, how the Voyt had bought Yagna rings of the purest gold, kerchiefs of the finest silk, and given her lots of coral necklaces and quantities of ready money into the bargain! All these were of course glaring fabrications, but they believed her implicitly. All but Yagustynka, who cried out in a passion:

"Great saints, Snuffle and Cant, pray for us!—Have you seen all this, madam?"

"Yes, I have! And I can swear, even in church, that it was for her he has stolen: aye, and very likely at her instigation too! Ah, but she is capable of any crime;

naught on earth is sacred to her, that shameless, that con-
scienceless one! The lewd beast, for ever prowling about
Lipka, bringing shame and disgrace wherever she goes! . . .
Why, she even attempted to seduce my own Yanek, that
innocent lad, as pure as a child! But he escaped from her
and, coming, told me all! Only think of it: the wanton
will not even leave a priest alone!" She stopped, out of
breath, for her bitter spite had made her speak at a great
rate.

These words had the effect of a spark on gunpowder. All
the former grudges against Yagna now sprang into life
again—all the feelings of envy and rivalry and hatred; all
present gave utterance to what they had to accuse her of,
and the tumult became indescribable. Everyone tried to
shout down everyone else, and with louder and louder
shrieks.

"How can our Christian land support such a monster?"

"And who caused Boryna's death? Have ye forgotten?"

"So she has even attempted to entice a priest! O merciful Jesus!"

"Ah, how much drunkenness and quarrelling and iniquity
are all owing to her!"

"She is an ulcer that infects the whole village, and because of her, Lipka is despised by all!"

"So long as she's amongst us, there will ever be sin and
wickedness and lechery! To-day the Voyt robs us for her
sake; another may do the same to-morrow!"

"Drive her out! Out—like a leper—to the woods and
the forests!"

"Drive her out!—There's no help for it! Drive her out!"
they yelled, infuriated, and now wrought up to any extremity. On the proposal of the organist's wife, they all
went in a body to the Voyt's. They found his wife bathed
in tears, and so wretched, so miserably dejected, that they
embraced her and wept over her, and condoled with her
with the utmost tenderness.

After a while, Yanek's mother mentioned Yagna.

"Ah, 'tis God's truth," the other lamented in despair.

the organist's wife was telling of the affair with Yanek, the Voytova pouring her grievances into everyone's ears; and, others joining in to swell the hubbub, the whole place was roaring with the noise.

Antek alone said not a word. He stood close to the bar, gloomy, his teeth set hard, pale with the torments he endured, and at times assailed with a wild craving to snatch up a bench, beat the whole shrieking mob to a jelly and trample them under his feet: so odious they were to him! But he kept himself in hand, though drinking glass after glass of liquor; only he spat on the ground, and swore under his breath.

Ploshka addressed him after a time, and said aloud, for all to hear: "We are at one to drive Yagna from the village: come, Antek, speak your mind on the matter."

A great silence fell upon the multitude; every eye was fixed upon him: they felt sure he would be against them. He, however, drew a deep breath, threw back his shoulders, and answered in a ringing voice:

"I, living with the community, am of one mind with the community. Will ye expel her? Do. Will ye exalt her? Do.—To me 'tis all one."

He pushed the crowd apart and left the place, without even a glance at anyone.

They continued the debate a long time, even till the morning light; but in the end it was quite decided that she should be expelled.

But few took her part; those who did were shouted down. Matthew alone fearlessly dealt curses around upon them all and, reviling the whole village in the utmost paroxysm of fury, left the place at last, and went to beg Antek to save Yagna.

"Do ye know what has been decided?" he asked him at dawn, pale as death and trembling from head to foot.

"I know. Law and custom are on their side," he replied curtly, whilst washing his face at the well.

"To hell with such laws! It's all the work of the organist and his wife. . . . Shall we put up with such injustice?

—In what has she been to blame? All their accusations are
mere lies! . . . Lord! are they to hunt her from our midst,
like a mad dog?"

"Would you, then, resist the assembly of the people?"

"Ye talk as if ye were on their side!" Matthew cried, in
a tone of sharp reproach.

"I am on no one's side. She is no more to me than a
stone."

"O Antek, rescue her!—Do something, for God's sake! I
shall go mad—mad! Think of it: what can she do? where
can she go? . . . Ah, those villains, those sons of dogs,
those wolves! . . . I will swing my ax, and smite, and
spare no one!"

"I will not help you in any wise. They have decided:
what is one man against them all?—Nothing!"

"Aha!—You have a grudge against her!" Matthew suddenly flashed out.

"Grudge or no grudge, that concerns none but myself!"
Antek replied sternly, and leaned back against the well-
cover, looking into vacancy. His passion for Yagna, suppressed but not less active, was now raging within him,
together with bitter jealousy: both tossing him to and fro,
like a tree that groans in the blast.

He looked around him. Matthew was gone. The village
seemed a strange place to him—loathsome and blatant exceedingly.

And in the very weather of that memorable day, too,
there was something odd and abnormal. The huge swollen
disk of the sun shone pallid in the sky; the heat was of a
sultriness beyond all that had yet been; the sky was clouded
with low-hanging hideous-looking vapours; the wind every
now and then sprang up in fitful gusts, and the dust rose
in thick whorls and spirals. A storm was at hand; far
away, there were flashes along the wooded horizon.

Now had the fermentation amongst the people risen to
the highest pitch. They ran about wildly; brawling was
heard in almost every hut; women fought together on the
mill-pond banks; the dogs were howling all the time.

Scarcely anyone went to work in the fields. The cattle, left at home, lowed plaintively in the byres. Nor was there any Mass on that day, the priest having left the place at daybreak. And every minute the feeling of unrest increased in every mind.

Antek, seeing that the people were gathering on the organist's premises, shouldered a scythe and went off to one of his fields that was close to the forest. The wind hampered his work, waving the corn to and fro, and blowing into his eyes; but he stood his ground firmly and reaped away, listening—now more calmly—to the distant sounds he heard.

"Perchance they are about it at this instant!" was the thought that flashed through his brain, making his heart beat like a hammer. A wave of rage swept over him: he drew himself up and was on the point of tossing his scythe away and running to the rescue of Yagna; he only mastered himself just in time.

"Whoso has done evil must suffer the penalty!—So be it! So be it!"

The rye bent in ripples round his knees, like the waves of a stormy lake; the gale blew his hair about, drying the sweat of agony on his face. He could barely see anything, for he was in spirit at Yagna's side—all of him but his arms, with hard trained sinews working instinctively, wielding the scythe and laying the rye low, swath by swath!

Once, however, there came upon the wings of the wind a shriek, loud and long-drawn-out, that came from the village!

He flung the scythe on the ground and sat down in the corn that rose like a wall around him. He grovelled close to the earth, and clung to it with a mighty effort, and held himself down with an iron grasp. And he kept himself fast, and did not weaken, though his eyes wandered away to Lipka; though his heart cried out aloud in terror; though an awful fit of trembling shook him from head to foot.

"All things must take their course: they *must!* We plough to sow, we sow to reap; and if anything hinder, we pluck it out like an evil weed!"

Thus spoke within his soul an inexorable immemorial Voice.—Whose? . . . Was it not that of the earth and its inhabitants?

He still felt himself rebelling, but now listened to it with more willing obedience.

"Even so. Everyone has the right to defend himself against a wolf. . . . Everyone!"

A few last regrets, a few idle thoughts, came still like stinging gusts of wind, wrapping him in darkness, and urging him to rise and act.

But he started to his feet, whetted his scythe, crossed himself, spat on his hands—and set to work with a will, laying low swath after swath with such furious energy that his scythe-blade hissed through the air, and the walls of ripe grain around him resounded to his strokes.

In the village, meantime, the fearful hour of judgment and chastisement had arrived. What took place there can scarcely be related. All Lipka was as in the delirium of a high fever; the people seemed to have gone stark staring mad. Those of more sensible natures kept within doors, or fled to the fields. The others were gathered on the banks of the pond, and so drunk (if we may say so) with rancour that, before wreaking revenge on Yagna, they had begun to wreak their fury on one another, with spiteful words of hate. . . .

But in a minute the whole multitude had set out to Dominikova's, like a foaming torrent in spate. The Voytova and Yanek's mother led them on, and a howling infuriated rabble followed.

They burst into the cabin like a tempest. Dominikova blocked the way—she was trampled down in an instant. Andrew sprang forward to her aid, and was knocked down at once. Lastly, Matthew, standing in front of the inner door, strove to keep them back; but in spite of the club he wielded with all his strength, not half a minute elapsed before he was lying close to the wall, unconscious and with a broken head.

Yagna had locked and bolted herself up in the alcove.

When they burst the door open, she appeared, standing with
her back to the wall; but she neither made any defence nor
uttered any cry. White as a corpse, with wide-staring eyes,
she shook all over in expectation of death.

A hundred hands shot out to seize her in their greedy
clutches, ravenous with hatred; she was whirled away like
a bush torn up by the roots, and dragged out into the enclosure.

"Bind her, else she may give us the slip and escape!" the
Voytova commanded.

By the roadside stood a cart prepared for her, filled to
the very top with hogs'-dung, to which cart a couple of
black cows had been yoked. Into the dung they tossed her,
bound fast and unresisting; and then, in the midst of a
deafening uproar—laughter, foul invectives, imprecations—
each a stab of murderous intent—the procession set out.

It halted at the church, and Kozlova bawled:

"Let her be stripped here, and whipped in the porch!"

"Aye," screamed another; "creatures of her kidney were
always flogged outside the church."

"Let her be whipped until the blood spurts out!"

But Ambrose had bolted the lich-gate, and stood close to
the wicket, the priest's gun in hand; and when they stopped,
he bellowed at them:

"The first that breaks in here—as I hope for mercy, I'll
shoot him! . . . I'll kill him like a dog!" And he looked
so grim, so formidable, with his gun ready to fire, that they
forbore, and turned aside to the poplar road.

They hurried on, for the storm might burst at any moment. The sky had grown still more gloomy; the tall
poplars tossed to and fro in the gale; clouds of blind-
ing dust flew up beneath their feet, and far-off thunder
rumbled.

They cried: "Faster, Pete, faster!" They looked skywards ill at ease, less noisy now, and walking by the roadside, for the middle was deep sand; and only now and then
did one or another of her bitterest enemies draw near the
cart and shriek:

"You swine! You wanton! To the soldiers!—Go, you plague-spotted harlot!"

Pete, Boryna's servant, was driving the cart, for no one else would do so. He walked beside and flogged the cows, and spoke a few words of pity to her, when he could speak them unnoticed.

"'Tis not far . . . your wrong shall be avenged: suffer now in patience!"

Thus did Yagna, bound, on a bed of dung, the blood oozing from her beaten limbs, disgraced for all her life, unutterably degraded, and supreme in wretchedness, lie neither hearing nor feeling anything around her; but the tears streamed down her bruised cheeks. At times, too, her bosom rose as if to utter a cry—but the cry never came. It stopped within her, petrified.

"Faster, Pete, faster!" they exclaimed, hurrying him along, and impatience partly calming their madness, they now came on at a quick trot, nearing the mounds which were the landmarks of Lipka.

Here they pulled out one side of the cart, made of loose boards, and shot her out, along with the dung, like loathsome offal. A loud thud was heard; she fell on her back, and remained motionless.

The Voytova came forward, and spurned at her with her foot, hissing: "Return to us again, and we'll hunt you away with dogs!" and, lifting up a clod as hard as a stone, and striking her cruelly, she added: "This for the wrong you have done my children!"

Another struck her a second blow: "This for the shame you have brought on Lipka!"

"May you perish for ever and evermore!"

"May you never lie in hallowed earth!"

"But die of hunger and of thirst!"

With these invectives, there rained upon her clods and stones and handfuls of earth; while she lay motionless, looking up into the trees that waved over her.

Then it grew dark, and a dense rain began to fall.

Pete delayed over "something to arrange about the cart,"

so the people did not wait for him, but returned in bands, much depressed and subdued. About half-way back, they met Dominikova, covered with blood and with torn clothes, sobbing and groping her way with a stick. On finding out whom she was passing, she shrieked in a fearful voice:

"Murrain and plague and fire and flood—let them not pass you over!"

At the words, they hung their heads, and fled panic-stricken.

.   .   .   .

It was a great storm. The sky had grown liver-coloured, the dust flew in bellying clouds; the poplars, with sobbing soughing sounds, were bowed and shaken to their roots; the winds howled, wrestling with the corn, and rushed roaring away to the quivering and murmuring forests. Twisted masses of hail-cloud, slate and copper-hued, hung low in bulging piles and airy hummocks here and there, cloven by streaming thunderbolts of wonderful brightness; though indeed the hail fell only in scanty showers, beating down a few leaves and boughs.

This, with few intervals, lasted all day long and till evening set in, followed by a black, cool, refreshing night.

And the next day it was splendid weather again; a sky without a stain, and the land sparkling all over with dew.

Everything in Lipka was now on its former footing. As soon as the sun was well above the sky-line, they all, as by common consent, sallied forth together to reap; the field pathways and roads were alive with rolling carts.

And as the Mass-bell tinkled from the church, each man stood up in the fields to listen to the sounds: those nearest could even catch the faint notes of the organ. Some knelt down to say their morning prayer, even aloud; some uttered a pious ejaculation, in which he found spirit and strength to work; everyone at least crossed himself . . . and then fell to work with the utmost energy.

Thus did it go on all day: a Divine Service of hard and

ceaseless and most fruitful work. Scarcely anyone remained at home. All the doors of all the huts stood wide open; even the children went afield, the aged and the invalids; and even the dogs, breaking loose from the ropes that bound them, darted off to the harvest-making.

No one was indolent, no one stood eyeing his neighbours' crops; they all, bowed over the furrows, and with untiring diligence, worked hard in the sweat of their brows.

Dominikova's fields alone remained unreaped—forgotten, as it were. The corn dropped grain by grain to the ground, the ears withered up with drought: no one went there, and the passers-by averted their heads not to see the desolation. More than one felt compassion, and cast wistful glances at his neighbours; but he would then fall to work again more diligently than before: it was no time for them to stand contemplating ruin and devastation.

For harvest was now in full swing: day succeeded day, full of the hardest toil, most joyfully supported.

And at last, the weather continuing magnificent, they bound the cut corn into sheaves, setting them up on the fields by clusters of eight, to be brought home to Lipka at their convenience. Now did the ponderous wagons roll along, on every field, through every lane, to every barn in the village. The gathered billows of golden corn flowed out along the ways and in the yards and on to the threshing-floors; a few stalks even floated in the pond, or dangled aloft from the roadside trees, with their yellow bearded stalks; and all the country-side was redolent of the reaped straw and the fresh ripe grain.

On not a few threshing-floors the flails were beating already, for the people were in a hurry to get their corn made into bread. Without, on the vast expanse of stubble, multitudes of geese were gleaning the remaining ears, and flocks of sheep and herds of oxen grazed there too. There, too, some fires had been kindled; and all day long the lasses sang and made a joyful noise, that mingled with calls and rumbling of carts, and made the merry sunburnt faces of the villagers shine still brighter.

The sound of the Angelus rose up from Lipka, with the clatter of carts, the ringing of scythes on the whetstone, and some far-off snatches of song: while the dust, golden in the western air, now began to blur the outlines of cabins and fields and woods.

The *Dȥiad* got on his crutches, drove the dogs away, set his wallet straight, and started off, saying:

"Dear folk, may God be with you evermore."

THE END

A NOTE ON THE TYPE IN
WHICH THIS BOOK IS SET

This book is set (on the Linotype) in Elzevir No. 3, a French Old Style. For the modern revival of this excellent face we are indebted to Gustave Mayeur of Paris, who reproduced it in 1878, basing his designs, he says, on types used in a book which was printed by the Elzevirs at Leyden in 1634. The Elzevir family held a distinguished position as printers and publishers for more than a century, their best work appearing between about 1590 and 1680. Although the Elzevirs were not themselves type founders, they utilized the services of the best type designers of their time, notably Van Dijk, Garamond, and Sanlecque. They developed a type face which is open and readable but relatively narrow in body, permitting a large amount of copy to be set in limited space without impairing legibility.

SET UP, ELECTROTYPED AND PRINTED
BY THE VAIL-BALLOU PRESS, INC.,
BINGHAMTON, N. Y. · ESPARTO
PAPER MANUFACTURED IN
SCOTLAND AND FURNISHED
BY W. F. ETHERINGTON &
CO., NEW YORK · BOUND
BY THE H. WOLFF ES-
TATE, NEW YORK